A D...
HER VAL... ...DOC

Valentine and Aug... before th...

BY
MELANIE MILBURNE

IT HAPPENED
IN PARIS…

BY
ROBIN GIANNA

MILLS &
BOON

A VALENTINE TO REMEMBER

One day they will never forget!

A DATE WITH HER VALENTINE DOC
by Melanie Milburne

Bertie Clark really *shouldn't* be fantasising about
Dr Matt Bishop—he's her boss, and is 100% off-limits!
But, working on the hospital's St Valentine's Day Ball
with him, Bertie knows she can't ignore the sparks
flying around for ever—surely a girl deserves a little fun?

IT HAPPENED IN PARIS…
by Robin Gianna

Biochemical engineer Avery Girard might have sworn
off men, but she can't help but get swept away by the
beauty, magic and romance of Valentine's Day in Paris…
especially when she's spending it with totally irresistible
Dr Jack Dunbar. One little fling can't hurt, *right*?

**Fall in love this Valentine's Day
with these sparkling romances
available from February 2015!**

A DATE WITH HER VALENTINE DOC

BY
MELANIE MILBURNE

Published in Great Britain 2015
by Mills & Boon, an imprint of Harlequin (UK) Limited,
Eton House, 18-24 Paradise Road, Richmond, Surrey, TW9 1SR

© 2015 Melanie Milburne

ISBN: 978-0-263-24687-2

Harlequin's policy is to use papers that are natural,
renewable and recyclable products and made from
sustainable forests. The logging and manufacturing processes conform
to the legal environmental regulations of the country of origin.

Printed and bound in Spain
by CPI, Barcelona

Dear Reader

The question I am asked most frequently is: *Where do you get your ideas?* It's not always easy to answer as inspiration for stories can be a deeply subconscious thing and I often don't have a clue where the idea came from. But in the case of Bertie and Matt's story I know exactly what inspired it.

On St Valentine's Day in 2014 I was interviewed on national television about 'How to Write a Best-Selling Romance Novel'. One of the panel hosts, Joe Hildebrand, had recently published *An Average Joe*, a memoir of his quirky childhood, and I just happened to be reading it at the time of the interview—which was kind of spooky! But then, Bertie's mother would say that was the stars or the planets aligning, or something. :)

Last year I was asked to write a short story for *The Australian Review of Fiction* (the first romance author ever to contribute—yay!). I wrote EM AND EM in the first person and couldn't wait to do it again in a full novel, so when my lovely editor Flo Nicoll offered me a chance to write a special St Valentine's Day book I jumped at it—but on the proviso that I could do it in the first person.

I hope you enjoy Bertie and Matt's story as much as I enjoyed writing it. BTW—watch out for Bertie's sister Jem's story, coming soon in Mills & Boon® Medical Romance™!

Best wishes

Melanie Milburne x

Each year I am part of the silent auction
for the Heart Foundation in Tasmania. I offer a
book dedication and this year's winner was Maria Chung,
who wanted this book to be dedicated to her husband:

Dr Stephen Chung, a wonderful husband, father and doctor.

Thank you to both of you for your continued support
of the Heart Foundation in Tasmania.

MM

From as soon as **Melanie Milburne** could pick up a pen
she knew she wanted to write. It was when she picked
up her first Mills & Boon® at seventeen that she realised
she wanted to write romance. After being distracted for
a few years by meeting and marrying her own handsome
hero, surgeon husband Steve, and having two boys, plus
completing a master's of education and becoming a
nationally ranked athlete (masters swimming), she decided
to write. Five submissions later she sold her first book
and is now a multi-published, bestselling, award-winning
USA TODAY author. In 2008 she won the Australian
Readers' Association most popular category/series romance,
and in 2011 she won the prestigious Romance Writers of
Australia R*BY award.

Melanie loves to hear from her readers via her website,
www.melaniemilburne.com.au, or on Facebook:
www.facebook.com/melanie.milburne

Recent titles by Melanie Milburne:

FLIRTING WITH THE SOCIALITE DOC
DR CHANDLER'S SLEEPING BEAUTY
SYDNEY HARBOUR HOSPITAL: LEXI'S SECRET
THE SURGEON SHE NEVER FORGOT
THE MAN WITH THE LOCKED AWAY HEART

**These books are also available in eBook format
from www.millsandboon.co.uk**

CHAPTER ONE

THE FIRST THING I saw when I walked into the ICU office on my first day back to work after my honeymoon was my postcard pinned to the noticeboard. Well, it was *supposed* to be my honeymoon. I'd booked the leave for months ahead. It's hard to get three weeks off in a row at St Ignatius, especially before Christmas. There are a lot of working mums at St Iggy's and I always feel guilty if I'm stuffing up someone's plan to be at their little kid's Christmas concert. Which was why I hadn't come back to work until the 'honeymoon' was over, so to speak.

My postcard was right in the centre of the noticeboard. In pride of place. Flashing like a beacon. The last time I'd seen it had been in my chalet room at the ski resort in Italy, along with two others I'd written to my elderly neighbours. I swear I hadn't actually intended to post them. It had been a therapeutic exercise my mother had suggested to rid myself of negative energy, but the super-efficient housekeeping staff must have seen them lying on the desk and helpfully posted them for me. That's service for you.

If I turned that wretched postcard around I would

see the lies I'd scrawled there after consuming a lonely cocktail or two…actually, I think it was three. *All went amazingly well! Having an awesome time!*

Now that I look back with twenty-twenty hindsight I can see all the signs. The red flags and the faintly ringing alarm bells I ignored at the time. I hate to sound like a cliché but I really was the last person to know. My mother said she knew the first time she met Andy. It was his aura that gave him away. My dad said three of Andy's chakras were blocked. My sister Jem said it was because he was a twat.

I guess they were all right in the end.

The chance to get rid of the postcard escaped me when Jill, the ward clerk, came in behind me with a couple of residents and chorused, 'Here's the blushing bride!' I was blushing all right. Big time. Looking at that sea of smiling faces, I didn't have the heart or the courage to tell them the wedding hadn't gone ahead. I smiled inanely and made some excuse about seeing an elderly patient and scooted out of there. I had only been at St Iggy's a little less than a year so I didn't know anyone well enough to consider them close friends, although some of the girls were really nice, Gracie McCurcher— one of the intensive care nurses—in particular.

And as to anyone finding out on social media, I'd closed my profile page a couple of years ago after someone had hacked into my account and used my image in a porn ad. Try explaining *that* to your workmates, especially the male ones.

My home village in Yorkshire is a long way from London—in more ways than one, but more on that later—so I figured it didn't matter if I didn't tell everyone I'd got dumped the night before the wedding. Cowardly, I know, but, to tell you the truth, I was still trying to get used to being single. Andy and I were together—not actually living together, because I'm idiotically old-fashioned, which is ironic when you consider my unconventional upbringing—for five and a half years.

I know what you're thinking. How could I *not* have known he wasn't in love with me after all that time? I'm not sure how to answer. I loved him so I expected him to love me back. Naïve of me perhaps but that's just the way I'm made. But maybe on some level I'd always known he was marking time until someone better came along.

I stood by the bedside of Mr Simmons, a long-term elderly patient, on that cold and dismal January morning and watched as he quietly slipped away. There is something incredibly sacred about watching someone die. Mind you, it's not always peaceful. Some struggle as if they aren't quite ready to leave their loved ones. Others slip away on a soundless sigh the moment their absent loved one arrives. It's as if they've waited until that moment of contact to finally let go. I've lost count of how many deaths I've seen. But I guess that's one of the downsides of working in ICU. Not everyone walks out with a smile on his or her face. Not everyone walks out, period.

I can cope with the death of an elderly person like Mr Simmons. I can even manage with a middle-aged person's death if they've lived a full and happy life and are surrounded by the people they love. It's the kids that get me. Babies in particular. It seems so unfair they don't get a chance to have a go at screwing up their life like I've screwed up mine.

Mr Simmons's grandchildren and great-grandchildren had been in the night before and said their final goodbyes. His wife died a couple of years ago so there was only his son and daughter by his bed. I watched as they each kissed his forehead, and then stroked his papery hand, and each shed a tear or two for the long and happy life that was coming to a close.

ICU is a pretty public place to die, which was why I had wrangled for months with the CEO to give me a quiet corner—if there is such a thing in an ICU department—so relatives could spend an hour or two without nurses or orderlies or whatever interrupting their last moments with their loved one. I had even had special permission granted to light candles of reflection and operate an aromatherapy infusion machine so the patients and their relatives and friends could breathe in their favourite scents instead of the smell of hospital-grade antiseptic.

Because it was my baby, while I'd been away things had fallen a little by the wayside, but I was back now and intent on finalising the introduction of my stress cost abatement model. I proposed to show how improving the environment in which relatives experienced illness or death in ICU ultimately reduced costs to the hospital—less demand for later counselling, reduced incidence and costs of litigation, and even reduced stress leave for ICU staff. I planned to present it at an upcoming hospital management meeting because I knew I could prove there would be benefits to the whole department with reduced stress in the ICU environment, not just for patients but for staff as well.

I softly closed the door—yes, not a curtain but an actual door!—on the grieving relatives and headed back to the glassed-in office where the registrars, interns and residents were being briefed by one of the consultants. I hadn't yet met the new director. He'd started the day after I'd left for my…erm…break.

I was looking at the back view of the consultant. At first I thought it was Professor Cleary—we call him Professor Dreary behind his back because he's such a pessimist—but when I got closer I realised it was someone much younger. He had very broad shoulders and he was tall. I mean *really* tall. He was at least a couple of inches taller than the registrar, Mark Jones, who we affectionately call Lurch.

I'm not sure if someone said I was coming over or whether the new director heard me approach. But he suddenly turned and his eyes met mine. Something fizzed in the air like a stray current of electricity. I actually felt the hairs on the back of my neck lift up. I had never seen such startling grey-blue eyes. Piercing and intense, intelligent and incisive, they looked at me in a frank and assessing manner I found distinctly unnerving.

'Dr Clark?'

'Bertie,' I said with a smile that felt a little forced. 'It's short for Beatrix with an X.'

He stood there looking down at me as if I were a strange oddity he'd never encountered in ICU before. I wondered if it was my hairstyle. I have longish wavy honey-brown hair, which I like to keep under some semblance of control when I'm working. That morning I'd tied it in two round knots either side of my head like teddy-bear ears.

Or maybe it was my outfit that had caused that quizzical frown to appear between his eyes. I'm the first to admit I'm a little out there in my choice of clothing. No white coat—not that we doctors wear them any more—or scrubs for me unless I've come from Theatre. I like colour and lots of it. It can have a powerful effect on patients' moods, particularly children. Besides, all you ever see in winter is black and brown and grey. That morning I had on skinny-leg pink jeans and a pea-green jumper with blue frogs on it. The new director glanced at the frogs on my breasts before returning his gaze to mine. Something closed off at the back of his eyes, as if he were pulling up a screen.

I didn't offer him my hand but, then, he didn't offer his. I'm normally a polite person but I wasn't sure I wanted to touch him until I had better control of myself. If his gaze could make me feel like I'd walked in wearing a string bikini then what would his touch do?

'Matt Bishop,' he said in a deep, mellifluous baritone that had an odd effect on the base of my spine. It felt loose…unhinged. 'I'd like to see you in my office.' He glanced at his watch before zapping me again with his gaze. 'Five minutes.'

I watched as he strode away, effectively dismissing me as if I was nothing but a lowly serf. Who the hell did he think he was, ordering me about like a medical student? I was as qualified as him. Well, almost.

I was aware of the staff's collective gaze as the air rippled with tension in his wake.

'You'd better not be late, Bertie,' Jill, the ward clerk, said. 'He's a stickler for punctuality. Alex Kingston got hauled over the coals for showing up two minutes late for a ward round.'

Gracie McCurcher gave a grimace and huddled further into the office chair she was swivelling on. 'He's nothing like Jeffrey, is he?'

Jeffrey Hooper was our previous director. He retired the week before I left for my…holiday. Think benevolent uncle or godparent. Jeffrey was the kindest, most supportive ICU specialist I've ever come across. He could be gruff at times but everyone knew his bark was just a front.

'That's part of the problem,' Jill said. 'Jeffrey was too lax in running this department. The costs have blown out and now Dr Bishop has to rein everything in. I don't envy him. He's not going to make any friends doing it, that I can tell you.'

I moved my lips back and forth and up and down. My sister Jem calls it my bunny-rabbit twitch. I do it when I'm stressed. Which is kind of embarrassing when my whole research project is on reducing stress. I'm supposed to be the poster girl for serenity. But the truth is I'm like the ducks on the Serpentine in Hyde Park. They look like they're floating effortlessly on the surface but underneath the water their little webbed feet are paddling like crazy.

'You'd better keep the photos until after work,' Gracie said.

Photos? I thought. Oh, *those* photos. I pasted on a smile that made my face ache. Everyone was looking at me. Here was my chance to come clean. To tell them there hadn't been a wedding. I could see my postcard out of the corner of my eye. It was still in pride of place on the noticeboard. Hadn't anyone else been on holiday, for God's sake? I'm not sure how long I stood there with my mouth stretched in that rictus smile but it felt longer than my 'honeymoon'. I wondered if I could edit some wedding-ish snaps on my phone. Set up a temporary social network account or something. It would give me some breathing space until I plucked up the courage to tell the truth.

'Good suggestion,' I said, and, taking a deep breath, headed to the lion's den.

I gave the closed door a quick rap and winced as my knuckles protested. It was a timely reminder I would need to develop a thicker skin if I were to survive the next few rounds with Dr Matt Bishop.

'Come in.'

I walked into his office but it was nothing like his predecessor had left it. Gone were the lopsided towers of files and patient notes and budgetary reports. There were no family photos on the cluttered desk. No empty or half-drunk cups of coffee. No cookie crumbs. No glass jar full of colourful dental-filling-pulling sweets. The office had been stripped bare of its character. It was as sterile and as cool as the man who sat behind the acre of desk.

'Close the door.'

I paused, giving him an arch look. I might have had an alternative upbringing but at least my parents taught me the magic word.

'Please,' he added, with a smidgeon of a lip curl.

Round one to me, I thought.

The door clicked shut and I moved a little closer to the desk. The closer I got the more my skin prickled. It was like entering a no-go zone monitored by invisible radar.

I wondered what my mum would make of his aura. Matt Bishop had a firm mouth that looked like it wasn't used to smiling. His jaw had a determined set to it as if he was unfamiliar with the notion of compromise. His skin was olive toned but it looked as if he hadn't been anywhere with strong sunshine for several months…but, then, that's our English summer for you. His hair was a rich, dark brown, thick and plentiful but cut short in a no-nonsense style. He was closely shaven and in the air I could pick up a faint trace of lime and lemongrass, a light, fresh scent that made my nostrils widen in appreciation. I'm a sucker for subtle aftershave.

I hate stepping into the lift with a bunch of young male medical students who've gone crazy with those cheap aerosol body sprays. I once had to hold my breath for six floors and the lift stopped on every one. I was wheezing like I had emphysema by the time I got out.

My mum reckons she can read auras. I'm more of a wardrobe reader. Matt Bishop was wearing a crisply ironed white shirt with a black and silver striped tie with a Windsor knot and black trousers with knife-edge pleats that spoke of a man who preferred formality to casual friendliness. But to counter that the sleeves of his shirt were folded back past his wrists, revealing strong forearms with a generous sprinkling of dark hair that went all the way down to his hands and along each of his long fingers. His nails were neat and square, unlike mine, which had suffered the fallout of the last two weeks after months of coaxing them to grow, and were now back to their nibbled-to-the-quick state.

I curled my fingers into my palms in case he noticed and sat down in the chair opposite his desk. I sat not because he told me to. He didn't. I sat because I didn't care for the schoolgirl-called-into-the-headmaster's-office dynamic he had going on. It was much better to be seated so I could look at him on the level. Mind you, with his considerable height advantage I would have had to be sitting on a stack of medical textbooks to be eye to eye with him.

His unreadable gaze meshed with mine. 'I believe congratulations are in order.'

'Erm…yes,' I said. What else could I say? No, I found my fiancé in bed with one of the bridesmaids' sister the night before the wedding? And that *he* dumped me before I could get in first? And how I tipsily wrote post-cards that were subsequently sent about what a fabulous time I was having on my honeymoon? Not going to happen. Not to Matt Bishop anyway. I would tell people on a need-to-know basis and right now no one needed to know.

I *needed* no one to know.

There was a pregnant silence.

I got the feeling he was waiting for me to fill it, though with what I'm not sure. Did he want me to tell him where I went on my honeymoon? What I wore? Who caught the bouquet? I thought men weren't all that interested in weddings, even when it was their own.

I stared back at him with my heart beating like a hummingbird had got trapped in one of my valves. *You could tell him.* The thought slipped under the locked door of my resolve. *No way!* the other side of my brain threw back. It was like a tennis match was going on inside my head. I was so flustered by it I shifted in my seat as if there were thumbtacks poking into my jeans.

His eyes drilled into mine. 'Is everything all right?'

'Yes.' I smiled stiffly. 'Sure. Fine. Absolutely.'

Another silence passed.

Here's the thing. I'm not good with silences. They freak me out. It's because my parents went through a no-speaking phase when Jem and I were kids. They wanted us to pretend we were living in an abbey like at Mont Saint Michel in Normandy in France, where talking is banned in order to concentrate on prayer. It would have helped if they'd taught us sign language first. Thankfully it didn't last long but it's left its mark. I have this tendency to talk inanely if there's even a hint of a break in the conversation.

'So, how are you liking St Iggy's so far?' I said. 'Isn't it a nice place? Everyone's so friendly and—'

'Harrison Redding, the CEO, tells me you're doing a research project on stress reduction,' Matt Bishop said.

'Yes,' I said. As much as I didn't care for his clipped tone, at least I was back on safer ground. I mentally wiped my brow. Phew! I could talk all day about my project. 'I'm looking at ways of mitigating the stress on patients, relatives and staff when a patient is in ICU, in particular when a patient is facing death. Stress is a costly burden to the unit. Staff take weeks—sometimes months—of stress leave when cases are difficult to handle. Patients lodge unnecessary and career-damaging lawsuits when they feel sidelined or their expectations aren't met. My aim is to show how using various stress intervention programmes and some physical ways of reducing stress, such as aromas and music tones and other environmental changes, can significantly reduce that cost to the hospital. My stress cost abatement model will help both staff and patients and their loved ones deal better with their situation.'

I waited for his response…and waited.

After what seemed like a week he leaned forward and put his forearms on the desk and loosely interlaced his fingers. 'You've had ethics approval?'

'Of course.'

I watched as he slowly flicked one of his thumbs against the other. Flick. Flick. Flick. I tried to read his expression but he could have been sitting at a poker tournament. Nothing moved on his face, not even a muscle. I was having trouble keeping my nervous bunny twitch under control. I could feel it building inside me like the urge to sneeze.

His eyes bored into mine. 'I have some issues with your project.'

I blinked. 'Pardon?'

'I'm not convinced this unit can afford the space you've been allocated,' he said. 'I understand Dr Hooper was the one to approve the end room for your use?'

'Yes, but the CEO was also—'

'And the room next to the relatives' room?'

'Yes, because I felt it was important to give people a choice in—'

'What sort of data have you produced so far?'

I wished I hadn't gone on leave for more reasons than the obvious one. It felt like ages since I'd looked at my data. Most of it was descriptive, which was something the survey questionnaire over the next few critical weeks would address. I understood the scientific method. Data had to be controlled, repeatable and sufficient; otherwise, it was useless. But I also wanted a chance to change the thinking around death and dying. Everyone was so frightened of it, which produced enormous amounts of stress. 'I'm still collecting data from patient and staff surveys,' I said. 'I have a series of interviews to do, which will also be recorded and collated.'

I wasn't too keen on the sceptical glint in his eyes. 'Multiplication of anecdotes is not data, Dr Clark.'

I silently ground my teeth…or at least I tried to be silent. Jem says she can always hear me because she listened to it for years when we shared a bedroom when we were kids. Apparently I do it in my sleep.

I *so* did not need this right now. I had enough on my plate in my private life, without my professional life going down the toilet as well. I understood how Matt Bishop was in brisk and efficient new broom mode. I understood the pressure of coming in on budget, especially when you'd inherited a mess not of your own making. But I wasn't going to be intimidated by a man who had taken an instant dislike to me for how I dressed or wore my hair.

He would have to get over himself. *I* wasn't changing.

'Will that be all, Dr Bishop?' I asked in mock meekness as I rose from the chair. 'I have some pre-assessments to see to on the ward.'

This time a muscle did move in his jaw. In and out like a miniature hammer. A hard sheen came over his gaze as it held mine—an impenetrable layer of antagonism that dared me to lock horns with him. I'm not normally one to pick fights but I resented the way he'd spoken to me as if I were a lazy high-school student who hadn't done their homework. If he wanted a fight then I would give him one.

I felt a frisson pass through my body, an electric current that made my nerves flutter and dance. I can't remember a time when I felt more switched on. It was like someone had plugged me into a live socket. My entire body was vibrating with energy, a restless and vibrant energy it had never felt before.

Without relaxing his hold on my gaze, he reached for a sheet of paper on the desk in front of him, which I presumed was an outline of my research. His top lip lifted in a sardonic arc. 'Your project name has a rather unfortunate acronym, don't you think?'

I looked at him blankly for a moment. And then I got it. I was annoyed I hadn't realised it before. Stress Cost Abatement Model. S.C.A.M. Why on earth hadn't someone pointed it out earlier? I felt like an idiot. Would everyone be snickering at me once Matt Bishop shared his observation around the water cooler? My stomach knotted. Maybe they already were… Was that why everyone had looked at me when I came to the office just now? Had they been talking about me…*laughing* at me?

I was incensed. Livid to the point of exploding with anger so intense it felt like it was bursting out of each and every corpuscle of my blood. I could feel the heat in my cheeks burning like the bars of a two-thousand-watt radiator. I had spent most of my childhood being sniggered at for my unconventional background. How would I ever be taken seriously professionally once this did the rounds?

I don't often lose my temper, but when I do it's like all those years of keeping my thoughts and opinions to myself come spilling out in a shrieking tirade that I can't stop once I get started. It's like trying to put a champagne cork back in the bottle.

I hissed in a breath and released it in a rush. 'I *detest* men like you. You think just because you've been appointed director you can brandish your power about like a smart-ass kid with a new toy. You think your colleagues are dumb old chess pieces you can push around as you please. Well, I have news for you, Dr Bishop. This is one chess piece you can't screw around with.'

I probably shouldn't have used *that* particular word. The connotation of it changed the atmosphere from electric to erotic. I could feel it thrumming in the air. I could see the glint of it in his grey-blue gaze as it tussled with mine. I'm not sure where his mind was going, but I knew what images mine was conjuring up—X-rated ones. Naked bodies. His and mine. Writhing around on a bed in the throes of animal passion.

Thing is…it's been ages since I've had sex. I'm pretty sure that's why my mind was running off the way it was. I'd put Andy's lack of interest over the last couple of months down to busyness with work as a stock analyst. I put down my own to lack of interest, period. I blamed it on the contraceptive pill I'd been taking. But then I changed pills and I was exactly the same. Go figure.

I saw Matt Bishop's eyes take in my scorching cheeks and then he lowered his gaze to my mouth. It was only for a moment but I felt as if he had touched me with a searing brand. I bit my tongue to keep it from moistening my lips but that meant I couldn't say anything to break the throbbing silence. Not that I was going to apologise or anything. As far as I was concerned, he'd asked for a verbal spray and, given another chance, I would give him one again.

He sat back in his chair, his eyes holding mine in a lock that made the backs of my knees feel fizzy. It took an enormous effort on my part not to look away. I had an unnerving feeling he could see through my brief flash of anger—the overly defensive front that disguised my feelings of inadequacy. I'd spent most of my life hiding my insecurities but I got the sense he could read every micro-expression on my face, even the ones I thought I wasn't expressing. His gaze was so steady, so watchful and so intuitive I was sure he was reading every thought that was running through my mind, including—even more unsettling—the X-rated ones.

'I'll keep that in mind,' he said. 'Close the door on your way out.' He waited a beat before he added with an enigmatic half-smile, '*Please.*'

CHAPTER TWO

I FINISHED MY pre-assessment clinic and walked back to
ICU. Stalked would be more accurate. I was still brood-
ing over Matt Bishop's treatment of me. Why had he
taken such a set against me? I wasn't used to making
instant enemies. I considered myself an easygoing person who got on with everyone. Mostly.

Come to think of it, there have been a couple of
times when I've run up against someone who didn't
share my take on things. Like my neighbour, who kept
spraying the other neighbour's cat with a hose every
time it came into his garden. That's just plain cruel and
I didn't refrain from telling him so. I got myself hosed
for my trouble, but at least I felt good about standing
up for Ginger.

And then there was the guy who'd been ripping
off another elderly neighbour a few doors down. Elsie
Montgomery employed him to do some gardening and
odd jobs but it wasn't long before he was doing her shopping and taking her to the doctor or on other outings.
At first I thought he was doing it out of the goodness of
his heart, but then I found out from Elsie—reluctantly,
because she was embarrassed—he had been taking

money out of her bank account after he'd got her to tell him her PIN.

I wanted Elsie to press charges against him for elder abuse but she thought he'd been punished enough by me shouting at him in the street in front of all the neighbours. That and the naming-and-shaming leaflet drop. That was a stroke of genius on my part. I got a team of local kids to help me distribute them. It will be a long time before he gets to cut any lawns in our suburb, possibly the whole country.

I was walking past the staff change rooms when Gracie appeared. 'How did it go? What did he say to you?'

I rolled my eyes. 'He has issues with my project.'

'What sort of issues?'

I gave her a disgruntled look. I wasn't going to spell it out for her. Word would spread fast enough. 'The rooms I've been allocated, for one thing. He thinks we can't afford the space.'

Gracie frowned. 'But you're doing amazing things with the patients and families. Everyone says so. Look at what you did for the Matheson family. You brought such comfort to them when they lost their son before Christmas.'

I pictured the Matheson family collected around Daniel's twenty-one-year-old body as he breathed his last breaths after a long and difficult battle against sarcoma. I spent hours with them, preparing them and Daniel for the end. I encouraged them to be open with Daniel about their feelings, not to be ashamed of the anger they were feeling about his life being cut short, but to accept that as a part of the journey through grief. I taught Daniel's father, who was uncomfortable showing emotion or affection, to gently massage his son to help him relax. When Daniel finally passed it was so peaceful in the room you could hear the birds twittering outside.

I let out a breath as we walked along the corridor back to the unit. 'I can't stop now. I'm only just beginning to see results. I've had three nurses tell me how much they got out of the meditation exercise I gave before I went on leave. When nurses get stressed, patients get stressed. It's not rocket science. It's common sense.'

'But surely Dr Bishop can't block your project now,' Gracie said.

I held my hands out for the antiseptic gel from the dispenser on the wall, my mouth set in an indomitable line. 'I'd like to see him try.'

I got busy doing a PICC line for a chemotherapy patient and then I had to help one of the registrars with setting up a patient's ventilator. I was due for Theatre for an afternoon list with one of the neurosurgeons, Stuart McTaggart. Not my favourite person at St Iggy's, but while he had an abrasive personality there was certainly nothing wrong with his surgical skills. Patients came from all over the country to see him. He had a world-class reputation for neurosurgery and was considered to be one of the best neurosurgeons of his generation.

I went to the doctors' room to grab a quick bite of lunch. It was a medium-sized room big enough for a six-person dining table and chairs, a couple of mismatched armchairs, a coffee table, a sink and a small fridge. The daily newspapers were spread out on the table, where a bowl of fruit acted as a paperweight.

Personally, I thought the place could do with a face-lift, maybe a bit of feng shui wouldn't go astray, but I was fairly new on staff, considering some people had been here for their entire careers, so I picked my battles.

I reached for an apple out of the bowl as the door opened. I looked up to see Matt Bishop enter the staff-room. His expression showed no surprise or discomfit at seeing me there. In fact, I thought I caught a glimmer of a smile lurking in his eyes. No doubt he was still enjoying the joke he'd made of my project. I hadn't heard anyone say anything about it so far but I knew it wouldn't be long before they did. He wouldn't be able to keep such a gem of hilarity to himself.

I felt my anger go up another notch. Why did I attract this sort of stuff? Why couldn't I go about my life without people making fun of me? Now, you might ask why would a girl wear bright, fun clothes and twist her hair into wacky hairstyles if she was afraid of people laughing at her? Duh! If they're laughing at my clothes and my hair I don't have to feel they're laughing at *me*. There's a difference and to me it's a big one.

I bit into the apple with a loud crunch. I was down a round and I had some serious catching up to do. I chewed the mouthful and then took another. And another. It wasn't the nicest apple, to tell you the truth. But I was committed now so I had to finish it. I can be stubborn at times—most of the time, to be honest. I *hate* giving in. I hate being defeated by something or someone. I'd spent a lot of my childhood being bullied so I guess that's why. It's not just about losing face. I hate failure. It goes against my nature. I'm positive in my outlook. I go into things expecting to achieve my mission. I don't let the naysayers get to me...or I try not to.

'So where did you go on honeymoon?' Matt Bishop asked, just as I'd taken another mouthful.

I swear to God I almost choked on that piece of apple. I thought he'd have to give me the Heimlich manoeuvre—not that we do that any more, but still. I coughed and spluttered, my eyes streaming, my cheeks as red as the skin of the piece of apple I was trying to shift from my airway.

He stepped towards me. 'Are you okay?'

I signalled with one of my hands that I was fine. He waited patiently with his steady gaze trained on mine. Of course I couldn't pretend I was choking forever, and since—technically speaking—I had been on honeymoon/holiday I decided to stay as close to the truth as possible once I got my airway clear. 'Skiing...Italy.'

'Where in Italy?'

'Livigno.'

He acknowledged that with a slight nod as he reached for a coffee cup. 'Good choice.'

I put the rest of my apple in the bin. It wasn't my choice. I'm a hopeless skier. I'd only agreed to it because it was what Andy wanted. And rather than waste the money—because he hadn't paid the travel insurance as I'd asked him to—I'd doggedly stuck with the plan. I must admit I was proud of myself in that I progressed off the nursery slopes, but not very far. 'You ski?' I asked.

'Occasionally.'

There was a silence broken only by the sound of coffee being poured into his cup. I waited to see if he put milk or sugar or sweetener in it. You've guessed it. There's a lot you can tell about someone from how they take their coffee. He was a straight-up man. No added extras. And he drank it smoking hot. I watched as he took his first mouthful without even wincing at the steamy heat.

'What does your husband do?'

The question caught me off guard. I was too busy watching the way his mouth had shaped around the rim of his cup. Why had I thought his mouth hard and uncompromising? He had the sort of mouth that would make Michelangelo dash off for a chisel. The lower lip was sensually full and the top one neatly defined. I don't think I'd ever seen such a beautifully sculpted mouth. I began to wonder what it would feel like pressed to my own…

'Pardon?'

'Is your husband a doctor too?'

Something about the way he said the word 'husband' made me think he was putting it in inverted commas or even in italics. It was the way he stressed the word. That, and the way his mouth got a slight curl to it as if he thought the notion of someone wanting to marry me was hilariously unbelievable.

'No, erm, he's a stock analyst.'

'In London?'

'Yes.'

There's an art to lying and I like to think I'm pretty good at it. After all, I've been doing it all my life. I learned early on not to tell people the truth. Living in a commune with your parents from the age of six sort of does that to you. I wouldn't have lasted long at

school if I had Shown and Told some of the things I'd
seen and heard.

No, it's not the lying that's the problem. That's the
easy part. It's keeping track of them that gets tricky.
So far I hadn't strayed too far off the path. Andy was
a stock analyst and he worked in London. He was currently seeking a transfer to the New York branch of
his firm, which, to be frank, I welcomed wholeheart-
edly. London is a big city but I didn't fancy running
into him and his new girlfriend any time soon. It was
bad enough having him come to my house to collect
all his things. I made it easy for him by leaving them
in the front garden. Yes, I know, it was petty, but I got
an enormous sense of satisfaction from throwing them
from the second-floor window. It wasn't my fault it
had snowed half a metre overnight. I'm not in control
of the weather.

I decided in order to keep my lying tally down I had
to ask some questions of my own. 'Are you married?'

'No.'

'In a relationship?'

He paused for a nanosecond. 'No.'

I wondered if he had broken up recently, or if the
break-up—if there had been one—still hurt. 'Kids?'

He frowned. 'No, of course not.'

'Why of course not?'

'Call me old-fashioned but I like to do things in the
right order,' he said.

I tilted my head at him. 'So let me guess…you haven't
lived with anyone?'

'No.'

I pondered over that for a moment while he took

a packet of sandwiches from the small fridge and sat down at the table. He opened one of the newspapers on the table and began to eat his sandwiches in what I could only describe as a mechanical way. I'm the first to admit hospital food isn't much to get all excited about, but the sandwiches for the doctors' room were always freshly made and contained healthy ingredients, or at least they had since I'd spoken to the head of catering a few weeks back.

'That's bad for you, you know,' I said. I know it was none of my business what or how he ate but the silence was there and I wanted to fill it. Needed to fill it, more like.

Matt Bishop didn't bother to glance my way. He turned the newspaper page over and reached for another sandwich. 'What is?'

'Eating and reading. At the same time, I mean.'

He sat back in his chair and looked at me with an inscrutable expression. 'You have something against multitasking?'

I didn't let his satirical tone faze me. 'Eating while performing other tasks is a bad habit. It can lead to overeating. You might be full by page three but you keep on eating until you get to the sports page out of habit.'

He closed the newspaper and pushed it to the other side of the table. 'How long were you going out with your *husband* before he asked you to marry him?'

There, he'd done it again. I wasn't imagining it. He'd stressed the word 'husband'. What was with the sudden interest in my private life? Or did he think it impossible anyone could be remotely interested in me? With the end of my engagement so recent I was feeling a bit fragile in terms of self-esteem. Come to think of it, my self-esteem has always been a little on the eggshell side. 'Erm, actually, he didn't ask me,' I said. 'I asked him.'

He lifted one of his dark eyebrows. 'Oh?'

'You don't approve.'

'It's none of my business.'

I folded my arms and gave him a look. 'I fail to see why the man has to have all the power in a relationship. Why should a girl have to wait months and months, possibly years for a proposal? Living every moment in a state of will-he-or-won't-he panic?'

'Don't blame me,' he said mildly. 'I didn't write the rule book.'

I pursed my lips, not my most attractive pose, but still. Jem calls it my cat's-bottom pout. I had the strangest feeling Matt Bishop was smiling behind that unreadable look he was giving me. There was a tiny light in his eyes that twinkled now and again.

'So how did he take it when you popped the question?' he asked.

'He said yes, obviously.' Not straight away, but I wasn't going to tell Matt Bishop *that* little detail. Andy and I had discussed marriage over the years. He just hadn't got around to formally asking me. I got tired of waiting. I know it's weird, considering my non-traditional background, but I really longed to be a proper bride: the white dress and veil and the church and the flowers and confetti and the adorable little flower girl and the cute little pageboy.

My parents had never formally married because they didn't believe in the institution of marriage—any institution, really. They have an open relationship, which seems to work for them. Don't ask me how. I've never said anything to them, but every time I looked at the photos of their thirty years of life together I've always felt like something was missing.

Matt picked up his coffee cup and surveyed me as he took another sip. 'How long have you been at St Ignatius?'

'Ten and a half months.'

'Where were you before here?'

'St Thomas',' I said, and tossed the question back, even though I already knew the answer because I'd overheard two of the nurses talking about him in the change room. 'You?'

'I trained in London and spent most of my time at Chelsea and Westminster, apart from the last twelve months in the US.'

I wondered why he had gone abroad and if it had anything to do with a woman, here or over there. I hadn't heard anything about his private life. Word has it he kept it exactly that—private.

My phone beeped with an incoming message and I glanced down to see it was a text from Jem.

How r u doing? it said.

I quickly typed back. Fine.

Within seconds she typed back. What did everyone say?

I typed back. I haven't told them.

She came back with, Y not?

I typed back the emoticon smiley face with red cheeks. She sent me a smiley face with love hearts for eyes. It was times like this I was truly glad I had a sister. She knew me better than anyone. She knew I needed time to sort my feelings out, to get my head around the idea of being single again.

I had a feeling she also knew it was not so much my heart that was broken but my pride. It's not that I didn't love Andy. I loved him from the moment I met him. He was charming and funny and made me feel as if I was the most important person in his life…for about a month. I know all relationships take work and I put in. I really did. It's just he hadn't factored in my career. His always came first. It caused many an argument. I mean, it's not as if someone's going to die if he doesn't show up for work. He never seemed to understand I couldn't take off a day whenever I felt like it because he was bored and wanted company.

I put my phone back in my jeans pocket and met Matt Bishop's inscrutable gaze. I wondered if he could see any of the thought processes of my brain flitting over my face. I like to think I can keep my cards pretty close, but something about his intense grey-blue eyes made me feel exposed, as if all my insecurities and doubts were lined up on show for his perusal.

'Any further questions?' I asked, with a pert look.

He held my look for an extra beat. 'Not at the moment.'

I turned on my heel and scooted out of there. Colour me suspicious, but I had a feeling there was not much that would get past Dr Matt Bishop's sharply intelligent grey-blues.

Theatre was tense but, then, Stuart McTaggart always operated that way. He wasn't one of those surgeons who chatted about what he did on the weekend or how

well his kids were doing at Cambridge or Oxford—
yadda-yadda-yadda. He didn't have classical music
playing, like a couple of the other surgeons on staff
did. He insisted on absolute silence, apart from when
he had something to say. I'd had to learn early on to
button my lips while in Theatre with him. He was gruff
to the point of surly and he barked out orders like a
drill sergeant. Some of the junior theatre staff found
him terrifying. Some of the more senior staff hated
working with him.

Funnily enough, I didn't find him too hard to handle.
I understood the pressure he was under. Patients were
more demanding of good outcomes than in the past,
or at least they had better access to legal representa-
tion and were more aware of their rights. The litigious
climate meant a lot of clinicians at the pointy end of
medicine were under far greater pressure and scrutiny
than ever before. That could be a good and a bad thing
depending on the circumstances. It was part of why I
wanted to pursue my research. Reducing the stress of
the hospital experience was a win-win for everyone.
Apart perhaps from the greedy lawyers, of course, but
don't get me started.

Stuart McTaggart was operating on a twenty-seven-
year-old man with a very vascular and awkwardly
placed benign brain tumour. Jason Ryder was a recently married man with a baby on the way. He was
a keen sportsman, playing semi-professional golf. He
had collapsed whilst playing in a tournament and been
admitted to St Iggy's via A and E. All was going well
until he developed a bleed. Alex Kingston, the surgical registrar, was the first to cop the flak from Stuart.

'Suck the blood out of the way, Kingston!' he said. 'I can't diathermy bleeders if they're underwater!'

Next in line was Leanne Griffiths, the scrub nurse.

'Be aware of what's happening in the operation, Sister Griffiths. I can't wait around while you call for more swabs. They should be open, on the table, ready when I need them. Which is now!'

Then it was my turn. Woot. Woot.

'What blood pressure have you got this patient running at, Dr Clark? He looks hypertensive to me and that's not assisting with this blood loss!'

And on it went. Everyone was to blame except Stuart. But, then, really, no one was to blame—it was just the nature of the tumour and the stress of trying to remove it with minimal damage to the normal brain. The human body was not always predictable. Things didn't always work out. They weren't working out now. The only way to eventually stop the haemorrhage was to ligate a couple of largish vessels, causing irreparable damage to a large part of what had been a normal brain.

The person I'd anaesthetised wasn't going to be the person who woke up…if he woke up. I hated even *thinking* those words. I always focussed on the positive. It gave great comfort to loved ones if they could hold onto hope for as long as possible.

I went down to ICU with the patient, keeping an eye on the monitor as we went. I was trying not to be influenced by the air of doom and gloom that had blown up in Theatre. I had seen patients much worse than Jason recover. It was a setback, certainly, but with time and patience and careful monitoring he had a chance, maybe even better than expected, given his level of fitness.

Once Jason was settled on the ventilator I went out to the family waiting in the relatives' room. His wife, Megan, was about six months pregnant and stood with Jason's parents as soon as I came in. 'How is he?' she said, holding her hand over her belly as if to protect her baby from hearing bad news.

'The operation was very difficult, Megan,' I said in a gentle but calm tone. 'The tumour had a lot of blood running through it. Mr McTaggart was able to get it out, but not without bleeding, and there is likely a bit of damage to some of the surrounding brain. It's impossible to tell at this stage how he's going to be. There's no choice but to wait and see what effect the tumour and the operative trauma has had. But it's important to keep positive and try not to feel too overwhelmed at this stage. Everything that can be done is being done to bring about the best possible recovery for Jason.'

There was a sound behind me and I turned to see Matt Bishop come in. 'I'm sorry to keep you waiting,' he said, briefly shaking hands with Jason's parents and then Megan. 'I'm Matt Bishop, the head of ICU.'

Jason's father Ken swallowed thickly. 'What's happening to our boy?'

'He's being ventilated and kept in an induced coma,' Matt said. 'During surgery there was a major bleed from the tumour bed. Mr McTaggart was able to stop the bleed, but it's possible normal brain may have been damaged in the process. When the brain swelling has decreased, we'll gradually reduce the sedation, and see what effect the surgery has had. But I should warn you that surgery to a vascular tumour like this, and the bleeding that goes with trying to remove it, can cause a lot of damage. I'm sorry but there's a possibility he won't wake up.'

Jason's mother put a shaky hand against her throat. 'You mean he could...die?'

Matt's expression was grave. 'A bleed like the one Jason suffered can damage vital areas of the brain. In the morning we'll repeat the CT scan and try to assess what physical damage has occurred. We might be able to predict from that how he might recover. In the end, though, we just have to wait, try to wean him off sedation and see if he wakes up.'

The word lingered in the air like a toxic fume.

If, not when he wakes up.

I watched as the hope on Jason's mother's face collapsed, aging her a decade. I saw the devastation spread over Megan's, distorting her young and pretty features into a mask of horror. Jason's father's face went completely still and ashen. All their hopes and dreams for their son had been cut down with one two-letter word.

Matt answered a few more questions but it was obvious to me that the poor family weren't taking much in. They were still trying to get their heads around the fact the son and husband they had kissed that morning on his way to the operating theatre might not come back to them.

My heart ached for them. I know as a doctor you're supposed to keep a clinical distance. And I do most of the time. But now and again a patient comes along who touches you. Jason was such a normal, nice type of guy. He was exactly the same age as me. His family were loving and supportive, the sort of family who loved each other unconditionally. I thought of the baby in Megan's womb who might never get to know his or her father. I thought of the implications for Megan, trapped in a marriage to a man who might be permanently disabled, unable to talk, to eat or drink unassisted. Then there were the bathing and toileting issues—the whole heart-breaking scenario of taking care of someone who could no longer do anything for themselves. Her young life would be utterly destroyed along with his.

Once Matt left I took the family to my relaxation room where my aromatherapy infuser was releasing lavender and tangerine, which had a calming effect and was shown to be beneficial in helping with anxi-ety and depression. I sat with them for a few minutes, handing them tissues scented with clary sage, another stress reliever, and listened as they talked about Jason. They told me about his childhood and some funny an-ecdotes about him as a teenager, and of his passion for golf and how hard he worked at his game. How they had mortgaged their house and forgone holidays for years in order to sponsor his career because they believed so unreservedly in his talent.

That's the thing about busy hospitals these days. No one has time to sit with patients and their families and chat. Nurses are under the pump all the time with other patients to see to. The doctors have the pressure of clini-cal work and administrative duties, and in a teaching hospital such as St Iggy's the responsibility of teach-ing medical students, residents and interns and regis-trars leaves little time to linger by a patient's bedside. Often it was the cleaning or catering staff that coun-selled patients most, but even they were under increas-ing pressure.

I made a point of keeping some time for the patients, even though it meant my days were a little longer than normal. Looking back, I think that was one of the reasons Andy strayed. I just wasn't around enough for him. That, and the assumption that because my parents had an open relationship I, too, would be happy with the same arrangement. Shows how little he knew me. But he knew how much I love my work. It's not so much a career for me but a vocation. I love being able to help people and being with them through the darkest times is the most challenging but in many ways the most rewarding.

I caught up to Matt half an hour later just as he was coming out of his office. I didn't wait to be invited in. I put my hand flat on the door just as he was about to close it. 'Can I have a word?'

He drew in a breath and released it with a sound of impatience. 'I have a meeting in five minutes.'

'I'll be brief.'

He opened the door and I walked past him to enter his office. My left arm brushed against his body as I went. I brush past people all the time. It's hard not to in a busy and often crowded workplace, especially in ICU or Theatre. But I had never felt a tingle go through me quite like that before. It was like touching a bolt of lightning. Energy zapped through my entire body from my arm to my lady land. I was hoping it didn't show on my face. I'm not one to blush easily…or at least not until that morning. I stopped blushing when my parents went through their naturalist phase when I was thirteen. I think my blushing response blew a gasket back then. But right then I could feel warmth spreading in my cheeks. I could only hope he would assume it was because of the message I was there to deliver.

I got straight to the point. 'Did you have to be so blunt with Jason Ryder's wife and family? Surely you could've given them a little ray of hope? You made it sound like the poor man is going to die overnight or be a vegetable. I've seen much worse than—'

'Dr Clark.' His curt tone cut me off. 'I don't see the point in offering false hope. It's better to prepare relatives for the worst, even if it doesn't eventuate. It's much harder to do it the other way around.'

'But surely you could have dressed it up a little more—'

'You mean *lie* to them?' he said, nailing me with a look.

There was something about his stress over the word 'lie' that made my skin shrink away from my bones. I tried not to squirm under his tight scrutiny but I can tell you that hummingbird was back in my heart valve. 'I think you could have found a middle ground. They're completely shell-shocked. They need time to process everything.'

'Time is not something Jason Ryder has right now,' he said. 'That was a significant bleed. You and I both know he might not last the night.'

I pressed my lips together. I wasn't ready to give up hope, although I had to admit Jason's condition was critical.

'Have you mentioned organ donation to the family?' Matt said.

I frowned. 'No, but I'm surprised you didn't thrust the papers under their noses right then and there.'

His dark blue gaze warred with mine. 'If Jason's a registered donor then it's appropriate to get the wheels in motion as soon as possible. Other lives can be saved. The family might find it difficult at first, but further down the track it often gives comfort to know their relative's death wasn't entirely in vain.'

I knew he was right. But the subject of organ donation is enormously difficult for most people, including clinicians. Relatives are overwrought with grief, especially after an accident or a sudden illness or surgery that didn't go according to plan. They want to cling to their loved one for as long as they can, to hold them and talk to them to say their final goodbyes. Some relatives can't face the thought of their son or daughter or husband or wife being operated on to harvest organs, even when those very organs will save other lives.

It was another thing I wanted to cover in my research. Finding the right time and the right environment in which to bring up the subject could go a long way in lifting organ donation rates, which were generally abysmal. All too often organ donation directives signed by patients were reversed because the relatives were in such distress.

I let out a breath in a little whoosh. 'I'll talk to them tomorrow. I think they need tonight to come to terms with what they've been told so far.'

There was a little silence.

I was about to fill it with something banal when he said, 'Would you like Jason moved to the end room?'

I looked at him in surprise. 'But I thought—'

'It will give the family a little more privacy.'

I couldn't read his expression. He had his poker face on. 'That would be great,' I said. 'Thank you.'

He gave me the briefest of smiles. It was little more than a little quirk of his lips but it made something inside my stomach slip. I suddenly wondered what his full smile would look like and if it would have an even more devastating effect on me. 'How do you get on with Stuart McTaggart?' he said.

'Fine.'

He lifted a dark eyebrow as if that wasn't the answer he'd been expecting. 'You don't find him…difficult?'

I gave a little shrug. 'He has his moments but I don't let it get to me. He's under a lot of pressure and he doesn't know how to manage stress. Stress is contagious, like a disease. You can catch it off others if you're not careful.'

He leaned his hips back against his desk with his arms folded across his broad chest. His eyes never once left mine. I would have found it threatening except I was so fascinated by their colour I was practically mesmerised. In certain lights they were predominately grey but in others they were blue. And now and again they would develop a tiny glittery twinkle as if he was enjoying a private joke.

'So what are your top three hints for relieving stress?' he said.

'Regular exercise, eight hours' sleep, good nutrition.'

'Not so easy when you work the kind of hours we work.'

'True.'

He was still watching me with that unwavering gaze. 'What about sex?'

I felt a hot blush spread over my cheeks. Yes, I know. I'm such a prude, which is incredibly ironic given my parents talk about their sex lives at the drop of a sarong. 'Wh-what about it?' I stammered.

'Isn't it supposed to be the best stress-reliever of all?'

I ran the tip of my tongue out over my suddenly parchment-dry lips. The heat in my cheeks flowed to other parts of my body—my breasts, my belly and between my legs. Even the base of my spine felt molten hot. 'Erm, yes, it's good for that,' I said, 'excellent, in fact. But not everyone can have sex when they're feeling stressed. I mean, how would that work in the workplace, for instance? We can't have staff running off to have sex in the nearest broom cupboard whenever they feel like it, can we?'

I wished I hadn't taken the bait. I wished I hadn't kept running off at the mouth like that. Why the hell was I talking about sex with Matt Bishop? All I could think of was what it would be like to have sex *with* him. Not in a broom cupboard, although I'm sure he would be more than up to the challenge. But in a bed with his arms around me, his long legs entangled with mine, his body pressing me down on the mattress in a passionate clinch unlike any I'd had before.

Just to put you straight, I'm no untried virgin. I've had three partners, although I don't usually count the first one because I was drunk at the time and I can't remember much about it. It was my first year at med school and I was embarrassed about still being a virgin so I drank three vile-tasting cocktails at a party and had it off with a guy whose name I still can't remember. What is it about cocktails and me?

But I digress. The second was only slightly more memorable in that I wasn't drunk or even tipsy, but the guy had performance anxiety, so I blinked and missed it, so to speak. I guess that's why Andy had seemed such a super-stud. At least he could go the distance and I actually managed to orgasm now and again. Told you I was good at lying.

Matt kept his gaze trained on my flustered one, a hint of a smile still playing around the corners of his mouth. 'Perhaps not.'

My phone started to ring and I grabbed at it as if it were the lottery office calling to inform me of a massive win. It wasn't. It was my mother. 'Can I call you back?' I said.

'Darling, you sound so tense.' My mother's voice carried like a foghorn. I think it's from all the chanting she does. It's given her vocal cords serious muscle. 'He's not worth the angst.'

I could feel my cheeks glowing like hot embers. 'I *really* can't talk now so—'

'I just called to give you your horoscope reading. It's really amazing because it said you're going to meet—'

'Now's not a good time,' I said with a level of desperation I could barely keep out of my voice. 'I'll call you later. I promise.'

'All right, darling. Love you.' She made kissy noises.

'I love you too. Bye.' I ended the call and gave Matt a wry look. 'My mum.'

'Who's causing you the angst?' he asked. 'Not me, I hope?'

I backed my way to the door, almost tripping over

my own feet in clumsy haste. 'I'd better let you get to your meeting.'

'Dr Clark?'

My hand reached for the doorknob and I turned my head to look at him over my shoulder. 'Yes?'

A glint danced in his eyes. 'Check the broom cupboards on your way past, will you?'

CHAPTER THREE

I WAS ABOUT to leave for the day when the CEO's secretary came to see me. Lynne Patterson was in her late fifties and had worked at St Iggy's for thirty years in various administrative roles. I had only met her a handful of times but she was always warm and friendly. She reminded me of a mother hen. She oozed maternal warmth and was known for taking lame ducks under her wing. Not that I considered myself a lame duck or anything, but right then I wasn't paddling quite the way I wanted to.

'How did the wedding go?' Lynne asked as her opening gambit. *What is it with everyone and weddings?* I thought. People were becoming obsessed. It wasn't healthy.

My smile felt like it was set in plaster of Paris on my mouth. 'Great. Fabulous. Wonderful. Awesome.' I was going overboard with the superlatives but what else could I do? In for a penny, as they say, but now I was in for a million. I had to keep telling lies to keep the others in place. I was starting to realise what a farce this was becoming. I would have been better to be honest from the start. But now it was too late. I would look completely ridiculous if I told everyone the wedding had been cancelled. Maybe in a couple of months I could say things didn't work out, that Andy and I had decided to separate or something. But until then I had to keep the charade going. *Oh, joy.*

'Well, that's why I thought you'd be perfect for the job,' Lynne said with a beaming smile.

'Erm...job?'

'The St Valentine's Day Ball,' she said. 'We hold it every year. It's our biggest fundraising event for the hospital. But this year it's ICU that's going to get the funds we raise. We hope to raise enough for an intensive care training simulator.'

I'd heard about the ball but I thought it was being organised by one of the senior paediatricians. I said as much but Lynne explained the consultant had to go on leave due to illness so they needed someone to take over.

'Besides,' Lynne said, 'you're young and hip and in touch with everything. The ball was becoming a little staid and boring. Ticket sales have been slow. We thought you'd be fabulous at putting on a great party.'

'We?'

'Dr Bishop.' Lynne beamed again. 'He said you'd be perfect.'

I did the teeth-grinding thing. Silently, I hoped, but I wouldn't have put money on it. 'Right, well, then, I guess I can do that,' I said, madly panicking because it was barely four weeks away. I comforted myself with the fact I didn't have to organise the venue or catering as the consultant had already done that, according to

Lynne. My job was to make the ball entertaining and fun for everyone.

As soon as I got out of the hospital I called Jem. She's a teacher—another irony, given our parents went through a no-schooling phase. It lasted three years but then the authorities cottoned on and we were marched back into the system. Interestingly, I was a year ahead of my peers academically but well behind socially. For Jem it was the other way around. She had no trouble fitting in but she struggled to catch up in classwork. She's never said, but I'm pretty sure that's why she ended up a teacher. She understands how hard it is for kids who aren't naturally academic. Mind you, she's no dunce. Once she caught up there was no stopping her. She whizzed her way through university, landing the vice chancellor's prize on the way through. Now she teaches at a posh girls' school in Bath.

'Jem, you got a minute to talk?' I asked.

'Sure,' Jem said. 'What's up? I mean, apart from being betrayed by your fiancé with the slutty sister of your bridesmaid, and then jilted at the altar, and going on honeymoon all by yourself.'

That's another reason I love my sister. She doesn't sugar-coat stuff. She doesn't just take the bull by the horns. She wrenches the darned things off. Unlike me, who tentatively pets the bull in the hope it will become my best friend and won't gore me to death. But one thing Jem and I have in common is a love of black humour. It's how we dealt with our wacky childhood. If we hadn't laughed we'd have cried. 'It's way worse than that,' I said, and told her about the postcard fiasco.

'What? You mean you still haven't told anyone? No one at all?'

'No.' I kept my head down against the icy cold wind as I walked along the frozen footpath. The last thing I wanted was to slip and end up in the orthopaedic ward. Although come to think of it…

'What about your friend, what's her name? The nurse you said was really sweet.'

'Gracie.'

'That's the one. What about her?'

I sidestepped a sheet of black ice. I decided I didn't want to break a leg. How would I explain no husband coming in to visit me? 'I'm going to tell her…soon.'

'It's not that hard, Bertie,' Jem said matter-of-factly. 'You have nothing to be ashamed of. Andy's a twat. You don't have to protect him. Tell the world what a flipping jerk he is.'

I guess you can tell by now Jem is not the sort of girl to get screwed around by guys. In fact, I think she terrifies most men, which kind of explains why she hasn't had a steady boyfriend for ages—years, actually. She dated a Sicilian guy once but it didn't last. It was a whirlwind affair that ended badly. She's never talked about it. Won't talk about it. I know better than to ask.

'I got caught off guard because of the new director at work,' I said. 'It was too embarrassing to go into the gory details.' *Understatement.*

'What's he like?'

'How do you know he's a he?'

'Because you wouldn't have been caught off guard if it was a woman.'

Got to hand it to my sister. She knows me so well. 'He's…annoying, but kind of interesting too.'

'Woo hoo!' Jem crowed.

I rolled my eyes. I knew what she was thinking—the best way to heal a broken heart was to find someone else and soon. But I'd had enough trouble finding Andy. I didn't like my chances in the dating game. Besides, I'm not sure I wanted all the drama. Maybe I was destined to be on my own. My heart sank at the thought. I didn't want to be alone. I wanted to be with someone who loved me. I wanted a family. I wanted it all. 'He thinks my research is dodgy,' I said.

'What's he look like?'

'Did you hear me?' I said.

'Is he hot?'

'He's okay.'

'How okay?' Jem said.

I blew out a breath. There was no point fighting it. Jem would get it out of me eventually. Might as well be sooner rather than later. 'He's six foot four and has dark hair and blue-grey eyes that change in different lights. He's got a nice mouth but I don't think he smiles at lot. Although he gets this little twinkle now and again that makes me wonder if he's laughing at me.'

'Way to go, Bertie!'

'Like that's going to happen,' I said. 'Besides, he thinks I'm married.'

'Some men get off on having an affair with a married woman.'

'Not him,' I said. 'He's too conservative.' Which was kind of what I liked about him, even though I was supposed to dislike him on account of him being so mocking about my project. But for all that I felt drawn to him. He intrigued me. All those shifting shadows in his eyes suggested a man with layers and secrets that were just waiting to be explored.

'So what doesn't he like about your research?' Jem asked. 'Apart from the funny title, of course.'

I almost tripped on a crack in the footpath. 'Why didn't you say something earlier?'

Jem laughed. 'I thought you did it deliberately. You know how everyone is always poking fun at New Agey things. I thought it was really clever of you, actually.'

'Yeah, well, Matt Bishop thinks it's a big joke,' I said. 'It will be all round the hospital tomorrow. I just know it. Everyone will be laughing at me.'

'You've been laughed at before and lived to tell the tale,' Jem said. 'We both have.'

I couldn't argue with that. Sometimes when I couldn't sleep I heard the mocking taunts from my childhood echoing in my bedroom. They were like ghosts from the past who wouldn't leave me alone. Mean ghosts who delighted in reminding me I wasn't part of the in-crowd. I was a misfit. A reject. A loner. Alone.

I said goodbye to Jem and walked through the park to my house a couple of streets back from Bayswater Road. I was really proud of my home. I had a shockingly high mortgage, which would take me the rest of my life to pay off, but I didn't care. I loved my three-storey Victorian house with its quaint pocket-handkerchief front garden.

I was teaching myself how to paint and decorate, not just to save costs but because I found it therapeutic. There was something incredibly soothing about paint-ing. I was doing a room at a time and really enjoyed seeing the transformation happen before my eyes. Cracked and peeling paint replaced by smooth fresh colour. I'd done the master bedroom and now I was working on the sitting room. I scrubbed and sanded back the woodwork and applied the first undercoat before I left for my… well, you know. Andy was going to help me finish it. Or at least that's what he'd said. Not that he'd helped me with any of it, although I do seem to remember once he carried some old wallpaper out to the recycling bin.

My dad isn't much help. He can barely change a light bulb, mostly because he and Mum went through a no-electricity phase, which lasted about ten years. Solar power is great when you live in a place like Australia where the sun shines just about every day. Not so good on the Yorkshire moors.

I had a bite to eat and set to work but I had barely got the undercoat lid off the paint tin when there was a knock on the door. I peeped through the spy hole. It was the neighbour who lives six houses up from Elsie. Margery Stoneham was in her mid-seventies and was our street's neighbourhood watch. Nothing escaped her notice. She had an annoying yappy little dog called Freddy who humped my leg any chance it got. Don't get me wrong. I love animals, dogs in particular, but Freddy was the most obnoxious little mutt I'd ever come across. He looked like a cross between a ferret and a rat and had the sort of wiry fur that felt like a pot scourer.

I felt on the back foot as soon as I opened the door. I had—inadvertently—sent Margery a postcard, along with Elsie. Who could believe three little pieces of cardboard could do so much damage? The dog was at Margery's feet, looking up at me with a beady look not unlike hers. 'Hi, Mrs Stoneham,' I said, with a bright smile. 'What a lovely surprise.' *Not*.

Margery peered past my shoulder. 'Is your hubby at home?'

'Erm, not right now.' *Here we go again*, I thought. But Margery was the last person I wanted to announce my failed wedding to. I might as well take out a billboard ad or announce it in *The Times*. 'How's that leg ulcer? Healed up now?' Freddy had taken a nip at her, not that she admitted that to me. She told me she'd scratched it on the coffee table. I checked out the coffee table when I was over there, dressing the wound for her. As far as I could tell it didn't have any teeth.

'Just about.' Margery looked past my shoulder again. 'Are you sure I'm not intruding? You're only just back from your honeymoon. I wouldn't want to—'

'It's perfectly fine,' I said. 'What can I do for you?'

That's one thing I did know for sure. Margery nearly always wanted something. She didn't just drop in for a chat. I can't tell you how many prescriptions I've written for her and I've only been living there just under a year.

'I wanted to ask a little favour of you,' she said. 'I'm going to visit my sister in Cornwall and I need someone to mind Freddy for a few days. I'd ask Elsie but she's not confident walking him and he does so love his walk.'

I wanted to say no. Jem would have said no but, then, she's a lot stronger than I am. I have this annoying tendency to want to please everyone. I say yes when I really want to say no because I'm worried people won't like me if I grow a backbone. 'Of course I'll mind him,' I said. See how good I am at lying? They just slip off my tongue. 'We'll have a ball, won't we, Freddy?'

I knew better than to lean down and try and pat him. He lifted one side of his mouth in a snarl that showed his yellowed teeth. Did I mention his foetid breath? Oh, and he farts. A lot.

When I got to work the next morning there was no change in Jason Ryder. He had been moved to my end room and was surrounded by his family. I spent a bit of time with them before I did a central line on a new patient. The morning was almost over before I ran into Matt Bishop. Literally. I was walking past his office with my head down, thinking about my ridiculous and steadily increasing web of lies, as he was coming out, and I cannoned straight into him. He took me by the upper arms to steady me and a shockwave went through me as if he had clamped me with live voltage. I couldn't smother a gasp in time. 'Oomph!'

His hands slid down my arms before he released me. I couldn't help noticing he opened and closed his fingers once or twice as if trying to rid himself of the feel of me. 'Sorry. Did I hurt you?'

I looked into his eyes—they were a darker shade of blue than grey as he was wearing a light blue shirt and a dark tie—and I felt like something tight and locked flowered open inside my chest. 'No. Not at all. It was my fault. I wasn't looking where I was going.'

He continued to look down at me. He had to look down as I'm only five feet five and I wasn't wearing heels. I felt like a Shetland pony standing in front of a thoroughbred. And, going with the equine theme, Matt's nostrils gave a slight flare, as if he was picking up my scent. I hoped to God it was the dash of the neroli oil I'd put on and not the musty smell of Freddy, who'd been dropped off that morning. 'Did Lynne Patterson speak to you about the ball?' he said.

'Yes. Thanks for the vote of confidence.' I couldn't quite remove the hint of sarcasm from my tone. 'I hope you don't live to regret it.'

'I'm sure you'll do an excellent job.' He gave me one of his enigmatic smiles. 'Planning a wedding can't be too dissimilar.'

Every time the word 'wedding' was mentioned I felt my cheeks burn up. I was going to have to wear thick concealing make-up or something at this rate. Or maybe I could pretend I had rosacea. 'I'm going to check out the venue after work,' I said. 'And I'm thinking we should make it a costume ball. What do you think?'

'That could work.'

I angled my head at him. 'What costume would you wear?'

The twinkle was back in his gaze. 'Now, that would be telling. You'll have to wait and see.'

'Will you bring a partner?' I'm not sure why I asked that. Actually, I did know. I wanted to know what sort of woman he dated. I bet he would be a wonderful partner. He would be polite and respectful. He would open doors for his date and walk on the road side of the footpath. I bet he could dance, too, proper dancing as in a waltz. Andy mashed my toes to a pulp on the one occasion we waltzed. And he got horribly drunk and I had to get two security guards to help me bundle him into a taxi. Talk about embarrassing.

'No.'

'Why not? Surely you could ask someone.'

He gave a loose shrug. 'I'm too busy for a relationship just now. I have other priorities.' He waited a beat before asking, 'Will you bring your husband?'

He'd done it again, that ever so slight stress on the word 'husband'. Every time he did that it made me feel as if he thought I was too hideous to have landed myself a man. I know I'm not billboard stunning or anything but I've been told I've got nice brown eyes and a cute smile. Well, I know parents are always biased, but still. 'Erm, I think he'll be away with work,' I said. 'He travels...a lot.'

'That's a shame. I was looking forward to meeting him.'

I wrinkled my brow. 'Why?'

His expression was impossible to read. 'You said he was a stock analyst, right?'

'Yes...'

'I thought I'd ask him about some stocks I've had my eye on for a while.'

I shifted my weight from foot to foot. I felt a heat rash moving all over my body. It was like ants marching underneath my skin. Maybe my talent at lying was deserting me. 'Don't you have a financial planner?' I said.

'Sure, but it's always good to get inside information, don't you think?'

I couldn't hold his penetrating gaze. I lowered mine and mumbled something about seeing a patient and left.

I was walking Freddy in Hyde Park in one of the dog exercise areas after work. It was freezing cold and flakes of snow were falling but I was determined to wear out the little mutt. While I'd been at work he'd chewed my favourite hippopotamus slippers Jem gave me for Christmas two years ago and one of my computer cables. I decided to let him off the lead so he could have a good run around and play with the other dogs. What I hadn't realised was that Freddy didn't *like* other dogs. Before I knew it he was at the throat of a corgi and it looked like Freddy was winning. The howls and growls and yelps and cries of 'Help!' from me created such a ruckus that people did what people normally do in that situation—they stopped and stared and did absolutely nothing.

Except for one man who came out of the shadows and pulled the dogs apart with his bare hands. Except his hands weren't bare. He was wearing gloves, lovely butter-soft black leather ones that Freddy's teeth immediately punctured. I grabbed Freddy and snapped his lead back on but the stupid mutt was straining at the leash, trying to get to the overweight corgi, who was doing the same on the end of its lead, which its owner had now refastened.

'I'm *so* sorry,' I said. 'It's not my dog. I didn't realise he would...' I blinked as the man's face was suddenly illuminated by one of the park's lights. 'You!'

Matt Bishop gave me a rueful look. 'It's not my dog either. It's my great-aunt's.'

'Your great-aunt isn't the Queen, is she?'

He threw back his head and laughed. I stood transfixed at the sound. It was deep and unmistakably masculine and made something deep and tight in my belly work loose. It wasn't just his laugh that was so captivating. It was the way his normally stern features relaxed, giving him an almost boyish look. At work with the pressures of lives in his hands he looked as if he was nudging forty. Now he looked no older than thirty but I knew he had to be at least thirty-three or -four to be as qualified as he was to head the department.

He was wearing casual clothes under a dark blue cashmere overcoat. Jeans and a sweater with the tips of his shirt collar showing. I don't think I've ever seen a more handsome-looking man. Not in a pretty-boy way but in a totally testosterone-oozing way that made the breath catch in my throat.

His gaze went to the cup-cake beanie I was wearing. It was pink and white and had a red pom-pom on top that looked like a cherry. I was pretty proud of it, actually. I taught myself to knit, making novelty beanies. So far I've made a mouse, a zebra and a bee.

The dogs were still snarling at each other. I had Freddy on such a tight leash I could feel the muscles in my arm protesting at the strain. Who needed the gym when you had an unruly dog? Freddy hurt more than three sets of ten-kilogram biceps curls.

'Quiet, Winnie,' Matt said. The corgi slunk down into a submissive pose but not before giving Freddy another murderous look. Freddy growled like something out of a horror movie and completely ignored my command to be quiet. I guess because my voice wasn't as deep and authoritative as Matt's, because as soon as Matt said it to Freddy he sat and shut up. He even held up his paw for a shake.

'Nice job,' I said. 'You don't happen to be best friends with Cesar Millan, do you?'

Matt smiled and my breath caught again. 'Dog training's pretty simple. You just have to show them who's pack leader.'

I'm not sure how it happened but somehow we started walking together. The dogs kept eyeing each other warily, but after a while they seemed to forget their ignominious start and got on with the job of sniffing every blade of grass…well, the ones that weren't covered in snow, that is. A light dusting had fallen, making the park look like a winter fairyland. I love winter. I think it's the most romantic time of the year. That's why I wanted to be married in early December. Everyone gets married in spring or summer. I wanted to be different. But, then, sometimes you can be too different, which I've found to my detriment.

'Where does your great-aunt live?' I asked into the silence. Actually, I was quite proud of the fact I'd waited at least thirty seconds before speaking. That's a record for me.

He named the street running parallel to mine. I was so shocked I stopped and looked up at him. 'Really?'

'What's wrong?' he asked.

I gave a shaky laugh. 'Whoa, that's spooky. I live in the next street. Number forty.'

'Why spooky?'

'As in weirdly coincidental,' I said. 'London's a big city.'

'True, but it's close to the hospital and I'm only staying there until I can move back into my place once the tenants move out in a couple of weeks.'

He was living a street away from me?

'Where is your place?'

'Notting Hill.'

Of course, I thought. I'd had a feeling Matt came from money. He had the right accent and the well-groomed and cultured look. It had taken me years to shake off my Yorkshire vowels. Now and again when I was overtired one would slip out. I privately envied people like Matt. They hadn't been dragged around the countryside in search of the next New Age trend, living in mud huts or tents or straw houses, not eating animal products or wearing them, not using chemicals or eating sugar or salt or processed food.

Don't get me wrong. I love my parents. They're good people, loving and kind and well meaning. But I couldn't imagine Matt Bishop's parents cavorting around a stone circle stark naked and chanting mantras. They probably wore Burberry and sipped sherry in the conservatory of their centuries-old pile in the countryside while a host of servants tended to their every whim.

'How long have you got the dog?' Matt asked.

'Until the weekend after next,' I said. 'My neighbour is visiting her sister in Cornwall. I don't know why she didn't take him with her. Maybe her sister won't let her. Can't say I blame her. He needs to go to reform school.'

I heard him give a soft, deep chuckle and another shiver shimmied down my spine.

'My great-aunt is visiting my parents for a few days,' he said.

I cast him a sideways glance. 'Your parents don't like dogs?'

Nothing showed on his face but the tone of his voice

contained a hint of something I couldn't identify. 'My father.'

'Is he allergic?'

His mouth tightened for a nanosecond. 'You could say that.'

'Do you have siblings?' I asked, after we'd walked a few more paces. See how good I was getting at silences? Maybe there was some hope for me after all.

'No,' he said after a slight pause. 'There's only me. You?'

'A sister called Jem—short for Jemima. Our mum was really into Beatrix Potter, in case you hadn't guessed. Jem's ten months older than me.'

He flashed me a quick glance. 'That was close.'

I rolled my eyes. 'My parents were using natural contraceptive methods. So natural they fell pregnant straight away.'

He smiled again. 'Are you close to your sister?'

'Very, although we're quite different.'

'What does she do?'

'She's a teacher.'

We walked a few more metres in silence. Yes, in silence! But for some reason I didn't feel awkward or pressured to fill it. I wondered about his parents, whether he was close to them or not. I sensed tension between him and his father but that might just be my imagination. Although a lot of men of Matt's age had the young stag, old stag thing going on. It could be quite a competitive dynamic, especially as the father neared retirement age.

'What does your father do?' I asked.

'He's in corporate law.'

'Does your mother have a career?'

'She used to work as a legal secretary but she didn't go back after she married.' He waited a beat before adding, 'My father likes having her at his beck and call.'

I frowned at his tone. 'Is that what *she* wants?'

He shrugged the shoulder nearest me. I felt it brush against mine. 'She seems happy enough being the trophy wife. It's either that or get traded in for a newer model. At least he's spared her the indignity of that.'

I was surprised—and secretly delighted—he'd revealed that to me. I wondered if he felt I was someone he could talk to about stuff. It's hard for doctors, particularly specialists at the top of their field. Everyone comes to *them* to solve their problems. No one ever thinks to ask if the specialist has problems of his or her own. I suspected Matt had some frustration towards his mother for settling for a life of sherry mornings and bridge club. Did his father play around? Openly or furtively?

I thought of my parents with their easygoing lifestyle. They loved each other. No one could ever be in doubt of that, least of all Jem and I. They were open about their—thankfully occasional these days—other partners, which Jem and I still found totally weird, but they always came back to each other and would never dream of stopping each other from reaching their potential. If my mum wanted to do something, my dad would support her in it one hundred percent, and vice versa. They didn't have secrets, or at least none Jem and I were aware of.

I decided against telling Matt about my background. He didn't ask, which either meant he wasn't interested or he was tired of small talk. Or maybe he regretted revealing what he had. I glanced at him covertly to find he had a frown on his forehead.

The dogs were walking to heel like star graduates from obedience school. I felt a little proud of myself, actually. Maybe I could win over Freddy by the time Margery got back. Have him eating out of my hand instead of biting it.

'Have you checked out the venue for the ball?' Matt asked.

'No, I thought I'd do that once I wore out Freddy.'

He stopped and looked down at me. I couldn't see his eyes because his face was in shadow but I could see the misty fog of his warm breath as it met the cold air. 'How about I come with you? That is, if your husband wouldn't mind?'

My heart gave a little stumble as I gave him one of my fixed smiles. 'Believe me, he won't mind at all.'

CHAPTER FOUR

MATT CAME TO pick me up in his car forty-five minutes later. I'd had just enough time to feed Freddy and wash his musty wet feathers smell off me. I spritzed myself with my neroli oil spray and brushed out my hair, which had been in a knot at the back of my head for work and then squashed flat by my beanie.

I'm not in the least bit vain but I will say one thing for myself—I have great hair. It's thick and healthy with just enough wave in it to give it loads of body, or I can straighten it, and it's long enough to put up or leave loose. Jem hates me for it, as hers is a riot of corkscrew blonde curls that makes her look like she's poked her fingers into a power outlet.

I was waiting on my front step as Matt's car double-parked. There are never any spaces in front of my house, which is usually my biggest bugbear, but tonight I was glad about it. The last thing I wanted was for Matt Bishop to park his car outside my door and invite himself in. One step inside and my charade would be blown. There wasn't a single thing to suggest I was a recently married woman, and it wasn't just the absence of a husband either. I had sent back all the wedding gifts…

apart from the really gorgeous art deco standard lamp Jem had given me.

Before I'd taken a step off my front porch Matt got out of the car and opened the passenger door for me. His gaze ran over my hair and my outfit in a way that made me feel as if he was seeing me for the first time. I actually saw him blink a couple of times as if he couldn't believe what he was seeing. I had changed into a raspberry-red knee-length dress and I'd teamed it with black leather boots—I tell my parents they're synthetic—and I was wearing fishnet tights. I was wearing a fake-fur coat—even *I* am with my parents on that—but I have to admit there was a hint of high-street hooker about my get-up. But, then, I love playful clothes. Not just so people will laugh at them instead of me, but more to put my finger up at the world for making snap judgements about appearances. We are all the same naked…well, more or less.

Mind you, I was having hot flushes thinking about Matt Bishop in his birthday suit. Even though he had a tall, rangy build, his neat, conservative clothes weren't quite able to hide the firm tone of his muscles. I could imagine how taut and toned his abdomen was, unlike mine, which was paying the price of a two-week stint of comfort eating.

I slipped into the low-slung sports car, the rich, soft leather seat cupping my body like an expensively gloved hand. I could smell Matt's subtle aftershave and took a deep breath to take more of it in as I pulled down the seat belt and clicked it into place.

He got in behind the wheel and I covertly watched the muscles bunching in his thigh as he put his foot down on the clutch and put the car into gear. There's something about a manual car that's intensely masculine. Surging through all those gears, the guttural sound of all those throaty revs, the G-force as the rubber hits the road. I felt myself being pushed back further into the seat as we headed to the corner.

The hotel where the hospital ball was being held was a boutique one owned by a former patient. We were getting the use of the ballroom at a cut price. The hotel was popular with A-list celebrities because it was both intimate and luxurious. I hadn't been there before so I felt like a Hollywood superstar walking up the runner of red carpet on the front steps leading into the polished marble foyer. Uniformed staff were behind the shiny brass and marble reception desk and there was a concierge and three porters in another section. There was a massive arrangement of flowers on a marble stand and a veritable waterfall of crystals hung from the ceiling in a gloriously decadent chandelier that tinkled musically as we walked under it.

I didn't want to appear too kid-in-the-candy-store overwhelmed by all the glitz and glamour surrounding me, but given I hadn't stepped into a proper hotel until I was eighteen I still had a lot of catching up to do. My parents didn't even stay in motels or caravan parks, let alone posh five-star hotels. They camped. And before you start picturing a nicely erected tent and a crackling fire and us four sitting around it singing 'Kumbaya', let me tell you it was nothing like that. We didn't have a proper tent. My parents always borrowed one that looked like it had a past life in the circus. It was huge. But that was because there were usually ten other families with us, which meant Jem and I had to hang out with a bunch of feral kids we had nothing in common with apart from having hippy parents.

It nearly always rained, and we were bitten to death by midges, or it was stinking hot and ants would get in our food, which was ironic given there was never any sugar in it.

So you can probably see why walking into the boutique hotel in Mayfair was such a big deal for me. Oh, and the fact that I was walking in with Matt Bishop was even more thrilling. We were getting looks. You know, the sort of double-take looks people give when they think they're seeing someone important walk by.

I can tell you, I *felt* important. I only wished I really was with Matt, I wished his hand was holding mine or his arm was around my waist. I was a little shocked at where my thoughts were straying. I hoped he couldn't read my mind. It was hard enough keeping my body language under control.

Matt had had the foresight to call the hotel ahead of time and make an appointment to see the ballroom. Typical me, I was just going to wing it, pop my head through the door and see what it was like. But, no, he had organised a guided tour.

The staff member left us in the ballroom while he took a call. Luckily for us the ballroom wasn't being used. The chairs and tables were against the walls, which made the floor space seem the size of a football field. The décor was a stylishly neutral one in cream and white with a touch of taupe, which gave wonderful scope for thematic decorations.

I did a three-sixty about the room and pictured stunning colours and costumes and wonderful food and wine and fabulous music with live musicians playing. I momentarily forgot about the hospital budget, but still...

'What do you think?' Matt said from beside me.

'It's perfect,' I said. 'We could have helium balloon trees and a chocolate fountain and a prize for the best costume.'

'Sounds like a plan.'

I was about to respond when the hotel staff member returned. He had an apologetic look on his face as he handed Matt a key card. 'I'm afraid I've been called away to deal with a little matter in Reception. The manager asked me to give you access to our honeymoon suite. It's the only suite that's vacant this evening so you won't be disturbed. A light supper will be sent up shortly, compliments of the hotel.'

'Oh, but we couldn't possibly—' I began.

'That's very kind,' Matt said, smiling at the staff member.

The honeymoon suite?

As we made our way to the lift my heart was skipping all around my chest cavity like a hyperactive kid on a pogo stick. I didn't say a word as the lift zoomed up to the top floor. Not one word. I did what most people do in lifts. I stared at the numbers, then at my feet, then at the 'In Case of Emergency' instructions, which I studiously memorised. Anywhere but at the tall, silent man standing within arm's reach of me. I kept my arms close to my body, clutching my purse across my belly, which was doing a series of super-fast somersaults that would have made an Olympic gymnast proud.

The lift opened and Matt led the way to the suite down the wide, velvet-soft carpeted corridor, holding the door open for me once he'd unlocked it. 'I feel as if I should be carrying you over the threshold or something,' he said with a deadpan expression.

I gave him a wry look. 'The last time someone carried me they herniated a disc.'

It was true. My dad picked me up as a joke a few years ago and ended up having months of physiotherapy. Not that I'm a big girl or anything but ever since then I've been self-conscious about my weight. It doesn't help that my father keeps reminding me of it every time he sees me by leaning over and groaning, 'My poor old aching back!'

Matt closed the door, looking at me with one of those quirked-brow looks. 'Not your husband, surely?'

I had to work hard to get myself together. 'Erm…no. He didn't carry me over the threshold. He's not very… erm…traditional.'

'Is that why you don't wear an engagement and wedding ring?'

I mentally kicked myself. I never wear rings of any sort at work because it's all too easy to lose them when I scrub up for a central line procedure or Theatre. But I should have thought of wearing a dress ring or something tonight. I'd given back Andy's engagement ring… after I'd got the plumber to find it in the S bend of my bathroom basin. I curled my fingers into my palm—as if that was going to help—and gave Matt a tight smile. 'I forgot to put them on when I got home from work. Silly me.' I spun round to look at the suite rather than have him study me in that penetrating way. 'Wow! Look at this place. It's totally awesome.'

I wasn't exaggerating. It *was* awesome. The suite

was in four compartments separated by different levels. The décor was lavishly decadent, lots of velvet and satin, with soft lighting creating a sensual mood. The sitting-room area overlooked the Thames with views over Tower Bridge and the brightly lit London Eye. A wide flat-screen television dominated one wall. Seriously, who needed a television while on honeymoon? Mind you, I was glad I had one on mine but that's because, well, you know, but at least I'd caught up on the complete box set of *Downton Abbey*. There was a well-stocked bar and a coffee table and side tables with gorgeous lamps that created an intimate atmosphere.

I caught a glimpse of the bathroom through the open door. It was bigger than my sitting room and was a luxurious affair of marble and gold with a white claw-foot bath in the centre of the room. A shower stall big enough for a hockey match was on one side and twin basins and gilt-framed mirrors above them on the other. Gorgeous fluffy towels, which looked as big as sheets, were on the gold towel rails or folded on a gold luggage rack-style holder.

On the top level of the suite there was a king-sized bed. I wondered if there was such a thing as emperor-sized—or maybe dictator-sized—as I'd never seen one as big as that before. The bedhead and sashed curtains either side of it were plush scarlet velvet, and teamed with the snow-white linen it looked not just stunning but temptingly inviting. I wasn't tired but I had a childish desire to bounce up and down on that big bed, like Jem and I used to do when we visited our grandparents, which was rare because our parents hadn't wanted us to be corrupted by capitalist greed. Like *that* worked.

There were dried rose petals artfully arranged on the bed and scatter cushions in the same rich scarlet were positioned against the bank of feather pillows. The bedside tables held twin lamps with sparkling crystal stands and the shades were the same pure white as the bed linen.

I stole a glance at Matt but he seemed totally unfazed by all the luxury. I suspected he was no stranger to five-star hotels. He was checking his phone, scrolling through messages or emails. 'Nice view,' I said to break the silence.

He looked up and smiled a lazy half-smile. 'Yes.'

I could feel my face blushing like the colour of a stoplight. Something about his gaze as it held mine made me feel like a teenager discovering she was attractive to the opposite sex for the first time. I felt aware of my body in a way I hadn't been before, all of its secret zones lighting up like a Christmas tree. Not just lighting up but fizzing with energy. I moistened my lips and watched as his gaze followed the pathway of my tongue. I saw his eyes darken as they came back to mine.

A knock on the door jolted me out of the moment. I whipped around and opened it before Matt could take a step. I knew I was acting like a gauche fool but I had never been so far out of my depth.

A hotel staff member wheeled in a trolley full of silver dome-covered dishes. There was a bottle of champagne in an ice bucket and two crystal flutes. The champagne had a scarlet ribbon tied around its neck the same shade as the cushions and drapes. I felt like I had stepped into a fairytale. I was suddenly a princess being served in the royal suite with a handsome suitor.

The handsome suitor discreetly tipped the hotel staff member and the door closed with a soft little click that had a hint of finality to it that was strangely disquieting. For some reason an anticipatory shiver coursed over my flesh. I sensed we had crossed a threshold, one I hadn't crossed in a long time. Maybe ever.

I was alone with a man I had only met the day before.

He was my boss, sure, but if things had been different—like if I weren't pretending to be married—I would have been perfectly happy if we were left alone for the next week. Month even.

'Might as well make the most of the situation,' Matt said, as he reached for the champagne bottle.

I watched as he poured the bubbles into the two glasses. My fingers brushed against his as he handed me my glass. My heart fluttered and thumped like it had developed wings and a limp. My pulse raced. I took a sip…more than a sip, to be honest. It's why I don't drink too often. If I'm feeling nervous I drink more than I should.

Before I knew it the glass was empty. I could feel the alcohol hit my bloodstream like rocket fuel. I felt light-headed but maybe that had more to do with the fact that Matt was standing close enough for me to hear him breathing. I could smell those grace notes of lemongrass and lime. I could see the shadow of stubble on his jaw, so dark and so sexy I wanted to trail my fingertips across it to see if they would catch like silk does on something rough.

He put his glass down after only taking a sip. I saw his eyes move between each of mine, back and forth, and then his gaze dipped to my mouth. I stopped breathing as his head came down as if in slow motion.

I know I should have stepped away. All it would have taken was half a step. But my feet were glued in place. Bolted to the floor. I lowered my lashes as his warm breath danced over my lips. I'm not sure how long we stood there like that, with our breaths mingling so intimately. It felt like no time at all and yet it felt like forever. I ached for him to close the distance. Every cell in my body was throbbing in eagerness. I could feel the entire surface of my lips tingling for his final touchdown.

And then it happened.

I'm not sure which one of us moved first but suddenly his mouth brushed mine, a feather-light touch that triggered a seismic reaction in every nerve in my lips. I felt them tingle and fizz as his mouth came back for more, harder this time, an increase in pressure that made my heart bang against my breastbone like a church bell pulled by a madman. His lips were warm and dry and firm and commanding. They were hard and then they were soft, tempting and then teasing. I stepped up on tiptoe, my breasts pushing against the hard wall of his chest; at the same time one of his hands settled in the small of my back and brought me closer.

I felt the outline of his body from chest to thigh. It was imprinted on my flesh, setting off spot fires everywhere we touched. My breasts swelled and ached and my nipples tightened. My belly quivered against the ridged plane of his. My pelvis throbbed as I felt the length and potency of his growing erection.

I hummed with pleasure against his lips, and then he

deepened the kiss with a bold sweep and thrust of his tongue into my mouth. The sensation of our tongues meeting was like an eruption. I leaned into him, into his kiss as if it was my only source of sustenance. I tasted the hint of champagne he had sipped, but it was the mint and maleness of him that was even more addictive.

I took succour at his mouth, letting my tongue wrangle with his in a catch-me-if-you-can game that made my spine shiver in reaction. Fireworks went off in my head. My brain was so jazzed by the sensations I was feeling it was like being short-circuited. Thoughts and rationality were pushed aside as lust and need took over. I had never had a kiss so exciting, so utterly captivating I forgot all sense of time and place. I was swept up in the moment of rapture, of feeling desired and desirable, of feeling feminine and powerful in a way I had never experienced before.

His hands were suddenly cupping my face, his fingers splayed across my cheeks as he savoured my mouth as if it were his last meal. The desire that arced and burned between us took me by surprise. I had a feeling it took him by surprise too. I felt it in the way he groaned as his tongue tangled with mine, the way his body ground against mine in that primal search for satisfaction. I could feel the potency of him against my belly, the blood surging in him, extending him. Hardening him.

My own body was in raptures of excitement. I could feel lust blasting through me like dynamite blasts through shale. My inner core quivered, moistened, swelled and ached. My breasts felt fuller and more sensitive where the wall of his chest was abrading them.

My lips were swelling under the mounting pressure of his mouth, my tongue fizzy with delight as it danced with his. He took my lower lip in his teeth in a soft little play-bite that made every hair on my scalp shiver at the roots. Then he swept his tongue over the spot he'd nipped, salving it, teasing it into wanting more.

I nipped at his lip, taking the flesh between my teeth and gently tugging, my insides shuddering with pleasure as he made a guttural sound of approval. I went at him again, not just his lip this time but his neck as well. I practically turned into a vampire. I sank my teeth into his skin and sucked and sucked. I probably would have drawn blood but for the fact he took me by the hair at the back of my head to control me.

But I didn't want to be controlled. Something inside me had got out of its cage. It was on a rampage. It was hurtling through every boundary or barrier I had put up in the past. My wild woman was on the loose. She was wanton and shameless and hot for action.

I went for his mouth again, crushing my lips to his, searching for his tongue with a brazen stroke of mine. He was ready and waiting for me. It was hard to tell who was more in control or if we both were on some crazy out-of-character roller-coaster ride of wild animal-driven lust.

His hands were at my breasts, shaping them through my clothes as his mouth kept up its passionate assault on mine. The feel of his hands cupping me was so wickedly delightful. It didn't matter that three layers separated his flesh from mine. I felt his touch as if he had stripped me stark naked.

I wasn't letting him cop a feel unless I got one too.

I put my hands on him through his trousers, shaping him, teasing him with the bold stroke of my fingers. He was so hard I could feel the blood pounding through him. And he was getting harder. That thrilled me more than anything. There's nothing more of a turn-on than feeling a man's ardent desire for you. It made my desire flare like fuel exposed to a naked flame. I practically exploded with a fireball of lust that shook me to the centre of my being.

Every part of my body quaked with need, with longing so primal and so intense I felt like a stranger to myself. I realised then how lacklustre Andy had been. He had never touched me through my clothes as if he was too impatient to take them off before he had me. He had never growled and groaned against my mouth as if he was imbibing a potent drug and it was the only thing keeping him alive. He had never made me feel as if I was the only woman who could bring him undone with just a kiss.

I should *not* have thought of Andy. Talk about taking a cold shower. It was like a bucket of ice water had been dumped down the back of my dress.

What was I doing?

I pulled back from Matt as if he had suddenly turned to fire. 'What do you think you're doing?' I said, acting like an outraged virgin in a Regency novel. I know it was a little late for such histrionics but I had to make up some lost ground. What sort of woman did he think I was? Or was he the type who got off on dallying with married women? I had met plenty of men like that. They disgusted me. They had no sense of loyalty. No sense of the damage they were causing.

His expression was unmistakably mocking. 'What's wrong?'

'What's wrong?' I all but spluttered the words at him. 'You know exactly what's wrong! This is wrong. Us kissing like this. It's tacky. It's gross. It shouldn't have happened.'

He arched a brow. 'Because I'm your boss?'

I swallowed so tightly I could hear it. *Gurhdt.* 'Not just that. I'm not…available.' For some reason I couldn't say the word 'married'. I was thoroughly fed up with the word. I wished I never had to hear it again. Married. Yukkety-yuk. Every time I said it I felt sick with shame at how everyone had looked at me back at home when I'd told them the wedding was off. Of course Andy had left that awful task to me. All those exchanged glances that spoke volumes. The I-told-you-something-wasn't-right-about-those-two looks that made my stomach lining corrode with nausea. The pitying looks were the worst. I would do anything to avoid seeing someone look at me that way again.

And I mean *anything.* Including carrying on a charade that was causing me more angst than anything else in my life so far. And that was saying something because my life has not been a tartan-blanket-and-wicker-basket picnic, let me tell you.

Matt's eyes held mine in a lock that made me feel raw and exposed. 'That wasn't the message I've been getting from the moment I met you.'

I was frowning so hard I reckoned even if I'd had

Botox in my forehead it would have run off scared. 'I've met men like you before. You get off on the challenge of scoring with someone who's off limits. It's all a game to you. Once you achieve your goal you move on to the next target.' I stepped up close again and poked him in the chest with my index finger. It hurt like hell because his chest was like a wall of marble but I wanted to drive home my point. But on a subconscious level I think I just wanted to touch him again. 'Find someone else to play with, Dr Bishop. I'm off the market. Got it?'

His smile was lazy and his eyes sexily hooded, and trained on my mouth as if he couldn't wait to devour it again. His hand captured mine before I could pull it away and he held it firmly against his chest, right over where his heart was beating. I could feel every thump. The doctor in me couldn't help noticing how fit he was. He had a resting pulse of forty-five bpm, which was pretty damn good. Right now mine was running as if I had arrhythmia. 'If you change your mind, call me,' he said. 'We could make an interesting pair.'

I curled my lip. 'Friends with benefits?'

His eyes glinted. 'Do you need a friend, Dr Clark?'

I needed my head read. That's what I needed. Because when he looked at me like that I wanted to kiss him again. I wanted to push him backwards towards the bed and crawl all over him and climb into his skin. But somehow I managed to get my wild woman back in her cage and snick the lock back in place.

I put up my chin and gave him an icy glare. 'Get your hands off me and keep them off me.'

He held my look for a heart-stopping moment.

I felt the tug of war between our wills. It was like

two strong forces that had never encountered that level of oppositional power before. The energy in the air was electric. Supercharged. Crackling like a high-voltage current along a tight wire.

I was the first to look away. I had to otherwise I would have confessed all then and there. But I didn't want his pity. I didn't want him to think I was on the lookout for a rebound fling. That I was so desperate to be found desirable that I would get down and dirty with a man I had known less than twenty-four hours. I wanted to salvage my dignity in the only way I knew how. Pretence. Anyway, I was good at it. I'd been doing it all my life in order to fit in.

I gave my hand an almighty tug and stalked over to where I had left my bag. I shoved it over my shoulder in an affronted manner, tossing my head—even though I know there is no way on earth anyone can *actually* toss their head, or roll their eyes, come to think of it—and wrenched open the suite door.

'Honeymoon over?' he said.

I looked at him over my shoulder. His mouth was lifted in what I was coming to know as his trademark sardonic smile. I let fly with a very rude two-word phrase that basically told him he could…well, I guess you get the idea.

I closed the door with a satisfying snick. I was glad I'd had the last word.

It's not often I get the chance.

CHAPTER FIVE

I'D BEEN HOME half an hour when I suddenly realised how quiet it was. Not just my house, which was like a proverbial tomb—even the rickety floorboards had stopped creaking. No, it was my phone. I would normally get a call from the hospital about a patient, or Jem would text or call or Mum or Dad would check in. Yes, in spite of their anti-capitalist ranting, they both have smartphones.

But nothing. Zilch. *Nada.*

I picked up my bag and searched in its depths for my phone. I usually slip it into one of the inner pockets so I can access it quickly. Sometimes it switches to silent if I'm not careful, or vice versa, which was incredibly embarrassing the last time I went to the cinema. The looks I got! Of course it went off right in the middle of the most important scene in the movie. And it was set on one of my *Looney Tunes* ring tones, which kind of wrecked the poignantly romantic mood.

Anyway, my phone wasn't where I normally put it so I had to go deeper. I swear to God all those jokes about what a woman carries in her handbag are true. I carry my life around in mine. I'm sure one of my shoulders is permanently lower than the other from lugging around the weight of my bag. I fished out my diary—I know there's an electronic one on my phone, but I still like writing things down because I remember them better that way—and then I took out my lip gloss and a wand of mascara and a little pack of tissues with red kisses on them.

I grimaced as I thought of the kisses I'd just exchanged with Matt Bishop. What on earth did he think of me? I had acted like a wanton slut. I had pressed my body against his in the timeless keen-to-mate manner. I'd acted like a tigress in oestrus. It was utterly shameful. What on earth had got into me? I'd been kissed before and nothing like that had happened. In recent times when Andy had kissed me I'd mentally made lists in my head—the wedding invitations, the flowers, the place-setting cards, which aunt to sit next to which aunt—that sort of thing. I had never burst into molten heat like lava blowing out of a volcano.

I tossed the tissues aside and dug deeper. I took out my purse, which is so loaded with loyalty cards I can no longer close it properly. Finally I upended my bag and let everything fall out on the kitchen bench. But apart from a shower of receipts and loose change and the spare key to Jem's place, and two tampons and a furry cough lozenge, there was no phone.

I frowned as I thought of the last time I used it. I didn't have a landline so there was no point in trying to call it. I didn't fancy going out in search of a public phone box, which were as scarce as alley cats with morals in my area. It was too late to knock on Elsie's door to ask to use hers and since Margery Stoneham was away… That's when it hit me. My place wasn't just quiet because my phone was missing.

Where the flipping hell was Freddy?

I called out as I searched in every room. I looked behind doors and in corners. I pulled back the curtains to see if he was playing a game of hide and seek but all I found that was remotely animal-like were dust bunnies. My heart was going into arrhythmia again. I was a cardiac infarct waiting to happen. My hands were shaking and my legs trembling as I stumbled through the rest of the house. Up the stairs I went, calling out at the top of my voice. I didn't care if I woke the neighbours. I didn't care if I woke the dead. I didn't care if I lost my voice in the effort. I had to find that dog! Margery would kill me if anything happened to her precious baby.

I came back down the stairs with a clatter, my feet almost tripping over themselves. I was breathing so hard it sounded like I was wheezing. I was close to crying too but I didn't want to admit it. I'm not a crier. Not any more. Not since the fifth grade in primary school when everyone laughed at my hair. My parents were in their no-shampoo phase. They believed every shampoo and conditioner contained toxic chemicals that would give us all cancer.

We didn't wash our hair with anything but homemade soap for months. Thank God that phase didn't last any longer. Jem and I got head lice, so our parents decided a few toxic chemicals would come in useful after all.

I checked the back garden but there was no sign of Freddy. Even his paw prints in the snow from when I'd taken him out for a pee before I left with Matt had disappeared as another fresh fall had come down.

I bit my lip to stop it from quivering and rushed back into the house. He had to be hiding somewhere. A dog didn't just disappear into midair. This wasn't a science-fiction show or one of those Las Vegas illusionist's acts. This was my life! My totally screwball life, admittedly. I had been watching Freddy the whole time…Or had I? I had been so worked up about getting outside on the footpath to wait for Matt. Had I let Freddy out without realising it? There was no other way he could have got out. I hadn't left any windows open and, anyway, none of them were low enough for him to jump out. Could he have slipped past me without me noticing? He was only a little dog, and a devious one at that.

I raked my hand through what was now a bird's nest of my hair. I felt sick and sweaty and icy cold at the same time. My overactive imagination was conjuring up horrid images of Freddy squashed flat on Bayswater Road, or mangled underneath a car and dragged for miles. Or kidnapped and held for a huge ransom. Or sold into one of those ghastly fighting dog rings that operate underground. I choked back a sob as the doorbell rang. It was the police, I was sure of it. They were here to tell me the dog *I was supposed to be minding* was deceased.

I wrenched open the door but it wasn't the police. It was Matt Bishop. For a moment I just looked at him numbly. The siren of panic screaming in my head had taken away my ability to speak. I was barely able to string two thoughts together. My head was pounding with the effort of trying to keep control of myself and not fall into fits of wild hysteria.

He held up my phone. 'You left it in my car.'

I didn't care about my wretched phone. I took it from him and all but tossed it on the little table in the front hall. 'Have you seen Freddy?' I asked.

His brow furrowed. 'Freddy?'

'The little dog I had in the park,' I said, my breathing still all over the place. 'He's gone. Disappeared. Vanished. I can't find him anywhere.' I could hear my voice cracking and swallowed to clear the blockage of emotion strangling me. 'He must have got out. I have no idea how. He was here when I left with you. I'm sure he was.'

'Where have you looked for him?' Matt asked in a deep, calm voice, which kind of made mine sound all the more hysterical.

'Everywhere,' I said. 'Inside and outside, back and front. He's not *he-e-e-re*.' I dragged 'here' out like a whiny kid having a tantrum. I know. Dead embarrassing.

'What about his owner's house?' he asked. 'Have you looked there?'

I swear to God I could have kissed him. I almost did. I had to physically restrain myself from throwing my arms around his neck and smacking a big fat smoocheroo on his gorgeous mouth. I hadn't thought about Margery's place. It was the most obvious place to look but in my panic I hadn't even thought about it. 'Let's check,' I said instead, and scooped up my coat and scarf off the peg.

I was in such a rush to put it on I got myself in a

tangle. Matt came to the rescue and held my coat behind me like a well-bred gentleman does and helped me guide my arms through the sleeves. Was it my imagination or had his hands given the tops of my shoulders a gentle and reassuring everything-is-going-to-be-all-right squeeze?

For a nanosecond I breathed in the scent of him. I allowed myself a tiny moment of feeling him standing behind me like a strong tower I could lean on. I wasn't used to leaning on anyone for support. I hadn't even let Andy do it, well, because he was rubbish at it, to be honest. But for that tiny fraction of a heartbeat I caught a glimpse of what it would be like to have a partner who would stand by me, who would be strong when I was falling apart, who would take control and sort out the mess I had stumbled into and make it all work out, like unpicking a really hideous knot.

We walked the few houses down to Margery's place. The snow was falling in earnest now. It was really quite romantic, come to think of it. It was like a scene from a film—a guy and a girl walking along the street in search of a missing dog. I just hoped this one had a happy ending.

Matt used the light app on his phone to shine on the footpath so I didn't lose my footing. I guess he must have worked out by now I was pretty clumsy when I got stressed.

When we got to Margery's front porch there was Freddy, sitting on the doormat, shivering so hard he vibrated like a two-stroke engine. I rushed to him without thinking and bundled him into my arms, only to get one of my hands nipped for my trouble. Even though

I was wearing woollen mittens—my ones with kitten faces on them, including whiskers, which might have had something to do with why Freddy attacked me—his teeth sank into my flesh almost to the bone. Well, not quite to the bone, but it sure felt like it.

'*Ouch!*' I said another word, actually, but you get the idea.

Freddy jumped out of my arms—I might have dropped him but I'm not sure—and started whining and scratching at Margery's front door.

'Are you okay?' Matt asked.

I shoved my hand in my pocket. 'Fine.' I looked at the pathetic sight of the shivering dog desperately trying to get inside his house and felt a wave of compassion flow over me. 'Poor little boy. He misses his mum.'

'Separation anxiety,' Matt said. 'It's because his owner treats him like a human instead of a dog.'

I glanced at him in the light being cast from the streetlight. His face was cast in shadow but the light was still strong enough to show the dark, unreadable sockets of his eyes and the long blade of his nose and his unbelievably gorgeous mouth. 'Yes, well, Freddy is all Margery has now her husband is dead. She has no family other than a sister who doesn't let her bring Freddy with her when she visits so what sort of sister is she?'

'I once minded my sister's pet rat. That's sisterly love for you. I hate the things, but I did it because I love her.' I guess the throbbing pain in my hand was making me run off at the mouth or something. I finally got my motor mouth under control and gave Matt a sheepish look from beneath my half-mast lashes. 'Sorry. Rant over.'

He gave me one of his crooked smiles. 'No problem.'

I looked back at Freddy. 'So, little guy, we'd better come to some sort of understanding. I'm filling in for your mum so you have to do things my way. No more Houdini pranks, okay?'

Matt produced Freddy's lead, which he had wisely taken from my hall table. I'd been in too much of a state to even think about it. He snapped it on the dog's collar and led him away from Margery's front door. 'I'll walk back with you,' he said.

I felt foolish and embarrassed as we walked back to my house. In the last thirty-six hours I had given Matt Bishop an impression of myself that was comical rather than competent. Panicky rather than professional. And—even worse—sexually available instead of committed.

I considered telling him about my cancelled wedding. I had just enough time in the distance between Margery's house and mine. Surely he would understand, given what he'd hinted regarding his parents' marriage? What if I just told him about my stupid postcard fiasco and how I'd been caught off guard when I'd arrived at work? How I had felt too embarrassed to explain and lied to save face. It was a perfectly understandable reaction. I wasn't the first person in the world to utter a little white lie or two. Maybe he'd told a few himself. Surely he'd understand. Who didn't tell a few lies now and again? It was part of being human.

I formed the words in my head but I couldn't get them past my lips. I couldn't bear to tell anyone, least of all him. I felt sick at the thought of it spreading throughout the hospital. I could just imagine the looks I would get. The behind-the-hand comments people would murmur. I had seen the gossip network operate in every hospital I'd worked in. It was the same as the schoolyard network. It was cruel and unstoppable.

I thought of the way Matt had criticised my research project. I couldn't bear to have him mock my personal life as well.

Besides, I wanted to keep my distance from him. He was far too potent for me to handle. He was clearly a man of the world. The world in which his father moved, one where women were prizes to be collected, toys to be played with and then discarded when they lost their appeal. He might have given the impression he didn't approve of his father's treatment of his mother, but wasn't he doing the very same thing with me? He knew I was off limits and yet he'd kissed me. He'd made the first move…hadn't he? Or even if he hadn't he had been the one who had come and stood right in front of me, looking at me in that intensely mesmerising way until I'd had no choice but to meet him halfway.

I wasn't used to feeling such wild, out-of-control feelings of lust and longing. I needed time to get my self-control reconditioned.

We came to my door and I took Freddy's lead from Matt's hand. Even though we were both wearing gloves I felt the jolt of his touch. It travelled through my body like a hot wire firing up my core so it was thrumming like a tuning fork.

'Erm, thanks for helping me find Freddy,' I said. 'I don't know what I would've done if we hadn't found him. He might've frozen to death.'

He looked at me for a long moment. 'It's a big responsibility, minding someone's pet for them. Did you offer or did your neighbour pressure you?'

How had he guessed that? I wondered. I shifted my weight from foot to foot, suddenly uncomfortable he was sensing more about me than I cared to have on show. 'I was just trying to help.'

He gave a nod as if that made sense. 'I'd better get going before I freeze to death. Good night.'

I watched him walk down my street from my front door. It was bitterly cold standing there on the doorstep but I couldn't take my eyes off his tall, rangy figure as he walked along the snow-covered footpath. I let out a long, foggy breath as he disappeared around the corner.

Oh, boy, was I in trouble.

I was in the female change room, putting my bag in the locker, the next morning when Gracie McCurcher came bursting in. 'Guess what?' she said, her eyes bright with conspiratorial excitement.

'What?'

'Matt Bishop has a girlfriend.'

I hoped my face hadn't shown my surprise. If he had a girlfriend then why the heck had he kissed me last night? I felt a rumble of anger roll through me. What was it about me that attracted two-timing guys? Did I have a sign on my head that said 'Exploit me'?

I shoved my bag in the locker and turned the key. 'How do you know?'

'He's got a hickey on his neck,' Gracie said. 'I saw it when he took off his scarf when he came in this morning.'

I was glad I was facing the locker bay instead of

Gracie. I was so hot in the face I was sure the lockers would melt and drool, like Salvador Dali's clock. 'Are you sure it's a hickey?' I said in a vaguely interested way. 'He might have scratched himself shaving.'

'I know a hickey when I see one,' Gracie said. 'I wonder who it is? Do you reckon it's someone from the hospital?'

'I have no idea.' I was scaring myself at how easy it was to lie.

Gracie was watching me in the mirror, where I was attempting to put my hair in some sort of order. 'I heard he went to the US after he broke up with a long-term girlfriend. She was a speech pathologist.'

'How long term?' I asked.

'Not sure.' Gracie gave me a speaking glance. 'For some men a couple of weeks is long term.'

I turned around and gave her arm a squeeze. She hadn't had much luck with boyfriends. Her first one left her for her best friend and her last one cheated on her the whole time they were together. She was a lot like me, she wanted the fairytale but so far it had eluded her. 'Don't give up hope, Gracie,' I said. 'You'll find your handsome prince one day.'

She gave me a thoughtful look. 'Is it better once you're married?'

I disguised a gulping swallow. 'Better?'

'Your relationship,' she said. 'More stable. Secure. Happier. My cousin told me she felt really let down after she got married. She said there's all that build-up to the big day. Months and months of planning and then it's all over. Was it like that for you?'

'A little, I guess,' I said, which at least was the truth. I was let down. Massively. Everything I had planned and dreamed for myself had been blown away as soon as I'd opened that bedroom door and seen Andy in bed with another woman. Someone younger and far more beautiful than I could ever be. And taller and thinner. She looked like one of those bikini models on a billboard. I'd felt short and dowdy and fat ever since.

'When can I see the photos?' Gracie asked. 'Have you got time now?'

'Sorry.' I glanced at the clock on the wall. 'I have to get going. I have to check on a patient before Theatre.'

I came back from Theatre and Jill Carter, the ward clerk, looked up from some filing she was doing. 'Have you heard the latest gossip?' She shut the filing-cabinet drawer and gave the same conspiratorial gleam Gracie had shown earlier.

I prided myself on my indifferent expression. I'd been practising behind my surgical mask in Theatre. 'No.'

'Apparently Dr Bishop is—'

'Right behind you,' Matt said from the office doorway.

Jill and I both turned around like schoolgirls caught out smoking behind the toilets. Jill recovered quicker than I did but, then, she probably hadn't spent half the night lying awake fantasising about his mouth kissing her.

'Oh, hello, Dr Bishop,' she said, smiling brightly. 'How did your heads of department meeting go?'

Matt's expression had the high wall with barbed wire

at the top look about it. 'Fine. Dr Clark?' His gaze nailed mine. 'My office in ten minutes.'

I couldn't stop my gaze drifting to his neck. His shirt collar covered half of it but anyone with a history of necking as a teenager would have recognised it for what it was. I could feel the slow, hot crawl of colour spread over my cheeks as my eyes came back to his. 'Sure,' I said. 'I'll just check on a couple of patients first.'

I was longer than ten minutes as I wanted to talk to Jason Ryder's parents about a new type of therapy I was keen to use with him. Childhood awakening therapy was still in its experimental stage but there was some anecdotal evidence of people in comas responding to stimuli from their childhoods. Playing music, favourite movies or reading well-loved childhood stories had produced responses in some patients. I felt sure it wouldn't compromise the care Jason was already receiving, and I was quietly confident it might be the key to getting him to wake. From what I'd gathered from his parents, he'd had a happy and contented childhood, which made him a perfect candidate.

Jason's parents were keen to try anything to get their boy to wake up and his young wife, Megan, was also supportive. I didn't want to offer them false hope but I was keen to try whatever I could to get the breakthrough everyone was hoping and praying for. The human brain had much more plasticity than the scientific community had realised up until recent times. It was an exciting time to be involved with neurosurgery as there were new techniques and advances in technology that brought relief and hope to patients who in the past would have had little or no hope of recovery.

I was on my way to Matt's office twenty-five minutes later when Professor Cleary stopped me in the corridor. He was Head of Geriatrics and I generally avoided him as I found him so negative. He drained my energy if I hung around him too long. I often wondered how his patients put up with his bedside manner. I always had to remind myself to call him Professor Cleary instead of Dreary. One of the residents almost got fired when he let slip the nickname on a ward round.

But this time Prof Cleary wasn't frowning or glowering in his usual doom-and-gloom manner. 'Hello, Bertie,' he said with a broad smile. 'I've been hearing about your research project at the heads of department meeting.' He gave a chuckle. 'Best joke I've heard in years.'

I lifted my chin and eyeballed him. 'What did you find so amusing about it?'

'S.C.A.M.' He chuckled again, a deep belly laugh that made the already frayed edges of my nerves rub raw. 'Harrison Redding is kicking himself for not seeing it earlier. Clever of you to poke fun at the establishment like that. But it won't win you any favours with the boss. He's a sharp tack, isn't he? Got a good reputation for getting the job done. You'll have to watch yourself. I can't see him letting you read his palm or his aura or whatever else it is you do.'

I clenched my jaw so hard it clicked audibly. I didn't respond other than to give him a hard, tight smile and continued on my way to Matt's office. But the sound of Professor Cleary's chuckle followed me all the way down the corridor.

My skin rose in a hot prickle. Who else would be laughing at me by the end of the day? I had walked down a lot of corridors during my childhood and adolescence with that sound ringing in my ears. My face boiled with embarrassment. I was furious with Matt but I was even more furious with myself. I had set myself up for mockery and I hadn't even realised it.

Honestly, a transactional analysis psychologist could conduct a whole conference on me.

I knocked on Matt's door and he issued a curt command to come in. I stepped inside his office to see him sitting behind his desk with a grim look on his face. 'You're late.'

I pulled my shoulders back. Jem calls it my bracing-for-a-punch-up pose. I wouldn't know the first thing about throwing a punch but I can look intimidating when I have to. Well, sort of. 'I'm not at your beck and call, Dr Bishop,' I said. 'I have responsibilities and commitments that have nothing whatsoever to do with you. And while I'm on the subject of commitments and responsibilities, you had no right to use my project title as a source of amusement at your heads of department meeting.'

A challenging light came into his grey-blue eyes. 'Are you asking to be fired?'

I held his look with equal force. 'Are you threatening me?'

His eyes moved over my face, settling on my mouth as if he was remembering how it felt against his own. I couldn't stop myself from moistening my lips. It was an instinctive reaction and my belly quivered when I saw him follow the movement.

His eyes came back to mine and I heard him release a short, whooshy sort of breath, as if he'd had a long, trying day. 'I wasn't responsible for that,' he said. 'One of the other department heads commented on it. It created a few laughs, sure, but I encouraged everyone to stick to the agenda. What you need to concentrate on is producing data.'

I wasn't ready to be mollified even if he had stood up for me, which I very much doubted. I could imagine him smirking along with the rest of them, having a laugh at my expense. 'I don't appreciate being the butt of puerile boardroom jokes,' I said. 'My research is important to me and I know it can bring about better outcomes. I just need time to prove it.'

'I have no issue with that,' he said. 'But that's not why I asked you to come in here.'

I hooked one of my eyebrows upwards. Jem calls it my schoolmarm look. *'Asked?'* I said. 'Don't you mean commanded?'

He gave me a levelling look. 'One of the nurses mentioned you're planning to do some extra therapy with Jason Ryder. I'd like you to explain to me exactly what it is you intend to do.'

I could see the scepticism in his expression. He had already made up his mind. He would rubbish my childhood awakening therapy like he'd rubbished my project. 'What would be the point?' I said. 'You'll just call it a whole lot of hocus-pocus.'

'Hocus-pocus it may well be, but I would still like to know about it first rather than hear it second-hand from a junior nurse. That is not how I want to run this department.'

The clipped censure in his tone made my back come up. I could feel every knob of my spine tightening like a wrench on a bolt. 'Even scientists have to have open minds, Dr Bishop. Otherwise they can be blinded by bias. They only see what they expect to see.'

His eyes battled with mine as his hands came down hard on the desk in front of him. 'I'll tell you what I expect to see, Dr Clark. Patients being treated with proven, testable treatments, not sprinkled with fairy dust or having crystals waved over them. I'm running an ICU department here, not a freaking New Age mind and body expo.'

I clenched my fists by my sides to stop myself from grabbing him by the front of his shirt. 'Is there any space in that closed mind of yours for good old-fashioned hope? Or do you always expect the worst just to keep your back covered?'

A muscle moved in and out in his jaw as he straightened from the desk. 'It's not fair to offer hope when there is none. People's lives—the ones left behind—get ruined by empty promises. Jason's family needs reliable information and support right now, not sorcery.'

My eyes flared in outrage. I was so incensed I wanted to hit something. 'Is that all you wanted to see me about? Because, if not, I have some spells to work on in my cauldron.'

A flicker of amusement momentarily disrupted the hardened line of his mouth. I got the feeling he was trying not to laugh. Somehow that made my anger cool a little. I liked it that he had a sense of humour. I liked it a lot more than I wanted to admit. 'There's one other thing,' he said.

I folded my arms like a sulky teenager. I even pushed my bottom lip out in a pout. I know it was childish but he deserved it. *Sorcery?* Good grief. I hadn't been to one of my parents' seances in months. 'What?'

'We have a situation.'

'We do?'

I was the one with A Situation. It was getting more and more ridiculous by the minute. Why, oh, why had I been so wretchedly cowardly about being jilted? Why hadn't I told everyone the truth right from the start? I felt like all my lies had followed me into his office. They were stealing all the oxygen out of the air. It was like being in an overcrowded lift. I was finding it hard to breathe when he looked at me in that all-seeing way.

'Last night—'

'Was a mistake and it won't be repeated,' I said, before he could go any further. 'I can't believe I did that… we did that. I blame it on the champagne. I never drink on an empty stomach. It was totally out of character and I apologise for any…' my eyes glanced briefly at his neck '…erm…inconvenience.'

His eyes continued to hold mine but his gave nothing away. It was like a drawbridge had come up. 'I like to keep my private life out of the corridors of the hospital.'

'Because of your ex?' I said.

A flash of something hard moved in his gaze. 'As I said, I like to keep my private life private.'

'Fine. Me too.'

He gave me a long, measuring look. 'If people were to put two and two together, things could get rather awkward for you.'

They couldn't get any more awkward than they already are, I thought. 'How is anyone going to know that what happened last night had anything to do with me?'

His poker face was back on but I was pretty sure there was a glint of amusement lurking in the back of his gaze. 'So I take it you didn't tell your husband?'

I pressed my lips together. 'No.'

'Why not?'

'Because…he wouldn't understand.' It sounded like a tawdry cliché. The bored and lonely, misunderstood wife looking for a bit of fun on the side.

Matt came around his desk and perched on one corner, his ankles crossed, his arms folded across the broad expanse of his chest. It was the sort of casual but in-command pose that signified a man who knew what he wanted and exactly how to get it.

It hit me then.

He wanted me.

I saw it in the gleam of his eyes as they held mine. I felt it in the electric charge of the air we shared. I felt it in the core of my body where a throb had started like a low, deep ache, slowly building to a pulsating need that radiated throughout my system. I folded my arms, as if that would help contain the fire that was raging in my blood.

'Have you thought about my offer?' he asked.

I swallowed tightly. 'Um…your offer of what?'

His eyes tethered mine. 'Exploring this thing be-tween us.'

This thing between us… It was more than a thing. It was taking me over. My insides coiled with desire. I wanted him as much as he wanted me. The thought of an illicit affair with him was suddenly very tempt-ing. I'd had such a boring sex life. This would be my chance to stretch my boundaries a bit. Gain a bit more experience with a man who truly wanted me. I could throw off my inhibitions and have a fling, like every other girl my age.

But how could I agree to such a thing while he thought I was married?

I unfolded my arms and held them stiffly by my sides, shooting him a caustic glare. 'I suppose you think just because I allowed you to kiss me that it means I'm desperate to jump into bed with you. Well, guess what? I'm not. Going to jump into bed with you or kiss you or allow you to touch me or even look at me like that.'

'Look at you like what?'

I glowered at him through eyes so narrowed I could barely see out of them. It was like peering through the eye of an embroidery needle. 'You know exactly what I mean. You're doing it now. You're looking at me as if you'd like to strip me naked and have me on your desk.'

I really should think before I speak. It's a bad habit of mine. The erotic premise of my words filled the air with a crackling tension that made the hairs on the back of my neck lift. The heat of his gaze seared its way through my body to gather in a molten pool between my legs. I even felt the skin on my body tingle and tickle all over, like the rapid spread of goose bumps.

In fact, I don't think I'd ever been more aware of my body before that moment. All my erogenous zones—including some I hadn't known I had—were flashing red hot, like a computer motherboard malfunctioning. My breasts tightened behind the lace shield of my bra. They felt twice their size—which would have been fabulous if it were physically possible—and overly sensitive. My mouth ached to feel his against it, in it, conquering it, devouring it. I ran the tip of my tongue over my lips and watched as he tracked its moist passage. My body silently screamed for him to close the distance, to crush his mouth to mine and do exactly as I'd so crudely said.

He moved away from the desk and came a step closer. I should have stepped back but, just like the time before, my feet felt clamped to the floor. He lifted my chin with the tip of his finger, just like those romantic heroes do in the movies. No one had ever done that to me before, which was kind of why I was acting so bunny-in-the-headlights. His fingertip felt warm and strong and yet gentle at the same time. I felt the tingle of his touch all the way to my toes. His gaze locked on mine, his pupils flared to deep pools of black ink. 'What are you doing for dinner this evening?' he asked.

I glared at him even harder, which was quite hard to do with him that close and smelling so lemony and citrusy. 'Did you even *hear* what I just said?'

'I'm free if you are.'

I tried for my best haughty tone. 'It's none of your business what I'm doing.'

'You made it my business by kissing me.'

'I did *not* kiss you!' I stamped my foot for emphasis. 'You kissed me. I just responded, which is perfectly understandable given I'd had a full glass of champagne.'

His eyes smouldered darkly as they held mine. 'How about we try it without the champagne this time? See if we get the same response. That would be more scientific, wouldn't you agree?'

I should have got away while I could but before I knew it his hands were on my upper arms and his mouth was on mine. It was a hard kiss, a proving-the-point kiss, but it was no less mind-blowing. My mouth opened under the heated pressure of his, my tongue mating with his in an erotic duel that made my insides shiver with lust.

I was hardly aware of doing so but suddenly my arms were snaking around his neck, my fingers lacing through the silky thickness of his hair as his mouth plundered mine. My breasts were so tightly jammed against him I could feel my nipples poking into his chest. My pelvis was on fire; I moved it against his in an attempt to assuage the grinding, empty ache of my body. His erection surged against me, potent and hard, powerful and dangerously tempting. I imagined him entering me, dividing my moist, hungry flesh and driving hard and repeatedly into me. I was so turned on I could feel the tingle of arousal tightening my core, the sensitive nerves pulsing in anticipation.

His hands cradled my head, his fingers strong and firm against my scalp. His teeth nipped and pulled at my lower lip, cajoling me into a payback game that made the base of my spine splinter into a million pieces like party glitter. I could barely stand upright. The sensations were earth-shattering as they coursed through me like the shot of a powerful drug. I was so pliable in his arms I was like a rag doll. I was melting into his hard frame as if I never wanted to be separate from him. I wanted to be fused to his body, to have him possess me and make me feel alive in a way I had never quite managed before.

'God, this is crazy,' he said against my mouth. I loved the tickling and tingling sensation his words created against my lips. It had an incendiary effect on me, making me kiss him with all the more shameful, wanton enthusiasm. I went back in search of his tongue, warring with it, teasing it to come and play with me.

His hands slid down my body to grasp me by the hips, his fingers digging into my flesh as if he never wanted to let me go. I could feel the throb of his arousal against me. It excited me to think I'd had that effect on him. But his hands didn't stay for long on my hips. One went to the base of my spine to bring me hard against him while the other cupped my breast through my clothes. It wasn't enough for me. I wanted his mouth on my breast. I tugged my shirt out of my jeans and guided his hand to my lace-covered breast.

He stroked his thumb over my budded nipple, creating a maelstrom of sensation that travelled through my body. He pushed my padded bra out of the way and lowered his head and took my breast in his mouth. Yes, it's actually small enough to do that. Well, maybe not quite all the way into his mouth, but you get the idea. But it didn't seem to matter to him that my breast was a little on the small side. He treated it like it was the most gorgeously ripe breast in the world. Seriously, you would've thought it was a Playboy Bunny's breast. His tongue played with my nipple, circling it and teasing it into a tight pucker. I tilted back my head as he moved his mouth over the upper curve of my breast.

He did the same to the under-curve, which was even more tantalising. I hadn't realised how sensitive my skin was there until his warm mouth and the sexily raspy skin of his chin and jaw moved against it.

He left my breast to come back to my mouth, subjecting it to a passionate onslaught that had me breathless and throbbing from head to toe with longing. I was aching with the need to have him inside me. I hadn't even felt this turned on as a teenager. It was like discovering my female hormones for the first time. They were surging through my system like an unstoppable force. I wanted him and I wanted him now.

One of my hands went for the waistband of his trousers but he stilled my hand, pressing it against the turgid length of him. 'Not here,' he said.

The words brought me back to my senses like a slap across the cheek. What was I doing, undressing my boss in his office? What was *wrong* with me? Besides the fact he thought I was married, I wasn't the type of girl to act so unprofessionally. I was annoyed that he was the one to bring things to a halt. In my mind it gave him the moral edge, making him far more principled than me. It made me feel as if I was the one who had no self-control, which was a whole lot nearer to the truth than I wanted it to be.

I relied on my usual cover-up tactic and gave him a disparaging look. 'Do you really think I was going to let this go further than a kiss and a quick grope?'

His eyes were a dark blue-grey as they held mine, the pupils still widened in arousal. 'If you change your mind you know where to find me. I'll be home all evening.'

I drew in a scalding breath. 'You'll be waiting a long time before I make a house call.'

A hint of a smile lifted the edges of his mouth. 'We'll see.' He went back around his desk and rolled out his chair. His eyes glinted as he added, 'Close the door on your way out, will you?'

I huffed and puffed for a moment before I whipped round and stomped out of his office, but I didn't close the door.

I slammed it.

CHAPTER SIX

'GOOD GRACIOUS, BERTIE.' Stuart McTaggart jumped about a foot in the air as the framed prints rattled on the wall as he came towards me. 'What on earth's the matter?'

I pressed my lips together so tightly they hurt. 'Nothing,' I muttered.

'Is it about your project?' He gave a chuckle not unlike Professor Cleary's. It was the first time I'd heard him laugh, so at least I'd achieved something, I thought wryly. 'I thought it was brilliant, actually. Very witty.'

'I can assure you it wasn't meant to be,' I said, as I walked down the corridor with him.

'I've just been in to see Jason Ryder,' Stuart said. 'His parents mentioned you want to try some new therapy with him.'

'That's if Dr Bishop will allow it,' I said through tight lips.

Stuart stopped walking to look at me. 'But he was very supportive of you in the meeting. He was the one who brought the meeting to order when we were all having a laugh about your research title. In fact, if I didn't know you'd just come back from your honeymoon I would've said you and he were an item. Did you see that love bite on his neck?' He gave another chuckle. 'Takes me back to my old courting days.'

I could feel my blush like a spreading fire. 'Personally, I think love bites are dreadfully tacky.'

He gave a grunt and continued walking. 'So, what have you got in mind for Jason?'

I explained what I planned to do and he listened—patiently, for him—before giving me the go-ahead. 'Can't see how it can hurt,' he said. He waited a beat before adding, 'I hope to God the family don't sue.'

I glanced at his worried expression. 'They don't seem the type and, besides, you didn't do anything wrong. It's a recognised complication of that type of neurosurgery.'

'Doesn't seem to matter to litigation lawyers, does it?' He gave me a cynical look. 'They want their pound of flesh and don't care who they slice it off.'

'I'm sure it won't come to that, Stuart,' I said, hoping it was true. Stuart was a highly competent surgeon but his gruff and autocratic manner often put people off side. When things went wrong, which they occasionally did because that kind of surgery on the human body wasn't an exact science, some people thought their only option was to sue for damages, but they didn't take into account the impact on the doctor.

Medicine today was far more of a team approach than in the past. Mistakes could be made anywhere along the chain of care but it was the doctor who ended up being the fall guy. It was especially difficult if the case was reported in the press. Biased reporting could smear a doctor's reputation, tearing down a lifetime of hard work in a sensationalised phrase or two. And then there was the well-documented expert witness dripping with hindsight bias. And coroners' cases, in which months could be taken over dissecting decisions that doctors had to make under pressure, in real time, with incomplete information in a badly constructed system. Insurance companies battled it out with their case-hardened lawyers but the doctor, usually with no medico-legal experience, was left as the scapegoat, with often devastating psychological fallout.

At my previous hospital a dedicated obstetrician had walked away from a thirty-year career after parents of a baby who suffered oxygen deprivation at birth and subsequent brain damage sued her for damages. The sensationalised reporting in the press besmirched her reputation to such a degree she felt she could no longer practise.

Stuart let out a tired-sounding sigh. 'Well, I'd better get a move on. I've got a clinic and then a tutorial with the students and I'm on call for the second time this week. It's a wonder my wife doesn't call a divorce lawyer.' He gave me a sideways glance. 'How does your husband cope with the demands of your job?'

'Erm...'

'Should've married a doctor, Bertie.'

I gave him one of my strained smiles. 'There's a thought.'

For the next week I changed my roster to night shifts. I know it was cowardly but I really wasn't ready to face Matt Bishop until I got my willpower under some semblance of control. Besides, there's nothing more lust deadening than lack of sleep. One good side of working the night shift was that I could walk Freddy in daylight… I use the word loosely because the sort of daylight we get in London in January is pretty insipid.

The other benefit of being on night duty was that I could spend a bit more time with patients without the hustle and bustle of ward rounds and relatives visiting. ICU was quiet all but for the hiss and groan of ventilators or beeping of heart monitors and heart-lung machines.

I sat by Jason Ryder's bed in the end room and watched as his chest rose and fell with the action of the ventilator. It was coming up to two weeks since his surgery and he was still in a deep coma, and every time we had tried to bring him out of it his brain pressures had skyrocketed. It wasn't looking good but I refused to give up hope. I couldn't get his wife, Megan, out of my mind. I could imagine how devastating it was for her to be expecting a baby at a time like this. The stress she was under wasn't good for her or the baby. Studies indicated that high cortisol levels in expectant mothers could cause epigenetic changes in the foetus, leaving them at higher risk of heart disease or some types of cancers in later life.

And then there were Jason's parents. I could imagine how my parents would feel if either Jem or I were in a coma. They would be frantic with worry, desperate for some thread of hope. No parent wanted to outlive his or her child. It wasn't the natural order of things. Every time I looked at Jason's parents I felt a pressing ache inside my chest, like a stack of bricks pressing down on my heart. I so wanted a good outcome for them and for Jason, who'd had such a bright future ahead of him.

I picked up the children's book Jason's parents had left earlier. It was one of my own favourites, *The Indian in the Cupboard* by Lynne Reid Banks. Apparently Jason had loved it when he'd been about nine or ten years old. I, too, remembered being captivated by the idea of a toy coming to life. I picked up where Jason's mother had left off before they'd left for the night and read a few pages.

I looked up after a few minutes to see Matt Bishop standing in the doorway, watching me. I had no idea how long he'd been there. I hadn't seen his name on the night-shift roster but, then, he might have been called in for a patient. I knew he worked ridiculously long hours. It had taken me quite an effort to avoid running into him. I even darted into the broom cupboard next to the doctors' room a couple of evenings ago when I heard him speaking with a colleague around the corner.

I can tell you I got a bit worried when he stopped right outside it and talked to Brian Kenton from Radiology. I had a sneaking suspicion he might have known I was in there. He took an inordinately long time to discuss a patient before moving on. I felt a fool, sneaking out of there a few minutes later, but what else could I have done?

I put the book down on the bedside table and rose to my feet. 'Did you want me—I mean something?' I asked, mentally cursing the fact I was blushing.

'How's he doing?'

'Much the same,' I said. 'His IC pressures spike every time I try to wean him off the ventilator. Stuart wants to keep them low to maximise perfusion of what might be marginally viable brain around the tumour bed. But before we ramp up sedation each time, there's no sign of consciousness. He's having another CT tomorrow to look at perfusion. And an EEG is planned after that.'

I handed him the notes, which he read through with a frown of concentration pulling at his brow. He drew in a deep breath, closed the notes and put them back on the end of the bed. He picked up the children's book and turned over a few pages. 'I remember reading this when I was about eight or nine.'

'I read it too,' I said. 'I can tell you I never looked at a toy the same way again.'

His mouth curved upwards in a half-smile as he tapped the book against his hand. 'So, this is part of your childhood awakening therapy?'

I searched his features for any sign of mockery but he was either keeping it under wraps or was genuinely giving me a fair and unbiased hearing. Or maybe he'd looked up some of the fledgling research online and was prepared to keep an open mind. 'Reading familiar stories, playing favourite music, relating family memories of holidays or whatever to the patient can sometimes trigger an emotional response,' I said. 'There've been a few cases reported now where patients have woken from comas when exposed to something particularly emotive from their childhood.'

'One assumes it would be beneficial to have a happy childhood in order to expect that sort of response.'

I frowned. 'You didn't have a happy childhood?' I asked it as a question, but it could easily have been a statement of observation, given the way his features were set.

'Not particularly.' He put the book back on the bed-side table before he gave me a little quirk of a smile. 'What about you?'

'Mostly.' I gave him a rueful look and then added, 'My parents are a little out there, if you know what I mean.'

'I would never have guessed.'

I couldn't help a short laugh escaping. 'I'm ultra-conservative compared to them. At least I turn up at work fully clothed.'

His eyes darkened as they meshed with mine. 'What time's your break?'

I glanced at my watch. 'Ten minutes ago.'

He took my elbow with a firm but surprisingly gentle hand. 'Come on. Boss's orders. Caffeine and sugar.'

We took our coffee and a packet of chocolate biscuits to his office. I got the feeling this was his way of calling a truce. He pulled out his office chair for me to sit on. 'Here, you play the boss for a while. Tell me how you would do things around here if you were me.'

I sat on his chair but I'm so short my feet didn't reach the floor. I tucked my ankles beneath its centre stand and hoped he wouldn't notice. I took a sip of coffee and looked at him over the rim of my cup. He was sitting in the chair I'd used the last time, his features showing the signs of the stresses of his job.

It looked like he hadn't shaved in over eighteen hours, his eyes had damson-coloured shadows beneath them, his hair was ruffled, as if he'd recently combed it with his fingers, and there were two lines down each side of his mouth I hadn't noticed before. I knew for a fact he wasn't on that evening because I'd checked.

After the broom cupboard hideout I wasn't taking any chances. He had worked day shifts for the last week, presumably so he could keep in closer touch with the hospital management staff while he ironed out the problems he'd inherited.

It made me wonder if he had anything outside work to distract him. A hobby or interest that gave him some respite from the human tragedy he dealt with day in, day out.

He was a dedicated workaholic. The type A personality who found it hard to be anything but task-oriented. Emotions were not to be trusted. It was facts and data and completing the job that motivated him. I knew from my study how important it was to search for balance. I'm not sure I had found it, given the way things had turned out between Andy and me, but at least I understood the dynamic.

I was starting to realise why Matt had taken such a stand with me on that first day. For a man who valued facts over feelings I must have come across as a complete nut job. He wanted the unit to be one of the best in the country, if not the world.

No wonder he had taken the line he had with me. I was like a loaded cannon to him. Someone who was unpredictable, perhaps even—in his opinion—unstable. I had some ground to make up to make him see me as the dedicated professional I was. Sure, I wore wacky clothes and did interesting things with my hair, but that didn't mean I wasn't a competent and committed anaesthetist. I took my responsibility with patients seriously. I literally had their lives in my hands. I would never do anything to compromise their safety. I just had

to convince Matt Bishop I wasn't the airy-fairy flake
he thought I was.

I put my coffee cup down. God knows I sure didn't
need the caffeine. My heart was already pounding as if
I'd had a dozen espressos with an energy drink chaser.
Matt had that sort of effect on me. 'I'm sorry about the
other day in your office,' I said.

'No apology necessary.' He sat watching me with his
steady, measuring gaze, his coffee cup cradled in his
right hand, one ankle crossed over his knee.

I glanced longingly at the chocolate biscuits on the
desk but I knew if I started on them I might not stop
till the whole packet was gone. My parents banning
sugar had had the unfortunate effect of making me a
sugar binger. I could eat a box of chocolates in one sitting, especially if I was feeling down about myself. I
just hoped my liver wasn't going to hate me for it some
time in the future.

Matt leaned forward and pushed the packet of biscuits closer. 'Go on. One won't hurt.'

I gave him a twisted smile as I took a biscuit out of
the packet. 'My mum does that.'

'What?'

'Reads minds.'

He smiled back. It relaxed his tired and drawn features and made me realise all over again how incredibly attractive he was. I looked at the biscuit in my hand
rather than look at his mouth, as I was so tempted to
do. All I could think of was how his mouth felt as it
moved against mine, how his hands had felt, touching
my body. How I wanted him to touch me again. How I

wanted to feel his body inside mine, making me come apart with ecstasy.

I was shocked at my behaviour. Shocked and bewildered. If my life had gone according to plan I would now be married and trying for a baby. Instead, I was single and feverishly attracted to a man I had only met a matter of two weeks ago. It was like my body had hijacked my mind. It was acting on its own initiative, responding and sending subtle and some not-so-subtle signals to him that I was attracted to him and available. No wonder he had offered me an affair. I would have to try harder to disguise my reaction to him. Definitely no more getting close to him. And absolutely *no* touching. I would have to limit my time alone with him, keeping things on a professional basis at all times.

I took a small nibble of my biscuit and chewed and swallowed it, acutely conscious of his steady gaze resting on me.

'You mentioned your parents are alternative,' he said. 'How alternative?'

'They're hippies,' I said. 'They both come from families with money, but for as long as I can remember they've moved from place to place around the country, following whatever lifestyle guru takes their fancy, or their money, or both.'

'Not an easy way to spend your childhood.'

I rolled my eyes. 'Tell me about it. There's only so much teasing or tofu a kid can take. But don't get me wrong. My parents are really cool people. I love them dearly and I totally understand their desire to live an alternative lifestyle. They're not the sort of people who could ever do the nine-to-five suburban thing. It's just not the way I want to live my life.'

'How did you cope, growing up?'

I gave him one of my sheepish looks. 'I rebelled now and again.'

'How?'

'I became a closet carnivore.'

He laughed. 'Wicked girl.'

I smiled back. He had such a nice laugh. Deep and rich and full-bodied, like a top-shelf wine. Seriously, I could get drunk on hearing it. 'I can still taste my first steak,' I said. 'What an awesome moment that was. Jem and I used to sneak out at night, not to sleep with boys or drink alcohol, like normal girls did. We'd find a restaurant and indulge ourselves in a feast of medium-rare steak.'

He put his coffee cup on the desk, a smile still curving his lips. 'Did your parents ever find out?'

'Not so far.' I licked the chocolate off my fingers. 'I'm good at keeping secrets.'

'Handy talent to have.' There was a glint in his eye that made something in my stomach quiver like an unset jelly.

I looked away and buried my nose in my coffee cup. I couldn't envisage how I was ever going to confess my folly. The only way I could think to wriggle out of it would be to put in my resignation and start over in a new hospital. It was the only way to save face. But the thought of resigning and reapplying somewhere else was daunting. I loved working at St Iggy's. It was the first place I'd felt as if I belonged. I was part of a team that brought top-quality health care to the public, and the fact that I had—so far—been allowed to trial some alternative therapies was an added bonus.

I put my coffee cup down with a little clatter. 'I'd better get back to work. Thanks for the coffee.'

'You're welcome.'

I walked to the door but before I could put my hand on the doorknob to open it his hand got there first. My hand brushed against his and I pulled it back as if I'd been zapped. His right arm was stretched out against the back of my right shoulder. I could smell the grace notes of his aftershave as well as his own warm male smell, which was even more intoxicating.

I made the mistake of looking up at him. Our eyes met in a timeless moment that swirled and throbbed with sensual undertones I could feel reverberating in my body.

His gaze dropped to my mouth. 'You have chocolate on your lip.'

'I do?' I swept my tongue over my lips. 'Gone?'

He brought the pad of his thumb to my lower lip and gently blotted it. 'Got it.'

Our eyes met again. Held. Burned. Tempted.

I drew in a shaky breath and pulled out of his magnetic field.

I turned and walked down the corridor, but it wasn't until I turned the corner that I heard his door click shut.

CHAPTER SEVEN

AFTER ANOTHER WEEK I was completely over doing night shifts. My circadian rhythms were so out of whack I was practically brain dead. My eyes were so darkly shadowed I looked like I'd walked off the set of a zombie movie. I had a couple of days off, which I spent painting my sitting room, something I'd had to put on hold while I'd had Freddy staying. Margery was back from her sister's now so I could stop worrying about muddy paws and mad yapping, not to mention obsessive chewing.

I'd given Freddy a big marrowbone to chew instead of my shoes and electronic appliance cords, but he'd buried it in the back garden and then brought it in covered in mud and slush and left it on my pillow. Nice.

The time off had also given me some space to work on the hospital ball. I'd gone back to the hotel and talked to the catering manager and I'd ordered the decorations and got posters printed and had them hung around the hospital. The ticket sales had been slow until I had taken over, which was rather gratifying. It seemed everyone was delighted with the idea of a fancy-dress ball and were madly ordering costumes online or in stores.

When I got back to work after my days off I was pleased to hear Jason Ryder had been gradually weaned off the sedation, but while his brain pressures hadn't soared and he was breathing on his own, he was still not responding to verbal commands. I encouraged his family to continue with the therapies I'd suggested and hoped they would see some improvement over the next week or so.

The EEG had encouragingly shown brain activity. There was something going on in Jason's head, but it wasn't getting out, a possible case of 'locked-in syndrome'. But *what* was locked in was still an unknown. Just how much loss of brain function had resulted from the surgery was anyone's guess at this stage.

Matt Bishop was alone in the central ICU office when I came in from checking on Jason. All the nurses, including Gracie, were occupied with patients. Jill was on an errand to another ward and the registrars were with one of the other consultants with a patient in Bay Five.

'Good news so far on Jason,' I said, by way of greeting. I was going to stick to my plan of keeping things professional and distant.

Matt was less optimistic. 'He's not responding to any stimuli.'

'Not yet,' I said. 'But his CT shows reasonable blood flow in most of the brain, and his EEG shows activity.'

He put the file he was holding down on the counter desk and momentarily leaned forward and rested his hands on top of it. There was a deep frown line between his eyes, his olive-toned skin looked even paler than usual and he had a pinched looked about his features.

If a zombie movie director had been looking for walk-on extras, I thought Matt and I would make a great pair.

'Are you okay?' I asked.

He drew in a breath and straightened, rubbing a hand over the back of his neck. 'Fine.'

'You don't look fine.'

'Thanks.'

I peered at him up close. 'Your eyes are bloodshot. Have you been on the turps?'

He gave me a look. 'No. I was up all night. And, no, I wasn't on night shift.'

'At least on night shift you get paid to feel like crap.'

He managed a quarter-smile and then it faded as he dragged his hand down his face this time, wincing as if the movement caused him pain. 'You have no idea of the mess this place is in. Jeff Hooper might win a popularity contest over me any day but he had no idea how to balance a budget. We're four months from the end of the financial year and the budget is blown. The CEO says there is no more money. How the hell can we pay staff and provide a service with an empty bank account? I've been told to come up with a solution.'

I stepped back and folded my arms across my chest before I was tempted to smooth that canyon-deep furrow off his brow. 'Is there anything I can do?'

He looked at me then. *Really* looked at me. His eyes went to mine, holding them in a lock that contained the sensual heat of everything we had experienced together in private—the kisses, the touches, the mutual arousal of primal desire. It went back and forth between our gazes like a fizzing current of electricity. I swear it was almost audible.

Lust unfolded deep inside my body like a lithe cat stretching its limbs. I could feel my body heating and beating with want, the little tingle of nerves, the flutter of my belly, the rush of my blood and the pounding of my heartbeat.

His gaze went to my mouth, stayed there for a pulsing moment, as if he was wondering if he could steal a kiss and get away with it. The thought thrilled me. The illicitness of it spoke to the wild woman in me I tried so desperately to keep contained.

I found myself stepping up on tippy-toes, leaning towards him, my mouth slightly parted in anticipation of the press of my lips to his.

'Oh, um, er, sorry,' Gracie said from the door.

I sprang back from Matt as if someone had fired a cannonball between us. Gracie was looking at me as if she had never seen me before. But then her eyes took on a wounded look, her pretty freckled face drooping in disappointment.

'It's not what you think—'

'I don't want to hear about it,' Gracie said crisply.

Matt straightened his tie, cleared his throat and moved past us both. 'I have patients to see,' he said, and left.

I closed my eyes for a second. My life was such a farce.

'Bertie, how *could* you?' Gracie said in a shocked voice.

'Nothing happened,' I said. 'We were just…talking.'

'I saw you lean towards him,' she said. 'What's *wrong* with you? You've just come back from your honeymoon, for God's sake. I never would've taken *you* for a player.'

'Who's being a player?' Jill asked, as she came breezing in with a stack of paperwork. She looked between Gracie and me and raised her artfully pencilled brows. 'You're not talking about Matt Bishop, are you? The man's entitled to have a private life, you know. Mind you, I'd give my back teeth to know whom he's seeing. No one seems to know but I'm sure it's someone from the hospital.'

I mentally rolled my eyes. Could this get any more ridiculously entangled?

'I believe he has a thing for married women,' Gracie said, shooting me a hard look.

Jill gave a disbelieving cough of laughter as she rolled back her chair to sit down. 'Can't see him following in his old man's footsteps.'

'What do you know about his father?' I asked.

Jill swivelled her chair to face me. 'Richard Bishop's a well-known womaniser, the younger the better, apparently. His wife Alexis turns a blind eye, has been doing so ever since their other son died.'

My insides lurched. 'What other son?'

'Matt's brother.'

I could feel my eyes popping. 'He has...*had* a brother?'

Jill gave me an odd look. 'Lots of people have siblings, Bertie.'

I brushed her comment aside with an impatient wave

of my hand. 'I know that, it's just he told me he was an only child.'

'Well, he is now,' Jill said flatly. 'Tim died when Matt was fifteen. Tim was two years older. He had a rock-climbing accident. He was in a coma for over a year before they finally turned off the ventilator.'

'How did you find out all this?' I asked.

'My sister-in-law went to school with Alexis,' Jill said. 'They'd lost touch over the years but recently reconnected on Facebook. I mentioned we had a new boss and when my sister-in-law heard Matt's name she gave me the background.'

Gracie was still eyeing me as if I were Jezebel incarnate but I was beyond caring about that right now. I was still trying to get my head around Matt's tragic background. The loss of his older brother, the long stint in ICU before Tim was finally allowed to die. Was that why Matt was so adamant patients' relatives should be told the truth straight up? Had his parents clung to hope for months and months on end because they hadn't been told—or hadn't taken in—the reality of their eldest son's irretrievable condition?

Gracie muttered something about changing a patient's IV fluids and left.

'So, who do you think Matt's seeing?' Jill asked.

'I hardly see how it's anyone's business.'

She let out a little sigh. 'You're right. Hospital gossip is like a virulent virus. Once it starts you can't stop it.'

Tell me about it, I thought.

Jill looked up at me again. 'Speaking of which, I heard in the tearoom there's a twenty-four-hour bug doing the rounds. They're isolating the cardiac ward. I reckon we might be next. Don't come into work if you get it.'

Right then I wished I never had to come to work ever again.

Gracie was in the change room when I went in to get my things before leaving for the day. She was getting her bag out of the locker and turned as I came in. 'Well, I'll say one thing. As new brides go, you have far more reason than most to blush.' She slammed the locker door. 'And here I was thinking you were different. More fool me.'

'Gracie—'

'I suppose that's why you didn't want to show me the wedding photos,' she went on. 'You didn't want to be reminded you were married while you're sleeping with another man.'

'I'm not sleeping with—'

'Do you know what it feels like to be cheated on? *Do you?*' Her eyes watered and her voice shook. 'It's the worst feeling in the world.'

I knew all right. I took a deep breath. 'I didn't show you the photos because there aren't any.'

Her forehead puckered. 'What do you mean? Did they get deleted or something? That happened to a friend of mine. The photographer accidentally deleted them. If it hadn't been for other people's phone cameras, there would've been no photos at all.'

'They weren't deleted,' I said. 'They weren't taken in the first place.'

Her eyes were as round as the top of the linen bin next to the washbasin. 'Why not?'

My shoulders went down on a sigh. 'The wedding was called off. Andy was having an affair. I found out the night before the ceremony. It'd been going on for months.'

'Oh, my God!' Gracie clasped her hands over her mouth.

'I walked in on him with one of my bridesmaids' sister,' I said. 'It was… Anyway, there wasn't a wedding.'

She dropped her hands and asked, 'But why didn't you say something? You sent a postcard saying what a wonderful time you were having. Why have you let everyone assume—'

'Because I'm stupid, that's why.' I sat down on one of the bench seats and looked at my feet. I was wearing my piglet socks. There was a hole in one of the toes from Freddy chewing them. I should have darned them but I hadn't found the time.

'But surely you could've told me?' Gracie sounded so hurt I could barely bring myself to look at her. 'I know we've only known each other a few months but I thought we were mates. I told you all my stuff. And yet you didn't say a word. What sort of friendship is that?'

'I know. You're right. But I was too embarrassed,' I said. 'I didn't want everyone to feel sorry for me. To pity me. Poor old Bertie, dumped the night before her big day. The day she's been planning ever since she was five years old.'

Gracie's eyes were almost popping now. '*He* dumped *you*?'

'Yeah.' I let out another despondent sigh. 'That's the most embarrassing thing. If he hadn't pulled the plug I probably would've gone through with it to keep up appearances. Sick, huh?'

Gracie took one of my cold hands in hers and clasped it warmly. 'It's not sick. It's completely understandable. All that money, all those guests, all that food and—'

'God, don't remind me,' I groaned. 'Lucky it wasn't a huge wedding. We travelled around so much as kids I don't have a lot of friends.'

'You have more than you realise, Bertie,' she said, giving my hand another squeeze.

I looked into her china-blue eyes and somehow managed a vestige of a smile. 'Thanks.'

Gracie chewed her lip for a moment. 'Sorry about what I said back in the office. But don't you think you should let people know? I mean, what about that thing I saw between you and—'

'You didn't see anything.' I stood and wrapped my arms around my body as if the temperature had dropped twenty degrees. 'I was the one at fault. He was just standing there. I don't know what came over me.'

'So you're not involved with him?'

'How can I be even if I wanted to?' I asked. 'He thinks I'm married.'

'Then you should tell him and everyone else you're not.'

I swung back to face her again. 'No. I can't. What will everyone think? You have to keep it a secret. Please, Gracie, don't tell anyone. Promise me?'

She gave me a worried look. 'I'm hopeless at keeping secrets. I always leak stuff. I can't help it. It comes spilling out.'

'You have to promise me, Gracie.' I was almost to the

point of begging. It was pathetic. I was even thinking of offering her money. 'You can't tell anyone. No one must know. No one. Do you hear me? No one.'

'But—'

'No one will be interested in my private life in a month or two,' I said. 'You know how it is with everyone here. We're all so busy we hardly have time to chat about what's going on in our home lives. After a couple of months I'll tell everyone I'm separated or had the marriage annulled or something.'

Gracie chomped on her lower lip again, her expression doubtful. 'But what if you want to date someone else? Dr Bishop, for instance.'

I tried to laugh it off but I didn't sound convincing even to my ears. 'He's not interested in me. Not in the long term anyway. I'm too out there for him.'

'I've seen the way he looks at you,' Gracie said. 'And he was the one who organised for Jason Ryder to be transferred to your room that first day. It was a heck of a job moving the ventilator but he insisted it be done. Not only that, if anyone dares to make fun of your project he cuts them off quick smart.'

Something in my chest spilled like a cup of warm treacle. It was the thing I found most attractive about Matt. Although he had reservations about my project, he still managed to keep an open mind. That, and the fact he stood up for me. How could I not find that the most appealing trait? For as long as I can remember I had dreamed of a knight in shining armour. The sort of man who would protect me, shelter me and support me in everything I attempted to do. Someone who believed in me, in my potential, who helped me reach it without hindering it with their own self-serving interests.

But wasn't I dreaming an impossible dream? I was twenty-seven years old. I'd already wasted a chunk of my life on a man who wasn't right for me. Could I risk squandering another period of my life with a man who had offered me nothing but a behind-closed-doors... what? A fling? He hadn't exactly been specific about the terms. 'We'd make an interesting pair,' sounded more like an experiment than a relationship. Was that how he saw me? As a test sample?

What if I failed?

I'd had a full day in Theatre the following day so didn't get to ICU until we had to transfer the last patient. None of the other cases needed high dependency care so they went straight to Recovery. Once I was finished with the transfer I went to Matt's office. The door was closed and I gave it a tentative knock. There was no response so I knocked louder.

'He's gone home.'

I jumped about a foot when Jill Carter spoke from behind me. 'Oh.'

'He left a couple of hours ago,' she said. 'He was in most of the night with Rosanne Finch, the leukaemia patient. I told him to go home. I told him he looked worse than some of our patients.'

I frowned. 'Is he unwell?'

'He wouldn't admit it but I reckon he's got the bug. Gives you a blinding headache and a fever for twenty-four hours, give or take nausea and vomiting.'

'Sounds like a heap of fun.'

Jill smiled wryly. 'At least our husbands have us to wait on them hand on foot. What's yours like as a patient? If he's anything like mine, you'd rather be at work.'

'That just about sums it up,' I said.

CHAPTER EIGHT

I FOUND MATT'S great-aunt's house without any trouble. I asked one of the neighbours who was walking by with an overweight labrador which house had a corgi called Winnie.

Here's what I've found out recently. Dog owners have their own network. It's like the medical community—everyone knows everyone. The only difference with dog owners is they only know the dogs' names, not each other's. They call each other things like Fifi's mum or Milo's dad. Weird but true.

The house was a lovely Victorian mansion—personally, I thought it was way too big for a single old lady—with a lovely knot garden at the front, which was currently covered in snow. There was a light on downstairs but the upper floors were dark. I pressed my finger to the brass doorbell and listened as it rang throughout the house. I heard Winnie bark and then the click-clack of her claws on the floor. After what seemed a long time I heard someone coming down the stairs. They weren't happy footsteps.

The door opened and Matt stood there dressed in nothing but a pair of drawstring cotton pyjama bottoms. I stared at his chest and abs. He was so cut it looked like he had stepped off a plinth in the Uffizi in Florence. My fingers itched to touch him, to trace my fingertips over every hard ridge and contour. I dragged my eyes up to his. His weren't pleased to see me, or at least that was the impression I got. 'I thought you might like some company,' I said.

'Now's not a good time.'

I looked at his forehead, where beads of perspiration had gathered. The rest of his features looked pale and drawn. 'Consider it a house call,' I said.

He managed to summon enough energy to lift one of his eyebrows but I could tell it caused pain somewhere inside his head by the way he winced. 'I thought you didn't make house calls?'

I pushed past him in the door. 'I'm making an exception.' I bent down to ruffle Winnie's ears. 'Besides, this old girl could do with a walk, surely?'

'It won't hurt her to miss a day.'

I turned back to face him. 'Stop frowning at me like that. It'll make your headache worse.'

'How do you know I have a headache?'

I gave him a look. 'Have you taken something for it?'

He dragged a hand down his face, wincing again. 'Paracetamol.'

'You probably need something stronger.'

'What I need is to be left alone.'

I put my hands on my hips. Jem calls it my 'taking-charge pose'. I can be quite bossy when I put my mind to it. 'Come on, off to bed with you. I'll sort out the dog and rustle up something for you to eat and drink.'

He made a groaning noise. 'Don't mention that word in my hearing.'

'When was the last time you ate?'

He gave me a glare but it didn't really have any sting in it. 'Yesterday.'

I shifted my lips from side to side. 'Fluids?'

'A couple of sips of water.'

'When?'

He let out an exhausted-sounding breath. 'You don't give up easily, do you?'

'I've been playing doctors and nurses since I was three,' I said. 'Now, where is your bedroom?'

He scored his fingers through the tousled thickness of his hair. 'Second floor. First on the right.'

I made my way to the kitchen and boiled the kettle and made a cup of chamomile tea, which is really good for settling an upset stomach. I had brought herbal tea bags with me as I know from experience that not everyone has them in their pantry. I was right about Matt's aunt. She only had English Breakfast and Lady Grey. I took the steaming cup up on a gorgeous silver tray I found in a display cabinet and carried it upstairs. I felt like one of the chambermaids in *Downton Abbey*.

Matt was lying in a tangle of sweaty sheets, his forearm raised at a right angle over his eyes. I got a good look at his chest and abdomen. Ripped muscles, just like an old-fashioned washboard, lean and toned with just a nice sprinkling of chest hair that fanned from his pectoral muscles into a V below the drawstring waist of his pyjama bottoms.

I hadn't realised how sexy male pyjamas could be, way more sexy than sleeping naked. It was the thought of what was hiding behind that thin layer of cotton that so tantalised me. He was lying with his legs slightly apart, his feet and ankles turned outwards, his stomach not just flat but hollowed in like a shallow cave. I looked at it in unmitigated envy. My stomach was more dome-like than the one on St Paul's Cathedral. I sucked it in and approached the bed. 'I have a cup of tea for you.'

He cranked open one eye. 'You don't have to do this.'

'Here.' I held the cup up to his mouth. 'Just take a few sips. It'll help with the nausea.'

He raised his head off the pillow and took a small sip but then he sprayed it out as if it were poison. 'What the freaking hell is that?'

'Chamomile tea,' I said.

He gave me a black look. 'It tastes like stewed grass clippings.'

I put the cup on the bedside table and mopped the front of my jumper with a tissue I'd plucked from the box near the bed. 'You won't feel better until you get some fluids on board. Maybe I should bring an IV set from the hospital and run a couple of litres into you.'

'Don't even think about it.'

I got up from the edge of the bed and went through to the ensuite bathroom. It was a beautiful affair, with black and white tiles on the floor and a freestanding white bath with brass clawed feet. The shower was separate and had brass fittings the same as the bath taps. There were black and white towels hanging on a brass rail, although there were another couple on the floor next to the shower, as if Matt hadn't had the energy to pick them up after he'd showered.

There was shaving gear on the marble counter where the washbasin was situated and one of those shaving mirrors, the one with one side magnified. I absolutely loathe them as they always show up my chicken-pox scar above my left eye. You guessed it. My parents went through an anti-vaccination phase.

I ran the tap to dampen a facecloth. I wrung it out and sprinkled a couple of drops of lavender oil, which I'd brought with me, on it and took it back to the bedroom.

Matt was still lying in that body-fallen-from-a-tall-building pose. I swear I could have drawn a chalk line around him like in one of those film noir murder mysteries. I gently pulled his arm away from his eyes and laid the facecloth over them. He gave a deep sigh, which made his whole body relax into the mattress.

'Did you hear that?' he said.

'What? Your sigh?'

'That hiss of steam.'

I laughed. 'You certainly are running a fever. Do you have a thermometer anywhere?'

'I have a doctor's bag in the study downstairs.'

I got up from the bed. 'I'll be back in a tick.'

I was at the door when his voice stopped me in my tracks. 'Bertie?'

I turned and looked at him. 'Yes?'

He opened his mouth to say something but then he closed it. 'Doesn't matter.'

'No, go on, tell me.'

He looked at me for a beat or two. 'Why did you come here tonight?'

I pulled at my lower lip with my teeth, not quite able to hold his gaze. I'm not sure I knew exactly why I'd come myself. I had acted on automatic, as if it had been programmed for me to walk the block that separated our places of residence and call on him. 'I know what it's like to come home to an empty house when you're feeling rotten.'

There was a little pulse of silence. I was feeling pretty proud of myself for not trying to fill it.

He closed his eyes. 'Forget about the thermometer. I need to sleep.'

'If you're sure.'

'I'm sure.'

I left him upstairs sleeping and took Winnie out for a walk. I found a spare key on the hall table so I didn't get locked out. Matt looked so exhausted I thought he might not hear me on my return. Winnie and I didn't go far as it was freezing but she seemed to enjoy the outing. She stopped at just about every lamppost for a sniff and a minuscule pee, before trotting on to the next one and doing it all over again. *That is quite some pelvic floor she has*, I thought.

I took her back and fed her and then had a good old snoop around. I love looking at other people's houses. I get lots of ideas for decorating my own. Well, that's my rationalisation anyway. Matt's great-aunt had excellent taste and clearly money was no object. The place was decked out in the most luxurious soft furnishings and the furniture was mostly antique, and not just charity-shop antiques either. I mean *real* antiques, like centuries-old pieces that were heirlooms that looked like they should be in the Victoria and Albert museum.

But it wasn't a house I could imagine a young family growing up in. I began to wonder what sort of house Matt had spent his childhood in. Was it like this one, a showpiece of wealth but without the warmth and heart of a house where children's laughter was always welcome? I wondered too about his older brother. Whether they were close and how Tim's death had impacted on him.

Was that why he was so driven and focussed on work? His blunt honesty about a patient's prognosis made a lot of sense now I knew his brother had spent so long in ICU before he finally died. I had seen enough relatives do the long stints in the unit, watching for any sign of change, their hopes hanging in the air like fragile threads that could be destroyed with a look or ill-timed word from a doctor.

That final walk from the unit once a loved one has passed away is one of the saddest things to watch. Some people hold themselves together, walking tall and straight, or putting their arms around other family members, keeping strong for the rest of the family. Others cry and wail and scream in denial and some have to be physically escorted, as they can't bear to bring themselves to leave. Others look for scapegoats, lashing out at staff or other relatives, apportioning blame as a way of dealing with overwhelming grief.

I wondered how Matt had handled his older brother's death. Had he stood tall and quiet and dignified or had he railed and ranted against the injustice of a young life cut short? Or had he buried his grief so deeply it rarely got an airing?

He was a complex man, caring and considerate, strong and capable and disciplined, but with a sense of humour that countered his rather formal, take-no-prisoners demeanour. I wondered if he would have turned out a different, more open and friendly person if his brother hadn't died. His real self was locked away behind layers of grief, only getting an airing when he felt safe enough to let his guard down.

I suddenly wished I were that person. The person he would open up to in a way he had never done with anyone else. Hadn't he already let me in a tiny bit? He had mentioned all had not been well with his childhood. He had mentioned his father and mother's relationship. Would he eventually tell me more, reveal more of the man he truly was? I hoped so. I had a sense we could be allies. Our childhoods couldn't have been more different but there was an air of loneliness…of otherness about him I could definitely relate to.

I found Matt's doctor's bag in the study downstairs. It was a beautiful room kitted up like an English country estate library. There were wall-to-ceiling bookshelves and there was even one of those extendable ladder-like steps to reach the top shelves. There was an antique desk with a Louis IV chair and an old world globe. The only modern thing in the room, apart from the electricity and Matt's doctor's bag, was a laptop on the desk. I admit I like a little snoop from time to time but I draw the line at reading other people's emails. Matt's computer was in sleep mode in any case, but there was a part of me that dearly would have liked to know if he'd mentioned me to any of his friends.

But then I saw a handwritten note lying on the desk next to an old inkwell and quill. My reading speed was faster than my moral rectitude. I was halfway down the page before I realised I was reading something that was meant to be private, but by then it was too late.

Matthew,

It's your father's birthday next month. I know you're not speaking to him after the last time you visited but he didn't mean it. He'd had too much red wine. You know he can never remember what he's said the next morning.

Anyway, I know you're busy but it would be lovely if you'd pop in. You don't have to stay long. I'm not doing anything too big. Just having a few friends around for cocktails. I wouldn't want Eleanor Grantonberry next door to think I couldn't put on a proper do for my husband.

Feel free to bring a date. Are you seeing anyone? You never tell me anything! Isn't it time you got over Helena? She wasn't right for you. You're too much of a workaholic. She and Simon are very happy. Did you know she's pregnant? The baby's due in June. I wish you could find a nice girl to settle down and have babies with.

Love Mum x

I sat on the chair and looked at that piece of paper for a long time. I wished my mum were there to do a handwriting analysis. But I could pick up enough between the lines to realise Matt had a complicated background.

And here I was, thinking mine was a little weird.

I went back upstairs with some chicken broth I'd made while Matt slept. I'd found some ingredients in the pantry and fridge and freezer and whipped up my classic cure-all. I set it out on a tray with a starched doily I'd found and carried it upstairs.

Matt opened his eyes as I came in. 'You're still here?'

'I haven't got anything on this evening.' I set the tray on the bedside table. 'Do you think you could manage a bit of broth once I take your temp?'

'Did you make it?'

'Don't worry, it's not laced with poison.'

He frowned. 'Sorry, I didn't mean to sound—'

'I did, however, sprinkle some eye of newt in it.'

He smiled a crooked smile. 'Don't make me laugh. It makes my head hurt.'

'Poor baby.'

I popped the thermometer in his mouth and waited for it to beep. I took it out and looked at the reading. 'Hmm, it's back to normal. The rest must've done the trick.'

I sat beside him on the bed as he worked his way through the bowl of broth. He didn't manage it all but he seemed to enjoy what he had. He even had a glass of mineral water with a squeeze of lemon I'd brought up.

Once he was finished I got up to take the tray back down to the kitchen. 'Why don't you have a shower and I'll sort out your bed for you? I'll even do hospital corners.'

He frowned again. 'Seriously, Bertie, you don't have to do this.'

'I know, but I want to.'

His eyes looked into mine. 'Why?'

'Everyone needs a friend now and again.'

His frown deepened as his eyes moved away from mine. 'I'm not sure I'm the sort of friend you need right now.'

'Because you haven't got over H-her?' I caught myself just in time. I didn't want him to know I'd been reading his private mail, although he might put two and two together once he realised I'd been in the study to get his doctor's bag. I'd left everything as I'd found it, but if he knew anything about women at all, he must know I would have read it.

He let out a long, uneven breath. 'I'm not good at relationships, any relationships. I hurt and disappoint people without even trying.'

'So you keep things casual with anyone who comes along who interests you.'

He gave me a measured look. 'Is that how you see us? As something casual?'

I wasn't sure how to answer. What exactly was he offering? Come to that, what was *I* offering? I couldn't hope to hide my attraction to him. My body had its own silent language. I could feel it calling out to him even then. The tightening of my core, the flush running over my skin, the way my eyes kept going from his to his mouth and back again. The way my tongue moistened my lips. Even the way I'd turned up tonight, playing nursemaid, surely told him all he needed to know. But how could I have what I wanted without causing even more mayhem in my life?

His eyes had a dark glint in them. 'I can see how it's risky, given your…situation.'

My teeth sank into my lip. Here was my chance to confess what a fool I'd been. The words were assembled on my tongue like paratroopers about to leave a Hercules aircraft. I knew once I let them out I couldn't take them back. How soon before he would tell someone at work about my game of charades? But there was no way

I could allow him to make love to me while he thought I was married. 'There's something I have to tell you... I should've told you earlier.'

'I know.'

I kept talking, barely registering he had even spoken. Now that I'd made up my mind to confess I had to get on with it without distraction. I had to get it out there before he kissed me or I lost my courage. Not that I'd had much to begin with. 'I've been lying to you about my...situation,' I said. 'There was no wedding. I was jilted the night before. I was too embarrassed to tell anyone. I went on my honeymoon alone and I stupidly wrote a couple of postcards when I was tipsy, pretending everything had gone ahead as planned.' I shook my head at my own foolishness, not wanting to look at Matt in case I saw the derision I was sure he must feel. 'Postcards. Can you believe it? Who writes postcards these days? How *dumb* is that?'

'I know.'

'But the thing is I never intended to post them,' I said, without even acknowledging Matt's calm insertion. 'The housekeeping staff took them when I was out of the room and kindly posted them for me. I should've known something like that would happen.' I took a breath and went on, 'I seem to always get myself into ridiculous situations. And then when I came back to work that first day there was my stupid postcard on the noticeboard. If I'd been sensible I would've phoned or emailed ahead or something. But walking in like that to their smiling faces, I...I just couldn't do it. How could I tell them that...?'

Somewhere in the workings of my fevered brain I

finally registered what he'd just said. Twice. I looked at him with a quizzical expression. 'You know what?'

His eyes had that spark of amusement shining in them again. 'I know you're not married.'

I gaped at him with my mouth so wide open you could have backed a London bus into it. *'You know?'*

His smile had a teasing element to it that made my blood start to tick with anger. 'I knew from the start.'

He knew?

A red mist came up in front of my eyes.

He'd known from the start?

My veins were so bloated with anger they felt like they were going to combust. It was rocketing through my body like a cruise missile. He'd known and not told me? Not given me a single hint?

Why?

I clamped my lips together to force myself to think before I spoke. But I was too upset to think. My thoughts were tumbling around my head like a handful of marbles in a glass bowl. It physically hurt to try and make sense of them. Had he been laughing at me behind all his casually posed questions? Questions about my 'husband' and where I went on my honeymoon. *Grrr!* He'd known the *whole time* how awkward I would find those questions and yet he had continued each time we interacted as if I were a new bride. What had motivated him? Had he *enjoyed* my discomfiture, my wretched squirming every time we spoke?

Of course he had. He'd led me on, teasing me, mocking me with his enigmatic looks and half-smiles. The crushing hurt was worse than my anger. It pressed down on my sternum like a chest of drawers. He had deliberately led me on—for what? To have a joke at my expense? So he could laugh about me with all my colleagues?

'How did you know?' I fired the question at him like a round of bullets. 'How could you possibly know? No one at the hospital knows, apart from Gracie McCurcher, and she's sworn to secrecy.'

He was still looking at me with an amused expression, which wasn't doing my escalating anger any favours. I felt like a pressure cooker inside me was about to explode. I could feel it expanding in my chest until I could scarcely draw breath.

'I heard about it via an old school friend of mine who works in the same company as your ex,' he said. 'We met for a drink a couple of days before you returned to work. He told me how he'd just come back from Yorkshire where the wedding of his colleague had been cancelled at the last minute. I wouldn't have taken any notice except he mentioned your name. *Bertie* is quite unusual so when you turned up at work I put two and two together.'

I gave him a livid glare. 'So why didn't you blow my cover then and there? That would've been quite a laugh for you, along with my project title.'

The amused look was exchanged for one that suspiciously looked like pity, or at least something very close to it. 'I figured you had your reasons for keeping quiet about it. I decided to play along for a bit.'

I sent him another paint-stripping look. Seriously, I could've taken my new paint burner back to the hardware store and used my gaze on my house instead. 'Why?' I shot back. 'So you could have a joke at my expense? Mock me while you pretended to be interested in me?'

His eyes darkened to a deeper bluey grey as they held mine, his voice deep and gravelly. 'I wasn't pretending.'

My heart kicked against my breastbone. 'You weren't?'

He shook his head.

'Oh, well, then…'

'You have to tell everyone, Bertie. Surely you see that?'

I stood from the bed and crossed my arms over my body. 'No. No. No. I can't. I just can't.'

'Why are you so worried about what people will say?'

I turned back to look at him. 'I spent most of my childhood being laughed at. I can't bear people sniggering at me, or—worse—pitying me. If I were to tell everyone now I was jilted the night before my wedding they'll howl with laughter or cringe in pity. It's too late. I have to keep it quiet. I *have* to.'

'Come here.' His voice had a commanding tone to it I found wonderfully soothing. It was like he was going to take charge—please, don't tell my bra-burning mother I said that!—and make everything right for me. I sat beside him on the bed and he took one of my hands in his. 'You don't have to keep pretending. The longer it goes on the harder it'll be to undo. People will understand. They really will, sweetheart. Trust me.'

It really got me when he called me that. A lot of men utter endearments without making them sound genuine. But I wasn't convinced a tell-all in the staffroom was going to work for me. Besides, I didn't have the guts to do it. My childhood scars were too deep, too raw to have them scraped open by even one giggle or chuckle. 'Please,' I said. 'Please, try and understand.'

He gave my hand a gentle squeeze, his eyes holding mine in a tender look. I don't think anyone—no man at least—has ever looked at me like that. He looked like he really cared about me, about my feelings, about my insecurities. 'I do understand. It's tough when things don't work out the way you'd planned. But you'll get over it in time.'

I gave him a narrowed look. 'Please, don't tell me you feel sorry for me.'

He stroked his thumb over the back of my hand. 'I feel sorry you feel so pressured to fit in that you can't be honest with people. But you don't have to hide or pretend with me, okay?'

I could feel a little wobble of my chin, which was the closest I've got to crying in a very long time. 'Okay.' It was barely a whisper but it sure felt good to say it. To admit I trusted him to keep my secret safe.

He trailed a finger over the back of my hand. 'There's a way around this.'

I suppressed a shiver as his finger travelled to the underside of my wrist where my pulse was skyrocketing. 'There is?'

His eyes scorched mine. 'We could have a secret relationship.'

I noted the word 'secret'. Not my favourite word right then, but still. I swallowed as his finger made a lazy circle against the skin of my palm. It felt like he had touched me intimately, stroking me to arousal. 'I want you to know I don't do this sort of thing normally.'

'I know.'

I looked at him again. Directly. Staunchly. 'I mean it, Matt. This is totally out of character for me.'

He gently brushed a strand of hair back from my face. I had always longed for a man to do that to me. Andy never seemed to notice my tendrils, even the ones I'd deliberately staged to hang loose so he could push them back. 'Maybe we need to get this thing between us out of our system. What do you say?'

'Well,' I said, tapping my finger against my lip for a moment, 'I do have a couple of stipulations.'

'Which are?'

'This bed, for one thing.' I stood up and put my hands on my hips again. 'If I'm going to have bed-wrecking sex with you, then we at least need to start with a bed that's not already wrecked.'

He gave another lopsided smiled as he swung his legs over the side of the bed. 'You are one crazy girl.'

'But you like me, right?'

He stood and brushed his fingertips down my cheek, his smile, even as it faded, still making my insides turn over. 'I hope you don't catch my bug.'

'Thanks to my parents, I have a robust immune system.'

He gave one of my Dorothy from Oz pigtails a gentle tug. 'You're going to need it.'

CHAPTER NINE

I REMADE THE bed with fresh linen and dumped the other in the laundry downstairs. I would have set on a load but I had other priorities right then. When I came back up Matt was standing next to the bed with just a towel draped around his hips. I went to him as if I'd been doing it all my adult life. It felt so natural to walk into his open arms and feel them come around me like strong, warm bands.

He smelt divine, soap and shampoo and his own male smell, and he was warm and still a little damp from the shower. I was damp too. I could feel my body stirring in response to his closeness; the maleness of him against my softer contours was enough to send my senses spinning.

His mouth came down to the side of mine, touching and teasing the corner of my mouth in a tantalisingly little prelude of what was to come. I turned my head so his lips came into full contact with mine. I wasn't in the mood for preludes. I wanted the whole damn symphony and in forte.

His mouth was warm and firm and moved against mine with devastating expertise. There was amazing choreography in our kisses. There were no nose bumps or tooth scrapes; instead, there was a natural affinity between our mouths, a graceful coordination like watching two brilliant dancers working the ballroom floor. My response to him was purely instinctive. I hadn't even thought I was a particularly good kisser until I had come into contact with his mouth.

His tongue stroked along my bottom lip and I made a sound of approval as I welcomed him inside. The warm glide of his tongue over and under and around mine made my insides contract with lust. His hands pulled me against him, his fingers digging into my buttocks to hold me against where his blood pounded with desire. I could feel the hard ridge of him swelling against me. It made my body restless to get even closer. I could feel the tingling and tickling of my inner core, an ache and pulse of longing growing more intense by the second.

His hands began working their way under my jumper, sliding his palms over my bare skin to find my breast. I made a little gasping sound as his fingers pushed aside my bra and made flesh-to-flesh contact. He cupped me first, and then he rolled the pad of his thumb back and forth across and around my nipple. It was the most exquisite torture. All the nerves beneath my skin leapt and twirled and pirouetted.

I wanted to touch him to give him the same pleasure he was giving me. I tugged at the towel covering him and it fell to the floor. I stroked my fingers down his hard, flat abdomen, stringing out the anticipation for him as I slowly made my way to my target. He sucked in a harsh-sounding breath as I claimed my prize. He was iron hard and yet his skin felt velvet smooth. I

felt the throbbing pulse of his blood against my hand.
I squeezed and stroked in turn. I circled my fingertip
over his tip, where pre-ejaculate fluid was beading. It
was an erotic reminder of the primal impulses going on
in my own body, the silky dew that moistened my inner
walls in preparation for the thrust and glide of his body.

He helped me out of my clothes with gentle but ur-
gent hands, using those same hands to stroke over my
flesh as he uncovered it. I felt like a present he was
unwrapping, a present he had waited a long time to
claim. He kissed every inch of my décolletage, along
the scaffold of my collarbones, dipping his tongue into
the suprasternal notch between.

His mouth came back to mine, plundering it with increasing vigour, as if the tight hold on his self-control
was under enormous strain. I kissed him back with passionate enthusiasm, my tongue dancing and duelling
with his. He tasted so fresh, a combination of mint and
salt and sexy maleness. He had shaved during his shower
but his skin still rasped against mine in a way that made
me feel incredibly feminine.

Once I was in nothing but my knickers, his hands
came up and cupped my face. I liked it that he hadn't
stripped me naked, that he'd allowed me that final barrier to make me feel less pressured, less exposed. I could
still feel him against me, the hot probe of his erection
making my body ache behind the lace of my underwear.

His lifted his mouth off mine so our lips were almost
touching, our breaths mingling in the intimate space.
'Are you sure about this?' he said.

That was another thing I liked. He hadn't taken my
consent for granted. He'd allowed me time to back out if

I wasn't comfortable with taking things further. I don't want to make Andy sound like a predator or anything but there were a few times when he hadn't really picked up on my change of mind or mood.

'I'm sure.' I put my hand to his face and stroked it down the chiselled plane of his jaw. 'But thanks for asking.'

He rested his forehead against mine. 'It's been a while for me.'

'Me too.'

He lifted his head to look at me. 'How long?'

'It's been a couple of months.' I gave him a wry look. 'Actually, it's probably longer.'

He brushed his lips against mine. 'Good girl.'

'Why'd you say that?'

He smiled at me. 'You're being honest.'

The words I was going to say were obliterated in the combustible heat of our mouths meeting in a scorching hot kiss that spoke of the deep, irresistible yearnings going on in both of our bodies. Our tongues tangled and teased, stroked and swept and chased each other in a sensual dance as sexy as any Latin tango.

I was standing up on tiptoe, my breasts pushed almost flat against his chest in an effort to get as close as possible. His hands gently peeled away my knickers; his palms warm as they cupped my bare behind. He moved against me, the strong pulse of his body sending mine into a frenzy of want.

He pulled back from me slightly. 'I need to get a condom.'

He left me briefly to find one in his wallet. He didn't have a supply in the bedside drawer, I noticed, which seemed to suggest he hadn't brought anyone back here before. I liked the special feeling it gave me, the feeling that I was the only woman he'd considered making love with since he'd got back from the States.

He came back to me sheathed and gently guided me to the bed, where we ended up in an erotic tangle of limbs. That was another thing I noticed. There was no awkwardness about who was going to put which limb where. We fitted together like one of those complicated puzzles that only a Mensa member can solve. The feel of his naked skin moving against mine, the glide and stroke of his hands, the caress of his lips and tongue and the heat of our connection went through every pore of my body like a current.

I stroked my hands over his back and shoulders, discovering every knob of his vertebrae as his mouth savoured mine. Our tongues did that sexy little tango again that mimicked what our lower bodies were aching and straining to do. I shifted beneath him, urging him to take things to the next stage, but he was taking his time to ensure I was properly aroused. He stroked my entrance, felt the wetness of me and then slid one finger inside. I almost came right then and there. He stroked his fingertip across my clitoris, just enough to make me aware of him.

The sensations gathered like an approaching wave, building momentum with a force that threatened to overwhelm me. I felt the tension building in my body as he stroked me again, softly, slowly, then varying the speed, getting to know what I liked and what I didn't.

Just when I thought I couldn't take any more he moved down my body, kissing my breasts, down my sternum to my belly button and then to the top of my mons pubis. Instead of using his fingers, this time he used his lips and tongue. I know I sound like a ridiculous prude but I've never really understood all the fuss about oral sex. Andy did his best, but I always felt he couldn't wait to get it over with so he could get on with the main event, so to speak. I would freeze up or fret that I hadn't waxed or that I might not be as fresh as I should be down there. I would end up pretending I'd had a good time just to get it over with.

But with Matt I forgot about all those insecurities and hang-ups. His caresses were so perfectly timed, so cleverly orchestrated my body went on a feverish journey of discovery that left me completely breathless. The orgasm rolled over me like a massive wave, spinning and tossing me into a world of sensation that left no room for conscious thought. I was reduced to that one part of my body, my most primal part. I writhed and clawed and cried and gasped as the ricocheting pulses went through me, finally leaving me in a limp heap as the afterglow flowed through every muscle in my body.

Matt came back over me, cradling the side of my face with one of his hands. He didn't ask if it was good for me. He didn't need to. Instead, he kissed me again, the taste of my own body on his lips stirring me into a new round of arousal.

I reached for him to guide him into my body but he really didn't need any help from me. He knew exactly where he was going. But he didn't thrust in hard, not at first. He took his time, inching in to allow me to get used to his length. I felt like a virgin having sex for the first time with someone who really knew what they were doing. I felt special and respected and worshiped, instead of exploited and used.

Once he sensed my body was fine with him being fully enclosed, he began to move. It's a rhythm as old as time but each couple has their own take on it. I never found my groove with Andy, or my other partners. I always felt I was three steps behind, like a novice dancer trying to join a complicated line dance. I was always out of sequence, out of time with my partners.

But with Matt I felt everything fall into place. He moved and I responded. Our bodies rocked together as if they had been programmed to do it. When he groaned with deep pleasure it made my flesh shiver all over. But instead of taking his pleasure, he hadn't finished giving me mine. He somehow got his hand between our bodies and found my clitoris again and stroked and coaxed it into an earth-shattering orgasm. It was so powerful I could feel it rippling through me, the tight contractions triggering his release. I felt the deep shudder of his body as it drove into mine in those last desperate pumps as he emptied. I felt his skin lift in goose bumps and stroked my hands over his back and shoulders and down over his lower spine and taut buttocks.

Neither of us spoke.

I didn't want to break the mood with banal conversation. I wanted to dwell in that quiet sense of physical harmony, the soothing mutual relaxation of two bodies that moments ago had been strung tight with sexual tension but which had now found peace.

It was a while before I realised Matt was soundly asleep. I know a lot a men fall asleep after sex, but at least he hadn't rolled away to the other side of the bed and started snoring like a wild boar.

He had quietly slipped into a deep and relaxing slumber while still holding me in his arms. For some strange reason I felt like crying. Not because he hadn't stayed awake long enough to tell me I was the best sex partner he'd ever had—as if *that* was going to happen—but because he felt comfortable enough with me to truly relax. I got the feeling he didn't do it too often.

After half an hour or so I gently extricated myself from his hold. He made a soft, deep murmur of something that sounded a little like protest but he didn't fully wake up. I covered him with the quilt and tiptoed about the room to collect my clothes. I dressed in the bathroom, and then, once I had restored some sense of order to my hair, I went downstairs. I gave Winnie a last pat and made sure she had doggy biscuits and a fresh bowl of water, and then I let myself out.

CHAPTER TEN

I HAD A pre-assessment clinic first thing the next day and then a meeting with the other anaesthetists about some minor changes to the training scheme. Then I had a list in Theatre that went over time due to the weirdest case of appendicitis I've ever seen, or the surgeon for that matter. Despite the patient only being seventeen, the appendix had been massively expanded and completely replaced by what looked like a tumour.

It meant I was nowhere near ICU until quite late in the day. I hadn't seen or spoken to Matt since I'd left his place the night before, but I knew he was at work because I'd overheard two of the theatre nurses talking about him.

'I walked past Matt Bishop on my way to work this morning,' Leanne said. 'Talk about hot. Do you know who he's seeing?'

'No, but I wish it was me,' the other one, called Kathy, said in a tone that suggested she was waggling her eyebrows.

I tried not to eavesdrop but my ears were out on cornstalks.

The girls must have sensed my interest as they turned

to me, where I was tidying up my equipment. 'Who do you think it is, Bertie?'

'Why would you think I would know?' I sounded a bit defensive. Way too defensive.

'Someone said he's seeing a married woman and she works at St Iggy's,' Kathy said.

'That's just malicious gossip and you shouldn't be spreading it,' I said. I immediately regretted it. I saw the way their eyebrows went up in unison.

'Touchy,' Leanne said.

'Anyway,' Kathy pitched in, 'why would you be so worried about what's said about him? Isn't he going to pull the plug on your research?'

I tried to keep my composure cool and indifferent but I could feel a hot tide of colour sweeping up from my neck to my face. 'Not if I can produce results.'

'You'd better watch out, Bertie,' Leanne said. 'If it's true Dr Bishop has a thing for married women, you might be his next target.'

'That's ridiculous,' I said. 'I'm not—'

'Interested?' Kathy said. 'Come on, you might've just got back from your honeymoon but you wouldn't be human if you didn't find him attractive.'

I could have told them then and there. *I'm not married.* But I could just imagine the fallout. The news would spread like wildfire. I would be the topic of every locker room and staff tearoom conversation. Everywhere I went people would give me those looks, the looks I'd faced for most of my twenty-seven years. Pity. Ridicule. Mockery.

Just as well I got a call about a patient in Recovery. I made good my escape and left.

* * *

I went to ICU after I finished in Recovery to check on Jason. His wife, Megan, was there, his parents having gone home after spending most of the day with him. She looked exhausted so I sat with her for a while, just listening as she told me about the plans she and Jason had made. Their excitement over finding they were to become parents, how they had chosen names and decided against finding out the sex of the baby, as they wanted the thrill of the surprise.

She even showed me the ultrasound images. Seeing a baby in utero in 3D stirred my own maternal longings in my body. I had squashed them down for years as I'd concentrated on my career, but now, as I got closer and closer to the big three-oh, I was hearing some very loud ticking.

Andy hadn't been so keen on having kids straight away but, like a lot of women, I'd assumed he'd change his mind once we were married. It was only when I saw him with that girl that I realised he wasn't mature enough to be a father. He was too selfish to want to give up his freedom and take responsibility for someone other than himself.

I berated myself for being so blind about him. I had let the years roll on, reassuring myself things would get better when they had got progressively worse. Why hadn't I acknowledged it? Why had I let it get to the night before the wedding to see my relationship with him for what it was?

Once I was sure Megan was comfortable with a fresh glass of juice and some sandwiches from the doctors' room—I was bending the rules, but the ones in the relatives' room weren't as nice, in my opinion—I left the unit.

Matt was coming out of his office as I was coming along the corridor to leave for the day. I'd thought of nothing else but him ever since I'd left his great-aunt's house the night before. I wanted to see him again. I wanted to explore the amazing chemistry we had together. My body was still aware of him. It still tingled every time I thought of the passion we had shared.

He stopped in the process of closing his door, pushing it open instead and indicating with his head for me to come inside. 'Got a minute?'

I walked past him in the doorway, my body zinging with awareness as one of his shirtsleeves brushed me on the way past. I turned and faced him once he'd closed the door. It was hard to read his expression. I wondered if he was regretting last night. I wasn't his usual type. But, then, I wasn't anyone's usual type. Maybe he was regretting making love to me now he was over his bug. Maybe I'd caught him at a weak moment. Maybe he didn't even like me. See how insecure I am? It's ridiculous.

'How are you feeling?' I asked lightly.

'Good. You?'

'Great. Fine. Peachy.' I always go overboard when I'm feeling nervous. I wasn't sure how to handle the morning-after routine, especially in the context of our relationship. I wasn't even sure what the context was. I couldn't have a proper relationship with him while I was pretending to be married, but what was he offering if I came clean? Hadn't he said he wasn't interested in anything lasting? He was too busy with other priorities or some other get-out clause he'd used.

He leaned back against his desk in his usual manner. 'That was the best chicken broth I've had in a long while, perhaps ever.'

'It's my own secret recipe.'

'I could tell.'

I wasn't sure we were talking about chicken broth, especially the way he was looking at me. I tried not to blush but all I could think about was how his body had felt inside mine. 'So...what did you want to see me about?'

'I suppose you've heard the gossip?'

I chewed at my mouth. 'Yes.'

'Any more thoughts on coming clean?'

I crossed my arms over my body. 'No.'

His eyebrows drew together. 'Even after last night?'

I affected a casual look, as if I had amazing, mind-blowing sex with men all the time. 'Why after last night?'

He looked at me in a frowning way. But then he closed off his expression. The screen came up and I was locked out. Something pinched inside my stomach. 'So you're still determined to run with this crazy charade,' he said.

I sent him an intractable look. 'I'm not ready to have my private life the subject of everyone's amusement.'

His brow furrowed back into a deep frown. 'Do you really think people will find it funny that you were jilted?'

I jerked up my chin. '*You* obviously did. Stringing

me along for three flipping weeks, asking all those stupid husband and honeymoon questions.'

He let out a whooshing breath. 'I suppose I deserve that.' He scraped a hand through his hair again, before dropping his hand back down by his side. 'Look, I wasn't really laughing at you. I was amused by the lengths you were going to when all you had to do was tell everyone the truth. People go through break-ups all the time. Relationships either work or they don't.'

I glared at him again. How absolutely typical to dismiss the emotional turmoil of what a break-up like mine had entailed. Easy come, easy go was obviously his credo. Well, it certainly wasn't mine. I was the one who'd had to face all those guests. I was the one who'd had to endure all those looks of abject pity. I was the one who was still trying to pick up the pieces of my life.

'I was twelve hours away from my wedding,' I said. 'The wedding day I'd been planning since I was a little girl. I'd been going out with Andy for five and a half years. We'd been engaged for eighteen months. That's a little different from being dumped after a lousy date or two.'

His expression stilled with seriousness. 'I know how hard a break-up is. But it's not as if you were in love with him.'

My eyes rounded in affront. 'Oh, and you're suddenly an expert on *my* feelings, are you? What gives you the right to say such a ridiculous thing? Of course I loved him. I was going to marry him, wasn't I?'

The look he gave me reminded me of the look a disappointed parent gives to a wilfully disobedient child.

It made me angrier than I had any right to be. He had touched on a nerve that was still a little sensitive.

But I wasn't prepared to admit just how sensitive.

'If you were still in love with him you would never have come to my place last night,' he said. 'You must've known what would happen between us, or are you lying to yourself now as well as everyone else?'

Of course he was right. I would never have slept with him if I'd had feelings for another man. But I was confused about my feelings for Matt. They were a jumbled mix I couldn't make sense of right now. Was I so fickle that I could fall in love so soon after losing Andy?

I paced a couple of steps across the floor, hugging my arms close to my body. 'I know I'll have to tell everyone eventually…I just don't know how to do it without looking completely ridiculous.'

'Sometimes the anticipation of something is worse than the actual thing itself,' he said.

I swung back to look at him. 'So why haven't you let everyone in on the secret?'

'It's not my secret to tell.'

I was used to a lifetime of being teased and exploited, of having my weaknesses and flaws broadcast publicly. The fact he hadn't breathed a word of my single status to anyone made something warm spill inside my chest. He'd had a perfect opportunity to make an absolute fool out of me and yet he hadn't done it. Why?

'Want to tell me what happened?' he said.

I let out a long breath. 'I guess, looking back, we'd always had a pretty sketchy sex life. But then I got caught up in the wedding preparations and…well, he got caught up in having an affair with someone more…available.'

I bit my lower lip until it was mostly inside my mouth. I released it, along with a sigh. 'It was the most embarrassing moment of my life and that's saying something because I've had some doozies.'

He closed the distance between us and stroked a wisp of hair off my face. 'My ex was having an affair too. To the guy she's married to now. They'd been friends for years but I didn't realise how friendly until I called on her one night unexpectedly. Simon answered the door. Not a great moment for either of us. I had to give him credit for coming up with an excuse for why he was standing there in nothing but his boxers.'

'What did he say?'

'He was hot.' His mouth gave a rueful little quirk. 'But, then, Helena obviously thought so.'

Behind the humour was lingering hurt. I could see it in his eyes. Or was he like me, and the betrayal was more of a wound to his pride and sense of honour? 'Were you in love with her?'

His mouth twisted again. 'I thought so at the time.'

'And now?'

He stroked his thumb over my bottom lip. 'You read my mother's note.'

I gave him a sheepish look. 'I didn't mean to. It's just I'm a bit of a speed-reader so I took it in at one glance.'

He leaned down and pressed his mouth to mine in a long, warm kiss that sent my senses into chaos. I reached for him automatically, stroking my fingers through his hair.

I leaned into him, relishing in the familiarity of his touch, the naturalness and ease of it.

After a few breathless moments he pulled back to look at me. 'You didn't stay last night.'

'I wasn't sure what the protocol was.'

He frowned a little. 'What do you mean?'

I shrugged beneath the cups of his hands, which were holding the tops of my shoulders. 'I wasn't sure if it was a one-off or...or something else.'

His hands tightened for a moment before he relaxed them, but he didn't let me go. 'You want to go and grab some dinner somewhere after work?'

I bit my lip again as I thought of the implications of us being seen out in public. There was already gossip about him seeing a married woman in the hospital. I hadn't realised until then that my lies were not just hurting me, they had the potential to hurt him. 'Can we just get some takeaway and have it at your place?'

He gave me a levelling look. 'The longer you leave it the worse it's going to be.'

I dipped out of his hold and crossed the floor, hugging my arms to my body again. 'I know. I know. It's just not that simple.'

'It seems simple enough to me.' There was a thread of impatience in his voice. Hard and tight, like a fine wire under strain. 'You just have to be honest, Bertie. People will talk for a while but it'll eventually go away.'

'I need more time.'

'For what?' he said. 'For you to rule out the possibility your ex will come crawling back to you?'

I looked at him in affront. 'You think that's what's stopping me? *Really?*'

His expression was marble cold. 'Be honest with yourself, if not with anyone else.'

'Maybe you should take a lesson from that pulpit you're preaching from,' I threw back.

His eyes were suddenly flinty. 'What's that supposed to mean?'

I flashed him a little glare. 'You've waited for over a year to get involved with someone else. Doesn't that suggest you're still moping over the one who got away?'

He shoved his hands into his trouser pockets as if he was trying to stop himself from reaching for me. 'We haven't got a hope of this progressing past a one-night stand if you don't tell everyone the truth about your situation.'

I drew myself up to my full height, which isn't saying much as I barely came up to the top of his chest. 'I'll tell you why it won't progress past a one-nighter. Because *you* won't allow yourself to feel anything for anyone because you're frightened they'll pull away from you when you least expect it. You'll never give anyone that power again, will you?'

A muscle worked in his jaw. 'I have work to do, so if you've finished listing my faults, I'd appreciate it if you'd let me get on with it.'

I swung away with a haughty toss of my head. Not literally. It was still firmly on my straightened shoulders. 'Fine. I'm out of here.'

I glanced at him when I got to the door but he had already dismissed me. He was sitting behind his desk and scrolling through his emails or whatever was on his computer screen.

CHAPTER ELEVEN

By the time I got home I'd cooled down, although that might have had something to do with the weather. The snow was falling in earnest and I'd heard on the news they were expecting more overnight. I didn't fancy a long, lonely night alone and I didn't have the enthusiasm for a session of painting and decorating. I looked around the half-painted walls and the threadbare carpets, the tired kitchen with its out-of-date appliances.

My house suddenly looked a bit like my life. A mess.

I was considering what to do about food, not that I had much appetite, when the doorbell rang. I peered through the peephole, toying with the idea of pretending not to be home if it was Margery. It wasn't.

I opened the door and Matt stood there, with snow falling all around him. There was even some clinging to the ends of his eyelashes. He was carrying a bag with takeaway food containers in it and a bottle of wine in a brown paper bag. 'Have we just had our first fight?' he said.

I felt every last residue of anger melt away. 'I'm sorry.'

'No apology necessary.' He held up his peace offering. 'I took a gamble on food. Curry all right?'

'Perfect for a cold winter's night.' I ushered him through to the kitchen. 'I'm sorry the place is a bit of a mess.'

'Was your ex a home handyman?'

I gave him a cynical look. 'Are you joking?'

He frowned. 'You're doing it yourself?'

'I'm trying to…but as you can see it's not going according to plan.' Was it my imagination or did the paint job I'd done the other night look patchy? There was a drip of paint on the skirting board I hadn't noticed before.

'It's a big job for one person.'

'Yes, well, it was supposed to be two people doing it but you know how that turned out.'

He took the wine out of the paper bag. 'You want some help with it?'

I wasn't sure what he was suggesting. But as olive branches went it was a good one—even better than the curry and the wine. 'Don't tell me you're handy with a paintbrush, otherwise I mightn't let you leave.'

He gave a sudden grin. 'I did up my place in Notting Hill before I went to the US. I enjoyed it. It was a change from work, where stuff can't always be fixed.'

I knew exactly what he meant. Sometimes the hopelessness of some patients' situations ate away at me. 'I spent some time with Jason's wife today,' I said, as I handed Matt a couple of wine glasses.

'How's she doing?'

'I think she's struggling a bit, as anyone would in her situation.' I took the glass of wine he had poured for me.

He looked at me across the Formica kitchen table that separated us. 'You're doing a good job. I can see how the things you've set up help. The little touches that make people feel less alienated by the environment.' He waited a beat and then continued, 'I had a brother two years older than me. He died when I was fifteen.'

'I know,' I said. 'Jill told me. She said her sister-in-law is your mother's school friend or something.'

He gave me a quirk of a smile. 'What used to be six degrees of separation is now two with social media.'

I rolled my eyes. 'Tell me about it.'

There was a little silence. I didn't feel so uncomfortable with them now. But after a moment I asked, 'What was it like for you and your parents when Tim was in ICU?'

He looked at the contents of his glass, swirling it as if searching for the memories in the dark cherry-coloured pool. 'Awful. No one told us anything. It was different back then. Doctors didn't always communicate that well with relatives. They only told us what they thought we needed to know. It wasn't enough. My parents thought Tim was going to make it right up until the day he died of pneumonia. It made the grief so much harder for them to cope with. I felt that if only we'd been told from the outset that things were pretty hopeless the grief would have been dealt with earlier. Instead, it's dragged on for years.'

'Grief doesn't have a use-by date.'

'No, I know. But it might've helped my parents prepare themselves a little better.' He put his glass down.

'Did *you* think Tim was going to make it?'

His eyes met mine. 'I hoped he would. I couldn't imagine my life without him. We were close. I looked up to him. He was my role model, the one I turned to for advice or help with homework or whatever. My father was hopeless at that sort of thing. The bottom dropped out of my world when I walked out of the hospital that day. I swore I would do everything I could to make sure other people didn't have to go through that the way we did.'

'So you became an intensive care specialist with a reputation for telling it as it is.'

He gave me a rueful smile. 'That pretty much sums it up.'

I came over to him and touched his shadowed jaw. He hadn't shaved and the stubble caught on the skin of my palm, making something inside my belly shift like a foot slipping on a sheet of black ice. 'Thanks for telling me about Tim. It helps to understand you better.'

He brushed a tendril of hair away from my face. 'I haven't spoken of him in years. It's a no-go area at home. My father goes off his head if Tim's name is mentioned. In his mind the wrong son died.'

'Oh, no, that's terrible,' I said. 'Did he actually *say* that?'

'Only when he's had one too many drinks.'

'Is he an alcoholic?'

'He wouldn't say so, but I have my suspicion he sneaks a few empty bottles into the recycling bin without my mother knowing. Or maybe she does know but keeps quiet because it's not worth the effort of standing up to him or the risk of losing her social standing or both.' His mouth was set back in a grim line. 'God, I *hate* talking about my family. We're not a family any more. Not since Tim died. We're just three people who happen to be related.'

I reached up and smoothed the taut muscles surrounding his tight mouth. 'I'm sorry things have been so tough for you. But look at what you do for others. The way you work so hard, so tirelessly to save lives. So what if you don't have a perfect family? Just wait till you meet mine.'

He smiled and I practically melted on the spot. I watched as his eyes darkened as they went to my mouth, the ink-dark pools of his pupils flaring as he brought his mouth down to mine. His hands buried themselves in my hair, his fingertips sliding along my scalp as he plundered my mouth with feverish intensity. His tongue played with mine, darting and diving and seducing it in a dance that made every cell in my body shudder in delight.

My arms went around his neck, my body pressed so tightly against him I could feel the buttons on his jacket digging into me. I began to undo them, roughly, urgently, impatient to get my hands on him. He shrugged off his jacket and tugged up his jumper and shirt, and I slid my hands along the flat plane of his chest and abdomen. He hauled the garments over his head and they fell to the floor. He set to work on my clothes: my jumper went first, followed by my top and bra. His hands were cold at first on my breasts but they soon warmed as I pressed into his caress.

I tugged at the belt on his trousers, sliding it out of the lugs and letting it slither to the floor. I unzipped him and freed him from his underwear, holding and stroking him as his mouth continued to subject mine to a sensual onslaught that made every hair on my head shiver at the roots.

This was the sort of passion I had been missing in my relationship with Andy. The firestorm of lust and longing that was totally consuming. Before I knew it, Matt had lifted me onto the kitchen counter, parting my thighs so he could come between them. Somehow he'd sourced a condom and got it on before he entered me with a fast, thick thrust that made me whoosh out a breathless gasp.

'You okay?'

Okay? I was in heaven. 'You feel so good,' I said against his mouth, as he came back to kiss me.

He began to move inside me, taking me with him on a roller-coaster ride of passion. Every thrust brought me closer and closer to that final moment of oblivion. It was just frustratingly out of my reach, but then he slid his hands underneath my bottom, lifting my hips just enough to intensify the friction. I came in a cataclysmic storm of sensations that showered and shook and shuddered through me in turn. I felt his own orgasm as it powered through him, the deep quaking of his body and the sharply cut-off groan as he spilled, making my own body respond with another shudder of delight.

He let out a deep, satisfied sigh and leaned his forehead on mine. 'Our dinner is probably cold by now.'

'I don't know,' I said. 'It's pretty hot in this kitchen.'

He smiled against my lips. 'Damn right it is.'

I was walking down my street on my way to work the next morning when I ran into Margery, who was taking Freddy out for a walk. She gave me a look that was colder than the snow that had settled overnight. 'A fine way to behave, I must say,' she said. 'And here I was thinking you were a nice old-fashioned girl. Seems I was wrong.'

'Pardon?'

Her eyes narrowed. 'I saw him.'

My heart gave a little lurch. 'Him?'

'The man who left your house in the early hours of the morning,' she said. 'It wasn't your husband. He wasn't blond and he was much taller.'

I pressed my lips together. How was I going to get out of this? If I told Margery, it would be all over the neighbourhood within minutes. I would have people coming to gawk at me as I walked past their houses. I would be a pariah. I know it's the twenty-first century and all that but people can still be really judgemental about other people's lives.

'Marriage isn't easy, Bertie, take it from me,' she said. 'I was married to my Ralph for thirty-eight years. The first couple of years are always the worst. But what you're doing is plain wrong. What would your patients think if they were to know you were taking men in while your husband is away working in New York?'

I let out a breath that came out in a misty fog. 'The man in question is a friend. Now, if you'll excuse me, I have to get to work.'

Gracie was in the change room when I came in. 'I can't do this any more,' she said. 'It's killing me. I'm so stilted with everyone. I have to keep watching what I say. Everyone thinks I'm cross with them or something.'

'I can't,' I said. 'Can't you see that? It would be social suicide.'

'Don't you mean you won't?' Gracie's look was

accusing. 'This isn't just about you, you know. It's about other people now. Me. Matt Bishop. Your friends and colleagues. The longer you keep this up the more hurt you're going to cause.'

I shoved my things in the locker and closed the door. 'I'm working on it, okay?'

'Then work on it a little faster, will you?' Gracie said, and stormed out.

Jill swivelled around from the computer when I came into the central office. 'Can I have a quick word?'

'Sure.' I tried not to look at my postcard on the noticeboard. I was waiting for the opportunity to come in when no one was around and take it down.

'What's going on between you and Gracie?'

I felt my cheeks flare with heat. 'Nothing. Why?'

She leaned forward and gave me a beady look. 'Sure?'

I controlled every micro-expression on my face. 'Why are you asking?'

'I thought you must have had a squabble or something,' Jill said. 'She's asked for her shifts to be changed so she's not on when you're on. *Have* you got an issue?'

'No, of course not.' I hated myself at that point. Truly hated myself. Gracie might be a relatively new friend but she was loyal and caring. I had dragged her into a nightmare of my own making and now she was doing everything she could to avoid me. It was an uncomfortable reminder of my childhood, where I would be standing alone on one side of the playground while the more popular girls were on the other. I wanted Gracie back on my side but I couldn't do what she asked. I just couldn't.

Jill was still watching me with a contemplative look.

'It wouldn't have anything to do with Matt Bishop, would it?'

I assembled my features into an expression of shocked affront. 'What on earth do you mean?'

'You two have a certain chemistry. Everyone's commenting on it.'

'So?' I said. 'I get on with most people. You do too. It doesn't mean anything illicit is happening.'

'You don't seem happy for someone who's just got married,' Jill said. 'You seem…preoccupied. Is everything all right between you and your husband?'

I clenched my hands instead of my teeth because that would be less audible. 'What is this? Why is everyone so fascinated with my private life?'

Jill tapped her fingertips on her knees. 'Bertie, this gossip that's going around is not doing Matt any favours with the management team. The CEO is talking about terminating his contract.'

I frowned. 'On what grounds? His private life is no one's business!'

She gave me a worldly look. 'You know how conservative the hospital management team is. They're concerned about the image of the hospital.'

'They should be concerned about the welfare of the patients and less with the private lives of their staff,' I threw back.

'I'm just saying—'

'Haven't people got better things to do than gossip?' I said.

Jill let out a sigh and turned back to the computer.

I stared at her back for a moment. I trusted Gracie but I didn't know Jill well enough to share my secret with her. I hated it that she thought I was a cheating wife but what else could I do? If I told her, I'd have to tell everyone. I wasn't prepared to do that. I had a plan. I was going to activate it. There was a way around this. I would resign and find another placement. Problem solved.

'I'm sorry, Jill, it's just things are a little difficult for me right now. I'm finding it hard to settle back in after being on my...on leave.'

She tapped a few keys before turning around again. 'Marriage is hard work. Just be careful, okay?'

I didn't see Matt at work because I did everything in my power to avoid being seen by him or with him. Thankfully I had other duties that kept me out of ICU for most of the day. I finally left for home after some overtime in Theatre when Stuart's list got blown out with a complication. I was walking out of the hospital when I saw Matt's tall figure coming towards me. He must have been waiting for me to come through the front exit. I pretended not to notice him and kept my head down.

'Bertie?'

'Don't draw attention to us,' I said, out of the side of my mouth.

'I thought I'd walk you home.'

'Please, don't,' I said, huddling further into my coat.

'We need to talk.'

'Not here. There are CCTV cameras everywhere.' I sounded completely paranoid. But, then, I was. Completely and utterly paranoid. Were the curtains twitching on every floor as staff and patients looked down at us or was I just imagining it?

Matt took me by the arm and turned me to face him. 'Listen to me.'

I was overwrought with the stress of it all. Gracie, Jill, the thought of Matt losing his job over my stupidity. I looked into his eyes and saw what he was going to say before he said it. And there I'd been, thinking my mum was the only one who could read minds. 'I know what you're going to say.'

'Bertie, you have to choose.'

'Choose what?' I pretended I didn't know what he meant. But really I was just delaying the pain. I couldn't have him and my secret. I had to make a choice.

His expression was gravely serious. 'If we're going to go somewhere with this relationship then you have to tell everyone the truth.'

'I thought you said you weren't interested in a relationship. You said you had other priorities.'

His eyes were implacable as they held mine. 'I'm not going to lose my job because you're too immature to face up to what you should've faced before Christmas.'

I glared at him. 'That's rich, coming from you! You took a whole year to get over what's-her-name.'

His jaw tightened like a clamp. 'We're not talking about me. We're talking about you.'

'I'm going to put in my resignation,' I said. 'I'll move to another hospital where no one knows about Andy. You and I can still see each other and no one will ever—'

'Will you listen to yourself?' he said, his eyes dark and glittering with disdain. 'What are you, fourteen?'

I stiffened my spine. 'Fine. I'll accept your ultimatum.'

He shook his head at me. 'Don't do this, sweetheart.'

I put up my chin. 'I'm not throwing my professional reputation away for a fling. I'm fine with it ending. I never wanted it in the first place.'

'You've made lying into an art form,' he said, with a cutting edge to his voice. 'But when you get home and start lying to the person you're looking at in the mirror, you'll know you're really in trouble.'

I was in trouble from the moment I laid eyes on him, but now was hardly the time to tell him. I was trying to salvage what was left of my pride. 'It's over, Matt. It was fun—or at least it was for you—while it lasted.'

'I didn't sleep with you to make fun of you,' he said. 'I slept with you because I…' He stopped and shoved a hand through his hair.

I raised a cynically arched eyebrow. 'Because you…?'

He dropped his hand. His mask was back in place. For a moment there I'd thought I'd seen a glimmer of pain in his gaze but it was well and truly gone now. I figured I'd probably imagined it. 'Never mind.'

'I have one question,' I said. 'Why did you ask me to take over the planning of the ball?'

He let out a long breath. 'I thought it would help you get over your break-up. I thought it would give you something to distract you. But if you don't want to follow through with it, I'll find someone else.'

'I'm sure it won't take you too long to find a replacement,' I shot back.

He gave me another I'm-over-this look and turned away and walked back through the front doors of the hospital.

* * *

I typed up my resignation that night and printed it out
and signed it with a flourish. I looked at it for a long
time before I folded it and slid it into an envelope. I left
it lying on the desk—I don't have any helpful housekeeping staff so there was no prospect of it being posted
until I was ready to do so myself.

Jason's parents asked to speak to me when I got to ICU
the next day. They were waiting in my relatives' room
but I hadn't had time to turn on the essential oil infuser
as I'd been caught up on the ward. Ken Ryder was holding his wife, Maggie's, hand. Megan was still by Jason's
bedside. I'd caught a glimpse of her on my way past,
crying as she held one of his hands.

'We want the truth,' Ken said. 'Mr McTaggart is saying one thing. Dr Bishop is saying another. We want
your opinion. What's our son's prognosis?'

I looked at their haggard faces, their drawn and tired
features. The shadows, in and under their eyes, and
the lines on their faces that had seemed to deepen like
trenches by the end of each long, heartbreaking day. I
took a deep breath, feeling as if I was stepping out of a
part of my personality like someone taking off a warm,
thick coat. I felt exposed and vulnerable without it but
I could no longer hide beneath its comforting folds.
'There's a very real possibility Jason will never recover.'

Saying the words felt like speaking a different language, one without hope as part of its vocabulary. I
watched as Jason's parents took them in. It wasn't the
first time they'd heard them but hearing it from me—

the one person who had offered them hope and positive thinking from the get-go—was clearly devastating.

'I'm sorry,' I said, blinking back tears. I never cried at work. I was always so self-contained but I could no longer keep that professional distance. In that small, private room I became Bertie instead of Dr Clark. I hugged Jason's parents and offered what comfort I could but it wasn't enough. It could never be enough because I could not—no matter how hard I tried—bring back their boy.

Jem had a student-free day that coincided with my next day off so she met me in Knightsbridge for lunch in one of our favourite haunts. 'So, what gives?' she said, when she noticed I wasn't eating my steak with any of my usual gusto.

I stabbed a French fry but didn't bring it up to my mouth. 'Don't want to talk about it.'

Jem reached over and pinched one of my fries. She had already finished all hers. She has this amazing ability to eat loads of food without putting on an ounce. I should hate her for it. 'You're in love with him.'

I pulled back my chin against my chest. 'With Andy?'

'No, you goose,' she said. 'With this Matt guy.'

'Don't be ridiculous. I've only known him, what, three and a half weeks? That's not long enough to fall in love.'

'Don't bet on it.'

I raised my brows. 'The Sicilian guy?'

Jem got that stony, closed-off look on her face. 'We're not talking about me. We're talking about you.'

Why are all the people in my life saying the same

thing? I wondered. 'Everyone is talking about me. Or at least they will be when my resignation hits the HR department tomorrow.'

Jem frowned. 'You're resigning?'

'What else can I do?'

She gave me one of her big-sister, older-and-wiser looks. 'What about your project?'

'I've got enough data to go on with and once I get a new placement I'll set it up again.' Even as I said it I realised how difficult it would be. I had developed a high level of trust at St Iggy's, which was why Jeffrey Hooper had allowed me to be so innovative. I might not find the same enthusiasm in another hospital.

Jem filched another fry. 'What about the St Valentine's ball? Aren't you the one organising that?'

I felt a twinge of guilt at how I'd walked away from my responsibilities. I'd heard Matt had found someone to take over—a nurse from the cardiac unit. I wondered with another pang if he was seeing her outside work. 'I was but it's been handed to someone else. I can do without the stress on top of everything else. Anyway, I haven't got a costume.'

'You could always go as yourself.'

I gave her a droll look. 'Ha, ha.'

'What about your neighbours?' Jem wiped her fingers on her napkin. 'You're not thinking of moving too, are you?'

I was ashamed to admit I was. I was even thinking about emigrating. No one would be able to gossip about me then. *Siberia should just about do it*, I thought. 'None of them are talking to me. Clearly Margery's been busy.'

Jem leaned across the table and patted my hand. 'Never mind. At least she won't be asking you to mind her horrible little dog any more.'

'Like she should throw the first stone,' I said. 'Her Freddy humps anything that's—' I stopped speaking when I saw the colour leave Jem's face. She was looking at the entrance of the restaurant, her eyes widening with horror. 'What's wrong?' I said.

She grabbed the bill the waitress had left moments earlier and thrust it at me. 'Do you mind getting this? I'll meet you in Harrods at the chocolate counter.'

'But—'

I frowned as I watched her slip out the back way through the kitchen. Then I turned and looked at the tall, stunningly handsome Italian man walking in with a beautiful blonde woman by his side.

It seemed I wasn't the only coward in the family after all.

CHAPTER TWELVE

MY RESIGNATION CAUSED quite a stir amongst the staff when I came in the day after it had been lodged. I had to dodge a few twisty questions, including one about whether I was pregnant. Gracie kept giving me looks I stubbornly refused to acknowledge. It was all right lecturing me about telling the truth but she wasn't the one who'd have had to live down the ignominy of pretending to be married. It was easier this way. I was making a new start and in a few months no one would even remember me.

My heart gave a painful squeeze when I walked past Matt's office. I hadn't seen him other than in passing since our conversation in the car park. I wondered if he was feeling even half the distress I was. The thought of not seeing him again was like leaving a part of myself behind. A part I'd only just discovered. I hadn't realised I was in love with him until I'd lost him. I guess it had crept up on me. Each kiss, each touch, each time we'd made love a bit more of my heart had been won over.

But if he loved me then surely he wouldn't have made me choose. It was his reputation he was most concerned about, not me. It proved what a fool I'd been to allow our relationship to get to that stage. Hadn't he said from the start he had other priorities right now? I had foolishly agreed to getting involved and now I was paying the price.

But if he'd only wanted a casual fling why had he revealed so much to me about his past? It wasn't just the red-hot passion I longed for in a relationship. It was that wonderful sense of intimacy, of being able to talk about painful things without fear of judgement or lack of interest. Matt had opened up to me in the same way I had opened up to him. Why, then, had he made me choose? It wasn't fair to push me. To blackmail me.

I was getting my things out of the central office on my last day when Jill came in with a bundle of files to be entered into the computer. 'I can't believe you're not coming to the ball,' she said. 'Why not use it as a send-off? We haven't had time to do a drinks thing for you or anything.'

'I don't want any fuss,' I said, eyeing that wretched postcard. If only I could get it off that board then maybe my life would magically return to normal, or whatever normal for me was.

'This all seems rather sudden,' Jill said. 'Did the CEO pressure you to leave or something?'

'No, of course not,' I said. 'It was my decision.'

She eyed me doubtfully for a moment. 'It won't be the same here without you, Bertie. You've brought a lot of fun to the department. Even Stuart is saying how much he's going to miss you. And Prof Cleary. Do you know what he said? He said you're like a bright red poppy in a field of oats.'

I blinked back a sting of tears. 'That was sweet of him.'

There was a short silence.

'You weren't really having an affair with Matt Bishop, were you?' Jill asked.

I couldn't hold her look and turned to the notice-board and unpinned the postcard. 'You don't mind if I take this?'

'Of course not,' she said. 'It'll just get thrown out. You might as well keep it for sentimental value.'

I pasted a tight smile on my face. 'That's what I thought.'

I felt like Cinderella on the night of the ball, except I didn't have two ugly stepsisters and a horrid stepmother keeping me away. I was keeping myself away. I watched as the clock ticked towards midnight. I imagined all the guests arriving, walking up the red carpet, couples arm in arm. My stomach clenched at the thought of Matt arriving with some gorgeous date on his arm. I thought of him dancing with her, his arms around her as I'd dreamed of his around me. I hadn't even had the chance to see if we could actually dance.

But if our lovemaking was anything to go by, I thought we would've had a chance to be *that* couple on the dance floor. You know, the couple you see at weddings or functions who look like they've just come off a reality dance show, their movements together so beautifully synchronised it was spellbinding to watch. I wanted us to be that couple. We were a great team at work. We balanced each other out. Matt's cold, hard science needed softening with my more feelings-based intuition. We were like a perfect cocktail. The flavours by themselves weren't too flash, but put them together and, wham. What a knockout combination.

I looked at the clock again. The ball didn't end until one a.m. If I got my skates on I would have just enough time to poke my head in the door to see if everything had gone according to plan. I was deeply ashamed at not following through with my commitment. People had been relying on me and I'd walked off the job. What if not enough money was raised, or what if there was some last-minute hitch and I wasn't there to sort it out? Since when had I become a quitter? I still had my ticket and I had a choice of costumes from previous fancy-dress parties. It was a choice between Princess Fiona from *Shrek* or Kermit the Frog.

I didn't fancy being either so I decided to do what Jem had suggested. I pulled out a nineteen-fifties ball gown I'd bought for twenty pounds in a charity shop a few years ago. I'd never worn it in public because I'd always thought it was too glamorous for me. But when I put it on and looked at myself in the mirror it was like looking at myself for the first time.

I put my hair up and put on a bit of make-up. I spritzed myself with perfume and picked up a little drawstring evening purse that matched the white organza of my gown. Actually, it wasn't really white any more. It was more of an off-white, leaning towards yellowed with age, and it had a couple of moth holes in the flared skirt, but I was hoping no one would notice that. I slipped on some heels and prayed my toes would forgive me for the ensuing torture.

I called a cab—there weren't any pumpkin coaches on duty that night—and went to the hotel.

The ball was in full swing when I slipped in to stand by one of the red-rose arrangements with heart-shaped helium balloons sticking out of it. The dance floor was full of dancers in a variety of costumes. Some had taken the fun aspect of the night to extremes but there was a nice sprinkling of elegance amongst the frivolity.

I saw Matt dancing with one of the nurses from A and E. My heart gave a painful spasm as I saw his hand in the small of her back as they waltzed around the dance floor. They looked so good together. Not quite as good as a couple from a dance show...in fact, I thought I saw Matt tread on her toe at one point but that could've been my wishful thinking in overdrive. But then, as if he had a sixth sense, he suddenly stopped dancing and said something to his partner. She nodded and slipped away to dance with someone else.

Then he turned and met my gaze across the crowded room.

I know it sounds like a cliché but I felt my heart come to a standstill. Tears sprouted in my eyes as he came towards me. He was dressed in an old-style tuxedo with a red rosebud pinned to his lapel—no silly cartoon or superhero characters for him. He took my evening-gloved hands in his. 'So Cinderella made it after all,' he said.

'Yes...a close call but so far my glass slippers are intact.'

'Dance with me?'

He didn't give me time to say yay or nay. Suddenly I was in his arms and we were moving around the dance floor. Yes, you guessed it. Just like one of *those* couples. In fact, we were so good everyone else stopped dancing to look at us. I would have enjoyed it more if I hadn't realised there were two reasons they were staring. One: we were pretty fantastic together. Two: I was still pretending to be married to someone else.

It was exactly five minutes to midnight.

I stopped dancing and slipped out of Matt's hold. 'Will you excuse me for a moment?' I said. 'There's something I have to do.'

Everyone was still standing on the perimeter of the dance floor as I walked over to the podium, where a microphone had been positioned for the fundraising auction that had been conducted earlier. I waited for the musicians to stop playing the last bars of their song and then I took a deep breath. 'Hi,' I said, waving to all of the familiar faces and the not-so-familiar ones.

'For those of you who don't know, I'm Bertie Clark.' I felt like someone at a support group owning up to some sort of vice. 'There's something I have to confess. I'm not really married. I was jilted the night before the wedding. I didn't mean to send that postcard. That sort of happened by accident. I've been pretending ever since. I'm sorry for all the hurt I've caused. It was stupid and immature and I'm terribly, unreservedly, unequivocally sorry.' I thought I'd better stop there. I was starting to sound like a thesaurus.

There was a moment of stunned silence and then everyone gave me a round of applause as they started to surge forward on the dance floor. I felt like a rock star at a concert. I wondered if I should take a bow or do an encore or something. It was almost worth all the angst of the last few weeks to be the centre of attention in such a celebratory way. Almost.

I saw Matt carve his way through the crowd towards me. I stepped down off the podium and straight into his open arms. 'So proud of you, sweetheart,' he said. 'So very proud.'

'This doesn't mean I'm coming back to work at St Iggy's,' I said.

'That's a shame as there's a patient who's pretty keen to see you,' he said, with an excited twinkle in his blue-grey eyes.

Something lifted inside my chest like a sudden up-draught of air. 'Jason's awake?'

Matt grinned. 'I got a call from the registrar half an hour ago. Megan was reading *Chicken Little* to him and he opened his eyes and spoke a couple of words.'

I threw my arms around him and danced up and down on the spot. 'That's the best news! I'm so thrilled for him, for all of them.'

Matt swung me around in his arms so high that my dress ballooned out in an organza circle. I was glad I'd put on my best knickers as everyone was probably getting a good eyeful of them. 'I swore I would never do this in public, but will you marry me?' he said.

I hadn't realised until that point the ballroom was completely and utterly quiet. You could have heard a pin drop. Or maybe that was my jaw hitting the floor. I blinked and opened and shut my mouth a couple of times. 'What did you say?'

He smiled that dancing smile that always made my insides turn over. 'I know it's too early to be propos-ing. How long's it been, four weeks? But I don't see the point in wasting months and years waiting to ask you. I love you. I fell in love with you that first day in my office when you stood up to me with your beautiful brown eyes flashing.'

I looked at him in stunned amazement. 'You love me?'

'I adore you,' he said. 'I love everything about you. I love the way you screw up your nose and twitch like a rabbit when you're stressed. I love the way you never gave up hope on Jason. I love the way you fight for what you believe in. You're wacky and a little crazy and I never know what to expect when I see you because you wear such way-out clothes, but I want to see you every day for the rest of my life. I want to have babies with you. I want us to be a family together. So will you do it? Will you marry me?'

'You love me...' I said it as if I was dreaming and that someone was going to tap me on the shoulder any minute and tell me to snap out of it.

Someone did tap me on the shoulder. It was Gracie. 'Congratulations,' she said, with a huge smile.

'But I haven't given him my answer,' I said.

The crowd began to applaud again, louder and louder, and there was a fair bit of foot-stomping as well. Even the band joined in with a big theatrical drum roll.

Then everything went absolutely quiet again and it was as if it were just Matt and I in that room. It was like we were the only people left on the planet. I saw the love he had for me shining in his eyes. I felt it in his touch as he tenderly brushed back a stray tendril of my hair from my face. I felt it in the energy that passed from his body to mine where we touched thigh to thigh, chest to chest, heart to heart.

I smiled a smile that felt like it was splitting my face in two. 'Yes,' I said, and then his mouth came down and met mine.

* * * * *

IT HAPPENED
IN PARIS…

BY
ROBIN GIANNA

Dear Reader

When my editor suggested I write a book set in Paris with a Valentine theme, I loved the idea! After all, what could possibly be more romantic than my hero and heroine meeting in Paris and falling in love (even if they know they shouldn't)?

I had such fun researching Paris and things to do there—though I admit it was a bit of a challenge that it had to be set in February! No spring trees bursting into bloom, no lazing in sunshiny parks lush with the scent of roses, no warm weather strolls along the Seine…

But I managed to find other things for Jack and Avery to enjoy when they first meet—including succumbing to a brief fling! He's an interventional cardiologist and she's a biomedical engineer—you can imagine their shock when they discover they'll be colleagues on the clinical trial they're in Paris to conduct. A trial that's extremely important to both of them.

Jack never mixes business with pleasure. Avery knows they might very possibly end up with different opinions on how the research is going. What will happen if Jack finds out that she holds the entire future of his trial in her hands?

If you enjoy Jack and Avery's story I'd love to hear from you! Find me on Facebook, Twitter, or my website: www.robingianna.com

Robin xoxo

For my wonderful children, Arianna, James and George. You three are truly the light of my life.

A big thank you to good friend Steven J. Yakubov, MD, who has been conducting TAVI clinical trials overseas and now in the US for years, and who inspired this story. I so appreciate it, Steve, that you called me to answer all my questions even after you'd had almost no sleep for three nights. Thanks bunches!

After completing a degree in journalism, working in the advertising industry, then becoming a stay-at-home mum, **Robin Gianna** had what she calls her 'midlife awakening'. She decided she wanted to write the romance novels she'd loved since her teens, and embarked on that quest by joining RWA, Central Ohio Fiction Writers, and working hard at learning the craft.

She loves sharing the journey with her characters, helping them through obstacles and problems to find their own happily-ever-afters. When not writing, Robin likes to create in her kitchen, dig in the dirt, and enjoy life with her tolerant husband, three great kids, drooling bulldog and grouchy Siamese cat.

To learn more about her work visit her website: www.robingianna.com

Recent titles by Robin Gianna:

FLIRTING WITH DR OFF-LIMITS
THE LAST TEMPTATION OF DR DALTON
CHANGED BY HIS SON'S SMILE

These books are also available in eBook format from www.millsandboon.co.uk

CHAPTER ONE

Jack Dunbar studied the map in his hand, trying to figure out where the heck he was in this city of two million people. He was determined not to waste his first hours in Paris, and never mind that he'd only had a few hours of sleep while folded into an airplane seat, couldn't speak French and had no idea how to get around.

But, hey, a little adventure never hurt anyone. Even getting lost would be a welcome distraction from thinking about the presentation he had to give tonight. The presentation that would begin the new phase of his career he'd worked so hard for. The presentation that would launch the newest medical device, hopefully save lives and change forever the way heart-valve replacement surgery was performed.

Before any sightseeing, though, the first thing on his list was coffee and a little breakfast. Jack stepped into the hotel restaurant and saw that a huge buffet was set up just inside the open doors. Silver chafing dishes, mounds of breads and cheeses, fruits and you-name-it covered an L-shaped table, but the thought of sitting there eating a massive breakfast alone wasn't at all appealing. He approached the maître d'. "Excuse me. Is there just a small breakfast I can grab somewhere?"

"Voilà!" The man smiled and waved his arm at the buffet with a flourish. *"Le petit déjeuner!"*

Jack nearly laughed. If that was the small breakfast, he'd hate to see a big one. "Thank you, but I want just coffee and something quick. What's nearby?"

"Everything you could wish for is right here, *monsieur.*"

"Yes, I see that, but—"

"I know a little place that's just what you're looking for," a feminine voice said from behind him. "When in France, eat like the French do. And that spread in there is most definitely meant for Americans."

He turned, and a small woman with the greenest eyes he'd ever seen stood there, an amused smile on her pretty face. He smiled back, relieved that someone might actually steer him in the right direction, and that she not only spoke English, but sounded like she was American, too. "That's exactly what I want. To immerse myself in French culture for a while. And soon, because I need a cup of coffee more than I need oxygen right now."

Those amazing eyes, framed by thick, dark lashes, sparkled as her smile grew wider. "Caffeine is definitely the number one survival requirement. Come on."

Leaving barely a second for him to thank the unhelpful maître d', she wrapped her hand around his biceps and tugged him toward the door and out into the chilly January streets of Paris. "Just down the street is the perfect café. We can get coffee and a baguette, then we'll be good to go."

We? Jack had to grin at the way she'd taken over. Not that he minded. Being grabbed and herded down the street by a beautiful woman who obviously knew a little about Paris was a pleasure he hadn't expected, but was more than happy about.

"I'm Avery, by the way."

"Jack." He looked at her and realized her unusual name went well with a very unusual woman. A woman who took a perfect stranger down the street to a coffee shop as though she'd known him for days instead of seconds. A red wool hat was pulled onto her head, covering lush dark brown hair that spilled from beneath it. A scarf of orange, red and yellow was wrapped around her neck and tucked inside a short black coat, and tight-fitting black pants hugged her shapely legs. On her feet she wore yellow rain boots with red ducks all over them, and a purple umbrella was tucked under her arm. Dull she most definitely was not.

"Nice to meet you, Jack." Her smile was downright dazzling. The morning looked a whole lot brighter than it had a few moments ago, despite the sky being as gray as pencil lead. "How do you like your coffee? American style? If you really want to be French, you'll have to drink espresso. But I won't judge you either way."

Her green eyes, filled with a teasing look, were so mesmerizing he nearly stumbled off the curb when they crossed the street. "Somehow I think that's a lie. And while I can handle being judged, I like espresso."

"I knew you were a man after my own heart."

He'd be willing to bet a lot of men were after her heart and a whole lot more.

The little coffee shop smelled great, and he followed

Avery to the counter. She ordered in French, and the way the words slipped from her tongue, it sounded to him like she spoke the language nearly like a native.

"You ordered, so I'm paying," he said.

"That's what I was hoping for. Why else did you think I brought you along?"

"And here I thought it was my good looks and so-phistication."

"I did find that, combined with your little-boy-lost look, irresistible, I must admit."

He chuckled. Damned if she wasn't about the cutest woman he'd been around in a long time. They took their baguettes and tiny cups of espresso to a nearby tall table and stood. Jack nearly downed his cup of hot, strong coffee in one gulp. "This is good. Just what I needed. Except there isn't nearly enough of it."

"I know. And I even ordered us double shots. I al-ways have to get used to the tiny amounts of espresso they serve when I'm in Europe. We Americans are used to our bottomless cups of coffee."

"Are you here as a tourist? With friends?" Jack couldn't imagine she was traveling alone, but hoped she was. Maybe they could spend some time together, since he'd be in Paris for an entire month. With any luck, she was living here.

"I'm in Paris to work, and I'm alone. How about you?"

"Me, too. Working and alone. But I do have a few hours to kill today. Any chance you'll show me around a little in exchange for me buying lunch?"

"We're eating breakfast, and you're already thinking about lunch?" More of that teasing look, and he found himself leaning closer to her. Drawn to her. "I've already proved I plan my friendships around who'll buy. So the answer is yes."

He smiled. Maybe this great start to his trip to Paris was a good omen. "Where to first? I know nothing about Paris except the Eiffel Tower, which I know is close because I saw it from the hotel."

"Paris is a wonderful city for walking. Even though it's cold today and may well rain. Or even snow. Let's walk toward the Seine and go from there. If we hit the tower early, we'll avoid some of the crazy lines."

"There are lines this time of year? I didn't think there would be many tourists."

"There are always tourists. Not as many in January and February as in spring and summer, but still plenty. Lots come to celebrate Valentine's Day in Paris. Romantic, you know?"

He didn't, really. Sure, he'd had women in his life, some briefly and some for a little longer. But, like his father in the past and his brother now, his life was about work. Working to help patients. Working to save people like his grandfather, who'd had so much to live for but whose heart had given out on him far too soon.

Avery finished her last bite of bread and gathered up her purse and umbrella, clearly ready to move on.

"I don't suppose they give little to-go cups of espresso, do they?" he asked.

"You suppose right," she said with a grin. "The French don't believe in multitasking to quite the same degree we do. They'd shake their heads at crazy Americans who eat and drink while walking around the city."

"I'll have to get a triple shot at lunch, then," he said

as they stood. He resisted the urge to lick the last drop from his cup, figuring Avery wouldn't be too impressed. Might even come up with an excuse not to take him to the Eiffel Tower, and one drop of coffee wasn't anywhere near worth that risk.

They strolled down cobbled streets and wide walks toward the tower, Avery's melodic voice giving him a rundown of various sights as they strolled. Not overly chatty, just the perfect combination of information and quiet enjoyment. Jack's chest felt light. Spending this time with her had leeched away all the stress he'd been feeling, all the intense focus on getting this study off the ground, to the exclusion of everything. How had he gotten so lucky as to have her step into his first day in France exactly when he'd needed it?

"That's L'Hôtel des Invalides," she said, pointing at a golden building not too far away. "Napoleon is buried there. I read that they regilded the dome on the anniversary of the French Revolution with something like twenty pounds of gold. And I have to wonder. Wouldn't all that gold have been better used to drape women in jewelry?"

"So you like being draped in gold?" He looked at the silver hoops in her ears and silver bangles on her wrist. Sexy, but not gold, and not over the top in any way.

"Not really. Though if a man feels compelled to do that, who am I to argue?" She grinned and grasped his arm again. "Let's get to the tower before the crowds."

She picked up the pace as they walked the paths crisscrossing a green expanse in front of the tower. Considering how cold it was, a surprising number of people were there snapping pictures and standing in line as they approached. "Are you afraid of heights?"

"Who, me? I'm not afraid of anything."

"Everyone's afraid of something." Her smiling expression faded briefly into seriousness before lightening again. "Obviously, the Eiffel Tower is super tall, and the elevators can be claustrophobic even while you're thinking how scary it is to be going so high. I'll hold your hand, though, if you need me to."

"You know, I just might be afraid after all."

She laughed, and her small hand slid into his. Naturally. Just like it belonged there.

"Truth? I get a little weirded out on the elevator," she said in a conspiratorial tone. "So if I squeeze your hand too tight, I'm sorry."

"I'm tough, don't worry."

"I bet you are." She looked up at him with a grin. "The lines aren't too bad, but let's take the stairs anyway."

He stared at her in disbelief. "The stairs?"

"You look like you're probably fit enough." Her green eyes laughed at whatever the heck his expression was. "But we don't take them all the way to the top. Just to the second level, and we'll grab the elevator there. Trust me, it's the best way to see everything, especially on a day like today, when it gets cloudier the higher you go."

"So long as we don't have to spend the entire day climbing, I'm trusting you, Ms. Tour Guide. Lead the way." The stairs were surprisingly wide and the trek up sent his heart beating faster and his breath shorter. Though maybe that was just from being with Avery.

For some inexplicable reason, she affected him in a way he couldn't quite remember feeling when he first met a woman.

They admired the views from both the first and second levels, Avery pointing out various landmarks, before they boarded the glass elevator. People were mashed tightly inside, but Jack didn't mind being forced to stand so close to Avery. To breathe in her appealing scent that was soft and subtle, a mix of fresh air and light perfume and her.

The ride most definitely would challenge anyone with either of the fears Avery had mentioned, the view through the crisscrossed metal of the tower incredible as they soared above Paris. On the viewing platform at the top, the cold wind whipped their hair and slipped inside Jack's coat, and he wrapped his arm around her shoulders to try to keep her warm.

"You want to look through the telescope? Though we won't be able to see too far with all the clouds," she said, turning to him. Her cheeks were pink, her beautiful lips pink, too, and, oh, so kissable. Her hair flew across her face, and Jack lifted his fingers to tuck it beneath her hat, because he couldn't resist feeling the softness of it between his fingers.

"I want to look at you, mostly," he said, because it was true. "But I may never get up here again, so let's give it a try."

Her face turned even more pink at his words before she turned to poke a few coins in the telescope. They took turns peering through it, and her face was so close to his he nearly dipped his head to kiss her. Starting with her cheek, then, if she didn't object, moving on from there to taste her mouth. Their eyes met in front of the telescope, and her tongue flicked out to dampen her lips, as if she might be thinking of exactly the same thing.

He stared in fascination as her pupils dilated, noting flecks, both gold and dark, within the emerald green of her eyes. He slowly lowered his head, lifted his palm to her face and—

"Excuse me. You done with the telescope?" a man asked, and Avery took a few steps back.

"We're all done," she said quickly. The heat he hoped he'd seen in her expression immediately cooled to a friendly smile. "Ready to go, Jack? I think we've seen all there is to see from up here today."

Well, damn. Kissing her in the middle of that crowd wasn't the best idea anyway, but even the briefest touch of her lips on his would have been pretty sweet, he knew. "I'm ready."

They crammed themselves onto the elevator once more, though it wasn't quite as packed as it had been on the way up. He breathed in her scent again as he tucked a few more strands of hair under her hat. "Thanks for bringing me up here. That was amazing." *She* was amazing. "So what now, Ms. Tour Guide? Time for lunch?"

"There you go, thinking about food again." She gave him one of her cute, teasing looks. "But I admit I'm getting a little hungry, too. There's a great place just a little way along the river I like. There will be a few different courses, but don't worry—it won't break your wallet."

He didn't care what it cost. Getting to spend a leisurely lunch with Avery was worth a whole lot of money.

They moved slowly down a tree-lined path by the river, and he felt the most absurd urge to hold her hand again. As though they'd known each other a lot longer than an hour or two. Which reminded him he still hardly knew anything about her at all. "Do you live here? You obviously speak French well," he said.

"My parents both worked in France for a while, and I went to school here in Paris for two years. You tend to learn a language fast that way. I'm just here for a month or so this time."

"What do you do?"

"I— Oh!" As though they'd stepped out from beneath a shelter, heavy sheets of rain mixed with thick, wet snowflakes suddenly poured on their heads, and Avery fumbled with her umbrella to get it open. It was small, barely covering both their heads. Jack had to hunch over since she was so much shorter than him as, laughing, they pressed against one another to try to stay dry.

He maneuvered the two of them under a canopy of trees lining the river and had to grin. The Fates were handing him everything today, including a storm that brought him into very close contact with Avery. Exactly where he wanted to be.

He lifted his finger to slip a melting snowflake from her long lashes. "And here I'd pictured Paris as sunny, with beautiful flowers everywhere. I didn't even know it snowed here."

"You can't have done your homework." Her voice was breathy, her mouth so close to his he got a little breathless, too. "It rains and snows here a lot. Parisians despise winter with a very French passion."

He didn't know about French passion. But hadn't Avery said when in France, do as the French do? He more than liked the idea of sharing some passion with Avery. "I'm not a big fan of winter, either, when snow and ice make it harder getting to and from work."

"Ah, that sounds like you must be a workaholic." She smiled, her words vying for attention with the pounding rain on the nylon above them.

"That accusation would probably be accurate. I spend pretty much all my time at work."

"I must have caught you at a good moment, then, since you're sightseeing right now. Or, at least, we were sightseeing before we got stuck in this."

"You did catch me at a good moment." Maybe the romantic reputation of Paris was doing something to him, because he lifted his hands to cup her cheeks. Let his fingers slip into her hair that cascaded from beneath her hat. After all, what better place to kiss a beautiful woman than under an umbrella by the Seine in the shadow of the Eiffel Tower? "I'm enjoying this very good moment."

Her eyes locked with his. He watched her lips part, took that as the invitation he was looking for and lowered his mouth to hers.

The kiss was everything he'd known it would be. Her sexy lips had tormented him the entire time they'd been together in that elevator and standing close to one another on the observation deck. Hell, they'd tormented him just minutes after they'd met as he'd watched her nibble her baguette and sip her espresso. He could still faintly taste the coffee on her lips and an incredible sweetness that was her alone.

He pulled back an inch, to see how she was feeling about their kiss. If she thought it was as amazing as he did. If she'd be all right with another, longer exploration. Her eyes were wide, her cheeks a deep pink as she stared at him, but thankfully she didn't pull away and he went back for more.

He'd intended to keep it sweet, gentle, but the little gasp that left her mouth and swirled into his own had him delving deeper, all sense of anything around them gone except for the unexpected intimacy of this kiss they were sharing. Her slim hand came up to cradle his neck. It was cold, and soft, and added another layer of delicious sensation to the moment, and he had to taste more of her rain-moistened skin. Wondered if she'd possibly let him taste more than her face and throat. If she'd let him explore every inch of what he knew would be one beautiful body on one very special, beautiful afternoon.

Lost in sensory overload, Avery's eyelids flickered, then drifted shut again as Jack's hot mouth moved from her lips to slide across her chilled cheek. Touched the hollow of her throat, her jaw, the tender spot beneath her ear. She'd never kissed a man she'd just met before, but if it was always this good, she planned to keep doing it. And doing it. And doing it.

His hands cupping her cheeks were warm, and his breath that mingled with her own was warm, too, as he brought his mouth back to hers. Her heart pounded in her ears nearly as hard as the rain on the umbrella. She curled one hand behind his neck, hanging on tight before her wobbly knees completely gave way and she sank to the ground to join the water pooling around their feet.

The sensation of cold rain and snow splattering over her face had her opening her eyes and pulling her mouth from his. Dazed, she realized she'd loosened her grip on the umbrella, letting it sway sideways, no longer protecting them. Jack grasped the handle to right it, holding it above their heads again, his dark brown eyes gleaming. His black hair, now a shiny, wet ebony, clung to his forehead. Water droplets slid down his temple.

"Umbrellas don't work too well hanging upside down. Unless your goal is to collect water instead of repel it," he said, a slow smile curving the sexy lips that had made her lose track of exactly where they were. Lips that had traveled deliciously across several inches of her skin until she nearly forgot her own name.

"I know. Sorry." She cleared her throat, trying to gather her wits. "Except you didn't bring an umbrella at all, so you would have gotten wet anyway."

"True. Not that I mind. I like watching the raindrops track down your cute nose and onto your pretty lips." His finger reached out to trace the parts he'd just mentioned, lingering at her mouth, and she nearly licked the raindrops from his finger until she remembered a few very important things.

Things like the fact that she barely knew him. Like the fact that they were standing in a public place. Like the fact that she wasn't looking for a new relationship to replace the not-good one she'd only recently left.

She stared at the silkiness of his dark brows and the thickness of his black lashes, all damp and spiky from the rain. At the water dripping from his hair, over a prominent cheekbone, down the hollow of his cheek and across his stubborn-looking jaw. The thought crossed her mind that she'd never, ever spent time with a man so crazily good-looking. Even more good-looking than her ex-boyfriend, Kent, and she'd thought at the time he was a god in the flesh. At least for a while, until she'd figured out the kind of overly confident and egotistical guy he really was. Until she'd found out he was actually the one convinced he was godlike.

Getting it on again so soon with another man was not something she planned on doing.

She drew a deep breath. Time to bring some kind of normalcy to a very abnormal day. "Let's go to the café, dry off a little and get some food. You being Mr. Hungry and all."

"I've realized there's only one thing I'm hungry for at the moment." His lips moved close to hers again as his eyes, all smoldering and intense, met hers. "You. All of you."

All of her? Was he saying what she thought he was saying? She tried to think of a quick, light response and opened her mouth to speak, but no words came out. Maybe because she could barely breathe.

He kissed one corner of her mouth, then the other. "What do you say we head to the hotel for a while? A little dessert before lunch. I want a better taste of you."

Her heart leaped into her throat. Never having kissed a man she didn't know also meant never having had a quick fling with one. Never dreamed she ever would. But something about the way he was looking at her, the way his fingers were softly stroking her cheek and throat, something about the way her body quivered from head to toe and heat pooled between her legs had her actually wondering if maybe today was the day to change that.

After all, her last two relationships had ended with loud, hurtful thuds. Didn't she deserve some no-strings fun, just this once? She'd only be in Paris for one month, busy at work most of the time. The perfect setup for exactly what he was suggesting. And what would be the harm of enjoying what she knew would be one exciting, memorable afternoon with an exciting, memorable man?

"I...um..." She stopped talking and licked her lips, gathering the courage to shove aside her hesitation and just say yes.

"I know. We've just met, and it's not something I usually do, either. Honest." He cupped her cheeks with his cold hands and pressed a soft kiss to her mouth. "But being with you here in Paris just feels right. Doesn't it? It just feels damned right."

She found herself nodding, because it did. For whatever crazy reason, it felt all too right. A no-strings, nothing-serious, no-way-to-get-hurt moment with a super-sexy man to help her forget all about her past disappointments.

Another drop of water slid over her eyelid, distracting her from all those thoughts, and she swiped it away. "Except I'm all wet, you know."

The second the words left her mouth his eyes got all hot and devilish, and she felt herself flush, realizing what she'd said. "That's a plus, not a problem."

A breathless laugh left her lips. Before she could change her mind she decided to give herself a little present to make up for what she'd been through with her past jerky boyfriends.

Silent communication must have zinged between them, because they grasped one another's hands and headed in a near run to the hotel. To her surprise, the closer they got, the more excited she felt. She was entering unknown territory here, and hadn't she always promised herself she'd live life as an adventure? Plunging into bed with Jack for an hour or two seemed sure to be one thrilling adventure.

With her heart thumping so hard she feared he could hear it, Avery followed Jack as he shoved open the door to his hotel room. Once inside, the nervous butterflies she'd expected to flap around earlier finally showed up. She stared at him, hands sweating, as he shut the door behind her, trying to think of what the heck she should say or do now that they were actually here.

"Wouldn't you know that the minute we come inside, it stops raining?" she said lamely. Why was she so suddenly, crazily nervous? A little fling was no big deal, right? People probably did things like sleeping with someone they barely knew all the time. Especially in Paris. She didn't, but surely plenty of women did.

"Maybe if we're lucky, it'll start raining again when we go out. I like kissing it off you." The brown eyes that met hers held amusement and a banked-down hint of the passion that had scorched between them just minutes ago.

He shut the door and flipped the lock, his gaze never leaving hers. The heat and promise and that odd touch of amusement in the dark depths of his gaze all sent her heart into a little backflip before he pulled her into his arms and kissed her.

Unlike their previous kiss, this one didn't start out soft and slow. It was hard and intense, his tongue teasing hers until she forgot all about what she should say or do. Forgot where they were. Forgot to breathe. His fingers cupped the back of her head, tangled in her hair, as the kiss got deeper, wilder, pulling a moan from her chest that might have been embarrassing if she'd been able to think at all.

His mouth left hers, moving hot and moist to the side of her neck to nuzzle there. "You feeling more relaxed now?" he murmured.

How had he known? Though relaxed probably wasn't quite the right word to describe how she was feeling. "Um, yes. Thank you."

He eased back, his fingers reaching for the buttons of her coat and undoing every one of them before she'd had a chance to blink. "I don't know about you, but I'm feeling a little warm," he said as he slipped it from her shoulders and tossed it on a chair.

"Must be from all that running to the hotel," she said, breathless, but not from their fast trek to his room. "I figured it was a good chance to start training for the spring marathon."

His lips curved. "I thought we were running for a different reason." This time, his hands reached for the buttons of her blouse, the backs of his fingers skimming her skin and making it tingle as he slowly undid them one by one. "The reason being that I can't wait to see what you're wearing under this."

Her lacy white blouse dipped low over her breasts,

and pure, feminine pleasure swept through her at the way his eyes darkened as he stared down at them. At the way a deep whoosh of breath left his lungs. His fingertips slipped down her collarbone and inside her bra to cup her breast at the same time that his mouth covered hers.

Oh. My. The man was certainly one amazing kisser. World class, really, and her bones nearly melted at the sensations swirling around her. His cool hand on her breast, her nipples tightening into his palm. His hot mouth tracking along her skin, her bra now slipping completely off her to the floor. Her pants somehow magically loose enough to allow his other wide palm to slide inside to grasp her rear before it moved to the front and touched her moist folds, making her gasp.

The loud patter of rain again on the window had him pausing his intimate exploration, and he lifted his head, his dark eyes gleaming. "Guess it's a good thing we came in here out of the rain."

"Good thing," she managed before he resumed kissing and touching her until she was trembling with the intense pleasure of it all.

"Avery." The way he said her name in a rough whisper, the way he expertly moved his fingers while kissing her mouth and face and throat, had her nearly moaning. It all felt so wonderful, every bit of nervousness evaporated, replaced by want and need.

How she ended up on the bed she couldn't say, but when his mouth left hers she looked at him, foggily realizing that she was somehow flat on her back completely naked, while he stood there, staring at her.

"You are every bit as beautiful as I'd fantasized you'd be," he said. "Looking at you takes my breath away."

If that was true, then neither of them had much of an ability to breathe at the moment.

"My turn to look at you. Strip, please."

Those bold words coming out of her mouth shocked her, but he just laughed. "Your wish is my command." His gaze stayed on her as he quickly yanked off his shirt, and her breath caught at his lean but muscular torso. As he shoved off his pants, his erection became fully, impressively but all too briefly visible before his body covered hers, hot and deliciously heavy.

"You didn't give me much time to look at you," she managed to say.

"Sorry. Couldn't wait to feel all your gorgeous, soft skin against all of mine."

Well, if he put it that way. She had to admit it did feel amazingly, wonderfully, delectably good.

Was she really doing this? Lying naked with a man she barely knew? The feel of his body on hers, his mouth pressing sweet kisses to everything within reach of it, his smooth, warm skin beneath her hands told her the answer was yes, but to her surprise she didn't feel tense or strange or regretful. All she felt was toe-curlingly excited and turned on.

His hands and mouth roamed everywhere until she found herself making little sounds and moving against him in a way that would have been embarrassing if she hadn't been so totally absorbed in the sensations and how he made her feel. Nearing orgasm more times than she could count before he backed off and slowed things down, she was close to begging him when he finally rolled on a condom, grasped her hips with his hands and pulled her to him.

Instinctively, she wrapped her legs around his waist, inviting him in, and the way they moved together made her think, in the tiny recess of her brain that could still function, that it seemed impossible they'd met only that morning. That this dance they danced hadn't been etched in both their bodies and minds many a time before.

And when she cried out, it was his name on her lips and hers on his as they fell together.

CHAPTER TWO

"JUST SO YOU KNOW…it's really true that I don't usually do this." Her pulse and breathing finally slowing to near normal, Avery managed to drag the sheet up to cover her breasts. She glanced over at Jack, whose head lay on the pillow next to hers, eyes closed, looking as sated and satisfied as she felt. She wasn't sure why the words had tumbled out, but once they had, she wasn't sorry. She didn't want Jack to think she routinely picked up men, showed them around, then dove into bed with them.

"Do what?"

The expression on his face was one of bland innocence, completely at odds with the amused glint in the eyes that slowly opened to look at her. She couldn't help but make an impatient sound. "You know very well what. Sleep with men I've just met. Heck, I've never even kissed a man I just met."

He rolled to his side, his warm body pressing against hers. "I believe it was I who kissed you. Figured it was a Parisian tradition. The city of romance and everything. And what's more romantic than a rainstorm in the shadow of the Eiffel Tower?"

"Well. There is that." Though she was pretty confident that if it had been any other man she'd invited to breakfast that morning, there wouldn't have been any kissing on their trek around town or any rolling around in the sheets, complete with a lovely afterglow. And, to her surprise, no feelings of regret at all. Maybe because she knew it would happen just this once.

The moment she'd stepped off the hotel elevator that morning, her attention had gone straight to him like a magnet. Tall, lean and obviously American, with an adorably befuddled expression on his handsome face as he'd spoken to the maître d', she'd moved toward him without thinking, inviting a stranger for coffee and breakfast as though she did it every day. Which he doubtless assumed she did.

"I hope you're not regretting it. Our kiss, and now this." He propped himself up on his elbow and slowly stroked his finger down her cheek. "I know I don't. Being so close to you under that umbrella, there was no way I could stop myself. And once I'd kissed you, all I could think of was kissing you more."

No way she could have resisted his kiss, either. Or the bliss that had come afterward. Not that she'd tried at all. "Well," she said again, as though the word might somehow finalize the whole crazy afternoon, "we've shared *le petit déjeuner*, walked a bit of the city and gone up the tower. Kissed under an umbrella and made love while it rained outside. I guess it's a good time to find out a little about each other. I hope you're not married?"

She said it jokingly, but a small part of her suddenly wondered if he possibly could be. If he was the type of man who philandered when working out of town. Her stomach clenched at the thought. After all, she knew that type way more intimately than she wished she did. Would Jack admit it if he was?

"Not married. Never have been. Remember, I told you, all I do is work. Which probably makes me pretty boring."

Whew. She looked at him carefully and managed to relax. Surely no one could lie about a wife so convincingly. "Don't worry, you're not completely boring." His twinkling dark eyes and devilish smile proved he knew he was darned exciting to be around. "Tell me something else about you. What's your favorite food? Besides espresso, that is."

"Sorry, coffee definitely is number one on my list of life's sustenance. Though I'm sure anything licked from your lips would qualify, too."

She laughed and shook her head. "I don't have to ask you about talents, because I already know a few of them. Blarney being one."

"And my other talents?" His eyes gleamed as his wide hand splayed on her back, pressing her close against him, and the heat of his skin on hers made her short of breath all over again.

"I'm not stroking your ego any bigger than it already is."

"How about stroking something else, then?"

"Already did that. And I see I'll have to watch what I say around you."

He chuckled as he kissed her shoulder, and she found herself thinking about his mouth and those talents of his and wasn't sure if it was that or his body heat making her feel so overly warm. Again. "So what are your hobbies?" he asked.

"I don't know if I'd call it a hobby, but I like to run. Helps clear my mind when it gets too busy. And I like marshmallows. A lot."

"Marshmallows?" He laughed out loud at that. "You're kidding."

"Unfortunately, no. I pop the little ones when I'm working on the computer. Which is why I have to run. Don't want to *become* a marshmallow."

"You're about as far from a marshmallow as anyone could be." His hand stroked feather-light up her arm and across her chest to slide down the other, making her quiver. "I'd like to run more than just on a treadmill, but my work just doesn't leave me that kind of time."

"So what is this work you spend all your time doing?"

"I'm a cardiologist."

Every muscle froze, and her breath stopped as she stared at him. A cardiologist? *Cardiologist?* Could this really be happening?

He was probably used to women swooning when he announced that, but not her. She'd worked with more cardiologists than she cared to think about, and being arrogant and egotistical seemed to be a requirement for becoming that kind of specialist. Something she'd allowed herself to forget for too long with her last two boyfriends.

Along with her shock came another, even more chilling thought, which now seemed all too likely since they were staying at the same hotel. Her heart thumped hard in her chest, her body now icy cold as she tugged the sheet up tighter around it. "What's your last name, Jack?"

"Dunbar." He smiled, obviously not sensing the neon "oh, crap" vibes she had to be sending off. "I'm working for the next month at the Saint Malo Hospital, testing a new heart-valve replacement device. I've worked damned hard to get the design finished and to get the arrangements for the trial finalized. Can't believe it's finally about to happen."

Oh. My. Lord. She couldn't quite believe it, either. Not the trial starting. This unbelievable coincidence.

How was it possible that the man she'd just slept with was Dr. Jack Dunbar? The Jack Dunbar she'd be working with and observing at the hospital? The Jack Dunbar who was testing the procedure many, including her, hoped would someday always be used, instead of open-heart surgery, to replace faulty heart valves? The Jack Dunbar who had helped develop the next generation of valve replacement catheter based on her original design?

A next generation she feared wasn't any better, or safer, than her own had been.

And if it became necessary to voice her opinion that the trial should be halted, he wouldn't feel like kissing her or making love with her again, that was for sure. Not that she planned on more kisses and lovemaking, anyway.

A cardiologist was the absolute last kind of man she wanted in her life. Again.

"How about you?" He lay back, reaching to grasp her hand, his thumb brushing against her skin. Just as it had earlier when they'd been walking in such a lovely, companionable way. This time the feeling it gave her wasn't electrifying and sweet. The sensation felt more like discomfort and dismay. "So, what kind of last name goes with Avery? And what kind of work brings you to Paris?"

She swallowed hard. "Funny you should ask. My work has a lot to do with your own, Dr. Dunbar."

"Your work is similar to mine?" Jack asked, obvious surprise etched on his face. "In what way? Are you a doctor?"

"No. I have a doctorate in biomedical engineering." She left it at that, which was absurd, since it was all going to come out sooner or later, and it might as well be now. Lying naked in bed with him.

That realization had her shaking off her stunned paralysis to leap out of bed and grab up her clothes.

"That's...impressive." He propped himself up on his elbow, obviously enjoying the view as she scrambled to get dressed. His dark eyebrows were raised even higher, an expression she was used to seeing when she told people what she did for a living. She was young to be where she was careerwise and being petite made her seem younger still.

"Not really. I just worked hard, like you. Then again, in my experience cardiologists are pretty impressed... with themselves." And was that an understatement, or what?

"I should be insulted, except it might be true." He grinned at her. "So what brings you to Paris?"

"Well, as I said, my work has to do with yours." And could there be a much worse situation? The very first time she had a one-time thing with a man, he turned out to be someone she'd be working with closely.

She still couldn't quite wrap her brain around this mess. With a nervous laugh threatening, she pulled on her shirt, relieved to be finally clothed. After all, being naked when they made their formal introductions would be all kinds of ridiculous, wouldn't it?

She smoothed down her clothes and took a deep breath as she turned to him.

"As you know, your company hired the designer of the first valve replacement catheter to come study and observe the trial of your new one. That designer would be me."

His mouth actually fell open as he stared at her. It seemed he shook his head slightly, and that jittery laugh finally burst out of her throat. Clearly, he was as shocked by this crazy coincidence as she was. Though maybe it wasn't so crazy or much of a coincidence— after all, the Crilex Corporation was putting them both up at the same hotel where they'd met.

"You can't be...Dr. Girard," he said, still wearing an expression of disbelief.

"I am. And I'm equally shocked that you're Dr. Dunbar." Awkwardly, she stuck out her hand. "Avery Marie Girard. Nice to meet you."

That slow, sexy smile she'd found all too attractive throughout the day slipped onto his face again before he laughed. He reached to shake her hand, holding onto it. "It's an honor, Dr. Girard. Obviously, I've read about all you've accomplished. Your designs for various medical devices. Studied them for more hours than I care to think about as I worked with engineers to design the one we'll be testing. I...can't believe that you're...her."

"Because I'm young?" Or more likely because he'd

already seen her naked, but maybe she could pretend it hadn't happened. As though *that* was possible.

"Because you're beautiful. And fun. And spontaneous. With silky hair you don't wear in a bun and crazy, colorful clothes instead of drab gray. Rain boots with ducks instead of orthopedic shoes." His eyes crinkled at the corners. "I'm obviously guilty of thinking of a very stereotypical brainiac scientist, and those stereotypes don't include any of the things you are."

"Jack Dunbar!" She shook her head mockingly, having heard it all before. "You shouldn't admit any of that. The Society of Women Scientists will publicly flay you if you say that aloud. Maybe mount your head on an energy stick and parade the streets with it, denouncing stereotypes of all kinds."

"And I'd deserve it." The eyes that met hers were warm and admiring. That admiration would doubtless change into something else if he knew about her true role in his project. A slightly sick feeling seeped through her. Why, oh, why, hadn't she learned who he was before she'd slept with him?

"Glad you admit it. Scientists come in all ages, sizes, genders and personalities."

"You're right, and I'm sorry." He got out of the bed as well, and she averted her gaze from his glorious nakedness. "Sounds like you buy into some stereotyping, too, though. That cardiologists are all egotistical and impressed with themselves."

Guilty. But she had good reason to believe that, and it wasn't based on a stereotype. It was based on personal experience. And then, today, she'd dived into bed with another one. How stupid could she be? "Let's agree to set those preconceived ideas aside, shall we?"

"Agreed." He shook his head as he pulled on his own clothes. "Wow. I'm just blown away by this. I'd been interested in meeting the famous Dr. Girard and pleased to have her participate in the trial with me. Little did I know she'd be an incredible tour guide, have the greenest eyes I've ever seen and…" he paused to look at her, speaking in the low, deep rumble that did funny things to her insides "…the sweetest lips on either side of the Atlantic Ocean."

Oh, my. And his were beyond sweet, as well. "Except you realize this was a bad idea. Now that we know we'll be working together."

In fact, he didn't have any idea exactly how bad an idea it had been.

Robert Timkin, the Crilex CEO, had spun to Jack and everyone else involved that Avery would be there just to observe the trial for her own education. But the company knew she had concerns about the new device and had really hired her to evaluate the data, giving her the power to stop the rollout of the next trials if she thought it necessary.

Jack had worked on designing the new device and organizing the trial for over a year, and he'd doubtless flip out if the data forced her to shut it down.

"Working together." His warm smile faded and his brows lowered in a frown. "I guess you're right. That is a problem."

"It is." She drew a calming breath. "Listen. This afternoon was wonderful. A lovely day in a wonderful city between two strangers. But now we're not strangers. And I have to be an objective observer as I gather data on the trial. From now on, we're just working colleagues, nothing more."

He stared at her silently for a moment, his expression serious, before he nodded. "You're right. Business and pleasure never mix well."

"No. They don't." Not to mention that she'd sworn off cardiologists for good.

He stepped forward and pulled her close, pressing his lips to hers in a soft, sweet kiss. Despite her words and thoughts and conviction, she found herself melting into him.

"That was from Jack to Avery. Thank you for an unforgettable day," he whispered against her lips before he stepped back. "Dr. Dunbar will be meeting Dr. Girard tomorrow in the cath lab as we both concentrate on why we came to Paris. Okay?"

"Okay."

He dropped one more lingering kiss on her mouth before he picked up her coat and draped it over her arm. She stepped out to the hall and the door clicked quietly behind her. She lifted her fingers to her lips, knowing with certainty this had been the only one-time fling she'd ever have. That she'd savor the memory, and pray that over the next thirty days it didn't come back to sting her in more ways than one.

CHAPTER THREE

AVERY STOOD BEHIND a wall of glass to one side of the operating table in the hospital's cath lab, watching the procedure on the X-ray fluoroscopy viewing monitor. She'd gowned and masked like everyone else in the room, but unlike anyone else, she held a tablet in her hand to record the notes she'd be taking.

"The prosthetic valve is made from cow tissue," Jack said to the nurses and doctors assisting or observing the procedure, as he and Jessica Bowman, the nurse he'd brought with him from the States, readied the patient. "This version doesn't require a balloon to open it as the previous one did."

He continued to explain, as he had last night during his presentation, how a transcatheter aortic valve implantation, TAVI, worked. The details of how the catheter was designed, and why the stent and valve were in an umbrella shape, designed to push the diseased valve aside before the umbrella opened, seating the new valve in its place. With the procedure not yet started, Avery had a moment to watch him instead.

Today, he was all business, his dark eyes serious above his mask, his voice professional and to the point.

In stark contrast to yesterday's amusing and witty companion. As they'd laughed and walked through Paris, his eyes had been perpetually filled with interest and humor, his mouth curved in a smile, his attention on her as much as it had been on the landmarks she'd shown him.

A very dangerous combination, this Dr. Jack Dunbar. So dangerous she'd thrown caution off the top of the Eiffel Tower. Thank heavens they'd agreed that no more hot, knee-melting kisses or spontaneous sex could be allowed.

Though just thinking about those kisses and their all-too-delicious lovemaking made her mouth water for more.

She gave herself a little mental smack. Date a cardiologist? Been there, done that. Twice. Fool me once, shame on me, fool me twice, shame on me again. Fool me three times? Well, her genius status would clearly be in question.

Then there was the other sticky issue. Obviously, the best-case scenario would be for the device to work fabulously, for the trial to be a success and for it to be further rolled out to other countries and hospitals. After all, in the U.S. alone over one hundred thousand people each year were diagnosed with aortic stenosis, and a solid third of them were high risk who might not do well with traditional open-heart surgery or weren't candidates at all.

But, from studying this stent and catheter, she worried that it didn't fully address the significant problem of postoperative valve leakage and subsequent pulmonary edema, which her own design had not solved and was something she was trying to fix in her new prototypes.

"I'm going to establish a central venous line through the right internal jugular," Jack said as he made an incision in the patient's neck. "Then insert a temporary balloon-tip pacemaker. Both groin areas of the patient have been prepped, and I'll next insert an introducer sheath into the femoral artery."

Avery watched as his steady hands worked. After completing the first steps, he made another incision in the patient's groin, moving the guide wire inside the artery. "Contrast dye, please, and monitor the heparin drip," he said as he watched his maneuvering of the wires on the overhead screen. "You'll see that it's important to puncture the artery with a high degree of angulation to minimize the distance from the artery to the skin."

The man was an incredibly skilled interventional cardiologist, that was obvious. She quickly focused on the careful notes she was taking to squash thoughts of the man's many skills he'd thoroughly demonstrated to her yesterday. Why, oh, why, would she have to be around him every day when the whole reason she'd given in to temptation had been because she'd thought she'd never see him again?

Finally, he finished stitching the access sites and the patient had been moved to Recovery. Jack shook hands with all those in the room congratulating him.

"Thank you, but I'm just one cog in this wheel that will hopefully change valve transplantation forever," Jack said. "One important cog is right here with us.

The designer of the first catheter-inserted replacement valve, Dr. Avery Girard."

Taken off guard, she felt herself blush as Jack turned, gesturing to her with his hand, then actually began to clap, a big smile on his face, as the others in the room joined him. She'd been keeping a low profile, and most of the hospital had just assumed she was a Crilex representative. Most cardiologists she knew—most definitely both of her old boyfriends—loved to play the big shot and preen at any and all accolades. Neither one of them would have shared the glory unless they had to.

"I appreciate your nice words, Dr. Dunbar," she said, feeling a silly little glow in her chest, despite herself. "I have every hope that the new design you've helped develop will be the one that works. Congratulations on your first procedure going smoothly."

"Thank you." His warm eyes met hers, reminding her of the way he'd looked at her yesterday, until the doctors observing converged on him to ask questions and he turned his attention to them.

Avery took off her gown, mask and hat, and caught herself watching Jack speak to everyone. Listening to his deep voice and the earnest enthusiasm there. She wanted to stay, to listen longer, but forced herself to move quietly from the room to go through her notes. Limiting her interactions with him to the bare minimum had to be the goal, and since there was just one surgery scheduled today, there was no reason to hang around.

Satisfied that her notes were all readable, in order and entered correctly into her database, Avery walked toward the hotel, feeling oddly restless. She'd planned to work in her room, but a peculiar sense of aloneness came over her. Since when had that ever happened?

Still, the feeling nagged at her, and she stopped to work for a bit at a little café, which seemed like a more appealing choice. After a few hours she headed to her room and settled into a comfy chair with her laptop. Projects on her computer included ideas on how to fix her previous TAVI design if the one Jack had in trial had significant issues.

That unsettled feeling grew, sinking deep into the pit of her stomach, and she realized why.

If she had to recommend the trial be discontinued, would Jack think it was because she wanted Crilex to develop one of her designs instead? That her concerns would be from self-interest instead of concern for the patients?

She'd been doing freelance work ever since abruptly leaving the company that had funded her first TAVI design. They'd insisted on continuing the trials long after the data had been clear that the leakage problems had to be fixed first, which was why she'd been glad to observe this trial before that happened again.

If only she could talk to Jack about it, so he'd never think any of this was underhanded on her part. But her contract with Crilex stated she was to keep that information completely confidential.

She pressed her lips together and tried to concentrate on work. Worrying about the odd situation didn't solve anything and, after all, Jack knew she'd designed the original. Wouldn't he assume she was likely working on improvements to it and observing his with that in mind?

She couldn't tell Jack the power she had over the

trial. But maybe she should tell him she had concerns with the design. To give him that heads-up, at least, and maybe nudge him to look for the same issues she would be as the trial continued.

Avery caught herself staring across the room for long minutes. With a sigh she shut the lid of her laptop and gave up. Clearly, she needed something to clear her head. Fresh air and maybe a visit to somewhere she hadn't been for a while. A place popped into her head, and she decided it was a sign that it might be just what she needed to get back on track.

A half hour later, jostling with others passengers as she stepped off the metro, she saw the sun was perilously low in the sky. She hadn't torn out the door in record time to miss seeing the Sacré Coeur at sunset and headed in that direction in a near jog, only to bump into the back of some guy who stepped right in front of her.

"Oh, sorry!" she said, steadying herself.

"No, my fault. I'm trying to figure out how to get to the Sacré Coeur to see it at sunset, and I…"

She froze and looked up as the man turned, knowing that, incredible and ridiculous as it was, the man speaking was none other than Jack Dunbar. Saw his eyes widen with the same surprise and disbelief until he laughed and shook his head. "Why is it that whenever I need a tour guide, the best one in Paris shows up to help me?"

Fate. It was clearly fate, and why did it keep throwing her and Jack together? Should she even admit that was exactly where she'd been going? "I wish I had the answers to the universe. But somehow I don't think you'll be surprised to learn that's where I'm headed, too."

He looked at her a long, serious moment before he gave her a slow smile, his eyes crinkling at the corners, and the warmth in them put a little flutter in her chest. "You know, somehow I'm not surprised. And who am I to argue with the universe? Guess this means we're going together."

A buoyant feeling replaced the odd, unsettled feeling she'd had for hours. Bad idea? Yes. Something she could walk away from? Apparently not.

"Then we've got to hurry." She grabbed his hand, knowing she was throwing caution away again. But how could she say no to the happy excitement bubbling up inside her? And after all, it was just a visit to the Sacré Coeur, right? "The sun's setting soon, and we don't want to miss it."

"Lead on, Ms. Tour Guide. For tonight I'm all yours."

CHAPTER FOUR

Jack looked at the adorable woman dragging him through the streets and wondered, not for the first time, how he could have gotten so lucky to have met her before they'd started working together. A personal connection before a professional one got in the way of it.

The professional part was unfortunate, since he'd vowed he'd never again get involved with a woman at work. For just one more night, though, he'd let himself enjoy being with Avery. After all, here they were, together. And, smart or not smart, he just couldn't resist.

"A lot of people think it's really old, but did you know the Sacré Coeur was consecrated after World War I in 1919?"

"I didn't know. Are you proving again to me that female scientists are well versed in many subjects?"

"I don't have to prove anything about women in science," she said in a dignified tone, "seeing as I'm not wearing orthopedic shoes."

He laughed. "True. And they're even bright green, which I've never seen in leather ankle boots."

"Clearly, you live a sheltered life. Maybe you should get yourself some brightly colored shoes."

"Somehow, I think my patients would worry about my skills if I dressed that way." His eyes met her twinkling ones, an even more vivid green than her boots, and just looking at her made him smile. "You get to hide in your lab and behind your computer. I don't."

"You could wear them while your patients are under anesthesia." She had that teasing look in her eyes that he'd found irresistible yesterday when they'd gone up the Eiffel Tower, then spent that magical time in his hotel room. That he'd found irresistible since the moment she'd grabbed his hand and led him to breakfast. That he had to somehow learn to resist, starting again tomorrow.

"Except most of my patients are awake during procedures, so I'll stick with black or brown."

"Where's your sense of adventure?"

"Here with you tonight."

She looked up at him, an oddly arrested expression on her face. "Mine, too." She stepped up their pace. "We're almost there, and since January's off season, hopefully there won't be big crowds. Good thing the sun's peeking through. I think it just might be a beautiful night."

"It already is."

A blush filled her cheeks as she realized what he was saying. And maybe it sounded hokey, but he meant it. His intense focus on work usually didn't allow him to notice things like a beautiful sunset or, though he probably shouldn't admit it, even a beautiful woman sometimes. But she'd grabbed his attention from the second he'd met her, and he didn't know what to do about that.

She led him around a corner then suddenly stopped,

turning her full attention in front of them. "*Voilà!* We made it! And, oh, my gosh, I think it's about the most spectacular I've ever seen!"

His gaze followed hers, and the sight was beyond anything he'd expected. At the end of the street behind a beautiful old building with large columns, the Sacré Coeur rose high above everything else. Its numerous cupolas and spires were bathed in pink and gold from the sunset, emerging from the pale sky and looking for all the world like a stunning mural in the mist.

"That's…incredible."

"It is, isn't it?" She took her hand from his, moving it to clutch his arm, holding him closer. He looked down to see her eyes lit with the same wonder he was feeling and that strange sense of connection with her, too, that had prompted yesterday's memorable interlude. "I haven't seen the basilica for a long time."

He moved his arm from her grasp and wrapped it around her shoulders, wanting to feel her next to him. They stood there together a long while, staring as the pastels changed hue and darkened. Eventually, the sun dipped low, taking the color and light with it, and Jack turned to her, pulling her fully into his arms without thinking. "Somehow, I don't think it would have seemed quite as beautiful if you hadn't been here with me."

She smiled and lowered her head to rest her cheek against his chest as she gazed down the street at the now shadowed church, and he couldn't believe how natural it felt to hold her like this. Like they'd been together a long time instead of one day. Like there weren't good reasons not to.

He stroked his hand up her back, sliding it beneath

her thick hair to cup her neck. "How about we take the funicular up to see the city below?"

She lifted her head and leaned back to look up at him. "How do you know about the funicular?"

"What, you think you have all the dibs on tour guiding?" He tucked her hair under her cute hat, a yellow one this time, letting his fingers linger on the softness of her locks before stroking briefly down her cheeks. "I read a Paris tour guide book because I didn't know I'd have a personal one tonight."

"And yet here I am."

"Yeah. Here you are."

For a moment her green eyes stared into his until, to his surprise, worry and utter pleasure, she lifted herself up on tiptoe, slipped her arms up his chest and around his neck and pressed her lips to his. The touch was instantly electric, surging through every cell in Jack's body as he tightened his arms around her. Until he forgot they worked together. Until he forgot they were standing near any number of other sightseers who were snapping photos and admiring the church. On the side of a busy street where cars and motorcycles and scooters veered all too perilously close.

Just as had happened yesterday under that umbrella, Avery managed to make him forget everything but the drugging taste of her mouth as it moved softly on his.

The roar of a scooter zooming by had him breaking the kiss. He leaned his forehead against hers, their little panting breaths creating a mist of steam in the cold air between them. "Wow. That was nice."

"What, you think you have all the dibs on initiating a kiss?"

He chuckled at her words, mimicking his. "Believe me, I'm more than happy to share the dibs. But as much as I'd like to keep kissing you, I don't want either of us sent to the hospital by one of the crazy drivers around here." Or get into a sticky situation because of their jobs. "Let's go on up to see the view."

She pulled away and something, maybe embarrassment, flickered in her eyes. He reached for her chin and turned her face to his. "Hey, what's that look for?"

"I don't know why I kissed you. Why I keep kissing you, even when we agreed not to." She shook her head, a little frown between her brows. "It's like something comes over me and I lose all common sense."

"If you have to lose your common sense to kiss me, I hope you don't find it," he teased, earning a small smile. He took a few steps backward, bringing her with him, until he came up against the wall of a building. Even as he knew he shouldn't, he lifted his hand to cup her cheek, gently stroking her beautiful lips with his thumb. "You taste damned good to me."

"Except we need to work together. So kissing or... anything else...isn't a good idea."

"I know. It's a hell of a bad idea." He kissed her again, and the sigh that slipped from her lips, the way her body relaxed into his nearly had him going deeper, and to hell with the risk of being struck by a car. But he forced himself to let her go, reaching for her hand. "Come on. Your funicular awaits, princess."

They rode to the top and enjoyed the incredible views of the city as he held her close to shelter her from the colder air and wind. They meandered along the cobbled streets of Montmartre as Avery filled him in on some of the history of the village that had long been a haven for artists, including Picasso, Monet and Van Gogh. Today it attracted young artists who peddled their work on the streets.

"I don't know about you, but I haven't eaten," Jack said as they passed a restaurant with an appealing exterior. He looked at the posted menu and laughed when he realized it was, of course, in French. "I don't know what this place serves, but you want to grab something to eat?"

"My parents and I lived right here in Montmartre the two years we were in Paris, but I've never eaten here," she said, looking at the menu. "It's pretty expensive."

"We deserve something besides hospital food, which we'll be eating a lot of. Come on."

The food turned out to be good, and they enjoyed a lively conversation and occasional debate about medical devices like stents and implants until they both laughed about it.

Jack grabbed the bill when he saw her reaching for it, handing his credit card to the waiter. "My treat. I like a woman who eats all her food and talks about something besides shopping," he said to tease her.

"You treated me yesterday, so it should be my turn. And it sounds like you've been dating the wrong kind of women."

"No doubt about that." In fact, she didn't know how right she was, and it was a good reminder why he couldn't date Avery, no matter how attractive she was. No matter how much he wanted to.

"I don't always practically lick the plate, though," she said with a grin. "Thank you. The food was amazing, but you spent way too much."

"You forget I'm a rich, egotistical cardiologist. When I'm not working like crazy, I like to throw money around to impress beautiful women."

"You're right. Somehow I'd forgotten."

Her smile disappeared. He had no clue why and tried for a joke. "It's my pleasure to shower money on gorgeous scientists who wear colorful shoes."

Still no smile. In fact, an odd combination of unhappiness and irritation had replaced every bit of the pleasure that had been on her face.

Well, damn. But it was probably just as well, considering everything. "Time to head back to the hotel," he said, shoving back his chair to stand. "We have two surgeries tomorrow I need to get ready for."

She nodded and they headed toward the metro. It felt strange not reaching out to hold her hand, and a pang of regret filled him. But wishing their circumstance could be different didn't change a thing.

"Oh! I think that's Le Mur des Je T'aime! I've never seen it."

"What's Le Mur...whatever you said?"

He followed her as she moved closer to look at a wall of tiles with words scrawled all over it and splashes of red here and there in between. "It's the Wall of I Love You. An artist named Baron conceived of the wall, with 'I love you' written in something like three hundred languages. As a place for lovers to meet."

A place for lovers to meet? That bordered on overly sentimental as far as Jack was concerned. "Sounds like something from a chick flick, with a gooey happily-ever-after."

After he'd said it he thought maybe he should have

kept his opinion to himself, and was relieved when she laughed. "Typical man. Not that I know much about lasting relationships and happily-ever-after."

"That makes two of us."

"Nobody you'd meet here at the wall? Old flame or old pain?"

"I've been too busy." The only woman who qualified as an "old pain" was the medical device sales rep he'd dated who, it had turned out, had used him big-time to advance her own career. He hadn't come close to being in love with her, but it had been damned embarrassing. Which was why he never dated anyone remotely connected to his work. And he needed to remember that.

She began walking toward the metro again, and they were mostly quiet on the way back to the hotel. Another sudden shower burst from the night sky that had them wet in an instant and nearly running the last blocks, intimately tucked beneath Avery's little umbrella.

Finally sheltered under the overhang in front of the hotel doors, she shook the rain from it. "Clearly, I'm going to need to get a bigger umbrella," she said, her voice a little breathless. "This one isn't nearly big enough for both of us."

Except, after tonight, they wouldn't be touring Paris together anymore. "I could invest in a big, yellow rain poncho and leave the umbrella to you. That would be pretty masculine and sexy, don't you think?"

"I don't know. People might mistake you for a giant lemon."

He loved her laugh and the way her eyes twinkled. Fortunately, other people loaded onto the elevator with them or he just might have found himself kissing that beautiful, smiling mouth of hers again. He grasped her elbow when they arrived on her floor and moved into the hall.

"What are you doing?" she asked. "You're staying on the eighteenth floor."

"I always walk a lady to her door."

"I don't think hotels count."

"Why not? There are so many doors in this huge place, you might get lost." He thought she'd smile at his teasing tone, but she didn't, and he sighed. "If that look on your face means you think I'm planning to jump your bones again, I'm not. Much as I'd like to, I get that it's different now. And agree it needs to be. Okay?"

"Okay."

She smiled, and it was her real, sunny smile. So real he had to kiss her one last time. She tasted the same as she had before, an intoxicatingly sensual mix of chilled, damp skin and warm mouth. The smell of rain and a slight, perfumed scent from her hair filled his nostrils, and the feel of her body through her coat filled his hands. He wanted to strip it off of her so that barrier wouldn't be between them.

A little sound came from her throat, and the sound inflamed him, his own low groan forming in response as he deepened the kiss. Damned if this woman didn't knock his socks off in every way a woman could.

She pulled back, her gloved hands a softly fuzzy caress on the sides of his neck. Her eyes were wide, her mouth wet from his kiss, her breathing choppy. "What is it about you?"

"Funny, I was just thinking the same thing. About you. Except I know the answer. You're amazing, and we have chemistry about equal to a nuclear explosion. Which makes it nearly impossible not to kiss you, even when I know I shouldn't." He pressed his lips to hers for another long moment before looking into the deep green of her eyes again.

She stared at him a moment longer before her beautiful mouth curved in an answering smile. "I guess we need to think of this as one last time Avery and Jack meet one another."

"I like that. A kiss dictated by the universe."

"By the universe." She rose up and kissed him again. Just as he was trying, in the midst of the thick fog in his brain, to mentally calculate how many hours it was until he had to be at work and alert, and how much longer he could enjoy the taste and feel of her, she drew back.

Her eyes were lit with the same desire he felt, and he was glad one of them had enough presence of mind to stop while they still could.

"There's something I want to be honest with you about," she said, clasping her hands together in an oddly nervous gesture. "And when you hear it, it'll probably help us keep our distance from one another."

"That sounds ominous. Is it that you're actually the one who's married?"

She smiled and shook her head. "No. It's about your TAVI device. I'm worried it doesn't address the flaw mine had. Leakage resulting in pulmonary edema."

He stared at her in surprise. "Why? We've barely begun the trial."

"I know. But I'm just not sure the corrections you've made will be enough, and feel it should have been tested longer on animals before a human trial."

What the hell? "The bioengineers and I worked hard to improve it. It's more than ready."

"I just wanted you to know I believe we should both pay extra attention to that aspect of the data."

Maybe this was how people felt when someone said their baby was ugly, and it wasn't a good feeling. "Duly noted. Good night, Dr. Girard."

He headed to his room, still reeling a little from her announcement. He was damned proud of the new device and would never have guessed she had any bias whatsoever about it. Surely she would remain scientifically impartial as she collected the data. Her announcement, though, did seem to make it easier to step away and keep his distance, which he tried to see as a positive development.

But as he attempted to sleep, he was surprised and none too happy to find himself thinking about Avery nearly as much as he was thinking of the work waiting for him early in the morning.

CHAPTER FIVE

JACK SAT AT the small desk the hospital had given him to use and finished his notes on the procedures they'd just completed. Now that surgery was over for the day, he let himself think about Avery and this uncomfortable situation.

For the first time in his entire career he'd had trouble getting one hundred percent of his focus on the patient and surgery in front of him before the procedure had begun. To not notice Avery standing behind the glass, ready to watch the TAVI procedure on the monitor, taking her notes. He'd finally managed, but somehow, some way, he had to keep Avery Girard and her premature concerns about the device from invading his thoughts.

He shoved himself from the chair to concentrate on what he'd come here to accomplish. He pulled up the patient records and headed toward the room of the second patient they'd done the procedure on.

Simon Bellamy was eighty-six years old and had been referred to them because of his severely diseased aortic valve. Although reasonably healthy otherwise, his age put him at high risk for open-heart surgery. He'd been doing well the past two days, and Jack expected he could be released tomorrow.

The satisfaction he was feeling as he looked at the patient's chart disappeared the instant he walked into the man's room.

Short, rasping gasps were coming from his open mouth, and he sat bolt upright in his bed, eyes wide. Jack grabbed his stethoscope from his scrubs pocket as he strode to the bedside. "What's wrong, Mr. Bellamy? Are you having trouble breathing?"

The patient just nodded in response, his chest heaving. Jack listened to the man's lungs, and the obvious crackling sounds were the last thing he wanted to hear. "Ah, hell." He pushed the button for the nurse, then got the blood-pressure cuff on the man. He stared at the reading, his chest tightening at the numbers. While it had been normal earlier today, it had soared to two hundred and twenty over one hundred.

The nurse hurried into the room. Jack kept his attention on his patient as he spoke, checking oxygen saturation levels, and was damned glad almost everyone in the hospital spoke English. "We need to reduce his heart's workload by getting his blood pressure down immediately. Also administer furosemide and get a Foley catheter placed, stat."

The man's oxygen level proved to be very low, which was no surprise. It was disturbingly obvious what was happening here. "I need to get a chest X-ray. Can you...?" He glanced at the nurse, who was busy getting the Foley placed. "Never mind. I'll call down to have the portable brought up."

And damned if the minute he finished the call to

X-Ray, Avery walked in with her tablet in hand, stopping abruptly.

"What's wrong, Dr. Dunbar?"

For a split second he didn't want to tell her, after her revelation to him last night. Which would be childish and unprofessional, not to mention pointless, since she'd figure it out anyway. "Acute onset aortic insufficiency. Getting a chest film to confirm."

Just his luck that she was witnessing exactly what they'd just talked about. A significant complication from the valve leaking. He knew her being there or not didn't change the reality and told himself he was mature enough and confident enough to handle it. For a small number of patients it wasn't an unusual complication, anyway, and Jack discussed with everyone all the risks and potential side effects.

Avery gave a single nod and stepped out of the way as the tech rolled the X-ray machine into the room and got the patient prepared to get the picture of his lungs. To her credit, there was no sign of I-told-you-so smugness on her face, just concern.

"Have you given him a diuretic and blood-pressure meds?"

Had she really asked that? He nearly let loose on her, until he saw the deep frown over her green eyes and the genuine worry there. He managed to bite back the words he wanted to say, which was that he knew what he was doing, for God's sake, and to butt out. Did she really think he was a lousy doctor? "Having a Foley catheter placed and gave him furosemide and BP meds. With any luck, he'll be more comfortable shortly."

She nodded again, moving farther away to one side

of the room as she opened her tablet. Her head tilted down and her silky hair swung to the sides of her cheeks as she began to tap away at the screen.

Frustration surged into his chest and he stuffed it down, a little shocked at the intensity of it. His years of practicing medicine had taught him how to remain calm even in critical situations, and he was fairly legendary for being cool under fire.

He inhaled a deep, calming breath and turned away from her to check on Mr. Bellamy. Already the man was breathing a little easier and able to lean back against the raised bed. The X-ray tech ambled off with the films, and Jack hoped they'd be done fast, though he didn't expect them to show anything he didn't already know. There was no doubt in his mind this was pulmonary edema, the patient's lungs full of fluid from the valve leakage.

"Feeling slightly better now, Mr. Bellamy?"

The man nodded, still mouth-breathing but not nearly so labored as before. Jack reached for his hand and gave it a squeeze. "I know that's a scary thing, when you can't get a breath. You've been given a water pill to get your lungs clear, and we're going to keep the Foley catheter in to catch the fluid. It will have to stay there until we get the volume of fluid we want to see and make sure it's nice and clear. Okay?"

The man nodded again, giving his hand a return squeeze before Jack headed out of the room to check the X-ray.

"Dr. Dunbar."

Avery's voice stopped him in the hall and he turned. He folded his arms across his chest, wondering if this was the moment for an *I told you so*. Which he absolutely would react calmly and professionally to, damn it, if it killed him.

"Yes?"

She stepped close to him and, to his surprise, placed her cool palm on his forearm. He couldn't figure out exactly what her expression was, but it didn't seem to be self-satisfaction. More like...remorse?

"I owe you an apology."

He raised his eyebrows. That was about the last thing he'd expected to come out of her mouth, and he waited to hear what she was apologizing for.

"It was completely inappropriate of me to ask if you'd administered blood-pressure meds and furosemide. You're the doctor in charge and far more knowledgeable about patient care than I am."

"Yes, I am."

A little laugh left her lips. "There's that egotistical cardiologist finally coming out. I knew he was in there somewhere." She dropped her hand from his arm and gave him a rueful smile. "During the clinical trial on my original device, I was often required to give instructions to nurses post-op when the doctors weren't around. I guess it's an old habit that's hard to break. Sorry."

She bit her lip, and damned if the thought of how incredible it had been kissing her came to mind.

How could he be thinking about that now? He looked into the green of her eyes, filled with an obvious sincerity, and felt his frustration fade. "Just don't let it happen again, or everyone in the hospital might start to wonder if you know something they don't. Like that I bought my MD online."

"It would take more than me blurting something dumb to tarnish your awesome reputation, Dr. Dunbar. Everyone here thinks you walk on water." Those pretty lips of hers curved. "But, believe me, I'll do my best to keep my trap shut. You know that old saying about how if looks could kill? Seeing the expression in your eyes at that moment, if that was true, I'd be lying on the floor lifeless."

In spite of everything, he felt himself smile, and how she managed that, he didn't know. "Cardiologists do have superpowers, you know. Better not test me to see if that's one of mine."

Her smile widened, touched her eyes and sent his own smile even wider. They stood looking at one another, standing there in the hallway, until Jack managed to shake off the trance she seemed to send him into with all too little effort.

He couldn't allow himself to fall any further for her obvious charms. Her work was too tangled up with his, and he'd promised himself never again.

He brought a cool, professional tone back to his voice. "I'm going to check on Mr. Bellamy's X-ray. I'll put the notes in his chart for your database."

He turned and strode down the hall, fighting a stupid urge to look over his shoulder to see if she was still standing there. When he stopped at the elevator he glanced back up the hall, despite his best intentions not to, and his heart kicked annoyingly when he saw her backside as she moved in the opposite direction. Riveted, he stared at the view. Her thick, shiny hair cascading down her back. That sexy sway of her hips, her gorgeous legs with their slender ankles, her delicate profile as she turned into a patient's room.

And found himself powerless against the potent memories of how she'd felt held close in his arms, the taste of her mouth on his, the feel of his body in hers.

Damn.

He focused on the gray elevator doors. This just might prove to be the longest month of his life.

CHAPTER SIX

"So, ladies and gentlemen," Bob Timkin said, smiling at the group attending the late dinner meeting at the hotel, "we are encouraged at the success so far after a full week of the clinical trial. Patients and their families are pleased with the results, and I have great optimism as we look forward to the rest of the month."

The forty or so attendees clapped, a number of them turning their attention, smiles and applause toward Jack. He shifted slightly in his seat, wondering why it felt a little awkward. Not long ago he'd felt pleased with the media attention he'd gotten for his role in the development of the prototype device and the work involved in getting it finished and the trial set up. Happy that his mother, father and brother—all doctors—were proud of him and what he was trying to accomplish in memory of his granddad.

A large group effort had made it happen. The biomedical engineers had taken his suggestions to heart when they'd created the device. Crilex had funded it. French officials had seen the value of conducting the first trials here. He'd always been sure to include every one of them in his presentations and mention them in interviews.

But when it came down to it, the focus of others had been primarily on his work and his skills.

Avery's gaze met his across the room, and damned if he didn't have to admit she was probably why he felt this sudden discomfort. Her original design was the whole reason he had a new TAVI device at all. And while a slight valve leakage in a small percentage of patients was normal, he didn't like it that now three of the patients in this trial so far had experienced that complication. Statistically, that was far higher than the expected six percent, and that knowledge, along with Avery's announcement of her concerns, added to his unease.

He and Avery had managed to be simply cordial and professional to one another for the remainder of this first week. She also hadn't said anything to him about the latest patient with the valve leakage, which he'd been surprised but glad about. She must have finally seen it was still way too early to become truly concerned.

Jack nodded in acknowledgement of the recognition being sent his direction, but as his gaze again met Avery's he knew he couldn't stand her believing he was egotistical enough to think he alone merited the applause. Why what she thought of him mattered so much, though, wasn't something he wanted to analyze.

About to get to his feet and give a little speech about all the people deserving credit for the trial, Jack saw Bob moving from the lectern. Discomfort still nagged at him, but he figured it would be ineffective and even weird to start talking as the crowd began to stand and disperse.

Next thing he knew, he was looking at Avery again, and, disgusted with himself, quickly turned away. He would not allow himself to wonder what she was doing the rest of the evening. Would. Not.

He should go to his room and look over the history of the patient he'd be doing surgery on tomorrow. But an odd restlessness left him thinking he needed to do something else first, so he could concentrate later. Maybe a little downtime, listening to music in the lounge, would help him relax.

He moved toward the table where Jessica was sitting with some other nurses, yakking away like they'd become best friends. "Hey, Jess. How about a drink at the bar? We only have a single surgery tomorrow afternoon, so I think we can stay up one night past ten p.m."

"You don't have to ask me twice." She smiled at the women she was with. "Anybody want to join us?"

One by one they shook their heads. "I need to get home to get my little ones ready for bed," a young woman said. "Their papa will let them have crazy fun all night if I'm not there, then they will be tired and crying in the morning before school."

Another nodded in agreement, rolling her eyes. "*Oui.* My Raoul thinks that, if Maman's not home, dinner can be a chocolate croissant."

Jack smiled as everyone at the table laughed in agreement. It sounded just like his sister-in-law's gripes on the rare occasions his brother took over with the kids. If he was ever a dad, he'd try to remember this conversation and be more responsible.

That the random notion came to mind at all took him

aback. Since when had he even thought about having a family? The answer was never. Work consumed his life.

For the first time, he wondered if that was all he wanted. If work could always be everything.

He shook his head, trying to shake off any and all peculiar and unwelcome notions. Paris was clearly doing strange things to him and had been since day one. He'd be glad when the month was over and the clinical trials continued elsewhere. Maybe he should consider talking to the Russian government about a winter trial in Siberia—if that didn't freeze some sense into him, nothing would.

He moved into the hotel lounge with Jessica, passing the dance floor as the heavy beat of music pulsed around them. "I can't believe I've worked with you for three years, but don't know your tipple," he said to Jess as they settled into a round, corner banquette.

"Like that's a surprise?" she said with a grin. "I don't think we've ever been out for a drink before. Ever. You're always still at work when I leave."

"We haven't?" He thought back and realized with surprise that was the case. "It bothers me to realize you're right. Though I'm pretty sure a big part of that was you falling for Brandon. And the two of you getting married thing was kind of a big deal."

"Okay, maybe that's true," Jess said, chuckling. "A cosmopolitan makes me pretty happy. Sounds extra-good after the constant demands you've put on me this week."

"Cosmo it is."

He ordered from the waitress and was just about to ask Jess a few of the questions he realized he'd never bothered to ask her before when, out of the corner of his eye, he saw Avery walk into the lounge. Not alone.

Every ounce of the relaxation and good humor he'd managed to feel for the past five minutes died when he saw the guy who accompanied her.

Jack recognized him as a doctor from the hospital, though he didn't know him. A urologist, maybe. French. Well dressed, like most Parisians, and good looking to women, too, he supposed.

Jack watched the guy laugh at something she'd said. As she gifted him with her amazing smile in return, he pressed his palm to Avery's lower back and led her to the dance floor.

The way she moved, the way she smiled, the way she rested her hand on the man's shoulder made it hard for Jack to breathe, reminding him of the moment they'd first met. Every muscle in his body tightened at the way the guy was looking at her as they moved to the beat of the music. Like she was first on his list of desserts.

"Earth to Jack. Should I call the bomb squad before it goes off?"

Jessica's words managed to penetrate his intense focus on Avery and the guy, and he slowly turned to her. "What?"

"You look like you're about to explode. Which I don't think I've ever seen from you. Jealous a little?"

"Jealous? That's ridiculous."

"It may be ridiculous, but I hate to break it to you. It's all over your face."

Somehow he managed to control his accelerated breathing. To school his expression into something he hoped was neutral. "I don't date women I work with. You know that."

"Uh-huh. Except this one's making you rethink that, isn't she?" Jack hadn't even realized the waitress had brought their drinks until Jessica took a sip of hers, studying him over the rim of her glass. "Listen. I get it. She's smart and pretty and, other than me, you're alone here in France. But acting on your attraction to her? That's just trouble calling your name."

Trouble with a capital *T*. Unfortunately, he'd felt that trouble calling his name ever since he'd arrived in Paris. Trouble in the form of a small woman with soft skin, smiling eyes and a mouth that tasted like bright sunshine on a gray day.

Had she joked with the guy that she chose dance partners based on who would buy her a drink? The thought squeezed his chest so tight he had to force out his response to Jess.

"Since when are you my guardian angel? Believe me, I know all of that, and you don't have to worry. I'm keeping my distance." At least, he'd managed to for the past week or so.

"Guess you'd better run, then, because she's heading toward our table."

He stiffened and turned. Then couldn't help the relief he stupidly felt when Dr. Frenchman wasn't with her. And hoped like hell he wasn't looking at Avery the same way that guy still was, watching her from a corner table.

"Dr. Dunbar, may I speak with you for just a moment?" Avery asked when she stopped in front of them, her gaze flicking from him to Jessica and back.

He sat back, trying to pretend she didn't affect him in any way, which stretched his acting skills to the limit. "What's on your mind?"

She stood silently for a moment. Jack took in how perfectly the yellow shift dress she wore fit her slim body. How she folded one hand over the other in a nervous gesture before she stilled them against her sides. How her silky eyebrows twitched the way he'd noticed before when she pondered what to say.

"I wanted to suggest that, when you have a day off soon, you let me show you—"

As though pulled by a string from some invisible puppeteer, he reached out to grasp her wrist, tugging her down onto the bench seat. Her hip bumped into his as her eyes widened in surprise. Jessica's presence had nearly helped him resist the urge but, God help him, the hot jealousy that had grabbed him by the throat took control. Wanting to send a message to the guy still sitting across the room. Prompting Jack to say what he couldn't stop thinking about, and before he knew it the words were coming out of his mouth.

"Show me the correct way to use an umbrella?" Of its own accord, his voice went lower as he dipped his head, his lips nearly touching hers. "Or explain the mysteries of chemistry and spontaneous combustion? In which case, we can find a more private place to talk."

She stared at him, and even through the darkness of the bar he could see the surprise and confusion on her face. "Um, no. I wanted to talk to you about the trial."

"What about it?"

"With three patients already experiencing valve leakage, I'm sure you see why I'm concerned."

He watched her lips move, thinking about how good it was to kiss her. Let his gaze travel to the V of skin below her throat, which he knew was soft and warm. "The trial's barely started. We haven't had nearly enough patients to come to any kind of conclusions yet."

"I know. But as I said before, sometimes there are red flags right away." Deeply serious, her green eyes locked with his. "I want to introduce you to a patient who underwent one of the first TAVI procedures with my original device. I'd like you to see what he's living with."

He laughed, disgusted with himself. While he couldn't stop thinking about the taste of her mouth and the softness of her skin, she didn't seem to be having any trouble focusing on work.

He realized he was still holding onto her wrist, and dropped it. "I know what people with postoperative complications live with, Avery. I treat them every day."

"Just think about my offer." As she lifted her hand to his shoulder, a part of him liked having it there, while the saner part reminded him she'd just had that same hand on Dr. Frenchman's shoulder. "You might find it enlightening to meet this man and his family."

She slid from the seat and walked away. To Jack's surprise, she didn't sit with Dr. Frenchman. Instead, she exited the bar entirely, and he was glad he didn't have to watch her cozy up to the man, at the same time annoyed as hell that he felt that way.

What was it about this woman? First he'd grabbed her and pulled her down next to him like he had a right to. And in spite of it being a beyond-bad idea, every time he looked at her, all he could think of was how much he'd enjoyed being with her and kissing her and having sex with her. How much he wanted more of all of it.

"Boy, you've got it bad." Jessica shook her head. "I hope you can keep from getting so tangled up with her that you lose perspective on what we came here to do."

As he watched Avery's bright yellow, curvy behind disappear into the hotel foyer, he could only hope for the same thing.

CHAPTER SEVEN

AVERY STEPPED OFF the hotel elevator to head to the front doors, then stood frozen when she saw Jack standing right where she wanted to go. An absurdly handsome Jack, wearing a pale blue dress shirt, necktie and sport coat.

She and Jack had been friendly but professional over the past two days of surgeries and patient follow-ups, and she hoped it could stay that way. Without the uncomfortable attraction that remained in a low hum between them. The attraction that had clearly prompted Jack to do the caveman thing and pull her down next to him after she'd danced with the French doc she'd met. Jessica was walking toward him, and Jack's mouth tipped into a smile when he spotted her. Normally wearing scrubs all day, Jessica had dressed up tonight, looking very attractive in a black dress with a coat slung over her arm. Obviously, the two were going to dinner somewhere, and when Jessica reached Jack she said something that made him laugh.

Could there be something going on between them, now that she and Jack had agreed to keep their professional distance?

The thought twisted her stomach in a strange little knot, which was ridiculous. Must be just a residual re-action to the shock of her ex cheating on her.

Still, the thought of walking past Jack and Jessica to leave the hotel made her feel uncomfortable, though that wasn't very mature. Hoping they'd move on to wherever they were going, she saw Jack pull his phone from his pocket. In just seconds his expression went from relaxed to a deep frown, and the sudden tension in his posture was clear even from all the way across the room.

Jack shoved his phone back into his pocket, spoke briefly to Jessica, and pushed open the doors to head out into the night. Was there a problem with a patient? Without thinking, Avery hurried to talk to Jessica, to see if there was anything she could help with.

"Jessica?"

The woman turned, and when she saw Avery the concern on her face morphed into a neutral expres-sion. "Yes?"

"I couldn't help but notice that Jack ran out of here quickly. Is something wrong?"

Jessica seemed to study her before she answered. "One of the patients we performed surgery on today is experiencing slurred speech and weakness in one arm."

Obviously, a possible stroke. "Which patient?"

"Henri Arnoult."

"All right. Thanks." Avery took a step toward the doors to head over there, but Jessica's hand on her arm stopped her.

"There's nothing you can do, Dr. Girard. He'll either make it or he won't, and you know as well as I do that stroke is one of the major risks of any kind of surgery involving stents."

"I do know. But it's my job to record every bit of data on every patient, whether it's a normal complication or not, and whether it's a good outcome or a bad one."

"Jack told me you have some concerns about this TAVI device. I hope your personal bias wouldn't interfere with—or influence—that data."

"I don't have any personal bias. Concerns, yes. Bias, no." Jessica regarded her with clear skepticism, and Avery sighed. "Listen. I appreciate that you support Jack, and I assure you that any and all data I record and analyze will be done carefully and scientifically. I'd love for this trial to be a success as much as you do."

"Good. Jack is the best surgeon I've ever worked with, and this groundbreaking work is extremely important to him. Important to heart patients, too."

"I know."

"Okay," Jessica said, nodding. "Please ask Jack to let me know how things go. Even if it's in the middle of the night."

"I will." As soon as Avery pushed open the door, cold wind whipped down her neck and up her dress. She closed her coat as tightly as she could and hurried the two blocks to the hospital.

She found Jack in the patient's room in the ICU, talking to the house doctor who had likely been the one to call him in. Avery hung back, not wanting to intrude inappropriately. It seemed like forever before the house doctor finally left the room. Avery inhaled a fortifying breath before she entered. Jack stood there, his back to the door, his hands in his pockets, looking down at the patient lying in the bed. She moved to stand beside him, her heart sinking when she saw that Mr. Arnoult was unconscious and connected to a breathing machine.

Without thinking, she tucked her hand through the crook of Jack's arm and his elbow, pressing it close against his side. "These are the tough days, I know, Jack," she said softly. "Do you know what's wrong?"

"He seemed fine when I saw him this afternoon. But I'm told his blood pressure soared and his speech became slurred, so they quickly got a CAT scan. Which confirmed he's had a large hemorrhagic stroke."

"It's not impossible that his condition could improve."

"No. Not impossible. We've given him meds to try to control the brain swelling, among other things, but I don't know. It's a big bleed."

"Have you...checked to see how the TAVI looks? Is it still in place?"

"Not yet. I just ordered an echocardiogram. I hope to God it hasn't moved, because there's no way he could survive open-heart surgery on top of this. Hell, he wouldn't have survived that kind of surgery before this." A deep sigh lifted his chest. "I suppose this is more confirmation to you that the trial might be premature."

He turned to look at her as he spoke, his eyes somber with concern. Her heart filled with the certain knowledge that it was for this ill man and not concern for himself or for the future of the trial.

"Will it shock you when I say no?" She pulled her hand from his arm to rest it against his cheek. "Risk of stroke is an unfortunate complication of any procedure like this. Give an elderly patient with serious underlying health problems the blood thinners necessary for this kind of surgery, and sometimes it doesn't go the way everyone hopes it will. It's no one's fault. It's not your fault or the device's fault. It just is."

He stared down at her for a suspended moment before, to her surprise, he gathered her in his arms. Another deep sigh feathered across her forehead as he rested his head on top of hers. She pushed aside his necktie before pressing her cheek against his chest, and she wrapped her arms around him, too, since he clearly needed that connection right now. He smelled wonderful, just as he had on their first day together, holding her close beneath that umbrella, and she found herself closing her eyes at the pleasure of it as she breathed him in.

"I'd hoped we wouldn't have any catastrophic events," he said as his hand stroked slowly up and down her back. "But you're right. It is a reality that this happens sometimes. And I appreciate you not making it even worse by stomping up and down and yelling about it."

"Wow. Sounds like you think I'm a troll or something."

"A troll?" She could hear the smile in his voice. "That, I've gotta say, never occurred to me."

It took great force of will for Avery to lean back and break the close contact between them. She glanced at Mr. Arnoult and the steadily beeping monitors and figured they should continue their conversation elsewhere.

"I could use some coffee. You?"

At his nod, she took his hand and they walked to the nearly empty coffee shop on the first floor. Sitting at a round table so tiny their knees kept bumping,

Avery sipped her espresso before asking the question she needed to know the answer to. "Jessica seemed to think I might skew the data based on what she called my bias about the device. Do you, too?"

"Honestly?" He quirked a dark eyebrow. "I'd be lying if I said it hadn't crossed my mind."

Her chest ached a little at his words. Obviously, there'd be no friendship between them if that was how he felt. And she realized, without a doubt, that she very much wanted that friendship. More than friendship, but under the circumstances friendship was all they could have.

And even friendship was probably a bad idea, considering Jack didn't know all that Crilex had hired her to do.

"I find, though, that for some damned reason," he continued as he leaned closer, his mouth only inches from hers, "the uncertainty seems to turn me on."

A startled laugh left her lips. "And my wondering if you're different or the same as most other cardiologists apparently has kept me interested, as well."

He leaned closer still, so close his nose nearly touched hers. "Or maybe it's that we just have this undeniable chemistry that refuses to be snuffed out by little things like that."

The timbre of his voice, the expression in his dark eyes made her a little breathless. "Well, I did get straight As in chemistry. It's something I'm good at."

"Now, that I already knew." He closed the tiny gap between them and gave her the softest of kisses. "I'm going to go check on Mr. Arnoult again and see if the echocardiogram's been done. You might as well go on back to the hotel, or wherever you were going to go to-night, and collect his data tomorrow. Unless your plan was to go out with Dr. Frenchman. He's a total player, and even more egotistical than I am."

"You mean the man I danced with?" Was it wrong of her to be pleased at the tinge of jealousy in his voice, to know that he'd noticed and had obviously been both-ered by it? Was it also wrong of her that she'd secretly hoped he would, even though she'd been disgusted with herself when the thought had occurred to her? "I didn't realize you knew him."

"I don't. I just know his kind."

"Uh-huh. Aren't you the man who told me I shouldn't judge you negatively just because of what you do for a living?"

"That's totally different. Trust me, I know how guys think and saw the way he was looking at you."

"What way?"

"Like I do." She'd never known something like a hot twinkle existed, but there it was in his eyes as he stood. "I'm going to spend the night here so I can keep tabs on Mr. Arnoult."

A sudden desire to stay right here with him, support-ing him, came over her, but she knew it didn't make a lot of sense. She wasn't Mr. Arnoult's family, she wasn't a medical doctor, and she and Jack needed to keep a pro-fessional distance. Though, at that moment, as her gaze stayed connected with his, she knew with certainty that was getting more difficult every day.

Concern for Mr. Arnoult and thoughts of Jack stay-ing up much of the night, working, left Avery unable to sleep well, either. Up early and in the hospital just after 7:00 a.m., she stopped in the hospital coffee shop to get double shots of espresso for both her and Jack, knowing she'd find him there somewhere.

She checked Mr. Arnoult's room first, relieved to see Jack was there, able to drink his coffee while it was still somewhat hot. Her heart squeezed the second she saw him standing next to the patient's bed, his dark head tipped toward the nurse and another doctor as he spoke to them.

Mr. Arnoult was still connected to the ventilator, and from her distance by the door it appeared he was still unconscious or heavily sedated. The squeeze in her chest tightened when she saw his head was thickly bandaged, which most likely meant they'd decided to try draining the hemorrhaging blood from around his brain.

Jack glanced up as she entered the room, and his gaze held hers for a moment before he finished his conversation and walked to meet her in the doorway.

"I could smell that coffee all the way across the room," he said. His hair was uncharacteristically messy, dark stubble covered his cheeks, and the lines at the corners of his eyes were more pronounced. "Nothing better than a woman who understands a caffeine addiction."

"I nearly got you a triple, but thought maybe I could get you to go to the coffee shop I took you to that first day. It would be good for you to get out of the hospital for a breath of air."

He shook his head. "Not yet. Maybe later."

"How is he?"

He grasped her elbow and led her down the hall to

the little office he'd been working from, pulling the single chair from behind the desk for her to sit on.

"No, you sit," she said, perching on the side of the desk. "You're the one who's been up most of the night."

"If I sit, I might fall asleep." He set down his coffee, giving her a shadow of a smile as he took hold of both her shoulders and gently lowered her into the chair. "A woman who brings coffee deserves not only the chair but being draped in gold, like you said women should be."

"Well, coffee is worth its weight in gold." She sipped her espresso and resisted the urge to ask again about Mr. Arnoult. Forced herself to be patient and wait for him to speak when he was ready.

With his body propped against the side of the desk and long legs stretched out, he drank his coffee and stared out the door. Just when she thought she couldn't keep silent another second, he put his cup down and turned to her. "Things aren't good. We couldn't control his brain swelling, so the neurosurgeon drained the blood from his brain about two this morning. I had hoped that releasing the pressure would work, but the swelling continued. Tests show there's now severe, irreversible brain damage—his pupils are fixed and dilated. No movement of his extremities, no gag reflex. Just received CAT scan images that confirm it. Which I'm going to have to share with the family when they get here."

"I'm so sorry, Jack." She stood and moved in front of him to hold both his hands in hers. "I know this is never the outcome anyone wants. But as I said yesterday, we both know this risk exists in a patient like him.

He was extremely ill before the procedure. You'd hoped to give him a new lease on life, which he had no chance of having without replacing his valve, and he wouldn't have made it through open-heart surgery for that. You tried your best."

He released her hands, his tired eyes meeting hers. "Thanks for all that. I do appreciate it. I know it, but it still feels crappy."

Without thinking, she slipped her hands around his neck and kissed him. Just like she had in front of the Sacré Coeur. This time, it was to comfort him, soothe him. But the moment her lips touched his, the moment his arms wrapped around her and held her close, the moment his warm, soft mouth moved against hers she nearly forgot the goal was comfort and not something entirely different.

But they were in an office attached to a busy corridor, which both of them seemed to remember at the same time. Their lips separated, and she rested her head on his shoulder as she hugged him, working on the comfort part again, stuffing down the other feelings that wanted to erupt.

It felt good to hold him. Felt good to try to offer him comfort. But as the moment grew longer, warmer, she reminded herself that she was there for another reason, too. She should ask him about the prosthetic valve and if he'd checked it or not, but she didn't want to break the closeness they were sharing. Not quite yet, anyway. The valve wasn't the reason the man had had the original stroke, and she'd find out soon enough if it had moved or leaked after the brain had begun to bleed.

Apparently, though, this connection between her and

Jack seemed to include mind reading. "I already know you well enough to guess you're dying to know about the valve," he said, loosening his hold on her to lean back. "We've done two separate Doppler echocardiograms, neither of which showed any fluid flow around it. It's fitting tight as a drum, which makes me all the sadder that he stroked before he could enjoy his life a little more."

She nodded. "That's encouraging for other patients but, yes, it's very sad for Mr. Arnoult. Would you like for me to join you when you talk to the family?"

"No. This is a part of what I do. The hardest part, but the buck has to stop with me."

She nodded again, and instantly pictured the caring and sympathy that Jack would show the man's family when he shared the bad news, because it was obvious that was simply a part of who he was.

"Then I'll leave you. How about letting me give you a little TLC later? I'm good at that." As soon as the words came out of her mouth and a touch of humor lit his eyes, she knew how he'd interpreted it. And found her heart fluttering, even though that wasn't how she'd meant it.

"I bet you are. And despite us agreeing we shouldn't mix business with pleasure, I can't seem to keep all that in the forefront of my mind when you're around." He tipped up her chin. "Something else seems to take over instead. Like serious anticipation of some TLC from you."

He gave her a glimmer of a smile, his dark eyes connecting with hers for a long, arrested moment. Then he kissed her in the sweetest of touches. The rasp of his beard gently abraded her skin, and he tasted of coffee and of deliciousness, and she could have kept on kissing him for a long, long time. But his lips left hers to track, feather-light, up her cheek and linger on her forehead before he drew back. "Thanks for being here. I'll find you later, okay? Maybe dinner?"

She'd barely had time to respond before he left the room, his posture proud and erect despite the exhaustion he had to be feeling. And at that moment she knew with certainty that Jack was nothing like her old boyfriends. He had an integrity and warmth and depth they couldn't even begin to match.

Avery concentrated on seeing all the patients who were still in the hospital after their procedures, carefully recording their vitals, test results, state of mind and comfort levels. But throughout those hours she often found herself thinking of Jack having to continue on and do his job. How he'd still operated on the patient scheduled for early that morning, his focus never wavering throughout the procedure as she'd watched, despite the obvious fatigue in his eyes.

She'd bumped into him once, rounding on patients, spending a long time talking with each of them, recording his own notes. She wondered if he'd spoken with Mr. Arnoult's family yet, and her chest tightened at how tough that was going to be on all of them.

As she moved down the hall to see a different patient, she heard the rumble of his voice in Mr. Arnoult's room and the sound of quiet weeping. Her stomach clenched, and when she glanced in she saw two middle-aged men standing, flanking an elderly woman who sat in a chair, dabbing her face with a crumpled tissue. Jack was crouched in front of her, one hand patting her shoulder, the other giving her another tissue he'd pulled from the box on a chair next to her.

Avery found herself pressing her hands to her tight chest at the sweet and gentle way Jack was talking with the woman, the deeply caring expression on his face. A part of her wanted to go into the room and stand next to him for support, but she knew he wouldn't want or need that. It wasn't her place to spy or eavesdrop, either, and she quickly moved on to the last patient she needed to see.

At that moment, she knew she wanted to somehow help him feel better about it all. While she knew this was far from the first time in his career he'd had to deliver bad news to a family, and certainly wouldn't be the last, giving him a reason to smile suddenly became her priority for the day.

How, though? They'd already been up the Eiffel Tower and seen the Sacré Coeur at sunset. Her mind spun through her favorite places in Paris, but many of them were more fun to go to in the summertime, when you were lucky enough to enjoy some sunshine and the gardens were glorious. Still, there was something to be said for just walking the city on a cold night, cuddling to stay warm on a bench in one of the gardens or by the Seine.

Cuddling? Her plan for the evening was about cheering Jack up, not kissing him or having sex or anything like that.

Except she'd be lying to herself if she pretended that she hadn't thought about throwing aside the very good reasons they shouldn't be together for one more memorable night. A night to help him forget a very long and difficult day. Knowing it would be more than memorable for her, too, would be the icing on the cake.

CHAPTER EIGHT

AVERY'S HEART, WHICH only moments ago had felt all bubbly at the thought of spending the evening with Jack and finding ways to make him happy, stuttered, then ground to a halt.

Standing stock still now just outside the doorway to Jack's office, she stared at what seemed like a reenactment of her warm and intimate time in that room with him earlier. A woman had her arms wrapped around his waist, and he held her close with his cheek resting on her head.

But unless Avery was watching some holographic image of that moment in time, Jack was not holding her. He was holding a different woman.

Jessica.

Barely able to breathe, Avery backed up a few steps, then turned to hightail it out of there.

She'd become completely, utterly convinced he wasn't at all like the last two doctors she'd been involved with, which proved how incredibly bad she must be at judging character. Clearly, every one of them charmed, lied and cheated as easily as they breathed, and she thrashed herself for forgetting. For thinking Jack was different.

She stalked down the hall, her throat tight with embarrassment as she thought of the really good fantasies she'd been dreaming up about their night together. Gullible idiot. Fool. IQ genius with no brains.

"Avery." Jack's voice and footsteps followed her, and she walked faster. "Avery, stop, damn it!"

His fingers curled around her arm, turning her toward him. She yanked her arm from his hold. "What is it, Dr. Dunbar? It's been a long day, and I have a date." A date with herself and her computer and her work, which she'd just remembered she'd promised herself would be her only focus until she'd let a certain man change her mind about that.

"Your date is with me. And if you're running off in a huff because I was hugging Jessica, you know damned well that she's married."

"Like that matters to some people."

"It matters to me. And to her. We've worked together for three years. She's my coworker and my friend. And as my friend, she felt bad about Henri Arnoult. Just like you did. That's all." He grasped both her arms this time, tugging her closer. "It's been a hell of a bad day. Mr. Arnoult's family had to make the hard decision to take him off the ventilator. We had to let him go. And, yeah, that's one damned difficult part of being a doctor, and I'm tired inside and out. The last thing I want is for you to be upset and thinking things that are all wrong."

She stared into his dark eyes, which were filled with frustration and exhaustion and worry. Could she have been wrong? Jumped to conclusions too fast? And hadn't she wanted to comfort him, not add to his stress, if she was wrong?

She definitely didn't want to make his day any worse

than it already had been. But her heart didn't feel up to being exposed to more punishment, either. "Listen. I think it's a good idea for you and Jessica to be together tonight. She knows you better than I do, and you'll have a nice time, I'm sure."

"Except that, even though I shouldn't, I want to know you better." He glanced down the hall, which was fairly quiet this late in the day, before turning back again, lifting his hands to cup her cheeks. "After the great time we've spent together, how could you even think I might have something going on with Jess?"

She stared up into his eyes and could see he really wanted to know. But she didn't feel like sharing her past. Her embarrassment that she hadn't seen her exes for who they were.

"I didn't. Not really. I was just being weird."

His eyes crinkled at the corners in a smile. "The only way you're remotely weird is the odd color combinations you sometimes favor." His thumb stroked along her cheekbone before he bent his head and kissed her. Maybe it was stupid, but the soft warmth of his lips managed to sap every ounce of the worry and self-deprecation she'd felt just moments ago. The feel of his mouth slowly moving on hers sent all of that to the outer reaches of her brain and her thoughts back to the fantasies she'd been having before she'd seen him with Jessica and freaked.

He broke the kiss, and the eyes that met hers were so sincere she knew she couldn't let what had happened with her stupid exes mess with her mind anymore. No way did she want to live her life suspicious of people and their possible agendas, backing away from potential pain instead of exploring all the wonderful things the world had to offer.

That Jack just might have to offer, if their potentially disastrous professional relationship didn't ruin everything before they had a chance to spend more time together.

"It would sure be nice to kiss you without knowing there are hundreds of people who might be spying on us at any moment. Which is pretty much the only times we've kissed so far. Let's get out of here."

She wanted that, too, but felt she had to ask about Jessica's plans. After all, the woman probably had nothing to do, and maybe she shouldn't hog Jack all to herself. Even though that was all she wanted, darn it. "Shouldn't we ask Jessica to join us for dinner?"

"One of the reasons she was happy to come and assist me in the trial here is because she has a cousin with three little kids living in Paris. She's enjoying spending time with them. And even if she wasn't," he added, his eyes gleaming, "I wouldn't ask her along. Three's a crowd, and you're the one who said you're good at TLC and offered to comfort me, right?"

"I did make that offer, though you probably don't need it. You're pretty tough, I know."

"Tough or not, a guy always appreciates some TLC from a beautiful woman. Looking forward to being with you tonight is the only thing that made today bearable." He placed his mouth close to her ear, and his words, the rumble in his voice, made her shiver. "I know you don't back out on your promises. And I can't wait to be on the receiving end of some tender, loving care from the talented Dr. Girard."

* * *

Chilly wind nipped what little skin they had exposed, and Jack watched Avery tug her blue and purple scarf more tightly around her neck. Figured it was the perfect excuse to hold her even closer to his side as they walked through the Palais-Royal gardens. Though gardens would be an overstatement at the moment, since everything was dormant from winter, and the only things remotely green were the carefully trimmed evergreen shrubs.

"I love this park in the summertime, when all the roses are in bloom and you can sit and enjoy the quiet and seclusion from the busyness of the city," Avery said, smiling at him, her cute nose very pink from the cold. "And the trees are trimmed in an arching canopy that's fun to walk beneath on the way to the fountain. I'm sorry it's not all that pretty right now."

"You're sorry because you could do something about it being the end of January? Are you a magician as well as a scientist?"

"Wouldn't that be nice?" She laughed. "Sadly, no. I just wish I could show you the Paris I love all year round, but we'll have to settle for now."

Her words struck him with a surprising thought, which was that he wished for that, too. For more than just these brief weeks with her. But that wasn't meant to be. He had his work and his TAVI trials, which would take him to various parts of the world, and finally, assuming all went well, to trials back in the States. He didn't have time in his life for any kind of real relationship and felt a pang of regret about that reality.

"I'm enjoying the now with you," he said. "What's the next part of now, Ms. Tour Guide?"

"Let's pop into a few of these boutiques. Anything in particular you like to look at? Or want to buy?"

"Yes. The one thing I particularly like to look at is you." Which had been true from the moment he'd met her. He tugged her close enough that her steamy breath mingled in the cold air with his own. "And I'd like to buy a thin gold chain to slip around your neck, except you'd accuse me of being an egotistical player again. When the only reason would be to please you. Okay, and touch your skin, too. I'm definitely looking for ways to make that happen."

She blushed cutely, and he loved the humor that shone in her green eyes. "You don't have to buy me gifts to make that happen."

Maybe she saw exactly where his thoughts had immediately gone, because she stepped out of his hold to walk through the doorway of a little shop.

"In truth, I'm into this kind of thing more than gold," she said as she picked up a delicate, inlaid wooden box.

"Music boxes? Any special kind?"

"I love old ones. But any kind makes me smile. Like lots of little girls, I had one with a dancing ballerina and fell in love with them after that." She opened the lid and a tune began to play. An adorable smile lit her face and eyes, making him smile, too. "Isn't it beautiful?"

"Beautiful." He damned near took it from her hand to buy it for her, but was sure she'd protest. It would probably make her feel uncomfortable to receive a gift from him at that point in their relationship—or whatever you'd call the powerful force that kept drawing him to her.

They stared at one another, and the hum in the air between them was so strong it nearly drowned out the soft tune tinkling between them. She put the box down and, to his surprise, grabbed his hand and trotted quickly out of the store, the sexy blue ankle boots she wore clicking on the pavement.

"Where to now?" he asked.

"I just thought of something that would be fun to do with you."

He hoped that "something" was her hauling him off to the hotel to get naked for the TLC she'd promised, but had a feeling that was wishful thinking. "And that would be?"

"This." They ran until they got to a carousel, the music filling the air around it not all that different from the music box, except a lot louder. She jumped onto its platform, turning to him with the bright eyes and brilliant smile he'd come to see in his dreams. "Come on! Which horse do you want?"

"Whichever you're on."

She laughed and walked between the rows of wooden animals, finally straddling a white horse with a bright green saddle and carved mane that looked to be flying in the wind. Jack swung himself up behind her. As her rear pressed against his groin, as he wrapped one arm around her waist and one hand on top of hers on the pole, as he breathed in the scent of her hair and her skin, he knew he'd never see another carousel without remembering this moment with her.

"I never knew I loved merry-go-rounds until this moment," he murmured in her ear.

"Doesn't everybody?"

"Everybody lucky enough to have a gorgeous woman sharing their horse."

The music grew louder, and as the carousel began to turn, their horse rose and fell, pushing his body into hers, rubbing them together. And damned if even through their clothes and jackets it wasn't just about the most erotic thing he'd ever experienced outside a bedroom.

He tried to scoot back, away from her a little, so she wouldn't feel exactly how aroused he was, but had a feeling she already knew. He dipped his head and let his lips wander over what skin he could reach, which wasn't nearly enough. Her cheek and jaw, her nose, her eyebrow. Her soft hair tickled his face as he nibbled her earlobe, tracing the shell of her ear with his tongue until her sexy gasp, the shiver of her skin he could feel against his lips, took every molecule of air from his lungs and sent him on a quest for her mouth.

The arm he had wrapped around her tightened as he lifted his hand from the pole to grasp her chin in his fingers, turning her face so he could taste her lips. Her eyes met his, a dark moss green now, full of the same desire he knew she could see in his.

Her head tipped back against his collarbone, and he covered her mouth with his and kissed her. Kissed her until he wasn't sure if the spinning sensation he felt was from the earth turning, the carousel revolving, the horse rising and falling or his brain reeling from Avery overload.

The sound of people laughing and talking seeped into his lust-fogged brain, and apparently Avery's, too, as they both slowly broke the kiss, staring at one another, the panting breaths between them now so steamy he could barely see her moist, still-parted lips. He brushed his thumb against her lush lower lip, and it was all he could do not to kiss her again.

"Didn't I say I'd like to kiss you, just once, without people standing around, watching?" he said when he was able to talk. "I don't think this accomplishes that."

She gave him a breathy laugh. "No. So let's accomplish it now."

As the carousel slowed to a stop, he slid from the horse, then helped her down. "Any ideas on how?"

"Oh, yeah." Her lips curved, and the only word to describe her expression would be *sensual*, which kicked his pulse into an even faster rhythm than it was already galloping in. "They don't call me the 'idea gal' for nothing."

CHAPTER NINE

JUST LIKE THE first time—the one she'd been sure would be the only time—Jack had her coat and blouse off before she'd barely drawn a breath. Time to get with the program and get his coat off, too. Her fingers weren't quite as swift as his talented surgeon ones, and she wrestled to get it unbuttoned.

He shrugged it off and tossed it on top of hers before reaching to touch his thumb to the top of her bra as he had before, slowly tracing the curve of it, and her breath backed up in her lungs at the expression in his eyes, at the low, rough sound of his voice. "Bright blue lace this time. Hard to decide if I like this or your pretty white one better."

"I have matching panties on. Does that help?"

His eyes gleamed in response. "Don't care if they match. I can't wait to see you in them." He lowered his mouth to hers, softly, sweetly, before moving it across her jaw, down to her collar bone, slipping farther until his tongue traced the lacy top of her bra. Sliding down to gently suck her nipple through the silky fabric until her knees wobbled. Avery clutched the front of his shirt, hanging on tight, wondering if she just might faint from lack of oxygen and the excruciating pleasure of it all.

She wanted to see his skin, too. Wanted to touch him and lick him, as well. "No fair that you're ahead of me," she managed to say, reaching for the buttons of his shirt. "No more distractions until I get your shirt off."

He lifted his head, ending his damp exploration of her bra, and his dark eyes gleamed into hers as she attempted to wrangle his buttons. "Happy to assist, if you'd like."

Oh, yes. She'd like. Mesmerized, she stared as he flicked open one button at a time, slowly exposing the fine, dark hair on his smooth skin, before finally pulling the shirt off entirely. About to reach for him, she lifted her gaze to his. Saw that his focus was on her breasts, and the hunger in his eyes sent her heart pounding even harder.

"You have one beautiful body, Dr. Girard."

"Funny, I was just thinking the same about you, Dr. Dunbar."

With a smile, he closed the gap between them, reached behind her, and in one quick motion had her bra unhooked, off her arms and onto the floor. His hand cupped her breast and his thumb moved slowly back and forth across her nipple until her knees nearly buckled.

"As I said before, those are some quick fingers you have, Dr. Dunbar. Should have known you were a surgeon or guitarist or something." She pressed her palms to his hard chest, sliding them through the dark, soft hair covering it. On up to wrap her arms behind his neck, holding him close, loving the feel of his body against hers as she moved backward, bringing him with her.

"You haven't seen anything yet," he said in a gruff voice so full of promise she found herself mindlessly touching her tongue to his jaw to taste him as she pressed her body to his. His mouth moved to capture hers as they continued their slow meander to the bed. She didn't even realize he'd unbuttoned her pants, too, until she felt his hands moving on her bottom, inside her silky underwear and on down her thighs until every scrap of clothing was pooled at her feet.

She gasped in surprise, which sent the kiss deeper. Until the backs of her legs hit the bed, and the impact jolted her mouth from his. He stared at her a moment before he slowly kneeled, pulling her undies and pants off her ankles as he nipped and licked her knees, making her jerk and laugh.

"Stop that," she said. "My knees are ticklish."

He grasped her calves as his tongue slipped across the inside of one knee, then the other, interspersed with tiny nibbles. "How ticklish?"

"Very." She gasped and wriggled, the sensation of his teeth and tongue on her bones and skin both sensitive and exciting. "And if you don't stop, it's not my fault if my reflexes send one up to crack you in the jaw."

"Risk noted." His hands slipped up to widen her legs as his tongue moved on in a shivery path to her inner thighs. "But I think we already agreed that life is full of risk. If it's potentially dangerous to taste you all over, then, believe me, that's a risk I'm more than happy to take."

Her breath coming in embarrassing little pants now

as he moved northward, she knew it was time to change direction. While part of her wanted, more than anything, for his mouth to keep going to the part of her currently quivering in anticipation, it seemed that mutual pleasure was more in order.

"Come up here and kiss me." She placed her hands on his smooth shoulders, trying to tug him back up.

"I am kissing you." And, boy, he sure was. His lips were pressing inch by torturous inch against her shivering flesh.

"My mouth. Kiss my mouth." She tugged harder at his shoulders. If she didn't get him away from where he was headed, she knew she just might combust. "I'm the one who's supposed to be administering TLC here, remember?"

He lifted his gaze to hers. His eyes were heavy-lidded with desire, but touched with amusement, too, and the smile he gave her was full of pure, masculine satisfaction. "For some reason, I forgot. Probably because I'm already feeling much less stressed. But if it will make you happy, who am I to argue?"

With one last kiss so high on her inner thigh she nearly groaned, he got to his feet. Which reminded her he still had his pants on, while she was sitting there utterly naked. His gaze traveled across every inch of her skin, hot enough to scorch, and she was a little surprised that his perusal was exciting instead of embarrassing.

She reached for his pants and undid them, happy that he took charge and quickly finished off the job. Then stared at the now very visible confirmation that he was every bit as aroused as she was.

"So now what, Dr. Girard?" He placed his hands on

the bed, flanking her hips, and leaned close. "The TLC ball is in your court."

She gulped. All the things she'd fantasized about seemed to have vacated her mind, along with every rational thought. Except how much she wanted to grab him and pull him on top of her and feel him deep inside.

"I…I can't remember exactly what I had in mind to soothe you and make you feel better. Give me a minute."

"That's okay," he said between pressing soft kisses to her mouth. "As I said, I already feel a whole lot better. Expecting to feel even better real soon."

His strong hands wrapped around her waist and he lifted her up to him, nudging her legs around his waist as he kissed her again. She was vaguely aware of the sound of the covers being yanked back and the cool sheets touching her skin at the same time Jack's hot body covered hers.

"I've realized the one thing that will soothe me the most," he whispered against her lips.

"What?"

"Making you feel good." He kissed her again. His body was deliciously heavy on hers as his hands stroked her everywhere, exciting and tantalizing. Their kiss grew deeper, wilder as his talented fingers finally delved into her moist core until she feared he might bring her to climax with just his touch.

Then the sudden, harsh ring of her hotel phone startled them both, sending their teeth clacking together. "Holy hell!" Jack frowned. "Are you okay?"

With her breath still short, she slid her fingers across his moist lips. "No blood, I don't think. You?"

"Fine. More than fine." His eyes gleamed into hers.

"Except for the damned interruption just when things were getting very…soothing."

She chuckled breathily as they both turned their heads to the still-ringing phone.

"Do you need to get that?" he asked.

Was he kidding? Even if it was the French president, she wasn't about to talk on the phone at that moment. "Whoever it is will leave a message. Or call back. Now, where were we?" She reached for him, squeezed, and the moan he gave in response sent her heart pumping faster and her legs around his waist in silent invitation.

He quickly ripped open a condom. "About to get to the next step in making us both feel good," he said, grasping her hips as they joined. Slowly, wonderfully, but as the tension grew she had to urge him to move faster, deeper. The room seemed to spin dizzily like the carousel had, but this time there were no barriers between them. She held on tight, loving the taste of him and the feel of him, until she cried out in release, wrenching a deep groan from his chest as he followed.

Jack buried his face in her neck, their gasping breaths seeming loud in the quiet of the room. Until another sound disturbed her bone-melting, utter relaxation and tranquility—the muffled ringing of a cell phone.

Jack lifted his head and looked down at the floor with a frown. "Who the hell keeps bothering us? I hope nothing's happened at the hospital."

He dropped a kiss on her mouth, lingering there, before he got up and dug his phone from the pocket of his discarded pants. Avery enjoyed the very sexy view of him, standing there comfortably naked, his skin covered with a sheen of sweat.

"Dr. Dunbar."

She watched his frown deepen and sat up, beginning to get alarmed. Hopefully this wasn't a crisis with a patient.

"And you can't give me some idea what this is about now?" he asked. "Fine. I'll be there."

"What is it?"

"I don't know." His warm body lay next to hers again, propped on his elbow. "Bob Timkin wants to meet with me—with both of us—tomorrow morning at eight. Says he has to talk to me right away about something to do with the trial."

"What? Why?"

"He wouldn't say. You don't happen to know, do you?"

The pleasure of the evening began to fade at the expression on his face. Beyond serious. Maybe even a touch suspicious? She couldn't even imagine how he'd react if he knew Crilex had given her the power to shut down the trial if she deemed it necessary, and the thought chilled her formerly very toasty body. "No. I don't. If I did, I'd tell you."

"Did you tell him you were concerned about the number of patients who've had the valve leak? You know I feel strongly that we haven't treated nearly enough patients to make any kind of judgment on that yet."

"Of course I didn't speak with him about Mr. Arnoult. For one thing, I haven't had a chance to finish compiling the data on his...situation. And I also told you I know the valve design was not why he died."

A long sigh left him before his mouth touched hers with a sweet, tender connection at odds with the tense tone of his voice. His finger tracked down her cheek before he slipped from the bed and got dressed, his expression impassive when he turned to her.

"I wish mixing…this…with work didn't create a hell of a complication for both of us. But there's no getting around it that it does." He stepped to the bed and took her chin in his hand, tilting her face up for another soft kiss. "Thank you for the TLC tonight. Sweet dreams."

And then he was gone, the door closing behind him with a sharp click. A whirl of emotions filled her chest, and she didn't know which one took center stage in her heart. Frustration that he still clearly didn't completely trust her to report the data scientifically and not emotionally? Disappointment, even sadness, that this obvious "thing" they had between them was a huge problem because of their jobs? Anxiety, knowing he would definitely not like having been kept in the dark about her authority to decide if the trial was rolled out further or not?

She flopped back onto the bed, her body still feeling the remnants of their lovemaking, and remembered how wonderful every second of it had felt.

Now, instead of stealing a kiss or two with him tomorrow, she knew the smart thing to do was go back to a strictly professional friendship. And she also had to wonder what in the world Bob Timkin had planned.

CHAPTER TEN

JACK SWALLOWED THE last of his morning coffee, wishing it didn't make him think of Avery and how her mouth always tasted after they'd shared espresso. Made him think of that first morning they'd spent together, that entire, magical day, and how beautiful and adorable she'd been. Realizing, from that moment on, he'd been fascinated by her in every way. Her looks, her brains, her personality.

He couldn't shake that fascination and attraction. An attraction that had grown even deeper after their time together last night, making love again to her beautiful body. Except his heart rate had barely slowed when the phone call had come, bringing a lot of questions with it. A harsh reminder of what he kept forgetting whenever he was with her. Which was that mixing business with pleasure was always one hell of a bad idea, no matter how incredible that pleasure was.

He thought he'd learned that painful lesson all too well. A lesson that had come in the form of doubt cast on his professional character and integrity, resulting in some very personal questions from a hospital ethics board. A lesson in why he should never get involved with a woman connected in any way with his work. Except he knew Avery was nothing like Vanessa. She wasn't the kind of woman who would advance her own career at the expense of someone else's.

He took the elevator to the hospital's administrative offices on the top floor, where Bob had a nice, cushy office that someone had clearly given up for him. About to knock on the doorjamb, he was surprised to hear Avery's voice speaking through the partially open door, then the rumble of Bob's voice in answer.

He knocked on the door and didn't wait to be asked in before pushing it all the way open to step inside. Timkin looked up, then stood, a broad smile on his face. "Jack. Thanks for coming. Have a seat."

"I'm good standing, thanks."

"Dr. Girard was just updating me on the patient data from the trial so far."

"Seems impossible to have any kind of real report, considering we've operated on all of twelve patients so far."

"Well, yes. But all of them came through it nicely, I see."

"Actually, that's not entirely true," Avery said. "Several of the patients have had significant paravalvular regurgitation, as Dr. Dunbar and I have discussed."

"And in that discussion I noted that a certain percentage of patients are expected to have that complication and can live fine with it." His chest began to burn a little. Was she about to tell Timkin she thought there might be a flaw in the design? He was confident that Bob was completely behind this trial and the next phase of the rollout to other hospitals.

"We do know that is a normal, and expected, complication, Dr. Girard," Timkin said. "While I'm aware the numbers of patients experiencing that are currently slightly higher than we would have wished, the procedure hasn't been done on nearly enough patients for those numbers to be meaningful."

Jack relaxed a little, and he waited to hear why Timkin had called the meeting. Avery's brows were lowered in a frown, and he could practically see the wheels spinning in that brain of hers, probably coming up with various data she wanted to spout.

"Which is why I asked you both to come here this morning," Timkin said. "We've decided to significantly increase the number of patients in this clinical trial, which I'm sure will please you, Jack."

"What do you mean, you want to increase the number of patients in the trial?" Avery asked, her eyes wide.

"It seems logical to me that we get as many patients in the trial as we can for these last two and a half weeks," Timkin said. "We need as much data as possible before we decide how many hospitals to roll this out to next. I have a few of my people looking for good patient candidates and screening them as we speak, and of course I'd like your nurse to work on finding some, as well."

"Frankly, I don't think that's a good idea," Avery said. Her gaze flicked to Jack, then away, before she continued. "With the comparatively high percentage of the prosthetic valves experiencing leakage, I think the trial should be conducted on a smaller number of patients so we can keep our eye on that until we know more."

"I respect your opinion, Dr. Girard. But increasing the numbers can't be anything but good, giving us the conclusive data we all want."

Jack smiled at this great news. "I appreciate the vote of confidence, Bob. Dr. Girard is, of course, the leading expert on this device but isn't as familiar with patient care. Those in the trial experiencing the valve leakage are all doing well as we manage their situation."

As he turned to leave, his gaze paused on Avery, and he was surprised to see the look on her face was completely different from that of a moment ago. Instead of concern, her green eyes held deep disappointment. He'd even call it hurt. Was it because of what he'd said when he'd reassured Bob he had the leakages under control?

This trial was beyond important to him, the patients it was helping and the future of interventional cardiology. Avery knew that as well as anybody. Why she was so overly concerned about the valve leakage, he didn't understand and refused to worry about yet.

But as he headed to the cath lab, the image of the hurt in her eyes went along with him.

Jack headed for the hotel fitness room, needing a physical release from another long day at the hospital, his muscles tense from hours of standing on his feet doing surgeries. He had to give Crilex credit—they'd gotten additional patients lined up incredibly fast, and he and Jessica had been working flat out. Which he welcomed for the clinical trial and welcomed for himself.

The busy pace had left him with little time to think about Avery. During the brief moments he'd had free, though, she'd been on his mind. Thinking about all the great things he'd learned about her over the past weeks. Knowing she wasn't the kind of self-interested person who would skew data to benefit her career, and feeling bad that had even crossed his mind. They might not always agree, but the woman had absolute integrity.

That it seemed he'd accidentally hurt her made him feel like crap. Made him want to head to her room and apologize, then grab her to explore more of Paris and laugh together. Kiss and make love together. That desire was so strong he could only hope that running hard on the treadmill would somehow blank it all from his mind.

At 9:00 p.m. there were only two other people in the exercise room, and he was glad he wouldn't have to wait around for any of the machines or weights to become available. He slung a towel around his neck and started out jogging on the treadmill, increasing the pace until he was running, breathing hard, sweating. To his disgust, even that didn't stop his thoughts from drifting to Avery. To the softness of her skin and the taste of it on his tongue. To her laugh and the amazing green of her eyes.

Which made him one damned confused man. He adjusted the treadmill settings and picked up the pace, noticing out of the corner of his eye that the middle-aged man who had been lifting crazily heavy weights was now sitting strangely sideways on the bench, leaning on one hand.

Jack looked more carefully at him, realizing the guy didn't look like he felt very well. He slowed to a stop, quickly wiped the sweat from his face and walked over to the man, concerned at the ashen color of his face.

"You okay?"

The man shook his head and laboriously said a few words in French. Jack hoped like hell he could at least understand a little English, even if he couldn't speak it. "I'm a doctor. I'm going to check your pulse."

Thankfully, he nodded, and Jack pressed his fingers to the man's wrist to see if his heart was in a normal sinus rhythm. It was fast, very fast, and he'd begun to sweat buckets, too, neither of which were signs of anything good. Just as Jack was about to ask the man if he thought he might be having a heart attack he slumped sideways and started sliding clear off the bench.

"Whoa!" Jack was able to grab him midway, managing to keep him from cracking his head on the hard floor.

"What is wrong, monsieur?" The other person in the room had come to stand next to him, staring.

"Get the hotel to call the medical squad."

The guy ran off just as the man opened his eyes again, thank the Lord. His brows lowered as he blinked at Jack, saying something Jack wished he could understand. Pressing his fingers to the man's wrist again, he grimly noted his pulse was thready, which meant his blood pressure was high, which again meant nothing good.

"Good God, Jack, what's wrong?" To his surprise, Avery crouched next to him, deep concern on her face as she looked from the ill man to him.

"I think he's having the big one. Going in and out of V-fib, and his pulse is really tachy." He looked up at her, relieved she might be able to communicate with the man. "Ask him how he's feeling, where it hurts."

She quickly spoke to the man in French and he managed to answer her back. "He says he's nauseated and his chest feels strange."

"Damn. The chances of this not being a heart attack are slim to none." He scanned the room and didn't see what he'd hoped for. "I wish this place had a defibrillator. His arrhythmia is bad, and if he crashes, I don't think CPR's going to do it."

"They do. Over here." She ran around the other side of the L-shaped room and returned with exactly what he needed if the man went into true V-fib.

"How did you know that was there? I've been in this gym ten times and never noticed."

"It's by the plié bar, which I'm guessing you don't use."

She gave him a quick grin, and he grinned back before turning to place his fingers against the man's carotid artery. "You'd guess right. I—"

With a sudden, strangled sound the man, who'd been lying on his side, flopped onto his back, obviously unconscious again. Jack shook him, then rubbed his knuckles against the man's sternum. "Hey, buddy! Wake up. Can you hear me? Wake up!"

But the guy just lay there like he was dead, and Jack cursed. "We've got to get his shirt off so I can check his heart rate with the defib."

They wrestled the T-shirt off the man as quickly as they could, then Jack grabbed the defibrillator. Both moved fast to get the paddle wires untwined as he pressed them to the man's chest. Then stared at the EKG monitor on the paddle in disbelief.

"He's code blue. I'm going to have to bust him." He looked up at her tense face. "Can you set it at three hundred joules while I get it placed? Then get the hell out of the way."

She nodded and her fingers got it adjusted impressively fast.

"Okay. Ready? Clear!"

She jumped up and backpedaled as Jack sent the electricity to the man's heart.

Nothing.

"Clear again." His own heart pounding like he'd just jumped off the treadmill, he busted the man once more. When the man's chest heaved and his eyelids flickered, then opened, Jack exhaled a deep breath he hadn't even realized he'd been holding in his lungs.

"Thank God," he heard Avery say devoutly as she came back and kneeled next to them, reaching to hold the man's hand.

"Yeah." Jack pressed his fingers to the man's throat. "Pulse is down to ninety. And his color's even a little better. I think we did it, Dr. Girard."

Their eyes met briefly across the poor, supine guy, and a wordless communication went between them. Relief that they'd been able to help and joy that he was hopefully out of the woods.

The man weakly said something in French, and Avery smiled and answered before turning to Jack. "He asked what happened. I told him his heart stopped, and you saved his life."

"We saved his life. You were awesome."

Her smile widened before she turned back to speak to the man again, and Jack could see her squeezing his hand. Now that he could take a minute to breathe, he had to marvel at how calm she'd been through the whole thing, and how comforting him obviously came as second nature to her. Doctors and nurses were trained how to react to this kind of crisis, but he doubted there was a lot of that kind of education in biomedical PhD school.

The door to the fitness room clattered open as several emergency medical techs wheeled in a gurney. The guy who'd run from the room to get help followed, along with several people Jack recognized as hotel management. He stood and updated the med techs on what had happened and where the man's heart rate was now.

The hotel guys talked with Avery. She handed them the defibrillator, and he heard her saying what a hero Jack was. Part of him absolutely hated that, since he was no hero. He was a doctor who'd been in the right place when he'd been needed.

But another part of him couldn't be unhappy about Avery praising him that way. The hotel staff pumped his hand and thanked him, and he repeated that it was just lucky he'd been in the right place and gave them credit for having the defibrillator there for him to use. If they hadn't, he was certain the outcome would not have been good for the man.

It seemed the room went from full of people to empty in a matter of minutes, and he noticed what he'd missed before in all the excitement. Avery wearing tiny, sexy exercise shorts that showed off her toned legs and a tank top that revealed a whole lot more of her skin than he'd ever been able to see before, since she was always dressed for the cold or the hospital.

Well, except for their two blissful moments together, when he'd been privileged to see every inch of her body.

His heart went into a little atrial fibrillation of its

own at the memories and the current vision standing right in front of him.

"That was one lucky man," Avery said. "How many people have a cardiologist around when they're having a heart attack? Were you in here working out when it happened?"

"I was running on the treadmill. Trying to loosen my muscles." *Trying to forget about you.* "He was lucky all right. Lucky that you came in when you did and that you knew where the machine was. I've got to tell you, I'm pretty impressed at how calm and cool you were, helping with what needed to happen without freaking out."

"Believe me, I was freaking out on the inside." She grinned. "But that's a sweet thing for you to say. Much better than the stinging barbs you've thrown lately."

"Listen." He rubbed his hand across the back of his neck to loosen the knots there. Hoped she'd accept his apology. "I'm sorry I said you didn't know much about patient care. I'm sure you do. I just wanted Bob to know the leakages so far are minor, but I shouldn't have implied you're clueless about postoperative treatment."

"No, you shouldn't have. I may not be a medical doctor or nurse, but gathering the data teaches me plenty, believe me."

"I'm sure it does." He cupped her chin in his hand because he wanted that connection. Wanted to show her he truly cared how she felt. "Did it hurt you when I said that?"

"Honestly? To my core." Her words pricked his heart, but the sweet smile she gave him soothed the wound. "Though I just might have not very nicely accused you of certain things, as well. Like maybe you were sleeping with a married woman the same week you were kissing me."

"You know, you're right. That wasn't nice of you at all." He caught her elbows in his hands, tugging her against him. "So we're even."

"Even."

As he looked into the green of her eyes he tried hard to conjure all the reasons he had to keep a professional distance from her. But he couldn't. All he could think about was how much he enjoyed kissing her and making love with her, and how he wanted more of all of it.

"What is it about you that makes it impossible for me to keep a professional distance? Even when I try?" he asked, genuinely baffled.

"Maybe because we share a love of espresso?"

"Maybe," he said, dipping his head down to speak against her lips. "Or maybe it's just you."

"No." She shook her head, her lips slipping back and forth across his mouth as she did, and that simple touch nearly made him groan. "It's us. That mysterious and unexplainable chemistry, whether we like it or not."

"Sometimes not," he said. "But I find I can't help that, way more often, I like it very much."

Knowing he damned well shouldn't, he kissed her, loving the way she instantly melted against him, her arms sliding around his back to hold him tight. Their mouths and tongues moved in a slow dance that already felt seductively familiar. A tiny little sound came from her throat as the kiss deepened, a sound so full of desire it sent his blood pumping and nearly had him slipping his hands into those tiny shorts she was wearing, not caring at all about the consequences.

Somehow, though, he managed to summon every ounce of inner strength he had to break the kiss, dragging in a few desperate breaths to clear his head. Not only were they in a public place, which seemed to always be a problem whenever he kissed her, but nothing had really changed.

The chemistry—hell, more like a nuclear reaction—was most definitely there. But so was the inescapable conflict in their jobs. And that situation was one harsh reality.

"Right now, there's nothing I'd like more in the world than for us to head upstairs and take up where we left off a few nights ago," he said, and the truth of that statement nearly had him grabbing her hand, hightailing it to his room and acting on exactly what he wanted. "But that would just make our jobs more difficult. The work I'm doing here is damned important to me. And I know your work is important to you."

"It is. Which is why I'm going to stretch on the bar, then get running. Good night, Jack." She rose on her toes to give him a quick peck on the cheek and turned to walk to the plié bar.

The sight of her sexy rear in those shorts and the thought of how she might contort herself around that bar practically made him groan. A mini war raged in his chest, with the part of him that wanted her yesterday, today and tomorrow fighting with the cool, rational part of his brain that seemed to short-circuit every time he was around her.

He thought about pretending to continue his workout while really watching whatever she was about to do, but he managed to move to the elevator instead. Giving work one hundred percent of his focus was something he'd been good at for a long time. Time to get with that program and somehow forget the vision of Avery's shapely butt cheeks peeking from beneath those shorts.

Yeah. Like that was going to happen. Which made him wonder. How cold, exactly, could he get the shower in his room?

CHAPTER ELEVEN

JACK STARED IN frustration at the Doppler echocardiogram. The paravalvular regurgitation from the prosthetic valve was more than obvious. The valve looked like it was fitting tightly, but there was no denying the image of the fluid seeping slightly from around it. Why had the past two patients experienced this problem when it hadn't been an issue with the last ten?

"What do you think, Jack?" Jessica asked, peering over his shoulder at the echocardiogram.

"I don't know what to think. I'm trying to figure out if I somehow did something different with these two patients. Maybe I'm not being careful enough as I insert the cath to remove the diseased valve. Or when I place the new one."

Jessica shook her head. "I'm watching almost every second you're working, and if I'd noticed you doing anything different at all, I'd say so."

His mind spun back to past procedures, wondering if the increased patient load had made him hurry in any way. He didn't think so, but he would be extra careful from now on to be sure to take his time and triple-check the monitor as he was putting the prosthetic valve in place.

Jessica glanced around, then leaned close, speaking in a near whisper. "Do you think it's a design flaw, like Dr. Girard has been worried about all along?"

His chest tightened. He'd have to be as stubborn as a mule to not have wondered exactly that. "I don't know. It's possible. The percentage of patients with medically manageable leakage is more than we expected, but not dramatically more. We're just going to have to wait and see the numbers as the trial unfolds."

Jessica nodded. "This patient's pulmonary edema is improving nicely, and the liquid from her Foley is crystal-clear now. She's going to be fine, I think."

"Good. I'll check on her again this afternoon."

"Dr. Dunbar!"

He and Jessica both turned to the nurse who'd run in. "Yes?"

"Madame Belisle is having trouble breathing. I fear it may be another aortic insufficiency."

He stiffened. Another one? Damn it to hell. "We'll be right there."

Jack grimly strode to Mrs. Belisle's room, with Jessica right behind. When he saw that Avery was in there, standing by the patient's bed, his heart knocked hard in his chest. He wasn't sure if it was from seeing her, or if it was because he knew she was taking notes on the third patient with this problem in a matter of days.

He took the woman's pulse, checked her blood pressure and went through the process to confirm the diagnosis, but it was pretty clear. Same song, different verse, and he hated that they had no idea why this kept happening at this rate.

As he gave orders to Jessica and the other nurse, he

was painfully aware of Avery observing all of it, tapping away at her tablet. Watching as the patient received the medications needed to reduce her blood pressure, the diuretic to clear her lungs and the Foley catheter to catch the fluids. Continued tapping away as the portable echocardiogram was brought to the room to get images of Mrs. Belisle's heart activity.

He resolutely ignored her presence, concentrating on the situation. A half hour later, relieved that the patient was breathing a little easier, Jack let himself glance up at Avery, surprised to see her green eyes staring straight into his. This time there wasn't a hint of the humor he loved to see there. They were beyond serious.

"I'm going to look at the echocardiogram," he said to no one in particular. He knew his voice was gruff, but he couldn't help the slightly sick feeling in his gut that maybe this clinical trial was heading downhill fast.

"I'd like to look at it with you, Dr. Dunbar," Avery's voice said from behind him as he moved down the hall.

Of course she would.

His gut tightened a little more. No matter how disturbing all this was, though, he knew he couldn't blame her or feel ticked at her. She was doing her job and, ultimately, if it turned out she'd been right all along, he had to accept that. Should welcome it, really, because if the device was truly flawed, he wouldn't want to put patients at risk any more than she did. If he had to spend another year working with Crilex's biomedical engineers to improve it before testing it on humans again, then that's what would have to happen.

Way premature to be thinking like that, Jack fiercely reminded himself. This clinical trial was only half over, and it was very possible they'd just had a run of bad luck and the next twenty patients would all do fine.

"What are you thinking, Jack?" Avery asked quietly as they studied the Doppler echocardiogram of Mrs. Belisle and the obvious, slight leakage from around the valve.

He looked at her, measuring his response. He trusted her. He did. But loose lips sank ships, as the old saying went, and there was too much riding on this trial to jeopardize it by being too forthcoming with the woman who'd been concerned about this risk all along.

"I'm thinking that I will carefully examine how I'm inserting the catheter and device. As I do that, we'll continue to compile the data. We're also going to perform the procedure on all the very sick patients who've lined up to receive it. Even those with this complication will be better off than they were before the surgery, you know."

"So you're not worried that this is clear evidence the device design just isn't yet where it needs to be?"

The expression on her face showed loud and clear that's what she thought, with maybe a little contempt thrown in. Or was it disappointment? Either way, he didn't want to see it and turned his attention back to the monitor. "Too soon to say. There's not enough evidence, and worrying about it when we don't have the data from a full study is pointless."

She was silent for so long, with such an odd, thoughtful expression as she studied him, it made him jittery. When he couldn't stand it any longer, he abruptly turned. "I have some other patients to see."

"Jack."

He paused and looked back at her, bracing himself for a lecture, willing himself to not let his frustration over all this send his temper flaring. "Yes?"

"I have a great idea," she said, her voice suddenly, surprisingly, light and playful. The same voice she'd used that first, very memorable day they'd spent together.

"Sounds scary."

"Not scary. I think you'll like the proposal I have in mind."

That mischievous smile that usually made him smile back was in her eyes once more. Right now, though, it made him wonder why her demeanor had changed so abruptly. He folded his arms and waited.

"You've been working long and hard and don't have any patients scheduled this weekend. You're looking pretty haggard, which is going to worry your little old lady patients who think you're the most handsome thing in the world."

"You think?" He actually did smile at that, and how she managed to change the entire atmosphere of the room in one minute, he didn't know. "Is that what's called a backhanded compliment?"

"Maybe. So here's my proposal." She moved closer to him and pressed her hands to his chest. He felt some of his stress seep away at their warmth through his scrubs, at how good they felt there.

It made him realize how much he'd missed her touch. Missed touching her.

He let himself cup her waist with his hands because he wanted to, and she was the one who'd started the touching after all. "Does it have anything to do with espresso? If it does, a triple sounds pretty good right now."

"It might." Her smile could only be described as flirtatious, which ratcheted up Jack's interest tenfold. At the same time, he felt even more perplexed. "I promise some serious espresso consumption if you agree. Wine consumption, too."

"Wine consumption? You sure know how to intrigue a guy. What other guilty pleasures might be included in this proposal?"

"You'll find out, if you just say, 'Yes, Avery.'" Her coy words were accompanied by the sparkle in her eyes he'd fallen for the first day they'd met, oddly mingling with a tinge of seriousness.

"I never say yes until I know what I'm agreeing to. What's the catch, and is it going to hurt much?"

"It might hurt, but you're tough enough to handle it," she said, the sparkle fading a bit. "I'd like you to come to Alsace with me, to a little village northeast of Paris. Not too far and easy to get to by train. It's beyond beautiful, so I'll get to show you more of France, and you'll get to shake the dust of this place from your feet and be all refreshed when you come back to work."

He tipped his head to study her, trying to figure out where she was going with this. "Despite the wine consumption promise, I suspect you're not inviting me there for a weekend of sightseeing and wild sex." Though just thinking about spending two days alone with her sent a hot zing through every nerve ending, which he quickly tamped down. Hadn't he sworn off sex or anything else with her?

Yeah, right. If that was her proposal, he'd be saying yes in half of one second and to hell with the consequences.

"Maybe it is about wild sex," she said, giving him the adorable teasing look he'd missed almost as much as her touch, and his heart pumped harder. "Along with meeting the patient I mentioned before, who was one of the first to receive my original TAVI device. I'd like you to hear his story."

"Uh-huh." Here was the damned big letdown he'd known was coming. "How about we go for the wild sex and forget the rest?"

"It's a package deal. We'll be out of Paris and away from the hospital to relax."

"You want me to meet this guy so much you'll risk more of us mixing business with pleasure?" The part of him that wanted his hands and mouth on her again was already yelling yes, but going there with her would be one bad idea. "I know the problems patients with leaky valves live with, Avery. And much as I'd like nothing better than to go on a weekend away with you, it'd just complicate an already complicated situation."

To his shock, she reached up to wrap her arms around his neck and kissed him. Kissed him until his knees nearly buckled and his heart raced. Kissed him until he couldn't breathe and his stress had completely evaporated. Kissed him until he'd say yes to pretty much anything she asked.

When she finally stopped, he could see in her eyes the same delirious desire he felt pumping through every cell in his body. Even though she was obviously using her all-too-irresistible feminine wiles to get him to see that guy, it was also clear she was every bit as turned on as he was.

"How about it, Jack?" she whispered against his lips. "I know you need a break. And meeting this man will just add to your data, so there's nothing to lose. Except, maybe, your virtue."

"Pretty sure I lost my virtue that first day we met." He had to chuckle, but he shook his head, not quite believing her tactics. "You drive a very hard bargain, Dr. Girard."

She pressed closer against him, and when his erection pressed into her stomach she gave him the wickedest smile. "Very hard, Dr. Dunbar. Which I hope means your answer is yes."

In a sign that this trip just might go as well as Avery hoped, the gray clouds parted and the sun cast its golden fingers across the vineyards and snowy mountains that surrounded Riquewihr. Jack parked the little rental car outside the town's ancient walls and turned to her with a smile.

"This place is amazing," he said. "I can't believe that one minute we're driving through endless vineyards, then all of a sudden here's this beautiful old medieval town parked right in the middle of it all."

"You should see it in the summertime, when everything's green and flowers are everywhere," she said, glad he already seemed to like this place. "Wait till we get inside the walls. The town itself is every bit as amazing and lovely."

She smiled, pleased that he again looked like the upbeat man she'd met in the hotel that very first day, and not the cardiologist whose tense and tired expression the past week had made her want to gather him up and hold him and give him more of that TLC she'd promised him before. It wasn't good for his patients or for Jack if he worked endless hours under stress, and in a sudden decision not too different from the moment she'd first met him in the hotel, she'd wanted to do something about it.

For days, a disturbing feeling had nagged at her. As the number of patients in the trial had more than doubled, the problems had increased, too. She knew Jack was as concerned about it as she was. But she also knew him well enough to guess that his fatigue and worry would turn into defensiveness if she suggested again that he ratchet the trial back to its original numbers, or even fewer.

Inspiration had struck on how she could accomplish two things at once. Get him to come here to Riquewihr for a much-needed break—and to meet Benjamin Larue. A lovely man with a lovely family, whose life had been damaged irreversibly during the first TAVI trials.

Jack's loose stride already seemed much more relaxed than the fast pace he kept in the hospital, moving from surgeries to patients to various test results and back. They headed toward the old clock tower, walking through the gate beneath it in the ancient wall.

"How many times have you been here?" he asked. "Just in the summertime?"

"I've been here twice. Once in winter and once in summer. Totally different things to do, of course. I love to hike the mountains, but the snow cover at the moment requires a different approach. So I figured maybe we'd cross-country ski or snowshoe. Have you ever tried it? I made a reservation for us just a half hour from now, so we'll have to hurry to get there. Unless you'd rather do something else."

"I haven't tried either one." He leaned closer, the devilish smile that had knocked her socks off—among other things—back in full force and electrifying the air. "But I'm all for any kind of exercise you might think up to get our blood pumping."

Her blood was already pumping just from looking at him and thinking about the kind of physical exercise he obviously had on his mind.

The curve of his lips, the light in his eyes as he looked at her and the various landmarks they passed reminded her so much of the Jack she'd shown around Paris that first day. The Jack she'd tumbled into bed with, before she'd thought long enough about it. Before she'd found out exactly how ill-advised that decision had turned out to be.

But pretending that hadn't happened, and deciding not to let it happen again, had come to seem pretty pointless. When the trial was over and she'd studied the data, her recommendation to Crilex would be the same no matter whether they were sleeping together or not. She knew Jack wanted what was best for the patients, and she had to believe, either way it went, that he'd come to the same conclusion she did.

She smirked at herself. Like before, she seemed to have a much easier time talking herself into being with him than the other way around. Probably because he looked sexier in scrubs than about anybody she'd ever seen, and asking her to not think about stripping them off him to see that lean, muscular body of his was like asking her to give up coffee.

She glanced at him out of the corner of her eye, smiling at the memory of his shocked expression as she'd coerced him to come on this trip. She'd never tried seducing someone to get them on board with a different agenda. Now she knew it was pretty exciting to know how well her sex appeal apparently worked on the man.

They walked down a cobbled street flanked by beautiful medieval buildings, with Jack commenting on all of it in amazement, before they checked into their small hotel. From the moment she'd first seen the place she'd been awed and delighted by the beautiful pastel blues, yellows and mauves of the buildings, like something from a fairy tale.

"Some cities in France had to rebuild after World War II, so a lot of the buildings are really replicas rather than the original medieval structures," she said. "I'm told that only two bombs dropped here, though, so it's nearly all original. Isn't the whole place incredible?"

"It is. I've never seen anything like it."

Pleasure fluttered inside her at the fact that he liked it as much as she did. As they made their way down the narrow, stone-lined hallway, Jack smiled at her. "Gotta tell you, the whole town reminds me of a Hollywood movie set."

"I know what you mean." The first time she had come here, she had thought the Renaissance-style stone and half-timber homes were almost too enchanting to believe. "I've always wondered if the animators who did *Beauty and the Beast* came here for inspiration."

"I confess I haven't watched that movie and also

confess I hope that's not part of your agenda for the weekend." He shoved open their room door and looked down at her with the teasing humor she'd enjoyed that first day they met. Humor that had been in short supply the past week. "Or watching *The Sound of Music*. Have to wonder if that's the plan, though, considering the dirndl that you're wearing."

"Dirndl?" She set her suitcase on the floor and fisted her hands on her hips, giving him a mock glare. "My dress is not a dirndl, Dr. Dunbar. It's a blouse beneath a corduroy jumper."

"If you say so." He reached to unbutton her coat, pulling it apart to look at her dress. "No need to get defensive, though. I like it. A lot."

He ran his finger along the lacy top of her blouse that dipped low to just above her breasts. Avery looked down, watching the track of his finger, her breath growing short. Vaguely, she pondered that maybe the skirt did look a little like a dirndl. Her main thoughts, though, were that his touch felt wonderful, that she'd missed it, and that, unlike the first two times they'd briefly shared a hotel room, she didn't feel at all nervous. All she felt was a delicious anticipation of the day and night they'd be spending together.

She looked back up at him, and a warm flush crept through her body at the way he was looking at her. The small smile was still on his face, but his eyes were filled with something entirely different that told her he, too, was feeling that same breathless anticipation.

"Bonjour, monsieur...mademoiselle."

They both turned to the open door and saw an older gentleman with a wide, curled mustache smiling at them. "I wanted to suggest that you join us this evening at five o'clock for a wine tasting from our local vineyards. There will be complimentary hors d'oeuvres as well, in our wine cellar."

"Thank you," Jack said. "We haven't made any plans yet, but that sounds great."

He shoved the door closed behind the man and turned to her again. "Are you sure Riquewihr isn't just some elaborate Hollywood hoax? I mean, how often do you see a guy with a mustache like that outside the movies?"

Her laugh morphed into more of a little hiccup when his fingers tugged apart the lapels of her coat again. "So," he asked in a low voice, "are we staying in or going out?"

"I…um…" She struggled to decide, wanting to show him the amazing and wonderful things about Riquewihr during the daylight hours of this single Saturday that they had. Wanted to enjoy the same delight she'd felt, that she was sure they'd both felt, seeing the Eiffel Tower and the Sacré Coeur. Have those kinds of lovely moments before they stopped at the Larue family winery to meet Benjamin.

But she also wanted that heady give and take they'd had before. The overwhelming sensations when they let go of all the external problems, shared their bodies and simply let the chemistry between them ignite into a searing, physical passion like none other she'd ever experienced.

She drew a breath to try to finish her sentence, but it was a shaky one at best. Because it was clear he could read exactly what she'd been thinking, and she nearly caught fire just from the look in his eyes before he lowered his head.

His lips covered hers, teasing, tasting, as his hands moved to her waist. Slid up to cup her breasts, his fingers again brushing the filmy top of her blouse as he deepened the kiss, the sweep of his tongue so delicious she had to bite back a moan.

When he broke the kiss, his eyes were so heavy-lidded she could barely see the gleam in the darkness of his eyes. "Didn't you say we have a time schedule to hit the mountain for a little skiing or snowshoeing?"

She nodded, knowing any verbal answer she gave at that moment would just come out as a whisper until she caught her breath. "Yes," she finally managed. "I thought you'd enjoy the fresh air and how gorgeous it is up there. But we don't have to. We have the day off to do whatever makes us happy."

"Just being with you makes me happy," he said, and she was surprised the words didn't hold a sensual tone. They sounded beyond sincere, and her heart tripped in her chest. "And since we have only so many hours of daylight, I think we should do what you'd already planned for us. Because I sure haven't been disappointed in any of our activities in France so far, Ms. Tour Guide."

She stared at Jack and realized he was being utterly genuine. He truly enjoyed just being with her, here or in Paris or wherever they happened to be, and hadn't come here with her just for the "wild sex" she'd teased him with. As she thought back to her two previous relationships, she realized that the physical part of them had been the primary element.

Which wasn't at all what she had with Jack. What they had between them went deeper than the sexual chemistry they'd talked about, which was thrilling and scary at the same time. Because she knew his job was not just his priority, it was his life. She was a brief interlude in that life—an interlude he'd made clear he felt uncomfortable participating in.

And if it became necessary to halt the trial, she could only hope and pray he understood why.

Her heart giving an odd little twist, she gave him a soft kiss before grasping his hand and smiling into his beautiful eyes. "Then let's head to the Vosges mountains. I think you'll love it, and afterward we'll both be more than ready for a little après-ski."

"Lead on, Dr. Girard. I'm all yours."

CHAPTER TWELVE

"Even without the potential for wine and wild sex, I'm glad I agreed to this trip," Jack said, looking handsome as all get-out with his cheeks flushed and his dark hair poking from beneath his knit hat. "Growing up, a few of my friends went skiing in the winter with their families. Both downhill and cross-country. We never went places like that, but now I wish I'd tried this kind of thing at home."

"I knew you'd like it." The crisp mountain air was filled with the rhythmic crunch of their snowshoes and Avery's heavy breathing from tromping practically straight up for the past fifteen minutes. "Also knew the only thing that would convince you to take your mind off work by coming here was the potential for sexual favors."

"Already, the woman knows me well." He sent her his most devilish smile, and she was pretty sure it was his expression and not the cold air that made her insides quiver.

"So, where did your family go on vacation?" The tracks of the cross-country ski course had been grooved into the snow next to them, and they followed that line to be sure to not get lost. A straight uphill line, and Avery's lungs and legs sure hoped for a downhill slope soon.

"We didn't, much." He shrugged. "Both my parents are workaholic doctors, with my dad being the worst. We mostly took the occasional short trip to New York or the beach. Just for a few days, so they wouldn't be gone long."

"Ah. So you took after them?"

He flashed her a grin. "Probably. My brother, too. But I'm beginning to see the value of a little vacation time."

The path curved in a C shape to finally slope slightly downhill, thank heavens, but it was one long way down. Avery had thought she was in pretty good shape, but the burning in her thighs and lungs after the uphill climb told her maybe not so much. "Let's cut through here. Catch the path on the other side."

"I may not be a skier, but I've heard you shouldn't go off the trail. What if we fall into a crevasse?"

"You're such a rule follower. Come on."

She grabbed his hand and veered to the right near a line of trees that went all the way down the mountain.

He slid her a look that said she was crazy, but his lips were tipped into an amused smile. "There are times to follow the rules and times when it makes sense to break them. Wandering around on a mountain doesn't seem like the best time to me, but you're the tour guide. Lead on."

Even though the snow was deeper there, going downhill made it easier to breathe. And she was glad she wouldn't be panting when she asked the question she'd been wondering about. "Was there some bad situation in your life that made you not want to spend time with me after we found out who each other was? When I said it wasn't good to be involved with someone you had to work with, you were very quick to agree, and I thought there must be a reason."

"First, there was never a moment I didn't want to spend time with you. I just knew it was a bad idea." She relaxed at his teasing expression, glad he wasn't going to get all stiff again now she'd brought up the unsettling back and forth between them. "But your observation is very astute. And here I'd always heard genius types were book smart but not people smart."

She rolled her eyes. "Again, the stereotype. I thought we were done with that."

"Sorry." He took a sideways step, his shoulder bumping into hers as his eyes got that wicked glint in them. "Learning that female scientists wear lacy, colorful underwear has changed my perspective forever. Don't think I'll ever be able to see techs with their test tubes and not wonder what they have on under their lab coats."

It was utterly stupid, but his words pricked at her heart. It wasn't like they were a real couple. One that would be together after the trial was complete in just over a week. He was a career-driven man who liked women in small doses, and fantasizing about lingerie and wild sex was part of that package.

"Hey." He must have seen something in her expression because he stopped walking and tipped her chin up. "I was teasing. There's only one woman whose underwear I wonder about."

She forced a laugh. "And I just might have to keep you wondering. But you haven't answered my question."

They continued their trek as several cross-country skiers slid by in the tracks above them, and the sound of his deep sigh mingled with the swish of the skis. "When I first found out who you were I was amazed. Well, I was amazed a whole lot of ways that day." He aimed that glint at her again.

Warmth crept into her cold cheeks at his words, remembering exactly how she'd behaved and how she'd never done such a thing in her life before. "I'd prefer you didn't remind me I slept with a man I'd just met. I'm embarrassed by that, and you know it."

"You shouldn't be." He wrapped his arm around her and tugged her close to his side. "The romance of Paris and our chemistry together made it inevitable. If it hadn't happened that day, it would have happened another day. From the second I turned to see the knock-out woman talking to me in the hotel, I knew it was meant to be."

His words, his low voice and the expression in his eyes caught her breath. "Maybe it was," she replied softly. "And you're still doing a darned good job of avoiding answering me."

"You just want to gloat when you hear I made a stupid mistake. Because you know I never do, and admitting I made one once isn't something I like to do."

"I know, Dr. Dunbar, that you think you're perfect."

"Hey, my mom calls me Prince Perfect. What do you expect?" That quick grin flashed again, almost as dazzling as the sunshine on the snow, and Avery had to admit he just might be as close to perfection as a man could be.

A minute went by, silent except for the crunch, crunch

of their shoes, and she'd begun to think he'd never tell her when he finally spoke. "My crown slipped a few years back, though. I dated a medical supplies rep who sold, among other things, stents for angioplasty. I switched to the stent she repped because I honestly thought it might be superior to the ones I'd been using. You can imagine how many stents we use a month, and because it was more expensive, the hospital bean counters questioned it. When it came out that she and I had a personal relationship, all hell broke loose. Hospital bigwigs accused me of behaving unethically, and as it all unfolded, a whole lot of dirty laundry spilled out."

She couldn't imagine Jack having a whole lot of dirty laundry. "Like what?"

"Turned out the beguiling Vanessa was sleeping with numerous docs, in multiple hospitals, who used high-end surgical and biomedical products. She was trying to get a big promotion at her company and used me, and the other saps, to get the sales record and promotion."

He shook his head, his lips twisted into a grimace. "What a fool I was. My relationship with Vanessa was pretty much strictly physical, but knowing the truth, that she'd used me, made me feel sick. I hated answering to the ethics board, having them question my professionalism. I was cleared of any wrongdoing, but vowed I'd never so much as look at a woman involved in any way with my job."

"Wow." His story might even be worse than her former boyfriend mistakes. And explained why the wall between them had been wider even than she'd thought their situation warranted.

"Wow?" He raised his eyebrows at her. "Maybe I shouldn't have confessed. You think I'm an idiot now?"

"No, of course not. But I've gotta tell you. While I feel bad you went through that, you've made me feel a little better about my own poor judgment."

"Which would be what?"

Part of her didn't want to share something so embarrassing, but he'd shared with her, so it was only fair. "I dated a couple of cardiologists for a while. The first one traveled a lot, teaching his specialized procedures. Turned out he had a woman in every port. Or every hospital, to be more accurate."

He stopped walking to stare at her. "I can't believe there's a human alive who could be stupid enough to not hang onto you with both hands when he had the chance."

He looked genuinely astonished, and what woman wouldn't feel pretty good about his words? "The second one started talking down to me, saying disparaging things."

"What kind of disparaging things?"

"Oh, like when people asked me questions about angioplasty and stents, which happened sometimes because that's what he did, he'd say I was the 'equipment' girl and wasn't qualified to talk about medical procedures."

"You've got to be kidding me." The astonishment was still there on his face, along with anger. "No wonder you wrote off cardiologists as being total jerks. But he was probably jealous of your amazing smarts. That kind of guy isn't worth having, and you know it."

"I do know. But I guess that whole experience has

made me hypersensitive. Which is why I was suspicious of you and Jessica. Sorry. But there are some real winners out there."

"Yeah. There are." His eyes and voice warmed and he stopped, turning to wrap both his arms around her and draw her close. Her own arms slipped around his back, and the sizzle between them could be felt all the way through their coats and hats, warming her from the inside out. "The kind of winner that makes a man do something he swore he wouldn't do. So maybe I'm still a fool. But I can't seem to keep you out of my head."

His cold lips touched hers, and in an instant both their mouths were toasty warm as they shared a slow, sweet kiss. Just as Avery angled her head, inviting him to delve deeper, the swishing sound of skis on snow came from above them. They pulled apart and looked up the hill to the trail they'd abandoned to see nearly a dozen skiers following one another in single file on the trail.

"Are you kidding?" Jack said. "Even out here in the middle of a mountain we have an audience?"

She wasn't about to let a few strangers ruin the heavenly moment. Of all the places she'd kissed Jack, holding him close on this wild, beautiful mountainside, his cold nose touching hers and his mouth so hot and delicious—this place was her very favorite. "Who cares? We're in France."

She tried to go up on tiptoe to kiss him again, but found it pretty difficult with snowshoes on her feet. Luckily, the superheated gleam in his eyes showed he knew exactly what she wanted and he kissed her again, sending her heart pounding even harder. Her legs wobbled, whether from the kiss or the hiking or both she wasn't sure. She hung onto Jack's coat as his mouth moved across her cold cheek and beneath her earlobe in a shivery path that made it very hard to breathe.

Frigid wind swept the cheek not currently covered by Jack's warm one and at the same time clumps of snow-flakes dropped onto her face. She opened her eyes to see Jack lifting his head, a slow, sexy smile curving his lips as his finger swept the snow from her eyelashes.

"Guess we should have thought to bring your umbrella up here on the mountain with us." His hat and shoulders were covered with snowflakes, too, and she looked behind him to see the wind catch more of the snow loaded on the evergreen trees and swirl it onto them, like Mother Nature was playing a joke and tossing it with her hand.

"Who knew?"

Their steamy, breathless laughter flitted between them as they separated, her gloved hand in his, to trudge on down the mountain in a companionable silence. She pulled in a deep, satisfied breath, realizing she felt as comfortable and relaxed as she'd felt in a long, long time, and hoped Jack was feeling the same.

Except he probably wouldn't be much longer.

"So here's the other thing we have scheduled today," she said, hoping her announcement wouldn't ruin the beautiful, quiet mood between them.

"Dare I hope it's the wild sex or the wine consumption? Or both combined?"

"Not yet. That might come later, if you're good."

"Oh, I'm good. You know I'm good."

She hated to squash the teasing heat in his eyes and

sucked in another breath, this one no longer relaxed. "After we turn in our snowshoes, we're going to take the car out to the Larue family vineyards."

Something in her expression obviously told him this wasn't just another pleasure excursion. "Your TAVI patient?"

"Clearly, I'm not the only astute one." Suddenly she felt nervous. Would meeting Benjamin make Jack go all defensive again? Snuff out the smile on his face, the relaxed posture, the teasing looks? Make it difficult for them to enjoy the hours together in this beautiful place?

Maybe it would. But with the complications that patients were experiencing increasing, her gut told her Jack needed to step back from how deeply he was wrapped up in the trial and think about it objectively. If meeting Benjamin didn't do that, probably nothing would. "Are you...okay with that?"

"I told you this morning, Dr. Girard," he said, his gaze steady on hers, "I'm all yours."

The house looked to be hundreds of years old, though at the same time it was still in pristine condition. Proof that most people had been shorter long ago, Jack had to duck beneath the ancient beam above the thick, wooden front door when he followed Avery, who was being kissed on both cheeks and warmly greeted by a woman who was probably in her early forties. Both were yammering on in French, and since he couldn't understand a word, he took time to look around the cozy room. A welcoming fire burned inside a huge stone fireplace, and a wooden table was covered with so many plates of finger foods you'd have thought every guest at the hotel was stopping by.

He blew out a breath. He'd known all along this was the catch to an otherwise great weekend with Avery, but now that he was here, dread began to seep into his gut. What did Avery really want from him? And what could this man have experienced that he hadn't seen before, anyway?

It wasn't as if he didn't know all too well about the challenges people with bad hearts faced every day. He stood by his statement that a less-than-perfect outcome was still better than what most had lived with before the procedure. This TAVI trial was doing important work, critical work, work that might have helped someone like his own grandfather, who had died with so much left to live for. Help a lot of people who couldn't get a new heart valve any other way.

Benjamin Larue must not have had luck on his side. Sometimes bad things happened to good people, and every doctor experienced days when it felt like a shower of bricks came down on everyone's head. When it did, it hurt like hell and left bruises that lasted a long time.

"Jack, this is Vivienne Larue. Vivienne, Dr. Jack Dunbar."

"Welcome, welcome! Please sit and make yourself comfortable while I get Benjamin. He is very happy you've come to visit."

Jack wasn't sure *visit* was the right term—why did he suddenly feel a little like he was standing in front of a firing squad? The feeling persisted, even though he sat in a comfortable chair by the flickering fire. Maybe it was the way Avery's green eyes were focused on him—*expectantly* would be the word—and that fueled his discomfort.

"So were you telling secrets about me in French?" Maybe making a joke would lighten up the awkward mood that hung like a cloud in the room.

"I don't know many of your secrets, though that one you shared on the mountain was a doozy. Can't wait to hear more and spread them all over the hospital."

Damned if the woman couldn't make him smile in the midst of an avalanche. "I might have to make up some juicy ones, just to surprise you."

"You've been surprising me since the minute we met." A sweet, sincere smile accompanied her words, and he felt himself relax a little.

"Likewise, Dr. Girard."

"Vivienne makes the best cheesy puff pastries," Avery said as she put a few things on her plate. "You should try one."

Before he could answer, he heard a sound behind him and turned to see Vivienne pushing a man in a wheelchair into the room.

It wasn't an ordinary wheelchair. It was semi-reclining, the kind someone who couldn't breathe well would use, and the man sitting in it had a prosthetic leg. His head was raised to look at his guests as introductions were made, and a friendly smile didn't mask his pallor or the thin, drawn look to his face.

So much for feeling less tense. His gut tightened all over again when he saw how young the man was to have this kind of disability. Probably only in his early forties, like his wife. It was damned unfair that sometimes a guy drew the short straw, and medical science just wasn't advanced enough to replace it with a longer one.

And wasn't that exactly why the work he was doing was so important? Advancing medical science to help patients was the critical goal.

"*Bon après-midi*, Dr. Dunbar. I'm honored to have you visit," Benjamin said in a hoarse, rasping voice as he extended his hand. "Avery tells me you have developed a new prosthetic valve device. I wish you well with it."

Jack stood and leaned over to shake his hand. "Thank you. Avery thought that speaking with you might help me do the best I can for other patients as we move forward."

Benjamin's smile broadened. "And I hope that you will taste our latest wine vintages to help me with those, as well. We make the finest wines in France right here, you know. Pinot Gris, Pinot Noir and Rieslings are our specialties."

"I didn't know. I don't pretend to be a wine expert, but I'm more than happy to lend my palate to you."

"Excellent." Benjamin beamed, then turned to talk to Avery. As Jack watched them banter, the room seemed to lose its claustrophobic feeling and he relaxed, taking a bite of the cheese Vivienne offered. Which made him realize he'd been prepared for criticism or attack or who knew what from all of them.

"So, Dr. Dunbar. Avery is determined that I tell you my story. Why she continues to take responsibility for God's hand in my life, I do not know. It is what it is. So I will recite it quickly, then we can enjoy more important things." Benjamin looked at her with an expression similar to that of a fond uncle, and her emotions were right there on her face, visible to anyone who wanted to look.

Warm friendship. Caring. Heartache and guilt.

She'd been through tough times with this man, he saw, surprised at that revelation, though he shouldn't have been. She had obviously had her own days where bricks had fallen all too hard on her head. She might not be a medical doctor, but she cared about the patients using the devices she'd designed as much as any of them. Cared about them deeply enough to forge this bond that obviously both hurt and soothed.

"I'd like to hear your story, Benjamin," he said. "More than anything, I want to help people like my late grandfather, and like you, with challenging heart valve problems."

He thought he was focused on Benjamin, but realized he was glancing at Avery, too. At her smile, and the softness in her eyes that told him she liked his response. He'd always thought he didn't care what others thought, that he worked for his patients and for the goals he'd set for himself, and that was all that mattered. But at that moment her approval brought a smile to his own face and made his chest swell a little, even though he knew that was absurd.

"At the age of nine I was diagnosed with diabetes," Benjamin said, staring at the swirl of red wine in a glass his wife had poured. "As the years went on, I was one of the less fortunate. Many complications, and eventually I lost my leg."

"Juvenile-onset diabetes can be a difficult disease to manage." Jack saw all too many patients with terrible complications from diabetes and hoped like hell researchers would eventually find a cure.

"It is." Benjamin nodded. "Then, when our boys were only seven and nine, my kidneys began to fail. We fit weekly dialysis into our schedules somehow. Along with caring for the vines and harvest and crush and all the other things that must happen for a winery to survive. For me to survive." His hand reached to Vivienne and she clasped it tight. "My beautiful wife has stood by me through all of this, and why that is I do not know. I only know that I am blessed."

"It is your stubbornness, Benjamin Larue. Your irresistible stubbornness."

Jack saw tears fill Vivienne's eyes, and he glanced at Avery to see hers had filled, as well. In her line of work she probably didn't often work with sick people. He dealt with it every day, but that didn't make it any easier. "When did you begin to have heart problems?"

"Not long after my dialysis began. When I worked with the grapes or played with my sons, I tired quickly, becoming very short of breath." His eyes met Jack's. "Do you have children, monsieur?"

"No."

"Then you do not know the joys and frustrations of their abundant energy. Energy I wanted to keep up with."

Jack might not know about wanting to play with his own children, with any children, but could easily imagine how that inability could cut away at your soul. "So you and your doctors decided a valve transplant would help. Except you weren't a candidate for open-heart surgery because of your other health issues."

"*Oui*. I was pleased to think a new procedure might help me breathe easier, work longer and play ball with my boys for more than five minutes." He grinned. "You may look at me and wonder, but I got pretty good at kicking with my pretend leg, which amused my children."

"Amused everyone," Avery said, smiling, too. "When his doctor and I came here to talk about the risks and benefits of the TAVI trial, I couldn't believe how Benjamin could practically do spin moves. His boys joked that he was Iron Man and had an unfair advantage. Tiring quickly was his primary problem, which we'd hoped to fix."

"But the surgery didn't go well." Jack wanted to get to the crux of the matter, though he already knew.

"*Non*." Benjamin's smile faded. "Afterward, I was much worse, not better. Now if I lie flat, my lungs fill. I cannot kick the ball with my boys at all anymore or work in the vineyard. My kidney problems make it impossible for me to take a diuretic to lessen the fluid buildup, and my body is not strong enough to handle open-heart surgery." He gestured at himself. "So this is it for me. I accept it, but hurt for my family that they must do all the things in the vineyard and at home that I no longer can."

"Bottom line, Jack? It was an utter failure," Avery said, her eyes intent on his. "We wanted to make Benjamin's life better, but we made it much worse instead. I know you see patients with bad outcomes. But you've been convinced that those with leakage from the prosthetic valve are medically manageable and still better off than before. Benjamin's situation proves that's not always the case. The percentage having this problem must be very small to justify the risk."

What was he supposed to say to that? All procedures carried risks. Every single one of them, from the simplest to the most complex. But he understood the frustration and deep disappointment. Benjamin may not have had the exercise capacity he'd wanted before the procedure, but now he had none at all and couldn't even sleep in a bed with his wife.

"Papa! Papa!" Two boys careened into the room, nearly skidding to a halt next to the wheelchair, speaking fast in French until he held up his hand.

"English, please. Our guest does not speak French, and it is good for you to practice."

Both boys took a breath, and Jack was impressed at how polite they were during a brief introduction, before launching into their story again.

"*Les chevreuils* got through the fence that has a hole and into the berry bushes. They were eating up the brambles before we chased them off! Why do deer eat thorny things like that, Papa?"

"The same reason you like your mother's macaroons, I suppose."

"Are you saying that eating my macaroons is like swallowing thorns, Benjamin Larue?" Vivienne said in faux outrage, her hands fisted on her hips.

"*Non, non*, my dearest, I am saying the brambles are like a delectable delicacy to *les chevreuils*, as all your wonderful dishes are to me." His chest filled with a deep chuckle that morphed into a horrible coughing fit that immediately swept all amusement from everyone's face.

Jack tensed, wishing there was something he could

do to help Benjamin breathe more easily, but there wasn't. The fluids had to work loose on their own, and he was sure everyone was as relieved as he was when the poor man's coughing finally subsided. Benjamin took a moment to catch his breath, then spoke to his sons, telling them where to get materials to repair the fence. Pride lit his eyes as they kissed both his cheeks, said their goodbyes and ran off as fast as they'd run in.

Jack thought of his own brother and how the two of them had always looked up to their dad. The man hadn't done much around the house, always busy working at the hospital. On the occasions they'd tackled a project together, though, he still remembered how he'd admired his father's smarts and physical strength. Not having that physical strength had to hurt Benjamin like hell, but thank God he still could guide and mentor his boys in other ways.

"You have a fine family, Benjamin," Jack said. "Think they'll continue the family tradition of wine making?"

"If they do not, we will disinherit them." His eyes twinkled. "Now it is time for that wine tasting, *oui*? I cannot walk down the stairs to the cellar, so we will have to enjoy it here. Vivienne, will you uncork them, *s'il vous plaît*?"

Jack saw the closeness between husband and wife just from the way they smiled at one another, and he found himself looking at Avery. Thinking about sharing that kind of lifelong bond with a woman had never been on his list of things to accomplish in his life. Wasn't sure it ever would be. But he had to admit there just might be something good about having that kind of steady love and support in good times and bad.

The Larues had managed to keep that through plenty of bad times.

Jack didn't have to know them well to hurt for them. He got why Avery wanted him to see what Benjamin lived with, but at the same time he felt she was being naive. If he counted the number of patients living less than optimal lives, he'd spend all day doing it. Life wasn't fair, that was for sure.

The clinical trial he was working so hard on was all about trying to level the playing field just a little. Trials existed for a reason, and that reason was to test new procedures and devices. If everyone threw in the towel halfway through because potential questions arose, nothing good would ever get accomplished from most of them.

Did Avery think meeting this great family that had to live with adversity and challenges would change his goals, or make him question what he wanted to accomplish? He damned well had plenty of his own patients who had to endure a life with far less than optimal physical ability. Surely she knew that.

Improving the lives of patients was all he wanted to accomplish. If she didn't understand or believe that, their time alone together this weekend wouldn't turn out the way he hoped it would.

CHAPTER THIRTEEN

Seeing the Larue family always left Avery with a tumble of emotions. Pleased about spending time enjoying the closeness of their family. Grateful for her own health. Sad for what they had to deal with every day. Guilt that she hadn't done a better job designing the TAVI device before it had gone to human trials.

At that exact moment she wasn't sure which emotion was winning.

Jack's arm wrapped around her waist, holding her close, might not be helping much with the guilt and sadness, but it did feel good there. Warm and comforting. Despite their height difference, their bodies seemed to fit perfectly together as they strolled through the village in search of a *biscuiterie* and the coconut macaroons Riquewihr was famous for. The shop she usually went to was closed for the winter, and she peered hopefully at dimly lit signs, trying to find another one that was open.

"There's one," Avery said, pointing down a crooked little street. "I don't remember it, but I'm sure every one of the *biscuiteries* are good."

"So you claim these cookies are the best things in the whole world?"

"The best. I guarantee you'll love them."

They went into the tiny shop and selected a few macaroons and espresso before sitting at a small table. Avery felt pretty much sapped of small talk and nibbled her cookie, hoping its deliciousness would cheer her up and make her a better companion, which she knew she couldn't claim to be at that moment.

"I have a confession to make," Jack said, looking extremely serious.

She paused with her macaroon halfway to her mouth. "A confession?"

"Yes. I'm not a big fan of coconut. In fact, I usually avoid it like flesh-eating bacteria. But if sharing coconut macaroons with you banishes the melancholy in your beautiful eyes for even a split second, I'll gladly choke one down."

As he said it, she could swear he actually shuddered, and she managed a laugh. "You believe it would cheer me up to watch you eat something you liken to flesh-eating bacteria? What does that say about the kind of person you think I am?"

"That you are caring. And that you obviously feel all beat up right now."

"There's that astute thing again."

"Don't have to be astute to see it, Avery. How you're feeling is written all over your face."

"Good to know." She closed her eyes and swallowed at the sudden lump in her throat. "I do feel beat up whenever I see them. Who wouldn't? I designed the prosthetic valve, and that valve is why his life is awful now. It's hard for me to see that wonderful family dealing with what they deal with. See Benjamin barely able to walk, when I saw him running with the boys before my TAVI device destroyed that."

"For all you know, his heart might have gotten worse anyway. The man's been dealt a bad hand of cards, and I feel for him, too." He reached for her hand, and its warmth had her holding it tight. "But if I blamed myself for every patient who didn't do well, or who died, like Henri Arnoult, I'd never be able to function and do my job. Medicine is both rewarding and damned difficult. The only way to help people is to forge on and do the best you can. Would it help people if you just stopped designing biomedical devices? Never came up with an improved stent or something no one's invented yet?"

"No. But I should have insisted it be tested further on animals first." Not that the manufacturer and sponsor would have listened anyway. "I'd hoped you'd come to see you should consider that, too, for yours."

"I am listening to you, Avery. Hearing you loud and clear, and paying attention to the reason for your worries. I want you to know that." Seeing how deeply serious and sincere he looked brought her hope that he truly meant it. "While it's impossible to know how Benjamin's health would be right now without the TAVI, I understand your point about possibly making it worse for some patients than others. This trial is already under way with patients who have no other options. I still believe we're doing far more good than harm. But since we have more than double the number of patients now giving us additional data, I will keep him in mind as we look at how things are going."

The weight in her chest lifted at the same time it squeezed even tighter. Not only did Jack respect her opinion, it sounded like this trek had accomplished her goal. How could she have thought he might be too narrow focused, too hell-bent on success, to at least listen? She'd already seen what a committed and caring doctor he was.

"Okay, for that you don't have to eat the macaroon," she said, managing a smile. "I can't believe you were going to, if you don't like coconut. Though I admit I'm incredulous that's even possible."

"Maybe I'd like it after it's touched your lips." His finger gently swiped her bottom lip and she could see bits of cookie on his finger just before he licked it off.

Had she really been yakking away with crumbs all over her mouth? Her embarrassment at that realization got shoved aside by serious body tingling at the oh-so-sensual look he was giving her.

"You know what?" He sounded genuinely surprised. "It is better. Definitely. Sweet and delectable, in fact."

"Not like flesh-eating bacteria?" She found herself staring at his mouth, and to keep herself from diving in there and tasting for herself the crumbs and espresso on his tongue, she tried for a joke. "I'm not a big fan of escargots, which I saw you gobbling up at the hotel hors d'oeuvre party. Maybe you could hold one between your lips and I'll nibble it from there. Just to see."

His laughter made her grin and realize he'd managed to squash much of the sadness she'd been feeling. Had also managed to blast away every negative thought her former relationships had stuck in her brain nearly from the first day she'd met him. Had managed to prove himself the complete package of what a sexy man should be. At that moment she knew the attraction and lust she'd felt when she'd first met him had evolved into very much more.

The thought both scared and thrilled her, and she wasn't at all sure what to do with the realization that had just slammed her between the eyes.

"Somehow, nibbling snails from my lips doesn't sound nearly as appealing as licking cookie crumbs from yours. I think we need further research on this, Dr. Girard."

"I think we need further research on why talking about flesh-eating bacteria and nibbling snails hasn't at all dulled my desire to kiss you, Dr. Dunbar." Further research on that, and on the tender emotions swirling around her heart as she seriously considered pressing her mouth to his right then and there.

"Then I definitely want to find out what will happen if I suggest you nibble *chocolat* from my lips. Which you can bet I'm pulling from the minibar in our room the minute we get there." His voice had gone so low, his expression so wicked that her belly quivered in anticipation of any and all nibbling action.

He tossed back the last of his espresso and stood, grasping her hand and leaning down to speak close to her ear. "Bring your cookies back to the hotel so I can see how they taste licked from your lips. After I lick off the chocolate. In fact, I like the idea of keeping a database of how all kinds of things taste from your lips and other beautiful parts of your body."

Whew, boy. She felt so hot she nearly didn't bother putting on her coat before they moved out into the chilly night. Jack walked fast, and because he was holding her hand she had to nearly run to keep up.

"Slow down a little. My legs aren't as long as yours."

"Having a hard time slowing down, thinking about our future data collection." His eyes glittered in the darkness. "And I figured the pace would keep you warmer."

No need to worry about her being warm. At all. About to skirt the ornate fountain in the center of a square, she found herself, ridiculously, wanting to make a wish like she always did when she was here. She tugged his arm so he'd stop. "Let's make a wish in the fountain. I always hope it's like the Trevi Fountain in Rome."

He pulled a couple of coins from his pocket and handed one to her. "What are you going to wish for?"

"It won't come true if you tell." She looked skyward to make her wish, surprised to see how remarkably clear it was for a winter night in France, which made her think about how wonderful it would be to make love to Jack outdoors deep in the vineyards when it was warmer, which briefly sidetracked her from her mission.

She yanked her thoughts back to ponder her wish as the stars seemed to twinkle down on them. She closed her eyes and tossed the coin into the fountain with a satisfying plunk.

"Your turn."

He tossed his coin. It landed just a millimeter from hers, and she wondered if that meant something. Which was beyond silly—it was just water in a fountain, and what would she want it to mean anyway?

"Maybe you'll get lucky and your wish will come true," she said.

His expression as his eyes met hers was odd, almost serious. It was too bad it wasn't really a magic fountain, because she'd love to ask it what his wish was.

"I'm already feeling lucky. Though I very much hope I'll get even luckier."

Her insides went all quivery again, as there was no mistaking the superheated gleam that returned to his eyes as he spoke. If the two of them making love again was what he'd wished for, he'd wasted his wish. Her breath caught just looking at his handsome face and sexy smile, and she fully intended to enjoy these hours with him before the stress of work faced them once again. Before he moved on to his next trial and she went wherever her job took her.

This time, it was Avery setting the pace, giving a quick greeting to the hotel manager before running up the two flights of stairs to their floor and into the room.

"For some reason, I'm feeling a little déjà vu," Jack said as he shoved the door closed behind them. "If it was summertime, I'd be sneaking into one of the vine-yards and feeding you grapes while making love to you under the stars."

Did the man have mind-reading powers, too, or was it just part of this electric connection they seemed to have? "Funny, I was just thinking the same thing. We could add grapes to the database." Breathlessly, she wrangled off her coat and tossed it on the chair. "It does seem like we've done the same dash into a hotel room several times since we met, wearing an awful lot of heavy clothes."

"Not exactly the same dash. For one thing, it seemed like you weren't too sure you wanted to unbutton your coat before. This time you're ahead of me." He reached for her and pulled her close. "Not to mention that, each time, it's gotten even sweeter. I'm betting tonight will be also, not even counting the macaroons you brought."

"Know what? You do taste sweeter than any cookie." She stood on tiptoe and slid her hands behind his head before she kissed him. Deeply, deliciously, pouring herself into it, wanting to show him how much she'd come to care for him. To tell him without words how impressed she was that he'd shared his honest view about Benjamin and medicine, while still listening to her, respecting her, caring what she thought. To enjoy the connection they shared that was of both mind and body.

He kissed her back. And kissed her. Until her breath was choppy and her knees nearly stopped holding her up. Figuring she'd like to be sitting or something before that happened, she backed them both toward the bed, but he stopped the movement and broke the kiss. He stood there just staring at her with eyes that were peculiarly serious behind the obvious desire shining there.

"What?" she whispered.

"When I came to Paris I was keyed up and couldn't think about anything but how all my work was about to pay off. Being with you that first day seemed like a great way to take the edge off before the trial started." He slowly shook his head. "But it didn't quite work out that way. Instead, you've added another edge."

"What do you mean?"

"I hate not having complete control over how I feel about you." He pressed her body so close to his it was hard to breathe. "I've spent my adulthood being in control of my life and my career. Not having that makes me damned uncomfortable."

Her heart constricted into a cold little ball at the fact that she was the one who had control over this current phase of his career that was so important to him. And he'd be very angry and upset that she hadn't shared that reality with him, if he ended up finding out. Or if she had to wield that control and power.

And yet somehow her heart swelled, too, at his words and the way he looked at her. Like she'd come to mean as much to him as he had to her. "Is being in control all the time important? Because right now I wouldn't mind you losing control a little."

"Yeah?" She thought he was about to resume their motion toward the bed, but he veered sideways toward the bathroom. At the same time he somehow managed to slip her blouse over her head, unzip the back of her skirt, yank off his own shirt and pants, and throw a condom onto the floor until they were standing naked just outside the tiny shower.

"I've heard the verse 'Jack, be nimble, Jack, be quick,'" she said, amazed and more than excited as she stared at his all-too-sexy physique. "Was that written about you?"

"You make me want to be quick. For some things, not everything." His lips curved. "Not jumping over any candlesticks, though. Wouldn't stay lit for what I'm planning next."

"And what are you planning next?" Avery quivered at the superheated gleam in his eyes, knowing whatever it was would be a whole lot better than any snail nibbling.

Jack turned the faucet on, then tugged Avery's

breathtakingly naked body into the cubicle and closed the door.

"My plan is to lick water from every inch of your skin," he said. The closeness of the space sent her pink nipples nudging against his chest and his erection into the softness of her belly, making him groan. Still-cold water rained onto his back as he shielded her from it until it warmed, but it didn't do a thing to cool the heat pumping through every one of his pores.

"It's small in here, I know. But I don't care. I liked kissing the rainwater from your face and mouth so much I've been fantasizing about getting you in the shower ever since."

"Should I get my umbrella? I kind of liked kissing you under that before we got all wet."

"Maybe next time." God, she was adorable. "I'm already all wet, and soon you will be, too."

He kissed her, letting one hand palm her breast while the other stroked down her soft skin and between her legs to make his last statement come true. The little gasping breaths and sexy sounds coming from her mouth into his nearly had him diving into her right then and there, but tonight was about slow and easy. Being together just this once without work and patients and the trial hanging around with them.

The water pounding on his back had finally warmed, and he pulled her under it to join him. He shoved her wet hair back so he could see her beautiful face and started with her forehead, sipping the water from her skin as it tracked down her cheek, her throat, her breasts.

Her fingers dug into his back as he tasted as much of her as her could reach, and the feel of her tongue licking across his shoulder, too, up his neck and around his ear, made him shiver and burn at the same time.

"You taste so delicious," he murmured against her damp sternum as her other slick wetness soaked his fingers and the scent of her touched his nose, making him want to taste her there, too. Probably not possible in the tiny shower, but later? Oh, yeah. "The best dessert any man could ask for."

"This water doesn't taste as good as the rain, though." Her chest rose and fell against his mouth. "Maybe we should try bottled water, since I don't think they drink tap water here."

"Too late for that." He chuckled and looked up at her, then paused in mid-lick. Arrested by the look on her face. It was filled with the kind of intimate connection between them he'd only felt with her—a humor and euphoria and something he couldn't quite define. He wanted to see more of it, wanted to look into her eyes as he kissed her mouth. Every bit of her tasted beyond wonderful, but that delectable mouth of hers was his absolute favorite of all.

Grasping her rear in his hands, he wrapped her legs around his waist, then realized he had to get the condom from the floor. He crouched down, juggling her on his knees as he reached for it, but she slid sideways. Mashing her close against him so she wouldn't crack her head on the tile wall, he fell back on his tailbone, his erection nearly finding home base as she slid forward on top of him.

"Well, hell. Note to self. Even the best idea can be ruined by poor planning." He steadied them both, resisting the urge to massage his sore butt, and saw she was stifling a laugh.

"Not ruined. Altered." She grabbed the trouble-making condom and tore the wrapper, and he thought he might come unglued as she opened it and rolled it on, then slowly eased herself onto him.

"Is this a good alteration to the plan?" she asked in a sultry voice as she moved on him, her eyes all smoky green, her beautiful lips parted, and he had to try twice before he could manage a short answer.

"Yes. Good." The back of his head was against the hard tile wall, his neck all kinked, and he was practically folded into a pretzel as the water still flowed and pooled on the shower floor, but none of that mattered.

All he could feel was her heat wrapped around him. All he could see was the vision that was her—her breasts, her hips, her face, the total goddess that was Avery Girard. He reached up to touch all of it, all of her, pulling her to him for the deepest kiss of his life as she increased the pace. As he felt her orgasm around him and followed her there.

Warm and bonelessly relaxed, Jack held Avery close beneath the sheets and down blanket. Round two in bed with the promised *chocolat* from the minibar had been every bit as good as the shower, which he'd never have believed until he'd experienced it.

"You were right, you know," he murmured against her silky hair.

"I usually am." He could feel her lips curve against his arm, and he smiled, as well. "What was I right about this time?"

"I did need a break. I needed to relax so I have a clear mind when I get back to work tomorrow. So thank you for that."

"Thank you for coming to meet Benjamin and listening to my worries with an open mind. That's all I wanted."

"All you wanted? Not me licking water and chocolate from you?"

"Okay, I wanted that, too."

He loved that little gleam in her eye and got distracted for a few minutes from something he'd been wanting to ask, having to kiss her again. When he finally came up for air he slipped her hair from her eyes and refocused his attention from the libido that kept leaping onto center stage around her.

"I've been wondering why you haven't come up with a next-generation TAVI device," he said. "You had to have heard through the biomedical grapevine I was working with Crilex on one. Is it because of Benjamin?"

"No. I can't quit trying to come up with a design to help people like him. I have a couple I'm working on. But I want the most promising device to be tested on animals until we're as sure as we can be of a positive outcome for patients. If I let a trial get started too soon, it's out of my hands after that."

"You didn't have much say during your first one?"

"No. Even after the percentage of patients with aortic insufficiency was too high and then Benjamin had his catastrophic problem, the sponsor insisted on finishing the trial."

Finally, he got why she wasn't working for that

company anymore, doing freelance work instead. "So you quit."

"I quit. I know trials carry risks, and patients know those risks. But for the cardiologist and corporation to ignore them when things have obviously gone wrong? That's unacceptable."

"And you think that's what I'm doing?"

"No." Her lips pressed softly against his arm, and he pulled her closer against him, glad that was her answer. "I don't think this trial is there yet. But it might get there, and if it does, I hope you'll do the right thing and shut it down."

"I want to finish the trial and study the data for the rollout, because I think we have to do that to come to any real conclusion." He hoped she understood his perspective. "If there was an extreme and obvious high risk, though, I wouldn't put patients' lives in harm's way to accomplish that."

"I know that now." Her teeth gleamed white in the low light. "That's why I'm lying here in bed with you, sticky with chocolate."

"Happy to lick you more to clean it off, if you like."

"Need to record the current data first. Macaroons, wine, espresso, chocolate." She pushed up onto her elbow. Her soft hand stroked across his chest, and he captured it in his, kissing her fingers and sucking the chocolate still clinging to one until she laughed and yanked it free. "So, you know my dirty little secret about the failure of my device and the failure of the people in charge to abort the mission. Tell me how you became so passionate about a second TAVI device."

He sighed. The subject of his grandfather still had the power to bring an ache to his chest. So much knowledge and grace had died with the man.

"My dad, my brother and I all decided to become cardiologists because of my granddad. I wish you could have met him—he was just a great guy and a great doc. Always seemed ironic that he had a heart attack when he was only in his fifties and suffered for years from a faulty valve afterward. He eventually had open-heart surgery, but he was one of the small percentage who didn't make it through."

"I'm sorry, Jack."

Her hand slipped up his chest to cup his cheek, and he liked the feel of it there. He turned his face to kiss her palm. "The more I worked with various stents in interventional cardiology, the more convinced I got that we could solve that problem. Help patients without other options and someday have the TAVI procedure completely eliminate the need to perform open-heart surgery for valve replacement. I want that to happen. And I want to be a part of it."

"You already are. No matter how things end up, this step you've taken is a huge one. Mine was, as well. Unsuccessful, yes, but each time, no matter what, we learn something that will help us do it better next time."

"Is that the biomedical engineering creed?" While he admired the hell out of her attitude, and agreed with it, he couldn't help teasing her a little, wanting to bring a smile back to her now somber face.

"My creed. Yours, too, I bet."

"Yeah. Mine, too." He wasn't even close to giving up

on this device. He was still convinced, even if Avery wasn't, that rolling it out to other hospitals remained the ultimate way to study it.

CHAPTER FOURTEEN

"Ah, Dr. Dunbar, you will promise I can tend my garden after you fix me, *oui*?"

"No promises, Mrs. Halbert. But I'll do the best I can. What do you like to grow in your garden?"

The smile Jack was giving the woman, the way his eyes crinkled at the corners and how he seemed genuinely interested in her garden all made Avery's heart feel squishy. It wasn't the first time that organ had felt that way around him. In fact, he'd made it squish a little their very first day together, and it had gotten to the point where it became pretty much a melted mess whenever he was around.

That she'd ever believed the success of this trial was important to him for his personal fame and fortune— more important than the success of the patients' health— made her cringe now. It was so obvious he was doing this to help people with no other surgical option. To someday change valve replacement surgery altogether, as she had wanted to do. To honor the memory of his beloved grandfather.

"I know I cannot dig my leeks from the ground. But grow chard and cucumbers, *oui*? My grandchildren love it when I fix them. And to prune my roses. *Est-ce que je serai capable de la faire?*"

He glanced at Avery, and she quickly translated. "She wants to know if she'll be able to do that after the surgery."

Jack placed his hand on the woman's gnarled one. "I hope so, Mrs. Halbert. Maybe I'll be here when you come for checkups this summer. I'd like it if you would bring me one of the roses you've pruned, to see and smell what you love to grow."

"Oui, oui." The woman beamed and patted his hand resting on hers. *"Quelle couleur? Rose? Blanche? Rouge?"*

Avery was about to translate again, but he was obviously able to figure it out as he smiled first at the woman, then at her in a slow perusal from head to toe. "I'm fond of every color, Mrs. Halbert. Preferably enjoyed all at once."

As his eyes met hers, that squishy feeling rolled all around in her belly. When he turned back to the patient she glanced down at herself and the yellow blouse and red shoes she wore. She decided she just might have to buy a new scarf in multiple hues to go with them for the next time she and Jack went out together.

The thought surprised her. Since when had she ever dressed for anyone but herself? Apparently the answer was, *not until she'd met Jack.*

Nurses came in to prep Mrs. Halbert for surgery, and as Jack spoke with them Avery quietly left the room. She pulled up the data from the past three days of surgery after she and Jack had returned from their weekend together. The weekend that had left her with the unsettling yet exhilarating knowledge that, for good or bad, her heart was in Jack's hands.

She hadn't planned on falling for him. For anybody. And she was pretty sure Jack was in the same boat. But since it was too late to keep it from happening, she fully intended to see just where these new feelings she hoped he shared might take them.

Yet there was that one potentially huge, very worrying issue with that, and she felt a little queasy just thinking about it. More than a little queasy, as she studied the information she'd gathered onto her tablet.

The dramatically increased patient load in the trial and the resulting data had waving red caution flags written all over it. If it continued like this, she would have to try to convince Jack to halt the trial. If that couldn't be accomplished, she'd have no choice at that time but to recommend to Bob it be halted and that future trials be discontinued.

Her stomach churned more, even as she hoped against hope that things would improve with the surgeries scheduled over the next couple of days. But if they didn't, if that's what had to happen, would Jack understand and agree?

She didn't know. But one thing she did know. No matter how much she'd come to care for him, those feelings would not get in the way of her professional integrity.

"Breathing better now, Mrs. Halbert?" Jack asked. It felt like he'd said those words a dozen times in just the past eight days, and it took a major effort to keep his voice calm and steady when he wanted to slam his fist into the wall and kick something.

"*Oui.* Better."

This déjà vu wasn't the great kind he'd shared with Avery, running to hotel rooms together. This was a recurring nightmare for both his patients and himself.

After taking the weekend off with Avery, Jack had returned to work feeling ready to take on the world. That feeling of energy and optimism had been quickly replaced by stress and anxiety as no fewer than three patients from last week and two from this one were already suffering with leakage from their new valves.

He studied Mrs. Halbert, very glad to see that her hands had loosened their grip on her chest and each inhalation seemed more even and less labored. He checked her vitals, asked the nurse to look at the fluid in her Foley and listened to her lungs, which were definitely clearer. Blood pressure improved, oxygen improved. Crisis hopefully over, and she'd be okay.

"Sorry you got that scare." He reached for her hand. "I know it feels bad when you can't catch your breath. But I believe you're going to feel pretty good by the time you go home to prune those roses."

"*Merci beaucoup.*" She gently patted his hand as she'd done every time he'd talked with her. If the woman had been in an advertisement playing a dear, lovely grandma, people would have bought whatever she was selling, and his chest felt a little heavy as he wondered if the sweet woman would be thanking him in a few months.

Think positively. He checked her pulse again and reminded himself she'd likely do just fine with meds to control the leakage, which was thankfully minor. But as he looked at the smile on her wrinkled face he saw someone younger. Benjamin Larue, who couldn't even sit upright without drowning in the fluid that collected in his lungs.

"I'll be back to check on you later, Mrs. Halbert." He shoved to his feet, spoke again to the nurse and said his goodbyes. Then saw Avery standing in the doorway.

Her expression bore no resemblance at all to the flirtatious, fun Avery he'd spent the weekend with. The woman looking at him rivaled a grimly stern principal about to haul a student off to her office, and Jack braced himself for the lecture she'd given before that he absolutely did not want to hear again at that moment.

He walked past her into the hallway, and she followed. He closed his eyes for a moment, trying to find his calm, before he turned to her and held up his hand. Needing to stop whatever she was about to say before it started, because it had been a damn long day and week and he knew his nerves were worn thin enough that he just might say something he regretted. He liked her—hell, more than liked her—and respected her, and getting into an argument with her was the last thing he wanted to do.

"I know the percentage of patients with problems is higher than we expected," he said. "I know you're worried that some won't be medically manageable, and I know you think we should perform the procedure on fewer patients as we finish the trial. I know, Avery."

"So what are you going to do about it?"

What *was* he going to do about it? Very good question, and one he didn't have a clue how to answer. He

ROBIN GIANNA							169

scrubbed a hand over his face, and when he looked at her again, saw her beautiful green eyes were somehow both soft and hard as they met his.

"Last week I was worried, but still watching. This week, in just ten surgeries, you've had two major leakages, and now Mrs. Halbert, which makes it thirty percent. Sweet Mrs. Halbert, who just wants to be able to prune her roses." She shook her head. "I think you know what you should do. The real question is whether or not you will."

"First, Mrs. Halbert's original valve was so diseased she could barely walk twenty steps. Second, thirty percent of patients in three days isn't thirty percent over the entire trial, which you may not be aware is how data must be collected."

Her mouth dropped open. "That's a nice insult. Reminds me of another cardiologist I used to be involved with."

Damn it. "I'm sorry, that was just frustration talking. You know I admire and respect you and your expertise." The disappointment he saw in her eyes made him want to punch himself the way he'd wanted to punch the wall. Saying something he shouldn't was exactly why he'd wanted to avoid the whole conversation. "But you think it's black and white. It isn't. If we reduce the number of patients, there might be fewer with problems, but there will also be fewer who get the help they need. Some who might die soon because their aortic valve barely works. Have you taken the time to talk to any of them or their families? Because I have."

He knew his voice was rising, and he sucked in a breath to control it, walking farther down the hall away from the rooms. He turned to her again, and she had that damned tablet clutched to her breast like a shield. "I've told them exactly how the trial is going, good and bad, and asked if they still wanted to participate. And you know what? They do. For almost all of them this is their last shot at a decent life. Or life at all. We won't have the conclusive data we need until trials are conducted over the next year at various hospitals."

"The data is screaming at you, Jack, but you're not listening."

"I am listening. I'm hearing the patients talk and the data talk. After it's rolled out everywhere it's scheduled to be, we'll listen to the entire conversation and go from there." He dropped a quick kiss on her forehead, knowing even that connection would ease his frustration with her and the situation. "I've got to get to my next surgery."

He scrubbed, then headed to the cath lab, working hard to bring his focus where it needed to be. Jessica was already there, arranging the last items needed for surgery, and she handed him his lead apron.

"Can I talk to you privately for a minute before surgery gets started?" she asked, glancing around at the doctors and nurses starting to filter in behind the glass wall in the cath lab to observe. Then she focused a laser look at Jack that was odd enough to grab his attention. He nearly asked why before just giving her a nod and moving to a quiet corner where he didn't think anyone would be able to hear them.

"What's up?"

"I found out something this morning that you're not

going to like." Jessica's lips were pressed into a tight line and a deep frown had formed between her brows. In the three years they'd worked together she hadn't been a woman prone to drama. Big drama was written on her face now, though, and he felt a little fissure of concern slide down his spine.

"This sounds ominous. We're getting started soon, so make it fast, please."

She glanced behind them again before speaking, keeping her voice low. "I was in the back room finishing up some things after your last surgery yesterday evening. Bob Timkin was there, talking to a hospital administrator type from a different French hospital who had just arrived in Paris to observe the trial. Timkin was showing him the TAVI device and talking it up. But when the guy asked him about conducting a trial at his hospital in Nice, I was surprised when Timkin put him off. Said we had to finish this trial first and see what the results were before they considered any rollout."

Jack frowned. "That can't be what he said. The whole reason French interventional cardiologists have been here observing how the procedure is done is so they can conduct their own trials. The trials at other French hospitals are about ready to begin."

"How long have we worked together, Jack?" Jess fisted her hands on her hips. "I heard him say it with my own ears. Are you implying I'm confused?"

"I believe you heard something. But it just doesn't make sense, so I have to think you missed some important part of the conversation." He trusted that Jessica must have heard a conversation that had been out of the ordinary. But it didn't add up. "Crilex has poured money into the development of the device and this trial for that exact reason—to conduct additional trials elsewhere for the next year. We've just begun to collect the data."

"I know. But, believe me, I didn't misunderstand. So, when he left to take the guy to dinner, I was glad he left his Crilex binders behind. He must have gotten them later, though, because this morning they were gone."

"You were planning to snoop through them?" Jack nearly smiled despite concerns about this conversation they were having. Jessica was the queen of snooping into things around the hospital she ordinarily wouldn't be privy to. "Must have ruined your morning that they were gone."

"A little." A small, return smile flitted across her face before that deeply serious expression came back. "But I did get a chance to snoop through them some. Quite a bit, actually, until a couple of people came in. Enough to surprise and worry me. I didn't call you about it then, because I'd hoped to look more this morning, to make sure I wasn't reading it wrong. So here's the other part you're not going to like."

Her expression was so dark and downright grim his chest tightened and the alarm bells rang louder in his brain. "Spill it, Jess. We don't have all day."

"Genius biomedical engineer Dr. Girard isn't here to just observe and possibly use ideas from this device on a new one she might design in the future. Crilex hired her to give her evaluation of your device regarding its safety and effectiveness. At the end of the thirty days, if she gives them the green light, they'll roll out the trials elsewhere. If she doesn't, Crilex won't fund any more clinical trials with it."

Jack stared at her in utter disbelief. "There's no way you can be right about that. No one can make any kind of final judgment call on a device's success or failure after just one month of clinical trials. That's ridiculous."

"It may be ridiculous, but I'm telling you it's true. And there's more." She stepped even closer, speaking in a conspiratorial whisper. "I wanted to make sure you knew before the procedures today, so you could watch your back and be careful what you say and do. Here at the hospital and before you get in any deeper with her."

The numb shock he was feeling started to take over his whole body. "Make sure I knew what?"

"The whole reason Dr. Girard is here is because she approached Crilex after seeing, in all the medical journals, details on the new design for the upcoming trials. And articles about you, working together with bioengineers to develop it. She told them, just like she told you, that she believes your design hasn't fixed the valve leakage problem hers had. Crilex decided they should listen. They don't want to pour millions more into something if it has an obvious defect. They'd rather put that money into a new design, then conduct trials with that one. I don't know about you, but I'm thinking she'd rather design her own for them, which is why she's 'concerned' about yours."

The numbness faded, morphing into a hot, burning anger. Could any of this possibly be true? That, all along, Avery had withheld from him the fact that she had full control of the future of this trial? That she'd told the product developer and sponsor of these trials she thought the device he'd worked on for over a year was bad?

He sucked in a calming breath. Jessica hadn't had time to read through all the binders. Maybe she was wrong. Maybe there was a mistake.

One thing was certain, though. After this procedure, he was damned well going to find out.

Avery stood in Bob Timkin's office, waiting for him and Jack. After the last surgery, Jack had asked her to meet them here in such a tense voice she wondered if he might be coming around to her suggestion to halt the trial.

Except when he walked into the room her stomach clenched when she saw the hard look on his face. It didn't seem to be a "you might be right" expression, but who knew?

He folded his arms across his chest and stared at her. "I've been trying to figure out how to ease into this, but I'm just going to ask. Did you go to Crilex with your concerns that I thought you'd only shared with me about the new TAVI device? And did they then hire you to evaluate the device and give your opinion on its safety and effectiveness? To decide if more trials should be conducted or not?"

Avery felt like she'd swallowed the big bomb he'd just dropped. How had he found out? And what should she say? She was contractually bound to secrecy on the subject.

"I've been here to observe the new device and the clinical trial. You know that." Which was true. Just not all of it.

"Cut the crap, Avery." Anger flared in his eyes. "I may have only known you a few weeks, but I can tell when you're lying. So tell me the damned truth. I think you owe me that."

"I like you a lot, Jack, and I respect you and the work you do. But I don't owe you anything." She breathed deeply before forging on. "The people I owe are the patients who went through the trial with my first device. People like Benjamin Larue. The people I owe are the patients going through this trial now."

"So it is true," he said in a rough, disbelieving voice. He shoved his hand through his hair. Stared at her like he was seeing her for the first time. "So you get to decide if it works or if it doesn't? If it's worth putting money into the next trials? That while you've feigned interest in how I think it's all going, you haven't really given a damn because you're calling the shots?"

Her hands felt icy cold and she rubbed them together. Wrung them, really, before she realized what she was doing and flattened them against her stomach. "Yes." She braced herself for whatever reaction he was going to have to what she had to say. "After I voiced my concerns Crilex management decided that if patients have significant problems during this trial, it might make more financial sense to put their money into a next-generation device. They don't want to spend millions on multiple and extended clinical trials only to have to redesign the device and start all over again."

"You know damned well that this trial, even with the increased patient load, won't provide close to enough data to make any kind of final judgment." The anger rolling from him now was nearly palpable. "Who do you think you are? Just because you designed the first device, it doesn't make you qualified to make that kind of call on a procedure like this. You're not the cardiologist doing detailed study of the patients' history. You're not the doctor performing surgery on the patients, taking their vital signs and carefully monitoring them post-op. Taking notes from the charts the *doctor* has written isn't even close to the same thing as medically caring for them."

Her own anger welled in her chest. Here it was. The same kind of insult her old boyfriend had liked to give her—that she'd been so sure Jack would never throw at her. "I may not be a cardiologist or a medical doctor but, believe me, I am more than qualified to know whether the device is safe or not and effective or not."

His eyes narrowed at her. "This whole thing smacks of unethical self-interest to me. You collect data on the trial, tell them the device is flawed and the roll-out should be stopped, and suddenly Crilex hires you to design the new one. No more messing around doing freelance work. You'll have a nice steady job and paycheck for a long while."

"That's beyond insulting." How had she thought he might be different from other egotistical, jerky cardiologists? "I have no expectation of being hired by Crilex. They have a great team of bioengineers, which you know very well since you worked with them to get this catheter designed. I resent you questioning my ethics and integrity."

"And I resent that you kissed up to me. Now I know why you approached me in the hotel and invited me out for the day, ending up in bed. You knew who I was and hoped I'd let slip some concerns of my own about the device or trial that you could use against me." He pointed his finger at her. "Stay out of my cath lab, Avery."

"For the record, I had no idea who you were. But it doesn't matter. You may be the brains and brawn behind this trial, Jack, but Crilex is the sponsor, which means they're running this show, not you. And they have given me authority to decide the next act."

Jack's heart was pounding so hard he thought it might burst from his chest. He'd thought the déjà vu with Mrs. Halbert had been unpleasant? This reenactment of the way Vanessa had used him to advance her career stunned him. Avery had pretended to like him when, in reality, she'd used him and the situation to snatch the reins of the trial from him, design a new catheter and run with it in her deceiving little hands.

"Doctors." Timkin came into the room to stand between them, frowning. "What's the disagreement here?"

"I've just discovered you gave her the authority to evaluate this TAVI device. Behind my back, keeping me in the dark. I've worked almost two years on this damned project, but you leave its future to someone else?"

"Jack. We simply wanted her expertise to contribute to the data collection. While it's true we asked her to give her opinion at the end of the trial, we have always fully expected there to be a full rollout when it's complete."

"Why didn't you tell me?" He wouldn't have let himself get so wrapped up in her if he'd known. He found himself looking at her beautiful, lying face, and wanted to kick himself. Wrapped up in her? Damn it, he felt so entwined with Avery he knew the pain of all this would twist him in knots for years to come.

"It seemed best to not have you distracted by any concerns about the future trials. You had enough on your plate getting everything set up for this one."

"I think you deemed it best for *you* not to have me go off on you. I don't appreciate my sponsor not being up-front with me, hiring someone to collect data behind my back and report to you."

"You knew I was collecting data for the study, which I've encouraged you to look at, so don't accuse me of doing it behind your back," Avery said, her eyes flashing green sparks. "Except you haven't wanted to really look at it."

"Tell me this." He turned to Timkin. "If Dr. Girard claims the device is unsafe, will Crilex hire her to design the next-generation one?"

"I already told you," Avery said hotly, "that Crilex's own biomedical engineers—"

"Yes," Timkin interrupted. "We would offer that position to Dr. Girard, should that be the case."

Jack could hardly breathe. He'd known it and had to believe she'd known it, too. "Funny, these self-interested concerns of yours, that you said you wanted to be 'honest' with me about. What a joke."

"My concern now is that thirty percent of patients have had serious to mild valve leakage just this week," she said. "Fourteen percent overall so far, which is more than double the expected number. The trial should be stopped and the data analyzed before any more procedures are performed."

"How do you feel about that, Jack?" Timkin asked.

How did he feel about her deception and the way she'd used him and her wanting to stop the trial right now so she could get started in her new, cushy job? Shocked and furious barely covered it. "It's a normal risk. All patients are being medically managed, and we've barely begun to have any kind of big picture here. You've already invested a lot in this device, and we need the year's worth of data," he said to Timkin. "Are you going to listen to her or to me?"

"Both. We'll decide on the rollout after everyone in this trial has received the TAVI. I need sufficient data to give shareholders as we decide to fund either this device or the next one."

"Now, there's some impressive corporate talk. Numbers instead of lives." Avery stared at them both, slowly shaking her head. "You told me, Jack, that you wouldn't put patients in harm's way if the risk became obvious."

"I said extreme risk. Fourteen percent isn't extreme."

She didn't rebut his statement, simply looking at him like he'd disappointed her ten times as much as her past boyfriends combined.

He told himself he didn't care. She'd used him and lied to him. He'd screwed up big time, believing in her, but that was over with. "Is this meeting done? I have work to do."

Slowly and carefully, she held the tablet out to him. "Good luck and goodbye. I can't be a part of something I no longer believe in."

She was quitting? Jack couldn't analyze the burning sensation in his gut, but he wasn't sure it was relief.

He watched the sway of her hips as she walked away, hating that he still wanted to. Watched as she moved all the way to the end of the hall and out the door, because he knew it was the last time he'd get to enjoy the view he never should have enjoyed to begin with.

He squared his shoulders. Work was what he did and who he was—always had been. It was past time to remember that.

CHAPTER FIFTEEN

AVERY WANDERED THROUGH Montmartre on her way to the apartment she'd been lucky enough to find available to rent for a few months.

She'd always loved this neighborhood. Loved walking the cobbled streets, window shopping in all the art stores and seeing the Sacré Coeur, which was beautiful any time of day.

Today, though, her soul wasn't filled with the pleasure of it all, bringing a smile to her face. Instead, it felt hollow and empty, because all she could think about was Jack. How angry and shocked he'd been, as she'd known he would be. How obviously beyond disappointed in her that she'd kept the secret she'd been asked to keep. Maybe she should have handled it differently somehow, but it was too late now.

There was plenty of disappointment to go around. She just didn't understand him. How could he be so blind to the fact that there were simply too many patients having problems to go on with business as usual?

She knew he was an excellent, caring doctor. An incredible man. But it seemed he cared more for his career and the future of the trial than he did for his patients. Or maybe his determination and narrow focus was keeping him unrealistically optimistic when it was clearly time to look at everything more objectively.

Out of the corner of her eye she saw a couple kissing and realized she was standing at the Wall of I Love You. It was the day before Valentine's Day, which hadn't been her favorite holiday anyway, but now was a day she wished would forever disappear from the calendar.

Her heart ached, thinking of being here in Montmartre with Jack. Thinking of their time together all over Paris, and in Riquewihr, and how much she'd come to care for him.

How she'd come to fall in love with him.

Her throat clogged, and she sniffed and swallowed hard, quickly moving away from the wall. There'd be no reunion with Jack, here or anywhere. The universe had gotten it wrong somehow, and it just wasn't meant to be between them the way she'd come to think maybe it was.

Time to get back to her computer and back to work on a new TAVI device that maybe some company would want to fund. And tomorrow, on Valentine's Day?

Tomorrow she'd load up on tissues and romantic movies and marshmallows and coconut macaroons, giving herself a whole day to cry.

Jack stared at the X-ray fluoroscopy as he seated the prosthetic valve into the patient's heart, surprised and none too happy that in the midst of it a thought of Avery flashed through his mind. The thought that he wished she was watching. That she could see she'd been wrong to quit. Wrong to want to shut down the trial since, so far, not a single one of the last eight patients had had any problems with their new valves.

He told himself it didn't matter whether she was there or not. That he should be glad. But he couldn't deny that, without her behind that glass wall, the cath lab felt empty. The air flat and dull. The woman brought an effervescence and energy everywhere she went, and even though he hated that he did, he missed it.

"Valve looks like it's fully in place and seating nicely, so I'm withdrawing the catheter and guide wires," he said to those watching. There were some new docs there today from outside France, interested in bringing a trial to their own hospitals, and he was damned glad things were finally going more smoothly.

Except, suddenly, they weren't. The wire wouldn't release from the valve the way it was supposed to. With a frown, he gently pushed, pulled, and twisted it, but it was stuck like a damn fish hook in rocks on a riverbank.

"Get the patient's feet up in the air to see if a change in position helps the wire release."

Jessica did what he asked, and he worked at it a few more minutes, but nothing. "Try helping him roll onto his right side. If that doesn't work, roll him to the other side." More minutes, more tugging and jiggling, more nothing.

Damn it to hell. "Jess, grab my cellphone and get Toby Franklin on the line. The bioengineer from Crilex who helped design the device. Quick."

Jess hurried to make the call, explained the problem, then held the phone to Jack's ear.

"Toby. I've been trying for ten minutes to get the guide wires loose. Any ideas?"

"Put the patient in the left lateral decubitus position," Toby said. "See if having him take a deep breath to increase the pressure in his chest cavity helps. Then give it a good twist to the left, pull, and pray like hell."

Sweating now, Jack did what Toby had suggested and nearly shouted *Hallelujah!* when the wires finally released from the valve and he was able to slowly withdraw them. "Okay. We're almost done. Get ready to clamp the artery so I can close the access site."

He dragged in a deep, relieved breath as Jessica and the other nurse put a weight on the artery in the man's leg, then clamped it. Able to take a brief break, the thought of Avery flashed into his brain again. This time he realized he was glad she hadn't been there to see the problem, though he shouldn't feel that way. He couldn't take every damned thing that went wrong as a personal failure. But the fact that it had happened at all would suggest a design flaw different than any they'd seen so far. He didn't want to talk about it with her, but definitely planned to discuss it with Toby.

"Dr. Dunbar, patient's pressure is dropping."

He looked up from closing the access site in the man's leg to see Jessica frowning at the monitors. "What is it?"

"Was one twenty. Now it's one hundred—no, ninety—and his pulse is dropping." Her eyes were wide with concern as she looked at him over her mask. "Oxygen saturation is falling, too."

What the hell? "Give him a liter of fluid and get an echo."

Jessica quickly rolled over the echo machine and got a picture. Jack stared at the image of the man's heart.

The valve looked snugged in right where it belonged. He peered closer and his own heart practically stopped when he saw the one thing he dreaded to see.

"Oh, no," Jessica whispered. Obviously, she'd seen it, too, and they stared together for a split second before Jack snapped himself back into action.

"We have a large, pericardial infusion," he announced to the room, his throat tight. "Jess, page Anton Maran. He's the thoracic surgeon on call. Somebody get in touch with Anesthesia. Everybody move to get the patient to the OR fast. We don't have a single second to spare."

The room became a flurry of activity as they got the patient ready, running down the hall with Jack as he pushed the gurney, because saving the man's life would require fast work and a lot of luck.

Breathing hard, his mind spun back to the whole procedure. How could he possibly have perforated the man's ventricle? There was just one, obvious answer. Somehow, when he'd had to twist and pull the wires to get them to release from the valve, the catheter had torn it.

"Is he going to make it?" Jessica asked as she ran along beside him.

"Stitching the cut will be easy for Anton. Getting him to the OR on time will be the hard part. The other part of the whole equation is whether or not he can recover from the open-heart surgery we were trying to avoid."

Jack said a prayer of thanks that Anton Maran and the anesthesiologist were already scrubbed up and in the OR when they wheeled the patient in. He briefed

Anton, but they'd already spent time going over each patient just in case there was an emergency like this one, so he was able to get to work fast.

Jack watched throughout the whole procedure. The shock of the man's ventricle getting perforated had worn off, leaving a stabbing ache behind. An ache of disappointment that the trial had ultimately not been the success he'd so wanted and expected it to be. An ache for the patient having to recover from this intense surgery, if he did recover.

An ache for Avery, who was long gone to who knew where. And all because he'd refused to listen to her.

Avery not being there, standing next to him through this thing, felt all wrong. How had that happened in a few short weeks? He had no idea, but somehow her absence felt like a huge, gaping hole in his life. In his heart.

All he'd wanted or needed in his life had been his work. Something he loved and was damned good at. Until Avery had shown up. Avery, in her colorful clothes with her beautiful green eyes, a teasing smile on her face and every bit as strong a work ethic as he had.

He'd wanted just a day or two of fun with her. To his surprise, she'd given him that and so much more. And what had he given her? Not a damn thing. Not even the respect he'd slammed her old boyfriend for not giving, either.

He shook his head at himself. What a damn fool.

Hours later, the surgery was over and a success, and Jack could only hope that the man remained in a stable condition. Feeling wiped out, he changed out of his scrubs and went to his hotel room. The thought of going out to eat without Avery sounded miserable, and he didn't feel like hashing out the day's events with Jessica, either. As he pondered room service, a knock at the door sent his heart slamming against his ribs.

Had Avery heard what had happened? He moved toward the door, wishing it would be her standing there, ready to give him another lecture that, for once, he'd be happy to listen to.

But it wasn't. "Jessica."

"Wow, my ego's gotten even bigger at how excited you sound to see me," she mocked. "Can I come in for a minute?"

"I'm always glad to see you. I'm just tired."

"Of course you're tired. I don't think you've rested for more than a few hours all week, and today was rough."

She sat on the side of the bed while Jack perched in the wooden chair by a small table and looked at her. "I've decided to stop the trial. I'm telling Timkin tomorrow morning."

He hadn't even realized he'd made that final decision, but now that the words had come out of his mouth, he knew without a doubt it was the right one.

Jessica nodded. "I figured you would. But that's not what I want to talk to you about."

He raised his eyebrows at her, hoping she didn't have some marital problem with Brandon. He wasn't up for that kind of conversation.

"Are you interested in where Avery Girard is?"

Hell, yes. He sat up straight. "I might be."

"Might be. Right." She snorted. "You've been glum

and cranky ever since she quit the trial, even before to-day's scary event. Which I guess proved maybe she was right, which means maybe you should find her and apologize and kiss her and then we can all be happy again."

If only it were that easy. "I don't think she has much interest in my apologies." Or in his kisses, and the thought made his chest ache all over again.

"I bet she does. But there's only one way for you to find out." She dug into her purse and pulled out a piece of paper, leaning over to wave it in his face. "Her address in Montmartre. She's rented an apartment for the month."

"How did you find that out?"

"Nurses at any hospital know everything." She stood and patted him on the head like he was a little kid. "Now, go. I'm heading to dinner with my cousin and expect a full report tomorrow."

He stared at the door closing behind her as adrenaline surged through his blood.

He knew he'd disappointed Avery, but he could fix that. Tomorrow was Valentine's Day, and he had to admit he didn't know much about romance. But the woman who'd held his clinical trial in her hands held his heart now instead, and she'd given him a few ideas about what just might work on her.

Avery frowned at the knock on her door, wondering who the heck could be bothering her at 9:00 p.m. in an apartment few knew she'd moved into. While she was eating marshmallows and macaroons and crying over movies. Cautiously, she peeked through the peephole and the shock of who was standing there stole her breath.

How had Jack found out where she was? And why? She knew it couldn't have anything to do with it being Valentine's Day. The man probably wasn't even aware of the holiday.

She took a moment to wipe her nose and eyes, smooth down her skirt and conjure the frustration and deep disappointment she'd felt the last time she'd seen him. Except the sight of his handsome, tired face made her want to wrap her arms around him and hold him close instead.

Disgusted with herself, she opened the door. "Lost in Paris?"

A small smile touched his mouth, but didn't make it to his eyes. "I am lost. Looking for a tour guide. You available?"

"No, I'm not."

"Can you give me just ten minutes? Please?"

She willed herself to resist the entreaty in his beautiful brown eyes, but felt that darned melting sensation inside her chest that seemed to happen whenever he was near. She sighed and figured she may as well spend ten minutes with him. Who knew? Maybe it would help heal the huge hole he'd left in her heart.

"Ten minutes."

She grabbed her coat from the rack by the door, and the feel of his fingers touching the back of her neck as he gently tugged her hair from inside made her eyes sting again. Lord, if she'd known what a heartbreaker the man was, she'd have avoided him that first day in the hotel like flesh-eating bacteria.

A little half laugh, half sob formed in her throat as she thought about their ridiculous conversation about that and snails and about the magical time they'd spent in Riquewihr. Which hadn't accomplished a thing, except to make her fall even harder for the man.

She was a little surprised he didn't touch her the way he always did as they walked to wherever it was they were going. Clearly, this must be a business visit and nothing more. Which, of course, she'd known anyway. Tears again blurred her eyes, and she forcefully blinked them back, getting really annoyed with herself now. Why would it even cross her mind to think it might be anything else?

When her vision cleared, she glanced at her watch, noting the time and fully planning on only ten darned minutes of torture with the man. Then realized they were standing by the Wall of I Love You. As she looked at him in surprise, the memory of kissing him there clogged up her breath.

"Someone told me this was a special place created just for lovers to meet. And this day, of all days of the year, seems like a good one for that to happen." He reached for her hands. "At the time, I thought that was a little hokey. I didn't realize how important such a place could be until my lover left me."

His lover. She closed her eyes at how wonderful that had been. But it wasn't meant to be. "We were supposed to be lovers just that one day. We should have left it that way."

"If that was all it was supposed to be, it would have been. But it was more than that. A whole lot more, at least for me. You brought a joy into my life I didn't even know was missing."

His words, the intense way he was staring at her squeezed her heart. But what was she supposed to say to that? He had his work and she had hers, and trying to combine that with being lovers had created nothing but conflict and pain.

"I love you, Avery." His hands tightened on hers. "I thought my work could be everything. But now I know. Even if I never see you again, it will never be enough. There would always be an empty place where you belong."

He loved her? Stunned, she stared at him as he drew her close, wrapped his arms around her and kissed her. So sure she'd never feel his lips on hers again, the pleasure of it had her melting into his chest and sighing into his mouth.

He pulled back slightly to look at her. "Remember when we made a wish at the fountain? I got my wish."

"I know. I figured you wished for sex, except I was going to give you that anyway."

"No, though I wasn't counting on that. Just hoping." A small smile touched his lips before he got serious again. "I wished for the wisdom to know when to keep at something and when to quit. It didn't kick in any too soon, but thank God it finally did."

"You're stopping the trial?"

"Yes. I'm sorry I didn't listen to you, because I should have. But that's not what I got the wisdom for. My wish kicked in when I knew I had to find you and tell you how much I love you and ask you to forgive me for all the things I've done wrong."

"You...you're not still mad about me not telling you the truth?"

"I wish you'd been honest with me, but who knows? Maybe we would have really kept our distance from one another, and we wouldn't be standing here tonight, kissing, on Valentine's Day."

"Maybe you're right. Who knew you were such a romantic?" Swallowing back tears, she reached to cup his face in her hand, barely believing this was really happening.

His lips curved in his first real smile of the night, and he gave her a long, delicious kiss that wobbled her knees before he let her go and reached into his pocket. To her shock, he pulled out the music box she'd looked at with him. The little tune tinkled when he opened it, and she started to shake all over when she saw what was inside it.

"Jack. What—"

"You said you wanted to be draped in gold." His fingers grasped the ring tucked into the red velvet folds of the box and held it up. A diamond flanked by sapphires, rubies and emeralds. "I thought a plain diamond was too dull for you, and I'm not sure this qualifies as draping, except around your finger. But I hope it's good enough for now. Will you marry me and be my forever Valentine, Avery?"

"You're asking me to marry you?" She stared into the intense brown of his eyes, barely breathing.

"I'm asking you to marry me. Begging. And since I'm about to have a heart attack because you haven't said you love me, too, please tell me. One way or the other."

"The answer is yes. *Oui, oui, oui*. And I do love you. Crazily love you. Wildly love you."

"Insanely love *you*." He pulled her close and pressed his face to her hair. "I don't deserve you, but I'm keeping you anyway." He held her for a long time before sliding the ring onto her shaking finger. She sniffed at the tears stupidly popping into her eyes again and wished she could see it better.

He held her hand tight as he pressed soft kisses down her cheek. "What do you say we team up to create a new TAVI device, Dr. Girard?" he whispered against her skin. "Sound like a good idea?"

"Une très bonne idée." She tunneled her hands into his hair and tipped his face so she could look into his beautiful eyes. Eyes that looked at her with the same kind of love she felt all but bursting from her chest. "I think we'll make a very good team, Dr. Dunbar. One very good team."

* * * * *

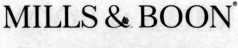
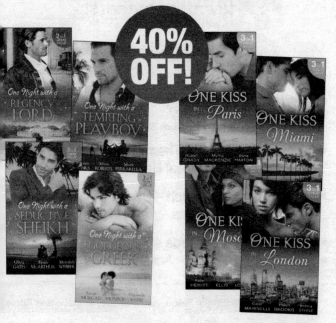

MILLS & BOON®

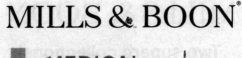

MEDICAL ROMANCE™

THE ULTIMATE IN ROMANTIC MEDICAL DRAMA

0215/03